THE
COMING
STORM

Also by Mark Alpert

THE COMING STORM

MARK ALPERT

ST. MARTIN'S PRESS • NEW YORK

THE COMING STORM. Copyright © 2018 by Mark Alpert. All rights reserved. Printed in the United States of America. For information, address St. Martin's Press, 175 Fifth Avenue, New York, N.Y. 10010.

www.stmartins.com

Library of Congress Cataloging-in-Publication Data

Names: Alpert, Mark, 1961– author.
Title: The coming storm : a thriller / Mark Alpert.
Description: First Edition. | New York : St. Martin's Press, 2019.
Identifiers: LCCN 2018031688| ISBN 9781250065421 (hardcover) |
    ISBN 9781466872240 (ebook)
Subjects: | GSAFD: Suspense fiction. | Science fiction.
Classification: LCC PS3601.L67 C66 2019 | DDC 813/.6—dc23
LC record available at https://lccn.loc.gov/2018031688

Our books may be purchased in bulk for promotional, educational, or business use. Please contact your local bookseller or the Macmillan Corporate and Premium Sales Department at 1-800-221-7945, extension 5442, or by email at MacmillanSpecialMarkets@macmillan .com.

First Edition: January 2019

10 9 8 7 6 5 4 3 2 1

For Neil and Nadine

Major Strasser: Are you one of those people who cannot imagine the Germans in their beloved Paris?

Rick: It's not particularly my beloved Paris.

Heinz: Can you imagine us in London?

Rick: When you get there, ask me.

Captain Renault: Hmmh! Diplomatist!

Major Strasser: How about New York?

Rick: Well, there are certain sections of New York, Major, that I wouldn't advise you to try to invade.

—*Casablanca* (1942)

THE
COMING
STORM

ONE

September 2023 | Brooklyn, New York

Jenna woke to the noise of boots stomping the apartment's loose floorboards. Two men rushed into her bedroom, dark figures silhouetted against the doorway. The shorter man halted in the middle of the room. The taller one charged toward her bed.

"Hands in the air! NOW!"

The man loomed over her, monstrous in the darkness. He wore a black helmet and thick slabs of body armor, and he pointed an assault rifle at Jenna's chest.

"Are you fucking DEAF? Get your hands up!"

She couldn't. Terror pressed down on her, pinning her to the mattress. She had no idea who these men were. She froze under her blanket, defenseless, wearing nothing but an oversized nightshirt and panties.

The shorter man stepped forward. He had a rifle too. "Don't be stupid. Raise your hands, nice and slow."

Now Jenna saw the black uniform under his body armor. The men were officers in the Federal Service Unit. The new police agency had started patrolling South Brooklyn three months ago, after the big flood in June and the looting in Brighton Beach. Jenna had seen dozens of FSU officers on Coney Island Avenue, stopping everyone on the street to check their residence documents. She'd also seen the cops outside the flood-damaged buildings on Ocean Parkway, rounding up the squatters and illegals.

Her terror pushed down harder, constricting her chest, but she managed to slip her hands out from under the blanket. They shook as she raised them.

In an instant, the bigger cop grabbed her wrists and flipped her onto her stomach. He yanked her arms behind her back and flung the blanket off the bed. "She's the one we want, right? The raghead's daughter?"

Jenna turned her head to the side so she wouldn't suffocate against the pillow. The shorter officer pulled out a flashlight and shone it on her face. "Yeah, that's her. Jenna Khan."

She squinted at the light, trying to look past it. She could hear shouts and scuffling outside her room. Then she saw another pair of cops in the corridor, running past her doorway and out of sight. They were heading for the apartment's other bedroom, where Jenna's father and brother slept.

Her throat tightened. When she spoke, her voice was thin and high-pitched, as if she'd gone back in time and become a child again. "Please . . . we're not illegals . . . I was born here, and my brother—"

"Shut your hole." The big cop tied her hands behind her back with a pair of plastic cuffs. They dug into her wrists, notching the skin.

The other officer kept shining the flashlight in her eyes. He stepped closer and leaned over the bed. "She's not bad-looking. For a Pakistani, I mean. Nice ass."

"But she smells like curry." The cop grabbed her by the elbow and lifted her off the bed. "Come on, get moving."

The man was alarmingly strong. He heaved Jenna to her feet and marched her across the room, gripping her arm as he and his partner walked behind her. If they were decent human beings, they would've given her a chance to get dressed—even with her hands tied, she could've stepped into a pair of sneakers—but the officers pushed her past her closet and bureau. Barefoot and shivering, Jenna stumbled toward the doorway.

When they reached the corridor, the big cop tried to steer her toward the apartment's front door, tugging her arm to the left. But instead she automatically turned to the right, toward the second bedroom, and caught a glimpse of her Abbu—it meant "Dad" in Urdu—illuminated by the flashlight beams. Hamid Khan knelt on the room's floor, naked except for his undershorts. Two officers in black uniforms stood behind him, both pointing their rifles at his balding head. A third cop bent over Hamid and tightened the plastic cuffs around his wrists.

Furious, Jenna lunged toward the bedroom. She twisted her arm out of the big cop's grasp and ran to her father. "Abbu!" She glared at the officers surrounding him. "What are you doing? Get away from him! *Get away!*"

The cops stepped back and aimed their guns at her. At the same time, Hamid raised his head and groaned. His nose was broken and his face smeared with blood, but that wasn't the worst of it. In the far corner of the room, another officer had tied up Jenna's brother. Raza lay facedown on his bed, his thin, brown arms bound behind his back, his skeletal legs splayed over the edge of the mattress. His head bobbed on the pillow, but otherwise he didn't move. He was a quadriplegic, paralyzed from the neck down, but the cops had handcuffed him anyway.

Jenna rushed toward him. She ignored the officers and tore across the room. But when she was a couple of yards from Raza's bed, the big cop caught up to her. He tackled her from behind, and with her hands tied behind her back she couldn't break her fall. She toppled forward, and her forehead smashed into the floorboards.

When Jenna woke again, she lay on the wet sidewalk in front of her apartment building. It was raining hard on her face, and a strong wind gusted across the night sky. She trembled under her damp shirt, her cuffed hands mashed between her back and the pavement. Her ears rang and her head ached.

Then she remembered: *Abbu. Raza.*

She lifted her head from the sidewalk and dizzily stared at the street, which dead-ended at Coney Island Beach a hundred yards away. Although the streetlights were off—the neighborhood's power had been out for the past two weeks—Jenna could see half a dozen cops nearby, all of them holding their guns at the ready. Their vehicle was twenty yards down the street, an armored truck as big as a fire engine, its tires sitting in two feet of turbid water. The neighborhood had flooded again, for the third time that month. Seawater from the Atlantic gushed over the beach and under the boardwalk and into the streets.

She turned her head in the other direction and saw three more Federal

Service officers on the sidewalk, but there were no detainees besides herself and no sign of her father or brother. Did the cops already load them into their truck? Jenna took a closer look at the vehicle and heard a grinding, whirring noise, the sound of the truck's driver trying to start its engine. Two officers sloshed across the street and yelled instructions at the driver, but despite all their advice the engine failed to turn over. Soon the floodwaters rose above the stalled truck's bumpers. After a few more seconds, the truck's headlights went out.

The water rose above the curb too and spilled across the sidewalk, streaming under Jenna's back. Panicked, she sat up and turned to the closest officer, who stood about ten feet away. "Hey! Hey, you!" She had to raise her voice over the noise of the storm. "What's going on?"

The cop ignored her. His black uniform had gold stripes on the shoulders. Jenna guessed he was in charge of the other FSU officers, probably their sergeant. He was busy shouting into his two-way radio. "No, listen . . . that can't be right . . . you mean to tell me that *all* the streets between here and . . . well, we can't just wait here until . . . what was that?"

Jenna couldn't wait either. Although it was difficult to stand up without the use of her arms, she managed to rise to her bare feet and approach the police sergeant. "Listen to me! Where are my father and brother? What did you—"

"What the fuck?" The cop lowered his radio and gave her a ferocious look. "Get back down! Right this fucking second!"

He clamped his free hand on her shoulder and pushed her down to the sidewalk. Her back hit the pavement, knocking the wind out of her. The pain was tremendous, but she couldn't even gasp. She rolled onto her side and closed her eyes until she could breathe again.

"Now stay there! Don't move till I tell you to!" The cop leaned over her for a moment, the rain pelting his body armor. Then he stepped away and went back to talking to his radio. "Repeat your last instruction, Dispatch . . . no, I already told you, we can't wait that long . . . I don't care how bad the roads are, you gotta send the vehicle anyway . . . we're fucked if you don't send backup, you hear?"

Jenna opened her eyes and glowered at him. She wasn't afraid anymore. She stopped shivering, even though the cold seawater surged under her head and numbed her feet. Rage boiled inside her. Jenna had a bad temper, and until this moment she'd been ashamed of it—she was too prickly and rebellious, too much of a smart-mouth—but now her anger was an asset. It kept her sane and focused. If her hands weren't cuffed, she would've strangled the police sergeant. She would've leapt on the cop's back and dug her fingers into his throat.

But it was no use. She couldn't fight, couldn't do a thing. The rage seeped out of her and the rain hammered down, and she felt nothing but self-disgust. She realized that this was no ordinary police raid, no routine roundup of squatters and illegals. If it were, the cops would've arrested everyone else in their building too. No, it was all her fault. She'd pushed things too far, asked too many questions. She should've just done her job at the lab, should've conducted the experiments without any objections. But she'd always been too stubborn—her father had warned her about it so many times. And now, thanks to her stupidity and arrogance, her whole family was headed for the FSU's detention cells.

The storm was getting worse. The wind howled over the flooded beach, picking up clumps of sand and garbage and flinging them at the redbrick apartment buildings. Seawater poured into the buildings closest to the beach, funneling through the broken windows and doors that had been trashed during the last storm two weeks ago. Jenna was no expert on weather forecasts—her degrees were in genetics, not climate science—but she could tell that the flooding was going to be worse this time. After the last downpour, the squatters abandoned all the ground-floor apartments in the neighborhood, but this time the floodwaters would rise even higher. Jenna looked up to the second and third floors of her building and saw shadowy figures behind the dark windows, her neighbors anxiously watching the storm.

Then one of the second-story windows opened, directly above. An elderly black woman stuck her head outside, oblivious to the rain, and looked down at the street. Against the glowing night sky—there was a full moon above the heaps of storm clouds—her face was a dark splotch, contorted with outrage. Jenna recognized her: it was Mrs. Wilson, their eighty-three-year-old next-door neighbor, dressed in a white nightgown that billowed over her ample body. The old woman leaned against the windowsill and pointed a thick finger at the police sergeant on the sidewalk.

"What did you do to that girl? You should be ashamed of yourself!"

Her voice, loud and indignant, echoed against the apartment building across the street. The sergeant looked up, and so did all eight of his men.

Two of them automatically pointed their rifles at Mrs. Wilson's window. But she didn't retreat into her apartment. Instead, she leaned farther out the window and clenched her hand into a meaty fist. "You think you can get away with this? And leave that poor girl half-naked on the sidewalk? Who the hell raised you boys to treat a woman like that?"

Someone opened a window in the apartment above Mrs. Wilson's. A moment later, a couple of people in the building across the street opened their windows too. Jenna felt a stab of humiliation—her nightshirt was hiked up to her hips, and all her neighbors were staring at her. But then she heard the scattered shouts from the opened windows.

"God damn! Look what they did!"

"Leave the girl alone, motherfucker! Yeah, I'm talking to *you*!"

"Fucking assholes, you gonna *pay* this time."

Now all the cops raised their rifles, aiming at the apartments on both sides of the street. Jenna tensed, heart pounding. The Federal Service Unit was a paramilitary force, trained and equipped to fight terrorists, and they'd brought all their firepower to South Brooklyn. After rioters torched the neighborhood's supermarkets last June, there was an exodus of everyone who could afford to leave; most of the white residents fled and most of the black and brown folks crowded into the few buildings that hadn't been razed or flooded. The New York Police Department pulled its officers out of the district, and the White House sent in the FSU to stop the chaos from spreading. The Feds had no qualms about shooting into crowds—Jenna had heard their gunshots in the distance many times over the past few weeks. So now she scrambled to get out of their line of fire, slithering across the sidewalk with her hands tied behind her.

She made it to the entrance of her apartment building and propped her back against the front door. Fifteen feet above her, Mrs. Wilson was still yelling at the cops from her window, calling them thugs and animals and worse. In response, the officers trained their rifles' laser sights on her. Bright red dots flashed on her wrinkled forehead.

Jenna opened her mouth, horrified. But before she could shout a warning to Mrs. Wilson, the old woman retreated into her apartment.

At the same time, more windows opened on the upper floors, and more onlookers yelled at the cops. Their voices rose and fell, a squall of insults and curses and threats, almost as loud as the storm crashing down on the street. The FSU sergeant raised his radio again and shouted another request for backup, practically screaming into the microphone. Meanwhile, the other officers turned this way and that, pointing their guns at the loudest protesters. The red dots of their laser sights raced up and down the building's façade.

This isn't good, Jenna thought. *I have to get out of here.* The cops weren't watching her at the moment, so maybe she could sneak away unnoticed. Maybe she could push against the door behind her and hide inside her building's vestibule. But she couldn't open the door without turning the knob, and that was impossible to do with her hands tied. She pulled at the plastic cuffs behind her back, hoping to slip one of her slick hands through the loops, but they wouldn't loosen. *Shit, I don't believe this!* She looked up at the knob, just inches above her head, and wondered if she could use her shoulder to turn it.

Then Mrs. Wilson reappeared at her second-floor window. She leaned over the sill again, now holding a dark, rectangular object in her right hand. "Here, take this." She cocked her arm, readying to throw the object.

The police sergeant saw her first. He staggered backward and dropped his radio into the floodwaters. "Bomb! She's got a—"

In an instant, the red dots converged on Mrs. Wilson, and the cops opened fire.

The assault rifles juddered in their hands, like thunder at the heart of the storm. The bullets tore into the old woman, plunging straight through her chest, piercing her nightgown in the front and back. Their momentum pushed her back into her apartment, out of sight, but the cops kept firing at her window, pocking and pulverizing the brick façade around it.

Jenna saw it all. With her hands tied, she couldn't cover her eyes. As the bullets shoved Mrs. Wilson backward, the old woman let go of the dark, rectangular object, which dropped in front of the apartment building. It splashed on the flooded sidewalk, just five feet from Jenna.

It wasn't a bomb. It was a pair of black sweatpants, neatly folded. They were meant for Jenna, to cover her bare legs.

"Cease fire!" The sergeant waved his arms at the other officers. "Goddamn it, *cease fire!*"

The gunfire stopped. The other officers lowered their rifles. For a moment, the only sounds were the howling of the wind and the lashing of the rain.

Then the whole street erupted with rage, all the onlookers at the windows bellowing at the cops below. It was a blaring, indecipherable uproar—Jenna couldn't make out a single word—but she knew what it meant. The police had gone too far this time. Now the people were angry enough to fight back.

It started with a lone gunshot, fired from the building across the street. The bullet didn't come close to hitting anyone—it streaked into the roiling waters next to the curb, at least ten feet from the nearest officer—but all the cops dived for cover behind the parked cars. They searched for the shooter by shining their laser sights on the building's upper floors, but there were at least a dozen open windows up there, all of them dark and empty. The unseen gunman had apparently ducked after firing his shot, and now it was impossible to tell where he was hiding.

Then two more shots were fired, both from Jenna's building. One of the bullets hit an SUV parked near the street corner, and the other struck a cop in the leg. The wounded man let out a shriek, and the other officers started firing blindly, spraying their military-grade ammunition all over the apartment buildings.

The barrage shattered every window on the street. Shards of glass and slivers of brick rained down from the buildings and splashed into the floodwaters. Jenna heard screams coming from inside the apartments, from the people who hadn't hit the deck fast enough, but she also heard more gunfire coming from the upper floors, and she caught a glimpse of someone poking a handgun over a windowsill. South Brooklyn had no shortage of guns, and the local gangbangers knew how to use them. They took potshots at the FSU officers, firing from the dark windows overhead and dodging the blasts of return fire from the cops' assault rifles.

The bullets zinged over the sidewalk in front of Jenna, whizzing in all directions. One of them struck the pavement just a yard away, and a sharp chip of concrete grazed her ankle. Frantic, she flattened herself against her building's door and slid her body upward, edging toward the brass knob. She twisted and squirmed, pressing her shoulder against the knob, but she couldn't get the damn thing to turn. *Shit, shit, shit!*

Then the door suddenly opened behind her. Someone grabbed her arms and yanked her into the vestibule, then slammed the door shut.

Before she could catch her breath, Jenna was dragged into the apartment building, as far as possible from the front door and the gunfire outside. It was darker here than on the street, and Jenna couldn't see a thing at first. But then she slid to a stop at the foot of the building's stairway, and when she looked up she glimpsed the dim outline of the biggest man she'd ever seen.

He let go of her arms but stayed hunched over her. "Don't make a fucking sound." His voice was low and hoarse, and he was breathing heavily. "You're mine now."

TWO

Lieutenant Rick Frazier spotted the *New York Times* reporter at the Bay Parkway checkpoint. The weaselly little asshole stood beside the chain-link fence that surrounded the South Brooklyn District. The man's face matched one of the ninety-six mug shots Frazier had memorized when the FSU sent him to this shithole of a city.

The moment of recognition was wonderfully satisfying. Like a key turning in the lock of Frazier's brain. He smiled as he recalled all the details about the man: name, address, birthdate, bio. *Damn, I'm good. I'm a fucking computer.*

Frazier stepped away from the checkpoint—a sliding gate in the fence, manned by two FSU officers under his command—and lifted his head, pretending to scrutinize the storm. He scowled at the night sky and the sheeting rain, which soaked his uniform and seeped into his boots. But all the while he kept one eye on the *Times* reporter. The man's name was Allen Keating, and he was a puny fucker, barely five and a half feet tall. Frazier was thirteen inches taller and outweighed him by at least a hundred pounds.

The reporter had dressed down for tonight's assignment. He wore a pair of ratty jeans and a black T-shirt that clung wetly to his torso. He was trying to blend in with the other people standing by the fence, the handful of curious locals who'd ventured out of their apartments at 2 a.m. to see the commotion at the checkpoint. Little Miss Keating stood there in the rain, acting casual, not wearing a press badge nor holding a reporter's notebook, doing his damnedest not to look like a newspaperman. But Frazier wasn't fooled. The sneaky bastard had an iPhone in his hand. He was using it to shoot video of the crowd on the other side of the fence.

Frazier stepped closer, still pretending to watch the weather. This section of the fence was sturdy and high, topped with coils of razor wire and illuminated by high-intensity searchlights. It ran for miles along the borders of South Brooklyn, separating the flood-ravaged, FSU-controlled district from the still-livable neighborhoods to the north—Bensonhurst, Midwood, Flatlands. The New York Police Department still patrolled those areas, but south of the fence the Feds were in charge. All the decent, law-abiding people had fled the district months ago, turning it into a refuge for criminals and illegals, an urban swamp festering on the edge of the city. And tonight's storm had flushed the swamp creatures out of hiding. At least three hundred of them swarmed on the other side of the fence, shouting and cursing at the FSU officers.

"Hey, cocksuckers! Let us out! We're drowning here!"

"Why are you assholes just standing there? Open the fucking gate!"

Frazier ignored them. Under ordinary circumstances, he would've gladly opened the checkpoint and started interrogating anyone in the crowd who wanted to leave South Brooklyn. That was the primary mission of the Federal Service Unit—to clean up the district by imprisoning its criminals and deporting the illegals. But the storm had caused problems across the whole city, and FSU teams had been dispatched on dozens of emergency calls. Frazier was left with a skeleton crew, so paltry that all they could do was monitor the fence and make sure that none of the scumbags climbed over it. He didn't have enough officers to interrogate the crowd or transport them to the detention facilities. So he kept the gate closed. Let them wait till morning.

But Allen Keating didn't ignore the crowd. The *Times* reporter poked his iPhone through a small hole in the fence to get a better view of all the wetbacks and ragheads on the other side. To the untrained eye, they didn't seem so dangerous. They just looked miserable and filthy and hopeless, and that's what the *Times* wanted everyone to see. In reality, there were dozens of rapists and murderers in that crowd, and probably a few Islamic State sympathizers who would've loved to plant a bomb in Grand Central Station. But the newspaper reporters didn't care about that. All they wanted to do was show the world how the big, bad FSU was persecuting those poor, oppressed souls.

Frazier sidled past his men—Sergeant Barr and Corporal Hendricks, both cradling their assault rifles—and positioned himself directly behind Keating, less than five feet away. The reporter aimed his iPhone at the only child in the crowd, a short, skinny boy in dirty, wet clothes, maybe eight or nine years old. The boy stood in an ankle-high puddle and held the hand of a black woman with dripping, matted hair. Frazier guessed the woman was Somali, because she was so tall and thin. She must've come to the United States more than seven years ago, before the refugee ban. Somehow she'd evaded all the Homeland Security roundups since then.

This woman wasn't a terrorist. She had a fist-size bruise on her jaw and track marks on both her arms. She was an addict and probably a hooker too, dressed in denim shorts and a bikini top and staring straight ahead with dull, heavy-lidded eyes. She didn't even seem aware of the kid standing by her side, gripping her hand and shifting his weight from foot to foot, antsy and frantic, as if he needed to go to the bathroom. The *Times* reporter adjusted his iPhone's camera and focused on the boy's face, which glowed like a brown moon under the searchlights.

Frazier focused on the kid too. His darting eyes, his shivering lips. The lights shone on him so intensely that they seemed to illuminate every thought in his head, every fear and nightmare. The kid was scared shitless. His mother was killing herself, and they were surrounded by predators. So the boy shivered and fidgeted, as if he could sense what was coming, all the abuse and horror that lay ahead for him. He cowered at the sight of it.

It was disturbing. No, worse than that—it was fucking unwatchable. The boy's face reminded Frazier of something from long ago, from his shitty hometown in poor-as-fuck Missouri. From that awful night on the gravel road in Cassville.

Jesus Christ. The kid looks like Andy. The same shock on his face. The same horror.

Frazier shook his head until the image went away. His memory was too good now, that was the problem. The drugs had improved it too much, made it too painful. Even after the picture faded from his mind, he still felt the ache in his chest, sharp and burning.

There was only one sure way to kill the pain. He took a deep breath and lunged at Keating.

With one hand Frazier gripped the reporter's elbow and with the other he grabbed the iPhone. He ripped the phone out of Keating's hands and held it in the air for a moment, furious and triumphant. Then he hurled it at the pavement as hard as he could, smashing it into a hundred pieces.

Keating staggered and lost his balance, falling against the chain-link fence. He tilted his head back and gaped at Frazier. "What the hell? Who are—"

"You think you're smarter than us, asshole?"

"I . . . I don't know what—"

"You thought you could get away with it? Sneaking into a restricted security zone? After we warned you and your bosses at the newspaper so many times?" Frazier tightened his grip. He could feel the slender bones under the reporter's clammy skin. "How dumb do you think we are?"

Keating trembled. His shoulders shook so hard that they rattled the section of fence he was leaning against. He'd just realized the sheer depth of the shit he'd stepped into. "Look . . . I have a press pass . . . issued by the New York Police Department this year, two-thousand-twenty-three . . . it's in my—"

"We're not the fucking NYPD. You're interfering with a federal operation and breaking federal laws. Which means you're going to federal prison."

The reporter's eyes widened. "You can't do that! You don't have . . ." He clenched his hands, fighting his own fear. "You're required by law to contact the New York Police Department when—"

Frazier interrupted him by breaking his arm. All he had to do was yank Keating's elbow backward, and the bones in his forearm snapped like pretzels. It happened so fast and took such little effort. The reporter dropped to his knees and started screaming.

Sergeant Barr and Corporal Hendricks stared at him. Although they didn't say a word, their faces twitched in surprise. They were both new recruits to the FSU who'd arrived in New York just yesterday, so they'd never seen Frazier in action before. It always shocked the recruits when they saw how fast and strong he was. The effects of the new drugs were much more dramatic than the changes you'd get from the older stuff, the stimulants and steroids. Frazier's men were clearly impressed, but they also seemed uneasy. After an awkward moment, they turned away and went back to scanning the crowd on the other side of the fence.

But Frazier didn't care what they thought. He felt stupendous, on top of the world. The burning pain in his chest was gone, replaced by that wonderful sense of satisfaction, like a key turning, everything clicking into place. It felt so good that he wanted to keep it going, maybe by hurting the reporter some more. Maybe he should break the bastard's other arm.

Then the portable radio clipped to his belt started buzzing. Frazier reached for it and stepped away from the fence, letting the reporter slump to the ground. According to the radio's LED screen, the call was from Frazier's boss, Colonel Grant. He was the regional commander, in charge of all the Federal Service Districts in the Northeast, appointed by the president himself. In other words, it was Pretty Fucking Important.

Frazier stepped farther away, so Barr and Hendricks couldn't eavesdrop. Then he raised the radio to his mouth. "Frazier here. You need something, Colonel?"

"We got a problem." Grant's voice was deep and gravelly and serious. The man was a no-nonsense commander, and now he seemed to be in a particularly shitty mood. "We sent Team Six to make an arrest in the Brighton Beach sector and they got caught in a firefight. Their truck died, and a bunch of hoods started taking potshots at them."

This was bad, but not terrible. There had been similar incidents in South Brooklyn over the past three months. "Did Headquarters send the Quick Reaction Force to bail them out?"

"Yeah, they're on their way. But I want you to lead another team to the sector. The idiots in Six let their suspect run off, and we need to recapture her as soon as possible."

"Her? A woman?"

"Her name is Jenna Khan. Thirty years old, five-foot-four, short black hair, light brown skin. Last seen ten minutes ago near Sixth Street and Brightwater Court. She's unarmed, wearing a gray nightshirt, no shoes, no pants. I already sent you her picture."

"Wow, she sounds intimidating. Why do you want her so bad?"

"Don't fuck with me, Frazier. I can't tell you shit, it's all classified. Just find the Khan girl as soon as you can." Grant paused for a moment, as if reconsidering his answer. When he resumed, his voice was low and wary. "It's connected to Palindrome. So now you know why this is important, right?"

Frazier knew. There weren't many people in the whole country who knew about the Palindrome Project, but he was one of them. He was one of the first men to volunteer for the experiments. "Okay, I'll round up my team. We have Stryker vehicles that can get through the flood zone."

"And Frazier? You should also know what our priorities are. We don't need to interrogate the girl. We just don't want her talking to anyone else about the project. So if you run into any trouble, don't worry about her fucking health, all right? You're authorized to use extreme prejudice."

"So you mean . . . ?"

"Get it done. If you can't take her alive, waste her."

THREE

The huge man dragged Jenna to her apartment building's basement. He didn't remove the plastic cuffs from her wrists—he just grabbed her left arm above the elbow and hauled her downstairs. She fought him, twisting in his grip and digging in her heels, but it was no use. Her bare feet slid down the wet steps.

She was terrified. The basement was even darker than the lobby, and the floodwaters streamed down the walls, funneling through every chink and crack in the building. At the bottom of the stairway the water was knee-deep, cold and churning and invisible in the darkness. Jenna couldn't see a thing, but the giant pulled her to the left without stopping, as if he knew exactly where he was going. It made no sense—there was nothing in the basement except a laundry room and a row of storage lockers. *Shit, he's going to rape me here. Then drown me.*

Jenna stumbled. She fell forward and her face splashed into the water, frigid and salty and thick with filth. But the giant jerked her upright and dragged her along, pulling her farther into the flooded basement. They turned left again and waded into even deeper water, up to her naked thighs and the bottom of her nightshirt. She cried in frustration, furious and desperate. This hulking maniac was going to murder her. He was going to rape her and drown her and leave her body floating in the putrid water. It was so sickening and pointless.

Then they stopped, and there was a loud *thump* in the darkness, a few feet ahead. The giant grunted, and there was an even louder *thump*, then another. Jenna realized that the man was hitting something with his forearm or shoulder, slamming into something solid with all his might.

He hit it one more time, and the thing gave way. It was a door, an emergency exit at the back of the building. It led to a small courtyard covered in two feet of water, which swirled around a Dumpster and a discarded refrigerator. The giant pulled Jenna through the doorway, and she felt a burst of relief as they sloshed their way outside. She was still his prisoner, but she was alive. And though the courtyard was middle-of-the-night dark, it seemed as bright as day compared with the basement.

The man dragged her past the Dumpster and down an alleyway between two other apartment buildings. They emerged on Fifth Street, a block away from the FSU officers. The cops were still shooting it out with Jenna's neighbors—she could hear the gunfire in the distance—but they were on the other side of the apartment buildings, so they couldn't see her or the huge man who'd kidnapped her. Without pausing, he tugged her to the right, and they splashed north along the flooded street, away from Coney Island Beach and the roiling ocean.

Jenna's legs and feet were numb from the cold, but her mind was clearer now, less saturated with panic. For the first time she got a good look at the giant, who seemed even larger now that they were running side by side. He was almost seven feet tall and built like an NFL lineman. Bulbous shoulders bulged out of the sleeves of his wet T-shirt, and trunklike thighs pumped inside his soaked jeans. His skin was dark and his hair had been shaved to black stubble. Jenna couldn't see his face so well—he kept a step ahead of her as he dragged her along—but he had deepset eyes and flaring nostrils, and his lips drew back from his teeth as he ran. He looked menacing and ferocious and, yes, maniacal. It wasn't reassuring.

And yet he hadn't hurt her. He could've easily killed her in the flooded basement, but instead he'd freed her from the FSU men and rescued her from the firefight, following an escape route he must've scoped out in advance. Clearly, he had plans for her. The only trouble was, Jenna didn't know what those plans were. He might be taking her someplace even worse. Maybe some abandoned apartment building where he could hurt her at his leisure.

She needed to find out. After they'd run a hundred yards down the street, she jumped ahead and stepped in front of him. He didn't let go of her, but she forced him to break stride. "Hey!" she yelled. "Where are we going?"

"Goddamn it!" His voice was fierce but quiet. "I told you to keep your mouth shut!" He spun around and stared at the block behind them, where they'd emerged from the alleyway.

Jenna automatically looked in the same direction, squinting to see better in the darkness. Another surge of seawater washed over the beach and gushed into the street, but luckily there were no FSU officers chasing them. "Okay, listen." She lowered her voice but stood firm. "I don't know who you are or what—"

"My name's Derek, and that's all I'm gonna say now, you hear?" He tightened his grip on her arm and yanked her forward. "You want those assholes to catch up to us?"

"No, but—"

"Then shut the fuck up and keep moving!"

She couldn't win this fight. Derek the kidnapper was too strong, and she was too dazed, and the wind howled overhead, buffeting and drenching them. She fell into step beside him, and they dashed through the storm.

A minute later, they reached Brighton Beach Avenue. An elevated subway line ran above this street, but the trains had stopped running in South Brooklyn three months ago, after the riots in June. Now the rusted tracks shadowed the avenue and its boarded-up storefronts, the remnants of what used to be pharmacies and supermarkets and restaurants. Rain pummeled the empty train stations and sluiced down the steel columns that supported the tracks. The street below was a muddy river, rising steadily.

But at least the wind wasn't as strong here. They headed west under the tracks, wading through the avenue's floodwaters, stepping around the abandoned cars and floating garbage. Jenna stared straight ahead and tried not to think about where they were going. In despair, she thought of her father and brother, wondering if they were still with the FSU officers on Sixth Street. She didn't hear any more distant gunshots, so maybe the firefight was over. But that meant the cops would go back to their headquarters now and take Abbu and Raza to the detention facility. It was a horrible ending to her family's story, all their years of struggle and sacrifice. They'd lost their jobs, their dignity, and now their freedom.

Jenna shook her head and cursed herself. She'd screwed up everything.

After ten minutes of slogging through the muck, she spotted the Ocean Parkway train station. On both sides of the street, stairways rose from the sidewalk to the elevated line, but after the riots the FSU had closed the station's entrances. Thick plywood boards and coils of razor wire blocked the stairways. As Jenna waded closer, she noticed a yellow sign nailed to one of the boards: TRESPASSING ON THE TRACKS IS STRICTLY FORBIDDEN. AS OF 6/15/23, THE FEDERAL SERVICE UNIT IS AUTHORIZED TO USE DEADLY FORCE AGAINST VIOLATORS.

Jenna was familiar with this station. She used to get on the Q train there and take it to her job in Manhattan, at Rockefeller University's Molecular Genetics Lab. The commute was a long one, an hour and a half each way, but it had never bothered her. She'd loved her job. She'd joined the lab as a postdoctoral fellow—the lowest position on the research staff—but the lab director had let her participate in the most interesting projects. She'd contributed her ideas and helped design the experiments. After just two years she was promoted to assistant professor, the youngest in the history of the university.

In retrospect, though, she would've been better off if she'd never stepped foot inside that lab. She should've studied something else besides genetics. Maybe avoided science altogether.

Grimacing, she turned away from the boarded-up stairs. At the same time, she felt a sharp tug on her left arm. Derek stopped at the foot of the stairway and pulled her close. While keeping his grip on Jenna, he clamped his other hand around the edge of one of the plywood boards. With a tremendous heave, he tore the board off the station entrance, then used it to shove the coils of razor wire out of the way.

He nudged Jenna toward the gap he'd made. "Duck your head."

She hesitated, glancing at the yellow sign on the board he'd just removed. "This is stupid. If someone sees us on—"

"Just go!"

She stooped down and slipped through the gap. Derek followed a moment later, pivoting his massive torso so it would fit between the splintered boards. Then he splayed his hand on Jenna's back and pushed her up the steps, which were caked with pigeon shit. She winced as the wet droppings squished under her toes.

They went up to the deserted station, clambered over the turnstiles, and climbed another stairway to reach the empty platform. Jenna looked up and down the elevated tracks, nervous as hell, half-expecting to see police sharpshooters on the rooftops of the nearby buildings. But no one was in sight, not a living soul.

She turned around, gazing in every direction. The neighborhood was cloaked in darkness and squalls. Gale-force winds whipped between the apartment buildings and deluged the streets. Although plenty of super-storms had hit New York in the past decade, and especially since the Great Arctic Melt three years ago, tonight's tempest was the worst yet. The Atlantic Ocean was taking its revenge on the city. Even the rich folks in Manhattan were going to suffer this time.

Jenna backed away from the tracks. She found some shelter under the platform's steel awning, which deflected the wind and rain. Then Derek came up behind her with a switchblade in his hand.

He grasped her shoulder. "Don't move."

The fear in her chest was so sudden and sharp that for a second Jenna thought he'd plunged the knife into her. But instead Derek cut the plastic cuffs around her wrists, slicing the ties in one swift stroke. It took a little longer for Jenna's terror to fade.

"My . . . God." Her heart knocked against her breastbone. She shook her hands to get the feeling back into them. "Give me a little warning next time, okay?"

Derek closed the knife and put it back in his pants pocket. His face was blank. It was as if he hadn't heard her. "We can't stay here. We have to keep going."

"Go where?"

"That way." He pointed at the elevated tracks to the west, which curved toward the Stillwell Avenue station. "We'll walk on the tracks."

She shook her head. "No, that's a bad idea. We can't—"

"We won't get electrocuted. They turned off the power."

"That's not what I'm worried about. You see how bad the storm is? The wind will blow us right off the tracks."

"I told you, we can't stay here." His voice rose. He stepped closer and narrowed his eyes. "We have to *go*."

Jenna stared at him. Maybe Derek wasn't a killer, but he was abnormally intense, and now that she saw him up close she realized his appearance was odd too. His dark face was mottled with round patches of lighter skin, each about the size of a dime. There was an ugly red ulcer on the side of his neck, a wound that hadn't healed right and was ringed with dead skin. His eyes were bloodshot and his lips were blistered, and every time he breathed he let out a low rasp from deep in his chest. Jenna was a researcher, not a doctor, but she could tell that something was wrong with him. And it seemed to be affecting his behavior, making him feverish and irate.

She needed to calm him. She held out her hands, palms up, in what she hoped was a soothing gesture. "Just listen for a second, okay? I'm grateful that you saved me from those FSU assholes, really grateful. But those same cops arrested my father and brother, and I need to help them. My brother, he's disabled, he can't walk or talk. That's why I still live with my dad, so I can help him take care of Raza. And both of them are probably scared out of their minds right now."

Derek shook his head. "There's nothing you can do about it. The Feds have them. They're going to jail."

"No, listen, I *can* do something. I can find out what charges the Feds are bringing against them. And maybe I can find a lawyer who'll fight their detention. So it would be best if we split up, you know? You go your way and I'll go mine. And if you need my help with anything—and I mean anything at all we can meet somewhere in a couple of days. I really think that's the best way to handle it."

He said nothing at first. His face went blank again, and for a moment Jenna thought he was seriously considering her proposal. Then he leaned over her, lowering his head until it was a couple of inches from hers. "Don't even think about it. If you try to run off, I'll bash your brains out."

He was so close, Jenna could see the broken blood vessels in his eyes. It took all her courage just to stand her ground. "What do you want from me? Are you sick? Is that it?"

Derek nodded. "Yeah, sick as hell. But you're gonna cure me." Sweat dripped from his eyebrows. He stank like a locker room. "You're gonna get me back to normal."

"Look, I'm sorry, but I'm not a doctor. I can't—"

Jenna stopped herself. She heard a distant roar, a rumbling, grinding mechanical noise coming from the north.

A quarter mile from the elevated tracks, a convoy of three black vehicles raced down Ocean Parkway. They were as big as tanks but much faster, plowing through the floodwaters on huge, monster-truck wheels. Jenna recognized them from news reports she'd seen on TV— they were armored personnel carriers, the favorite ride of soldiers and SWAT teams. Each vehicle had a fierce-looking machine gun on top and a pair of powerful searchlights. As the convoy sped closer, the searchlights turned back and forth, sweeping their beams across the abandoned buildings on both sides of the parkway.

Derek grabbed her arm. "Get down!"

He pulled Jenna down to the platform, wrestling her to the wet concrete. Breathless, she sprawled on her stomach next to Derek and peered at the convoy, which slowed to a crawl as it approached Brighton Beach Avenue. One of the armored vehicles pointed its searchlights skyward, and the beams played over the elevated tracks, flashing horribly bright against the steel rails. Derek flattened himself, pressing his forehead to the platform, and clamped his hand over Jenna's back to keep her down.

After a long moment, the personnel carriers turned left and moved on. They sloshed down the avenue below the tracks, going east. The rumbling gradually faded below the noise of the storm.

Scowling, Derek rose to his feet. "Those were Strykers. I rode in them in the army. In Afghanistan."

"But the ones we just saw belonged to the FSU, right?" Jenna sat up and shivered. She was cold and exhausted. "And they're going to Sixth Street?"

"Yeah. They're looking for you." He grabbed her arm again and pulled her toward the tracks, forcing her to sit down on the edge of the platform, with her legs dangling over it. "After they search all the buildings on the street and see you're not there, they'll come back this way." He sat on the edge beside her, then jumped down to the tracks. Then he turned around and grasped her waist with both hands. "That's why we have to go."

Jenna was in even more trouble than she'd thought. Too stunned to resist, she let Derek lower her to the tracks. Then they turned west and started walking.

It was the hardest thing Jenna had ever done.

Even in daylight and good weather, walking on the elevated tracks would've been difficult. The steel rails were supported by wooden railroad ties that had been installed decades ago. The ties were splintery and waterlogged and littered with all kinds of wet trash—plastic bags, soggy newspapers, McDonald's wrappers. And on this section of the elevated line, there were yawning, foot-wide gaps between the ties, which meant that a misstep could easily break your leg.

But the storm made everything a hundred times worse. Jenna could barely see where she was going, and the gales from the Atlantic battered her. Derek marched down the middle of the westbound track, exactly midway between the rails, stepping quickly and efficiently from one railroad tie to the next, but Jenna couldn't keep up. Halfway to the next station, a powerful gust threw her off balance and she fell to the track. Her hands smacked into the edge of one of the ties and her knees smashed into another.

"Fuck!" She lay facedown across the track, dizzy and hurting all over. Her head hung between two of the railroad ties, and through the gap she could see the flooded street below. She waited a moment for the dizziness to pass, then raised her head and looked for Derek, who was twenty feet farther down the track. "Hey! *HEY!*"

He stopped and turned around, but he didn't come back to help her. He just raised his right arm and pointed to the east. Jenna slowly and painfully stood up, planting her feet on the ties and bracing herself against the wind. Then she looked east, back to Brighton Beach, about a mile behind them. The armored personnel carriers were hidden behind the rows of buildings, but she saw the beams of their searchlights. They illuminated the sheets of rain falling on the neighborhood.

Jenna got the message. The FSU was hard at work. She and Derek had to get farther away. She took a deep breath and continued trudging down the track.

After a few minutes the storm's fury subsided. The clouds thinned, glowing with the light of the full moon above them, and the winds died down, allowing Jenna to walk a little faster. The elevated line curved toward the ocean and passed a complex of high-rise apartment buildings, all in disastrous shape. Their windows were long gone, shattered in previous storms, and their balconies were badly damaged. But the buildings hadn't been completely abandoned. Some of the windows were boarded up with plywood or cardboard, and some of the apartments glowed with flickering light, most likely from the candles and Coleman lamps of squatters.

Soon they reached the next station, just north of Surf Avenue. This used to be the stop for the New York Aquarium, but that place was demolished in one of last year's storms. Farther west were the remains of the amusement-park rides that used to crowd the area between Surf Avenue and the Coney Island boardwalk. The same storm that wrecked the aquarium also knocked down the Cyclone roller coaster, which now lay in a tangled heap of wood and steel, surrounded by the floodwaters like an island. There were smaller islands of debris where the other rides once stood: the Thunderbolt, the Sling Shot, the Seaside Swing, the Brooklyn Flyer.

Jenna stared at the piles of rubble. She'd loved the rides at Coney Island. Because her family lived so close to the amusement park, they used to go there every weekend when she was a kid. Those were the good years, before Jenna went to college and everything fell apart. Her mother was alive back then, and Raza could still walk. Her father was a happier man then, always teasing her and making stupid jokes, and Jenna was happy too, a cheerful Muslim girl who still said her prayers and wore her hijab. Their favorite ride was the Wonder Wheel, the hundred-year-old Ferris wheel that towered over the boardwalk. All four of them would sit in one of the Wonder Wheel's cars and watch the whole city come into view as the wheel spun them upward.

The Ferris wheel was still there, just two hundred yards from the elevated tracks. It was the only ride that hadn't been destroyed, probably because it had been built so solidly. It loomed high above the flooded beach and the ruined boardwalk, a huge, skeletal disk with dark, crisscrossing spokes.

As Jenna stared at the thing, the wind from the ocean picked up again. The storm strengthened, lashing her with so much rain that she had to crouch and hold on to the railroad ties. Derek stopped too and looked over his shoulder at her. Then he turned to the south and gazed at the Atlantic. His body went still. He froze in that position, so motionless that his silhouette seemed to become part of the tracks.

Jenna looked in the same direction. Although the ocean and sky were almost equally dark, she could make out the horizon. It was rising. A massive sea swell, stretching for miles from east to west, rushed toward Coney Island. She stared in horror at the long, black wall of water. It was at least sixty feet high and capped with white breakers, furiously charging toward the shore.

Derek snapped out of his trance and raced over to her. He grabbed her arm and yanked her to her feet. "Run, goddamn it! If you want to stay alive, keep up with me!"

They started running side by side, heading west at full speed. Only a minute ago, Jenna had struggled to walk on the tracks, but now she hurtled over the railroad ties. Off to her left, the sea swell rolled closer and climbed higher, but she fixed her eyes straight ahead and focused on her stride. She aimed her bare feet at the ties and sprang off them with all her strength, doing everything she could to run faster. Derek's grip on her arm kept her steady and gave her momentum. In seconds they left the Aquarium station far behind and dashed toward the Stillwell Avenue stop.

But they weren't fast enough. The sea surge roared over the beach, carving a new channel through the sand. The wall of water struck the broken boardwalk and tore off a giant piece of it, a thick slab of concrete and wood, almost a hundred yards long. Propelled by the surge, the slab careened through the ruined amusement park, sliding into the piles of debris. Then it slammed into the base of the Wonder Wheel.

The crash echoed over Surf Avenue and the elevated tracks. Without breaking stride, Jenna turned her head to the left and saw the stretch of boardwalk jammed against the Ferris wheel's spokes. The wheel tilted for a moment, leaning away from the ocean. Then it plunged to the ground and splashed into the floodwaters. The sea surge swept over the wreck and streamed toward the elevated line.

Derek ran even faster, pulling Jenna forward. *"Come on, come on!"*

Her lungs were bursting. It was no use. The ocean slid over Coney Island like an immense black sheet, carrying tons of bobbing wreckage. Its frothy edge smashed into the two-story buildings on Surf Avenue and obliterated their brick façades. An instant later, the deluge rammed into the steel columns that supported the train line.

The impact shook the tracks. The railroad ties shuddered and Jenna lost her footing. She started to fall backward, but Derek swung her around and swooped an arm under her knees. He lifted her to his chest and kept running between the rails, leaning forward and breathing like a bellows.

She couldn't believe it. He was unnaturally strong and phenomenally fast. The elevated line swayed and vibrated, hammered by the sea surge coursing underneath it, but Derek kept his balance and sprinted ahead.

Jenna clutched his torso, holding on for dear life, and felt the muscles working under his skin. She peered over his shoulder and saw the tracks buckle a hundred feet behind them, the steel rails twisting and the railroad ties snapping. But Derek outran the collapse. He reached the section of track that curved north, away from the ocean, and then dashed for the shelter of the Stillwell Avenue station.

And then, all at once, they were out of danger. The station was a massive concrete structure with a huge steel canopy arching over the tracks. The terminal had been renovated a decade ago, and Jenna guessed that the reconstruction crew had done a good job, because the place looked remarkably undamaged. Derek slowed to a jog, then stopped on the tracks beneath the arching canopy. They were safe from the storm here.

But Jenna didn't feel safe. Not at all. Although Derek had saved her life, she was more uneasy than ever. She squirmed in his inhumanly strong arms. "Let go of me! Put me down!"

He stepped toward the station's platform and gently set her down on its edge. "I have something for you." He climbed onto the platform beside her, grasped her elbow, and led her across the station.

They weren't alone here. Because the Stillwell Avenue Station was so well-protected from the weather, other refugees from the storm had sneaked into the terminal.

There were cardboard boxes on the platform and homeless people sleeping inside them. Jenna couldn't see their faces, only the parts that stuck out of the boxes, the legs and torsos wrapped in rags and soiled blankets. What surprised her the most was that the storm hadn't woken anyone. The city all around them was drowning, but this station's platform was safe and dry, so the people here slept right through the catastrophe. They were so exhausted, they hadn't even noticed it.

Derek dragged her to the far end of the platform, where the elevated tracks ran north to Gravesend and Bensonhurst. There were two more cardboard boxes at this end, and the smaller one was occupied—a pair of long legs in filthy jeans and muddy sneakers poked out of it. But Derek ignored the sleeper and led Jenna to the larger box. She sat down on the platform while he reached inside the box and pulled out a canvas duffel, an olive-green bag with the words "U.S. Army" stenciled on it. This was Derek's box, she realized. He'd brought her to his makeshift home.

Then, to Jenna's dismay, he grabbed one of her bare feet and examined its sole.

She tried to pull her foot away from him. "What the hell do you think you're doing?"

"It's all cut up." He let go of her foot, grabbed the other one, and pointed at the lacerations on the heel and arch. They were bleeding freely. "This one too."

Jenna hadn't noticed the bleeding, hadn't even felt any pain until he pointed it out to her. Her terror had been so strong, it had overwhelmed everything else.

Derek opened his duffel bag and pulled out something that looked like a red Q-tip. He started swabbing the thing against the wounds on her feet. "This is an iodine swab. It's gonna sting a little."

It stung *a lot*. Jenna tried to take her mind off the pain by staring at Derek, who squinted and beetled his brows as he swabbed her cuts. She knew she shouldn't change her attitude toward this kidnapper just because he was giving her first aid. It was in his own interest to make sure she didn't bleed to death. And yet the cuts on her feet really weren't *that* bad. He could've ignored them and let her suffer.

After Derek finished disinfecting her, he removed a gauze pad and a roll of tape from his bag and dressed her wounds, one foot at a time. He did it so deftly, she wondered if he'd served as a medic in the army. Once her feet were taped up, he put his first-aid supplies back into the bag and reached into his box again. He removed a pair of gray sweatpants and a rolled-up ball of socks and tossed them at Jenna.

"They're clean. Mostly." He dug inside the box once more and pulled out a pair of old black sneakers. "I got these at a men's shelter where I was staying. Not sure if they'll fit you, but they're better than nothing."

She kept silent as she took the clothes from him, but her mind was churning. It was disturbing to see how meticulously Derek had planned this, how carefully he'd targeted her. He could've abducted any doctor or surgeon in New York, but instead he'd chosen a biomedical researcher to help him. He'd probably gone to the library and looked up her credentials and checked out her lab's website, which still displayed a photograph of Jenna on its home page even though she no longer worked there. He'd even guessed her shoe size, for God's sake.

He stared at her and frowned. "What's wrong? You don't like the sneakers? Not your style?"

Jenna turned away from him. Averting her eyes, she put on the sweatpants and socks. Then she slipped her feet into the sneakers. They fit perfectly.

She was busy tying the laces when she heard a rustle coming from inside the smaller box nearby, the one that was occupied. The long legs and muddy sneakers started to move, and then a skinny young white guy crawled out of the cardboard and rose to his feet. He had messy blond hair and a tattooed neck and a white T-shirt with a big dark stain below the neckline. There weren't many white people left in South Brooklyn, and Jenna was wary of the few that remained. Most were either drug addicts or had serious mental problems, and this guy seemed to fall into the second category. A row of scars ran up his forearm like the rungs of a ladder, and his eyes were too wide and wet and fervent. He stared intently at Jenna, then smiled at Derek.

"Shit, bro! You brought back a surprise!" He loped toward them, rubbing his hands together. "She's a nice, juicy brown one! Is she Arab? Indian? Whoa, look at the titties on that bitch!"

Derek shook his head. His face was blank, neither angry nor amused. "She's not for you, Keith. Go back to sleep."

Keith the mental case didn't seem to hear. He stepped closer to Jenna and leered at her chest. "Hey, girlie? You speak English? You like me, right? Maybe just a little bit?"

She stood up and looked him in the eye. He scared the hell out of her, but she didn't let it show. "No, I don't like you. Get away from me."

He laughed. It was a loud, high screech, the laugh of a crazy man. "Oh baby! You and me are gonna have some *fun* tonight!"

Derek stood up too, still shaking his head. "You don't listen good, do you? I told you to go back to sleep."

Keith's face abruptly changed from lascivious to enraged. He curled his lip and sneered at Derek. "No, bro, you owe me. I watched your shit, didn't I? I watched it all day long and made sure no one stole your stuff. And now I deserve some kind of reward. Those are the *rules*."

"I'm not warning you again." Derek stepped forward and stood toe-to-toe with the asshole, towering over him. "Go back to your fucking box."

Luckily for Keith, he decided to back down. He held up his arms in surrender and let out another crazy laugh. "All right, bro, all right! I guess you don't want to share, do you?" He retreated to his cardboard box, slowly and reluctantly. "You want to keep the bitch all for yourself, right?

All that nice brown pussy, and no one else gets a piece of it. What a fucking shame."

Keith knelt beside the box, and for a second it looked like he was going to take Derek's advice and go back to sleep. But instead he reached inside the cardboard and pulled out a gun, a big black nine-millimeter. He held it with both hands and pointed the muzzle at Derek. "Well, lookee here. This is what you get for being greedy, you black cocksucker. Now you're gonna—"

Derek moved so fast that Jenna never saw him cross the platform. She blinked, and suddenly he stood right in front of Keith, with one hand around the barrel of the nine-millimeter and the other around the lunatic's throat. He wrenched the gun out of Keith's grip before he could pull the trigger and crushed his larynx before he could say another word. Then Derek shoved him backward, and Keith plummeted off the platform and onto the tracks. His skull cracked against one of the rails, and blood splattered over the railroad ties.

Jenna turned away, but it was too late. She saw the man die. And now she knew why Derek had kidnapped her. No ordinary human had that kind of speed and strength and agility. The genetic experiments must've succeeded beyond all expectations. The research had progressed to human trials, and the results were far better than what anyone in her lab had thought was possible.

For a moment, Derek examined the nine-millimeter pistol he'd acquired. Then he tucked the gun into the waistband of his jeans and turned back to Jenna. His eyes were redder now, so bloodshot that there were barely any whites left. Yellowish pus leaked from the unhealed wound on his neck, and his breathing was harsh and ragged.

"You ready?" he rasped. "We gotta keep moving."

FOUR

Colonel Eli Grant marched into the White House, breezing past the Secret Service agents at the West Wing entrance. They knew him well, even the agents on the midnight-to-eight shift. He never would've imagined it, not in his wildest dreams, but he was a regular visitor to the White House now. He was a goddamn big shot.

He walked across the lobby and down the corridor, passing the offices of the national security advisor and the vice president. During the daytime these offices buzzed with activity, with generals and admirals and bureaucrats hustling from one meeting to another, but at 3 a.m. the hallways were empty and the office doors were closed. To tell the truth, Grant liked it better this way. The worst thing about the government was that it required so many damn people to run it. And the vast majority were idiots.

As he passed the closed doors, Grant pulled his secure phone from his pocket and checked for updates on the situation in New York. Superstorm Zelda was still pounding the city, flooding all the low-lying areas. Grant had sent reinforcements to the Federal Service Districts in Brooklyn and the Bronx, but there were reports of crowds gathering at the districts' checkpoints. That was bad news. If the illegals breached the fences, the whole Safe Cities program would go straight to hell. Grant was trying to beef up the FSU teams, communicating with all his lieutenants on the front lines, but it wasn't easy to command his troops from two hundred miles away. You can't run a war long-distance—he'd learned that in Syria, during his first tour there as a Special Forces commander. And the same thing was true for this shitty home-front war.

But he had to come to Washington after Keller summoned him. It was a bad idea to disobey the K-Man's orders.

Grant turned left and marched down another corridor. This one wasn't empty. Two Secret Service agents stood at the far end of the hallway, flanking the entrance to the Oval Office. Thirty feet closer, another pair of agents stood by the door to the office that was adjacent to the president's, the office of White House Senior Advisor Vance Keller. Stiff and unsmiling, the agents nodded at Grant. Then one of them opened the door.

Inside, the K-Man sat behind his desk, pen in hand, looking down at some papers. He didn't raise his head; keeping his eyes on the documents, he gave a hand signal to the Secret Service man. The agent nudged Grant into the office and closed the door behind him.

Keller still didn't look up. He kept studying his papers, occasionally jotting down a note or crossing out a sentence. Grant waited a couple of seconds, standing in the middle of the office, then took a seat in one of the fancy armchairs in front of the desk. He didn't feel insulted. The K-Man did this to everyone, generals and ambassadors and congressmen and cabinet secretaries. It was a power play. He wanted to make it clear that his time was more important than yours.

Grant busied himself by scrutinizing the office, but there wasn't a whole lot to see. Behind Keller's desk was a window made of bulletproof glass. During the day you could see the White House's South Lawn, but now it was pitch-black. To the left of the desk was the door that led to the Oval Office, the private entrance Keller used whenever he wanted to talk to the president. Other than that, though, the office was unremarkable, and the walls were bare. That was Keller's style. He liked being the Mystery Man, the guy who rarely speaks at cabinet meetings but takes careful notes on everyone else.

The only decorative item on Keller's desk was a framed portrait of his late wife. She'd died young, in her thirties, just five months after she married the K-Man. In the portrait she stared straight ahead, her blond hair draping her pale, flawless face. Printed on the frame in ornate script was the word "Princess," which had been her nickname in the White House. In addition to being Keller's wife, she was the president's eldest daughter.

Grant didn't like looking at the portrait. For him, it was a painful reminder of failure, one of the worst defeats in the War on Terror. It happened three years ago, just a week after Grant quit the army and started working for Keller. The K-Man had been one of the president's advisors from the beginning, a boyish Republican operative who knew everyone in Washington, but he and Princess didn't become an item until 2020. She was on the rebound, having just divorced her first husband, who'd also been a presidential advisor but suffered a nervous breakdown after a couple of years in the White House. Her new relationship with Keller coincided with the president's reelection campaign, which was floundering despite all their efforts. Princess tried to help her father by speaking at his rallies, and that's when the attack happened, right after she gave a rousing speech about political harmony and hope. The date was burned into Grant's memory: October 29, 2020. The day of her assassination.

He averted his eyes from the photo and focused on the K-Man instead. Keller was still young, only forty, but he looked awful. His tall, emaciated frame hunched over the desk like a scarecrow in a $5,000 black suit. The job had aged him—he'd been at it for seven years—and he'd never fully recovered from the death of his wife. After the assassination, America stood behind the president, giving him enough sympathy and support to rescue his failing campaign and reelect him by a sizable margin. Keller got his share of sympathy too, and he took on an even greater role in the administration during the second term, seizing control of the White House staff and the National Security Council. But his boyishness vanished forever, replaced by a cold intensity. His narrow face was haggard and lined, his eyes sunk deep into their sockets, his lips stretched thin and colorless.

Keller scowled at the papers he was reading. His expression was so full of annoyance that Grant grew curious about the documents. Sneaking a look out of the corner of his eye, he tried to read the papers upside down, or at least the words in bold type scattered across the pages. But he didn't have much success. The only words he could make out were "CAR BOMB," "THREAT LEVEL," and "ISLAMIC STATE."

Finally, Keller put down his pen and pushed the papers aside. He raised his head and attempted to smile. "Thank you for coming on such short notice, Colonel." His voice was soft and amiable, the exact opposite of his personality. "I'm especially appreciative because I know how busy you are right now."

Grant nodded. He knew enough not to go into the details about the crisis in New York. The K-Man didn't like details; he expected his subordinates to take care of all that. And Grant was taking care of it. "No problem, sir. Everything's under control. What can I do for you?"

Keller leaned back in his chair. He was still trying to smile and not succeeding. His pale lips twisted at the corners. "I want you to see something." He reached for the phone on his desk and pressed a button. "You can send him in now," he said softly into the receiver. Then he hung up and turned back to Grant. "I think you'll find this very instructive."

Ten seconds later, the door to the office opened again and two men stepped inside. The one on the left was another Secret Service agent, a beefy guy in a blue blazer, perfectly interchangeable with all the other agents in the White House. The man on the right, though, was a surprise. He was a twerpy, white-haired fellow dressed in khaki slacks and a rumpled polo shirt. His eyes were bleary, his cheeks frosted with gray stubble. He looked like he'd been woken from a deep sleep and forced to dress quickly. Grant recognized him immediately: it was the attorney general of the United States.

Without a word, the Secret Service agent turned around, left the office, and closed the door. The attorney general stared at Grant for a moment, blinking slowly, like a befuddled gnome. Then he grimaced at Keller. "Whatever you want, Vance, it better be important. You know I don't care for these middle-of-the-night meetings."

The K-Man gave him a sober look. He wasn't trying to smile anymore. "I called you here because we have a problem. A serious threat to the nation's security. I hate to disturb you at this hour, but I was under the impression that our national security was one of the things you vowed under oath to protect."

"I assume this has something to do with the Federal Service Unit?" The AG pointed at Grant. "That's why Eli is here too?"

He curled his upper lip as he said Grant's first name, infusing each syllable with contempt. Technically, the attorney general was in charge of the FSU, but when Keller set up the new agency, he and the president appointed all the regional commanders. So Grant's real boss was the K-Man, not the AG, and that drove the little gnome crazy.

Keller nodded. "Yes, this matter involves the FSU. Specifically, the Palindrome Project. Do you recall our recent conversation about this program?"

"Of course. And I'm not surprised you're having problems with it." The attorney general stepped toward Keller's desk, but kept pointing at Grant. "This man isn't qualified to supervise the project. I don't know what you were thinking when you chose him. This operation needs a high-level leader, not a Special Forces commando. He has no scientific expertise whatsoever."

Grant was ready to defend his qualifications, forcibly if necessary, but he stopped himself when he saw Keller narrow his eyes at the AG. The K-Man clearly wanted to fight this battle himself. "Colonel Grant has recruited dozens of scientists and technical advisors to work on Palindrome. They have more than enough expertise to guide the project."

"No, you need *independent* advisors. Experts who can point out the pitfalls and dangers, instead of blindly following orders." The AG opened and closed his hands, twitchy and fervent. "Palindrome has tremendous risks, Vance. If something goes wrong, it could have *catastrophic* consequences for public safety. And that means you can't run the project with such a small and inexperienced leadership team. You need input and guidance from other agencies, from Homeland Security and the FBI and the National Intelligence Program."

Keller frowned. He didn't like to be lectured. "We went over this already. If we bring more agencies into the planning, we increase the chances that someone will compromise the project's secrecy."

"Not if you do it right." The attorney general raised one of his hands to his chest and tapped it with his index finger. "I'm the best person to run Palindrome. If you put it under my supervision, I'll make sure it stays secret. And I'll give the project the leadership it needs."

Grant had to bite his tongue to keep himself from laughing. The little schemer was so transparent. The AG didn't really care about public safety. He was just trying to expand his bureaucratic turf. That was the biggest problem with this administration, all the clowns wrestling with each other for control of the circus.

But Keller wasn't amused. His frown turned menacing. "I'm familiar with this argument. You promised me the same thing in our last conversation, using the very same words. And I told you *no*, remember? I told you I didn't want any other officials brought into the project. And then I specifically warned you not to breathe a word about Palindrome to *any-one*. Remember?"

The AG didn't reply. His face reddened, and he stepped backward. He seemed to finally realize why the K-Man had summoned him to the White House.

Keller propped his sharp elbows on his desk and leaned forward. "But you ignored my warning. You discussed Palindrome with the secretary of Homeland Security."

"No, that's not true!"

"We recorded it. Frankly, I'm stunned at your stupidity. Didn't it occur to you that we might have listening devices in the secretary's office?"

The attorney general took another step backward. His eyes darted to the left and right, as if he was looking for the nearest exit. He bit his lip. "I'm sorry, Vance, but I had to do something. You're taking too many risks without—"

"*You're* the problem. *You're* the threat to national security." Keller stretched his long arm across the desk and pointed at the AG. "You jeopardized one of our most important operations by revealing the classified details to an unauthorized official."

"Unauthorized? That's ridiculous! He's a member of the president's cabinet!"

Keller shook his head. "Not anymore. And neither are you. You can continue your conversation with him if you want, because I'm sending both of you to the same place." He turned away from the attorney general and looked straight at Grant. "Colonel, will you do me a favor? This traitor has violated the Espionage Act. Please arrest him."

Grant stood up and grinned. "With pleasure, sir." He reached for the inside pocket of his jacket, where he kept the essential tools of his job—his badge, his extra clip of nine-millimeter bullets, and a pair of handcuffs. Moving with practiced ease, he stepped behind the attorney general, grabbed his arms, and snapped the cuffs on.

To Grant's disappointment, the gnome didn't resist. He just stood there, shivering in disbelief. He'd assumed he was smarter than his bosses, and now he was shocked to discover that he wasn't. And Grant didn't feel sorry for him, not one bit. The guy was smug and sneaky and sanctimonious, but worst of all, he was disloyal. In Grant's opinion, that was an unpardonable crime.

Keller was even less sympathetic. He pointed at the door. "Well, it's time to say goodbye. I'll tell the newspapers that you resigned for medical reasons, and that you're being treated at the Beaumont Army Medical Center in Texas."

The AG's knees buckled, but Grant held him by his elbows and kept him from hitting the floor. He sagged in Grant's hands like a sack of laundry. "Please . . . Vance . . ." He was sobbing. "I . . . I can't . . ."

"Don't worry. You're not actually going to Texas. That's just our cover story." The K-Man twisted his lips again. "In reality, you're going to Colorado. Specifically, the maximum-security federal prison in Fremont County. I hear it's lovely this time of year."

The attorney general let out a whimper. Disgusted, Grant pulled him away from the desk. With one hand he held the AG upright, and with the other he opened the office door. Then he handed the spineless twerp to the pair of Secret Service agents in the hallway. "Here you go. You know what to do with him, right?"

The agents nodded. They weren't surprised. Keller must've given them a heads-up.

Grant watched them drag the attorney general down the corridor. Then he turned back to Keller, closing the door behind him. "Thank you, sir." He returned to the armchair in front of the desk. "You were right. That was very instructive."

Keller picked up his pen and went back to studying his documents. But Grant could tell that their meeting wasn't over yet. The K-Man gave him a sidelong glance. "Now that he's out of the way, you can take charge of the entire Federal Service Unit. All the other regional commanders will report to you. For the time being, though, I want you to focus on Palindrome. We need to move to Phase Three as quickly as possible."

"Yes, sir." Grant nodded vigorously, showing nothing but confidence. "Everything's in place. We've completed all the field tests, and we'll be ready for the deployment very soon. We can start Phase Three in forty-eight hours, maybe less."

"Is there anything else we should be worried about? Any potential complications that we haven't already discussed?"

Grant took a moment to think it over. Unlike the AG, he had no worries about Palindrome's safety. The leaders of the research teams had assured him that Phase Three posed no threat to public health. His biggest concern was that someone would try to sabotage the project during this crucial period. One of the lab directors, a researcher named Tung, had gone missing yesterday, just vanished without a trace, and that had made Grant nervous about the project's security. So he'd ordered the roundup of all the scientists on the teams, right down to the lowliest graduate students. Most of the researchers didn't know the full scope of Palindrome or its ultimate goal, but they were clever people, and one of them might figure it out. Better to lock them all in a secure detention facility for the next few days, so they couldn't disrupt the all-important Phase Three rollout.

He had another concern about the project, but it was less pressing and more nebulous, more like a nagging unease. It had to do with one of the field tests that the Special Forces had conducted in Afghanistan. The army commander there was an old buddy of Grant's, and he'd sworn up and down that all the participants in the Palindrome test had been accounted for. But his reports weren't entirely complete or convincing. Grant worried now about the loose ends.

In the end, though, he decided against sharing these concerns with Keller. Whatever happened, Grant could handle it. He was going to make Palindrome a success, no matter what. He had to admit, he'd become obsessed with the project. He'd spent so much time and energy on it, almost three years of planning and coordinating. It was the most important assignment he'd ever taken on, and it had already given him more satisfaction than anything else in his life—more than the twenty years he'd wasted in the U.S. Army, more than his ungrateful kids and their bitch of a mother. Keller had promised him a spectacular reward for his efforts, and now the payoff was in sight. Palindrome would be his redemption, his crowning glory. It would vindicate *everything*.

"No complications, sir." Grant made a chopping motion with his right hand, as if beheading an enemy. "We're gonna win this thing. We're gonna show them all."

The K-Man kept his eyes on his papers, but he seemed satisfied. He crossed out another sentence. "Very good. Once you get back to New York, you can—"

A howl interrupted him, a loud, guttural moan that shook the walls. Keller's head popped up, and Grant jumped to his feet. At first he thought it was the attorney general, but the unnerving noise wasn't coming from the corridor. It came from behind the door that led to the Oval Office.

Grant leapt toward the door, but Keller held up his hand. "No! I'll take care of it."

"But he's—"

"Don't worry, he's not hurt. This happens every night." Keller stood up and reached the door in two long strides. "It's just another challenge we're dealing with. Please let yourself out of the West Wing and return to your duties, Colonel."

Then the K-Man entered the Oval Office and shut the door behind him, leaving Grant on the other side.

A moment later, the president let out another unearthly howl.

FIVE

Lieutenant Frazier stared at his men in disgust. Six of them slouched on the bench seats inside the Stryker as it raced back to the South Brooklyn District's fence. Their uniforms were muddy and dripping. Filthy brown water trickled from their body armor and puddled on the vehicle's steel floor. They'd just spent two hours searching the streets and apartment buildings of Brighton Beach during the worst storm in the city's history, but they had nothing to show for their efforts. They hadn't found the Khan girl. They were a bunch of useless dipshits.

Frazier focused his loathing on the idiot to his left, Sergeant Lynch, the leader of the team that let the girl get away. The sergeant was big and burly, a natural-born brawler, but the expression on his wet face was terrified. Frazier was reaming him out.

"So how long was it again?" He got in Lynch's face, staring him down. "A minute?"

"I swear, Lieutenant, it was less! I took my eyes off the bitch for thirty seconds, tops!" He cringed, leaning back in his seat, pressing his shoulders against the inside of the Stryker's armored hull. "She was right there, on the sidewalk, and then she was gone!"

"And she just disappeared? Carried away by the storm, maybe?"

"I looked up and down the street. No sign of her. I figured she was hiding behind one of the parked cars, because that's what everyone else was doing. We were under heavy fire."

"Really? From a few civilians with handguns?"

The look on Lynch's face was childishly pathetic. A bead of muddy water dripped from his chin. "Sir, there were at least a dozen shooters in the apartment buildings! We blasted some of them, but we couldn't get them all. They kept moving from window to window, taking shots at us. I'm telling you, sir, it was fucking serious!"

Frazier shook his head. These dipshits weren't real soldiers. They'd never served in Syria or Somalia or Afghanistan. Most were recruited from SWAT teams in stateside police departments, so they had no idea what to do in a firefight. For a moment, Frazier wished he was back in Kandahar with the Rangers, with a team of real soldiers who knew what the fuck they were doing. Like Deadeye Spinelli or Mad Dog Jones, or Frazier's old commander, Captain Powell, the Butcher of Balochistan. Those guys kicked some *serious* jihadi ass, and that was in the ragheads' home territory. This numb-nuts Lynch wouldn't have lasted a week there.

"Let's speed things up, Sergeant. How long were you pinned down?"

"Uh, five minutes?"

It was probably ten minutes, maybe more. That would've given the Khan bitch plenty of time to run off. Even so, it was such a clean getaway that Frazier suspected that someone had helped her. Maybe a neighbor or a friend. Or some thug from one of the South Brooklyn gangs, maybe the Bloods or the Latin Kings. Or maybe—and this was the worst-case scenario—it was another person connected to Palindrome. Maybe Colonel Grant had a serious security breach on his hands. That would explain why he'd sounded so pissed when he'd contacted Frazier.

"Just one more question. You notice anyone trying to help the girl? Any bystanders take a particular interest in her?"

The sergeant nodded. "Yeah, this old lady in one of the apartments started yelling out her window at us. But we took care of her, Lieutenant. We fucked her up good."

Frazier clenched his hands. He wanted to crush this moron's empty skull. In fact, he wanted to kill all six of the soldiers in the Stryker, the whole sorry team. And he could do it too. He was strong and fast enough. He could decapitate all of them without breaking a sweat.

But he had his orders to carry out, and murdering his own men wouldn't be helpful. Instead, Frazier reached for his wireless tablet, which was linked to the FSU's surveillance network. At the moment, the network had a lot of holes in it; the agency's drones were grounded tonight because of the weather, and the storm had cut power to most of the security cameras on the streets. When Frazier turned on the tablet, though, the screen displayed a list of battery-operated surveillance cameras that were still transmitting their video feeds to the network. There were more than a hundred of them in the South Brooklyn District, and about half were infrared cameras that could show the glowing heat signatures of human bodies moving through the darkness.

He selected the four infrared cameras closest to the Khan girl's apartment building and displayed all their video feeds on the tablet's screen, arranged in quadrants. Then he stared at the feeds, looking for glowing figures in the dark, flooded streets. The task was made easier by the fact that the storm was still raging and very few people were outside. All the places worth looting had already been ransacked. The only figure Frazier spotted was a fat homeless guy lying on the hood of a car, just above the floodwaters on Brighton Beach Avenue. He was either drunk or dying.

After a few seconds, Frazier chose four more infrared feeds, transmitted by cameras a bit farther away from the girl's building, and inspected them just as carefully. Then he scrutinized another quartet of videos, then another. He did it quickly and efficiently, his eyes roving over the images and his mind focusing on any out-of-place details. He'd always been good at this kind of mental work, but his brain had sharpened after the last round of injections, and now he eyeballed each feed in less than a second. Although the government had computer programs that could do the same thing—recognizing faces, detecting security threats—Frazier knew he was doing it better than any software package could. He was a fucking surveillance *machine*.

As he scanned the videos, he noticed the trail of damage from the storm surge. It had smashed Coney Island's shoreline, pulverizing the boardwalk and knocking down a long stretch of the elevated train tracks. A camera mounted on a nearby high-rise building showed the cold, dark seawater surrounding the Stillwell Avenue station. Floating in the water were several human bodies, still warm but rapidly cooling.

Frazier grimaced. Under normal circumstances, he would've ordered a rescue-and-recovery operation. His men would've charged into the flooded neighborhoods and tried to save the storm's survivors. He'd led plenty of rescue operations in Afghanistan, ordering the Special Forces to combat zones to extract wounded soldiers, and it still seemed like the natural thing to do. He kept staring at the screen, at the corpses bobbing in the water, and his discomfort worsened. He felt like he was neglecting his most important duty.

But this situation was different, he reminded himself. The floating bodies on the screen weren't his fellow soldiers. They were the corpses of the people he was fighting, and most of them weren't even American. The storm was doing the FSU's job, getting rid of the illegals who didn't belong in this country and the murderers and terrorists who wanted to destroy it. So there was nothing to worry about. One of the corpses might even be the Khan girl, Frazier thought. He tried to adjust the video feed to get a better look at the bodies, but most were floating facedown and tangled in garbage.

After several seconds he gave up and moved on to the next set of video feeds, which were from four cameras farther north, in the Gravesend neighborhood. There was nothing interesting on three of the feeds, but the fourth caught Frazier's eye. The camera was on a rooftop on 25th Avenue, a hundred yards from the elevated tracks where the D train used to run. Although the video was grainy, Frazier spotted two people on the tracks, a large male and a small female, their bodies shining brightly in the infrared images. They were walking north, away from Coney Island and toward the District's fence. In ten minutes they would reach Bay Parkway, the same checkpoint Frazier had been supervising a couple of hours ago.

His pulse raced. He adjusted the magnification of the surveillance video and zoomed in on the female. She had short hair and wore a long, loose nightshirt. That lined up with Colonel Grant's description of the Khan girl. Frazier couldn't identify her male companion—the video quality was too poor to show the guy's face or any distinguishing characteristics—but he thought of Palindrome again. It took some balls to walk on the elevated tracks, especially on a night like this. These people weren't ordinary bums or scumbags. They were the fucking assholes he was looking for.

Frazier lunged toward the front of the Stryker. He brushed past the corporal sitting at the gunner's station and grabbed the shoulder of the private who was driving the vehicle. With his other hand, Frazier pointed at the map on the driver's navigation screen.

"Head for the Bay Parkway checkpoint! Fast as you can!"

Frazier jumped out of the Stryker as soon as they got there. He needed to find Sergeant Barr and Corporal Hendricks, the officers he'd left in charge of the checkpoint, but he stopped in his tracks when he saw the mob on the other side of the fence. It had more than tripled in size over the past two hours.

At least a thousand ragged people crowded a block-long stretch of Bay Parkway, jammed up against the chain-link fence that ran down the middle of the street. They stood in foot-deep floodwaters, all of them eyeing the locked gate, their wet faces gleaming under the checkpoint's searchlights. The ones at the front of the crowd clutched the fence and rattled the mesh of steel links. More than a dozen had climbed halfway up the fence, and a few were trying to clamber over the coils of razor wire at the top. Meanwhile, the assholes at the back of the crowd tossed pieces of broken pavement over the gate. One of the chunks hit Sergeant Barr in the helmet, making him stagger and drop to his knees. Corporal Hendricks just stood there, his mouth wide open.

Frazier ran toward them, cradling his M4 carbine. He halted between Barr and Hendricks, making sure that everyone in the crowd could see him. Then he pointed his assault rifle at the night sky and fired over the heads of the fence climbers.

Most of them instantly let go of the fence and dropped to the ground. A few stubborn fuckers clung to the fence's steel links, but Frazier kept firing until they let go too. One idiot got tangled up in the razor wire and hung upside down, screaming. The coil tightened around his legs and the razor blades dug into his thighs. Blood soaked his pants and dripped from the fabric.

The crowd backed up, retreating several feet from the fence. But they didn't scatter. Frazier reloaded his rifle and fired another thirty bullets over their heads, but nobody bolted. Instead, more ragheads converged on the checkpoint. Thousands of them were trying to flee the district, sloshing north on the side streets toward Bay Parkway.

He reloaded again but held his fire. It wouldn't do any good. The fuckers had nowhere else to go. They'd rather risk a bullet than drown in the storm surge.

Frazier lowered his rifle and helped Barr to his feet. Then he faced the half-dozen soldiers who'd just stepped off the rear ramp of the Stryker. *"Fan out and guard the gate! And cover it with the Stryker's machine gun too!"* He pointed at the big fifty-caliber gun mounted on the vehicle's roof. He'd raised his voice to maximum volume, loud enough for everyone in the mob to hear. *"If any of these scumbags so much as touches the fence, blow his fucking head off!"* Then he turned to Hendricks. "You take care of Barr, see if he needs a medic. I'm going to the train tracks."

The corporal shouted, "Yes, sir!" but Frazier had already started running toward the Bay Parkway station. The stairway going up to the tracks was only two hundred feet from the checkpoint.

The elevated tracks ran perpendicular to the district's fence, which extended under the train line. Another fence ran over the line, blocking anyone from using the tracks to escape the district. Next to this upper fence the FSU had built a sentry tower, which loomed twenty feet above the tracks and forty feet above Bay Parkway. It was an ideal position for observing the checkpoint, and for firing on the crowd, if that proved necessary.

There were two FSU corporals in the sentry tower, Murphy and Paulson. Frazier had assigned them to guard duty at the start of their shift, and now he waved to them as he climbed the steps to the tower's platform. Murphy was peering through a pair of infrared binoculars, keeping watch over the elevated tracks to the south. Paulson stood behind a machine gun, an air-cooled fifty-caliber Browning M2HB, which rested on a tripod and pointed at the people in the street below.

Frazier had already radioed them from the Stryker, telling Murphy and Paulson to look for a man and a woman walking on the tracks. As soon as he reached the platform, he asked, "Any sign of them?" and both corporals shook their heads. He wanted to check for himself—the injections had also improved his eyesight—but before he could ask for the binoculars, he noticed another man sprawled in the corner of the platform.

The guy lay on his back, unconscious, his face very pale and his right arm bent at an unnatural angle. It was Allen Keating. The reporter from *The New York* Fucking *Times*.

Frazier pointed at him. "What's he doing here?"

Murphy shrugged. "We didn't know where else to put him, sir. He passed out a few minutes after you left."

"Is he sick? He don't look too good."

"His arm bled a lot after you broke it. I think you messed up one of his arteries or something." Murphy grinned. "But don't worry, Lieutenant. Reporters are like cockroaches. No one really cares if you step on one."

Paulson chuckled behind his machine gun, but Frazier didn't laugh. If this asshole reporter died on them, Colonel Grant would demand an explanation, and the colonel hated foul-ups of any kind. At the very least, Frazier would have to invent a cover story. And get his men to back him up.

But he wasn't going to worry about it now. He grabbed the binocs from Murphy and gazed down the elevated line, all the way to the next station at 25th Avenue. No woman in a nightshirt, and no man either. They'd probably climbed down from the tracks. In fact, there was a good chance they were mingling with the other ragheads on Bay Parkway.

Frazier stepped toward Paulson, who was gazing at the crowd through the Browning's gun sight. "Is there anyone matching the description down there? Young woman with short black hair, light brown skin? Wearing a long gray nightshirt?"

Paulson smiled but didn't take his eye off the crowd. "Sorry to disappoint you, sir, but most of those shitheads are male. And most of the females are wrinkled old skanks. There are a few young homegirls down there, but no one in a nightshirt. The only one who comes close is that bitch on the sidewalk, see? But she's wearing some kind of hooker outfit."

He pointed, and Frazier started at the sight of her. It was the African woman he'd noticed before, the addict from Somalia with the bikini top and the track marks on her arms. She was wandering in a daze at the back of the crowd, getting jostled by the others. But the boy wasn't with her.

Frazier looked at her through the binoculars. The woman's face was blank—no fear, no panic. It was a junkie trance, so deep and complete that she'd forgotten all about her son. Frazier scanned the crowd around her, looking for the boy. Just two hours ago, the kid had been clutching his mother's hand, holding on for dear life, his round face shining under the searchlights. But now he was nowhere in sight.

Frazier adjusted the binocs to get a wider view. He scrutinized the whole crowd, all the assholes standing behind the chain-link fence. *Where the hell is he? Did he wander off?* Frazier knew this was stupid, getting so anxious about some random kid he'd never seen before tonight, who didn't even look that much like Andy. The little fucker wasn't even white, for Christ's sake. But Frazier couldn't stop it. He felt the ache in his chest again, like a bayonet between his ribs. It was so sharp, it made him dizzy. His vision blurred.

Then the memories came back, impossibly crisp and solid: Andy in the backseat of their car, struggling for breath. His mouth gaping, his tongue hanging out. His small hand gripping Frazier's so tight. And Grandma driving their shitty old car like crazy, barreling down the gravel road toward the hospital.

Jesus Christ, it's happening again! HE'S DYING AGAIN!

"Uh, Lieutenant? Are you okay? You—"

Frazier dropped the binoculars and spun around, swinging his arms. His fists hit something and knocked it over, but he couldn't see it. All he could see was the gravel road to Cassville, the thick woods flying by on either side of the car. And his brother's contorted face, turning blue and purple.

Then he heard a strange noise, the sound of a diesel engine starting up. It wasn't another memory from Cassville, Missouri. This noise came from the street below, from Bay Parkway. At first he thought it was the Stryker's turbo-diesel engine, but the noise was rougher, more grating, the harsh sound of an old truck engine that hadn't been started in a long time. And that's what made it so strange. Who the hell was driving a truck through South Brooklyn tonight?

He shook his head, hard, trying to get back to normal. Grant had warned him that the drugs might have "moderate side effects" but this was a lot worse than moderate. It felt like a piece of his brain—the piece that held his memories—had expanded across his skull and taken over everything else. He closed his eyes and shook his head even harder, rattling and rearranging all the pieces inside. *Goddamn it! Get back in the right order!*

Then Frazier opened his eyes. He could see again, thank God, but what he saw wasn't good. Corporal Murphy lay on the platform of the sentry tower, his helmet knocked off his head. His eyes were rolled up in their sockets, the side of his head was bashed in, and blood was streaming from his ears. Frazier had walloped him without realizing it, and now the corporal was just as pale and unconscious as the *Times* reporter, whose right arm was mashed under Murphy's left leg. And Paulson was staring wide-eyed at all three of them, probably wondering if he should swing the machine gun around and point it at his commander.

Then a shot rang out, and Paulson shuddered. A bullet aimed at the sentry tower struck the back of his neck and blasted through his throat.

Frazier dove for cover, landing on the floor even before Paulson's body hit it. A second bullet whizzed above them, then a third and a fourth. Then Frazier heard the old truck engine coughing and grinding, revving up to an unbearable shriek.

He lifted his head and peered down at Bay Parkway, just in time to see the truck smash into the fence.

SIX

Jenna did what Derek told her to do. But at the same time, she watched and waited. She was ready to bolt as soon as she got the chance.

When Derek told her to walk north on the D line tracks, she walked north. When he told her to leave the tracks at the 25th Avenue stop, she followed him down to the street. And when he found the tractor trailer a block south of Bay Parkway and told her to get inside the truck's cab, she obediently slid into the passenger seat. But she rested her arm near the door handle while Derek hot-wired the truck's ignition and started the engine. As soon as he got distracted, she was going to open the door and jump out. She couldn't outrun him—she'd seen how fast he was—but if she got enough of a head start, maybe she could find a place to hide. She had to at least try it, even if the odds were against her. If she got away, she could start looking for her father and brother and maybe find out where the FSU had taken them.

As the truck began moving, though, the doors locked automatically. Derek pointed at the footwell on the passenger side of the cab, below the glove compartment. "Get down there. Scrunch all the way in. Things are gonna get hairy in a second." Then he reached for the waistband of his jeans and pulled out the gun that used to belong to Keith, the now-deceased lunatic.

"Whoa, whoa, hold on. What are you—"

"I said, GET DOWN!" Derek glared and pointed the gun at her. The whites of his eyes were dark with blood, but she could see the reflections of the dashboard lights in them.

Jenna didn't think he'd actually shoot her. He wanted her to cure him, that's why he'd kidnapped her. But the man was so desperate and unpredictable that she couldn't be certain what he'd do next. So she slid out of her seat and squeezed into the footwell. She folded her legs to her chest and wrapped her arms around her knees and cursed herself under her breath. *You goddamn idiot! You should've jumped out of the truck before the doors locked!*

A moment later, Derek brought the tractor trailer to a stop. Then he raised the pistol and took careful aim out the driver-side window. Jenna couldn't see what he was targeting, but she imagined the worst. Derek was good at killing. No, he was more than good—he was *enhanced*. He had unnatural abilities programmed into his cells.

He fired four times in quick succession. Jenna covered her ears, but the shots still hammered her eardrums. Then Derek lowered the gun and stomped the gas pedal.

The engine roared, and the truck lurched forward. Derek slammed his palm on the truck's horn and leaned out the window, screaming, "OUT OF THE WAY!" at someone in the street. Alarmed, Jenna half-rose from the footwell to look out the windshield. But before she could see anything, the truck hit something solid. The impact threw her forward, and her head bashed against the glove compartment.

She blacked out for a second. Or maybe five or ten seconds.

When she came to, Derek was gone. He'd left her alone in the truck's cab, crammed inside the footwell, her face pressed against the rubber floor mat. She lifted her head, and everything in the cab whirled around her—the steering wheel, the glove compartment, the empty passenger and driver seats, all careening in nauseous circles. But the noises were worse. Derek had left the driver-side door open, and through the gap Jenna could hear a sickening mix of screams and gunshots.

She raised her head a little higher and saw hundreds of people rushing past the truck, their faces illuminated by blinding searchlights. It was a stampede of terrified men and women splashing across Bay Parkway and stumbling over a mangled pile of chain-link fence and razor wire, half-submerged in the floodwaters. The truck had knocked down a section of the FSU's fence, and now the prisoners of the South Brooklyn District were leaping over the fallen barrier and making their escape.

Jenna climbed onto the driver's seat and peered through the windshield, looking for Derek. At first she couldn't find him, but when she heard the next gunshot she turned toward the noise and saw him fire his pistol at an FSU officer. The cop's face exploded under his helmet. The other officers swung their assault rifles toward Derek, but by the time they returned fire he was already gone. He darted and zigzagged through the terrified crowd, and then a few seconds later he was behind the cops, blasting away, aiming at all the gaps in their body armor.

His skills were horrifying. Derek was operating at a different speed than everyone else, running faster, reacting quicker, taking advantage of the chaos and all the human shields around him. Jenna was an expert on brain physiology, and she could see that Derek's mind was functioning at an accelerated pace, his brain cells signaling each other in microseconds, his cerebral lobes processing thoughts in an instant. His visual cortex had become so efficient that he could see things happening before any of the cops could. And the signals from his brain flowed so quickly to the nerves in his arms and legs that he could perform extraordinary feats of coordination, enabling him to dodge every obstacle and hit every target and slaughter the FSU men, one by one.

Jenna knew that no chemical stimulant—not Dexedrine, not meth, not cocaine, not Ecstasy—could change mental performance so dramatically. But a genetic alteration could do it. That was her specialty, the genetics of brain functions. She'd studied it for twelve years in college and grad school and Rockefeller University's Molecular Genetics Laboratory, where she'd manipulated the genes of lab rats to make them smarter and faster. And now it was obvious that another scientist in her field, maybe someone she knew, had dared to perform the experiments she'd objected to. Someone had made the same genetic changes to humans.

She grimaced. Derek was literally inhuman. Judging from the enhancement of his abilities, Jenna guessed that hundreds of his genes had been altered, a significant percentage of his protein-coding DNA. Genetically, he wasn't *homo sapiens* anymore. He was a different species entirely.

The shock was so strong, it cleared her head. Her dizziness and nausea subsided, and in their place she felt a cold, calm certainty. Derek was even more dangerous than she'd thought. She had to get away from him *now*, while he was still busy fighting the FSU officers. It was her last, best chance.

Jenna jumped out of the truck and landed in the floodwaters, soaking her borrowed sweatpants up to the knees. She stooped low beside the driver-side door, trying to stay unnoticed as she scoped out the safest route away from this nightmare. Heading west would definitely be a mistake. The Bay Parkway station lay in that direction, and there was a sentry tower on the elevated tracks. Going east wouldn't work either; one of the FSU's armored personnel carriers—Derek had called it a Stryker—was parked in the middle of the street, and it had a very large, nasty gun on its roof. But the street to the north looked clear, and most of the district refugees were running that way. All Jenna needed to do was join the throng and run like hell across Bensonhurst and Borough Park. She wouldn't stop until she was out of Brooklyn altogether.

She waited until a group of tall black men rushed past the truck, and then she caught up to them and slipped into the middle of the pack. She couldn't see Derek through the scrum of bodies, but that was good; it meant he probably couldn't see her either. The searchlights glared overhead, making Jenna all too visible to any FSU officer who might be scanning the crowd, but the circle of light covered only a short stretch of Bay Parkway. In a few seconds she would run beyond it and plunge back into the darkness. She was just fifty feet away.

Then she heard a horrid rattling off to her left. A torrent of streaking lights poured down on the street, like shooting stars in miniature, glowing yellow and red and white. They zoomed in nearly straight lines from the sentry tower on the elevated tracks to the running mob on Bay Parkway.

But they weren't shooting stars. They were tracer rounds. The glowing bullets showered the crowd in front of Jenna. A dozen people staggered and shrieked and dropped headfirst into the floodwaters.

She skidded and crashed into one of the tall men ahead of her. Someone in the sentry tower was firing at them. Some homicidal maniac with a fucking machine gun was mowing down the crowd, starting with the runners at the front. Jenna saw them fall in waves, the large-caliber bullets ripping through their bodies and shattering their skulls. The gunner slaughtered them methodically, first killing everyone at the leading edge of the crowd and then slowly pivoting the gun to cut down the people farther back.

Jenna turned around, but there were too many people jammed behind her. The refugees from the district were frozen, panicking, screaming. They couldn't go forward, couldn't turn back. Meanwhile, the machine gun swept its fire across Bay Parkway. It was a massacre, an extermination.

She scrambled through the crowd, squirming between the hysterical men and women, desperate for a way out. But she wasn't going to make it. Now the machine gun was targeting the heart of the mob, scything dozens of people just a few yards ahead of her, turning the flooded street into a river of corpses. They were falling everywhere Jenna looked. Their screams were almost as loud as the gunfire.

Jenna went into a crouch and closed her eyes. She couldn't watch anymore, couldn't listen. She shut out all the horrible sights and sounds, and instead she pictured her father and brother. She imagined having dinner with them one last time, back in their apartment, safe and sound. She thought of the prayers her father always said before they started eating, and for the first time in ten years Jenna said a prayer too. *Dear Allah, take care of Abbu and Raza, wherever they are! Don't let anyone hurt them, please!*

Then someone grabbed her right arm and nearly yanked it out of its socket. An irresistible force pulled her to her feet and dragged her through a gap in the crowd that hadn't been there a moment ago.

It was Derek, of course. When Jenna opened her eyes, she saw him charging like a bull through the panicking mob, knocking everyone else aside and hauling her along at top speed. The machine gun rattled behind them and the victims shrieked and dropped, but Derek snatched her out of the killing zone and barreled down the flooded street, away from the sentry tower.

Jenna stumbled after him, frantically pumping her legs and trying not to fall into the water. She felt grateful but exhausted, relieved but helpless. He'd saved her again, but for what?

Once they were clear of the crowd, he headed for the Stryker parked in the middle of Bay Parkway. As they rushed toward it, Jenna stared at the machine gun on top of the personnel carrier and wondered why it wasn't firing at the crowd too. The ramp at the back of the Stryker was down, and Derek dragged her inside the vehicle. Then he pushed a red button that raised the ramp and closed the rear hatchway.

Jenna looked down at the vehicle's floor and saw the bodies of two FSU officers, each with a bullet hole in his forehead. But instead of horrifying her, the sight of the corpses just left her numb. She'd already seen so much death tonight that she was beyond horror. She wasn't even surprised. Derek had followed a perfectly logical strategy. He'd eliminated his enemies and seized their best weapon, the Stryker.

He stepped over the bodies and sat down in the vehicle's driver seat. The Stryker had a steering wheel like a truck's, but the dashboard was like something out of a jet cockpit, with lots of dials and switches and a big navigation screen. Derek flipped one of the switches and the screen came to life, displaying a wide-angle view of Bay Parkway, probably transmitted from a video camera at the front of the vehicle. Then he looked over his shoulder at Jenna. "Why did you leave the truck? Were you trying to run away from me?"

Before she could decide how to answer, a barrage of bullets clattered against the Stryker's hull. Jenna jumped at the noise, but Derek calmly adjusted his screen to display the sentry tower where the gunfire was coming from. "Don't worry. We got plenty of armor around us." He flipped another switch below the screen, and the Stryker's engine began to rumble. "That son of a bitch in the tower is in trouble now. We got our own fifty-caliber gun on top of this vehicle."

The Stryker jolted forward. Derek steered it toward the elevated tracks while Jenna looked over his shoulder at the navigation screen. There was a clear path down Bay Parkway. Most of the refugees who'd crowded the street just a minute ago now lay in the floodwaters. Jenna felt nauseous again as the Stryker jounced up and down, trundling over the dead, crushing their bodies.

Derek stopped the vehicle a hundred feet from the train station, and another barrage from the machine gun battered the Stryker's armor. On the screen, the gun looked satanic, spitting fire from the dark tower above the tracks. Derek grasped a joystick to the right of the steering wheel and manipulated it until a set of crosshairs appeared on the screen, centered on the tower. Then he pressed the button on top of the stick.

The Stryker's gun rattled above them. This time, Jenna didn't jump at the noise. She stared at the screen and watched the bullets hit the sentry tower, sparks flying everywhere. And she felt an emotion that was new to her, a grim, deadly satisfaction. She cheered on the bullets, celebrating each impact. She couldn't see the gunner in the tower, the murderous bastard who'd massacred the crowd, but she hoped the gunfire from the Stryker tore him apart. God help her, she wanted him dead.

Then she saw him on the screen. The murderer's gun fell silent, and a large ghostly figure fell from the tower. It was silhouetted against the night sky for a moment, and Jenna felt a bolt of terror. She remembered the stories her mother used to tell of Azrael, the Muslim angel of death, who flew above the city at night, collecting the souls of the dying. The figure hung above the horizon, huge and angry, even darker than the midnight sky behind him. Then it dropped out of sight, onto the elevated tracks.

Derek kept firing the Stryker's gun for another fifteen seconds, first pocking the sentry tower and then scoring the whole train station. Then he let go of the joystick and leapt out of the driver's seat. "Get moving. You're coming with me." He leaned over one of the corpses on the floor and wrenched a semiautomatic pistol from the victim's stiff hand. "We're gonna make sure that all the assholes in that sentry tower are dead."

Jenna backed away from him. She didn't want to go up there. She'd seen enough. "No, I'll stay here. I promise I won't go anywhere or try to—"

He pointed the pistol at her. "You're gonna follow right behind me, you hear? If you try to run away again, I'll shoot off one of your fingers. Maybe two." He stepped past her and pushed the red button that lowered the Stryker's ramp. "Let's go."

He aimed his gun at her left hand. This was another logical strategy. Whatever he wanted Jenna to do for him, she clearly didn't need all her fingers to do it. If she resisted, he'd just mutilate her hand and bandage it up. Then he'd tell her again to get moving.

So she followed him out of the Stryker. She was still watchful, still waiting for a chance to get away. But now she had even less hope than before.

They raced toward the stairs that went up to the Bay Parkway station. Derek held his pistol high as he climbed the stairway, and Jenna struggled to keep up with him. As soon as they reached the station, he ran straight for the sentry tower and leapt up its steps, taking them three at a time. The tower's upper half was a wreck, gutted by the Stryker's machine gun, but Derek made it to the platform in seconds. Jenna followed more cautiously, clutching the splintered handrail until she reached the top of the stairs.

There were three bodies on the platform, two men in FSU uniforms and a third man in civilian clothes. But Derek barely glanced at them. Instead, he leaned over the edge of the tower and peered down at the tracks below. Jenna assumed he was staring at the gunner who fell off the platform, but when she looked herself she didn't see a body on the tracks. The elevated line stretched into the darkness, rain-slicked and empty.

Derek shook his head. "Shit. Look at this. I don't fucking believe it."

His voice was different now—halting, uncertain. For the first time, he didn't sound like a bullying asshole. Normally, this change in tone would've been a welcome improvement, but Jenna wasn't happy about it. Derek sounded worried, seriously anxious about something. And if something could worry *him*, it had to be pretty damn bad.

She pointed at the tracks. "It looks like he got lucky. Probably landed on his feet and ran off."

Derek kept shaking his head. "Impossible. He fell at least twenty feet. He would've broken an ankle at the very least."

"Well, maybe he *crawled* away then. But—"

"No, he left the scene too fast. The son of a bitch must be in Palindrome. He's a test subject. Like me."

Jenna's stomach churned. She was a geneticist, so the word "palindrome" had a special meaning for her. It referred to a DNA sequence with a distinctive kind of symmetry. And those sequences formed the heart of a molecular tool that scientists had invented ten years ago, a tool that had revolutionized the study of genetics. But like any other tool, it could be turned into a weapon.

She stared at Derek and noticed that the symptoms of his sickness had worsened. Tears of blood leaked from his eyes, and the wound on his neck was throbbing. Jenna wanted to turn away, but she forced herself to look at him. "How many test subjects are there? Do you know?"

Before he could answer, she heard a groan from the other side of the platform. Derek spun around and pointed his gun at the bodies on the floor. The FSU officers were clearly dead—one of them had a bloody hole in his throat, and the other had a shattered skull—but the civilian rolled his head and opened his mouth. His face was pale and battered, and he seemed to be only semiconscious. After a second, though, he opened his eyes halfway and tried to raise his arm. He held something black and shiny in his left hand.

Derek lunged toward him, aiming his gun at the guy's head. "Drop it! Right now!"

The civilian groaned again and dropped the shiny, black object. "Take it . . . please." He winced. Talking was clearly painful for him. "I want you . . . to take it."

Jenna stepped forward and picked it up from the floor. It was an iPhone. She examined it, confused. Why did he want them to take his phone? To call an ambulance? Maybe he didn't know there was no cell phone service in South Brooklyn anymore.

Meanwhile, Derek bent over and stuck his pistol right in front of the civilian's broken nose. "Who are you? What are you doing here?"

The guy clenched his jaw. It looked like he was in agony. "My name . . . is Keating. I'm with . . . *The New York Times.*"

Jenna knelt beside him. Now it was starting to make sense. The FSU officers hated the city's newspapers. They also hated the TV news shows and the radio stations and anyone else who tried to tell the world what the federal agents were doing. She'd seen the agents arrest and beat up reporters when they tried to visit the district, and she guessed that's what happened to this guy from the *Times.* Except in his case, the beating got out of hand.

She leaned closer, examining his injuries. "The FSU did this to you?"

Keating nodded weakly. "The big one grabbed . . . my other phone . . . and smashed it. But I always . . . carry an extra in my pocket." He raised his left hand again and pointed a trembling finger at the iPhone. "I shot video . . . of what just happened. The shooting. The massacre. You have to . . . you have to give . . ."

He closed his eyes and writhed in pain. Jenna looked over her shoulder at Derek. "We need to get him to a hospital. Can you carry him?"

Derek shook his head. He was still pointing his gun at Keating's head. "He won't make it. He's lost too much blood."

"So you're not even gonna try?"

"There's no point. It would be kinder to put him out of his misery."

"What? Are you nuts?"

Keating screamed. His back arched and his body convulsed. At the same time, he reached for Jenna with his left hand and grasped her wrist. "Give the phone . . . to Tamara. That's . . . the safest way. Her address . . . her address is . . ." He faltered and let go of her. He seemed to be losing whatever consciousness he had left.

Jenna wondered if she could carry Keating by herself. He wasn't all that big. She shoved the iPhone into her pocket and was about to slip her arms under him when she heard a distant rumbling. Her throat tightened and her stomach twisted. She'd never heard this horrible noise before tonight, but over the past two hours it had become all too familiar.

She rose to her feet and looked to the east. Three more Strykers sped down Bay Parkway, their searchlights silvering the flooded street. They were about half a mile away from the checkpoint and closing in fast.

Derek stepped between her and Keating. Pointing his gun at her head, he pushed her toward the steps leading down from the sentry tower. "Time's up. We need to *go*."

Jenna pushed back. Derek was at least twice her weight, but she held her ground. "No, I'm not going without him! Go ahead, shoot off my fingers!"

Keating lifted his head a few inches off the floor and gazed at them foggily. "It's 168 . . . Prospect Park West . . . just give her . . . give it to . . ."

Derek frowned. He narrowed his bloody eyes and pressed his blistered lips together, as if steeling himself for something awful. Then he lifted his right foot and slammed it down on Keating's head.

Jenna didn't look. The sound she heard was sickening enough. She was going to faint.

Derek wrapped one arm around her waist and the other under her knees. Then he carried her down the steps.

SEVEN

Lieutenant Frazier knelt in the floodwaters, holding the boy's mangled body. The kid had been trampled, his face bludgeoned almost beyond recognition. But Frazier recognized him. It was the moonfaced African boy, the one he'd tried to save.

It happened right after the truck broke through the fence. The ragheads scattered out of the tractor trailer's path, and Frazier spotted the boy wading across the street, turning his head right and left. He was only ten feet from the section of chain-link fence that the truck had knocked down. The kid was so close to the breach that, if he'd wanted to, he could've been the first person to escape the South Brooklyn District. But he didn't run. He just stood there, facing the crowd that was stampeding toward the gap in the fence. As they rushed toward him, he kept turning his head, searching all their faces. He was looking for his mother.

Frazier had shouted, "WATCH OUT!" from the sentry tower, but there was no time to do anything else. Within seconds, the shitheads at the front of crowd knocked the boy over, and the ones farther back scrambled over his body, stomping his chest and stomach and head. The mob was so thick that Frazier lost sight of the kid. But he spotted the boy's mother in the crowd, running blindly with the rest of them, trampling her own son.

After that, Frazier went berserk. His mind tilted and joggled, swinging back and forth on an invisible pivot. On the conscious level, he saw what was happening on the street below. He saw the giant ringleader of the scumbags jump out of the tractor trailer and attack the FSU team at the checkpoint, and he saw the Khan bitch come out of the truck too. But on a deeper level, he lay beneath the floodwaters with the boy, pressed to the asphalt by the mob's pounding feet, his body jerking and twisting with each blow. Some of the ragheads must've seen the kid struggling under the water, but no one stopped to help him, no one even considered it. *Because they don't give a shit about anyone but themselves. Because they're fucking animals who don't deserve to live.*

So Frazier got behind the machine gun and started firing on the crowd. He wanted to kill all of them.

But he made a mistake. His mind was jittering so wildly that he didn't recognize the scumbags' ringleader at first. It was obvious that the guy had superhuman abilities—how else could he have taken down the eight FSU officers at the checkpoint?—but Frazier was crazed and furious and not thinking rationally. He didn't make the connection until the fucker grabbed the Khan girl and pulled her into the Stryker. And by then it was too late. The traitorous bastard had outgunned and outsmarted him. All Frazier could do at that point was run away. He jumped off the sentry tower and landed on the tracks and got the hell out of there.

After a few minutes, though, his brain returned to normal. He stopped running and turned around and headed back to Bay Parkway. By the time he got there, another Stryker convoy was on the scene to repair the fence and recover the bodies of the fallen officers and start searching for the guy who'd killed them. But that fucker was long gone. He was a clever son of a bitch even before he took the Palindrome drugs, and now he was ten times smarter. They wouldn't find him unless he wanted to be found.

So Frazier searched for the boy instead and found his body floating in the muck alongside all the others. He cradled the limp, waterlogged corpse and stared at the swollen, mutilated face. He was thinking clearly now, and he knew the kid wasn't Andy. But it didn't matter. Frazier was full of the same rage he'd felt all those years ago. He'd taken his revenge on the fuckers who'd hurt his little brother, and now he was going to do the same to the inhuman bastard who'd turned against him. Frazier had known the man for a long time, had even respected and revered him, but now he was going to track down the motherfucker and kill him.

First, though, he had to talk to Colonel Grant. He let go of the kid's body, letting it slip back into the floodwaters. Then he pulled the secure phone out of his uniform and punched in Grant's number. The colonel picked up the call, and Frazier gave him the news.

"He's still alive, sir. I just saw him."

"What? Who are you talking about?"

"My old commander. From the Rangers' Third Battalion. Captain Derek Powell."

EIGHT

Colonel Grant was in an interrogation room on Rikers Island, waiting for the prisoners to be brought in. He sat in a metal chair that was bolted to the floor, next to a metal table that was also immovable. He smoked a cigarette while he waited, an activity that was absolutely forbidden for every other FSU officer. But he made an exception for himself. It was one of the perks of being the boss.

It was late morning, almost noon, but there were no windows in this part of the prison. Rikers Island was a sprawling complex of buildings, situated in the middle of the East River between the boroughs of Queens and the Bronx. The island had formerly been the site of New York City's jail complex, but the city closed it down in 2021 because of its long history of brutality. The next year, the Federal Service Unit took over the facility to support its antiterrorism operations. Grant thought it was a very appropriate place for his headquarters.

He finished his cigarette and immediately lit up another. He had a good excuse for bingeing—the past twelve hours had been hellacious. While Superstorm Zelda thrashed New York, the thugs and illegals had busted out of the city's Federal Service Districts. They broke through the fence at two places in the South Brooklyn District and at three checkpoints in the Bronx. Thousands of illegals scattered across the city, hiding wherever they could, probably welcomed by all the shit-for-brains Democrats who wanted to turn America into a Third World hellhole. The FSU asked the New York Police Department to help round up the scumbags, but the mayor refused. He said the NYPD wouldn't arrest anyone who hadn't committed a crime.

That, in Grant's opinion, was total bullshit. The mayor was an idiot, the king of all the shit-for-brains. The illegals who'd escaped were going to join forces with the Islamic extremists who were already planning attacks all over the city. There were going to be more bombings in Times Square and Central Park and Grand Central Station. But the mayor didn't give a fuck. He was the best friend the terrorists ever had.

Zelda finally let up at dawn, but by then half the city was without electricity and large parts of Lower Manhattan were underwater. Although Rikers didn't suffer much damage—the Feds had built a seawall around the island when they took over the complex—the storm had disrupted Grant's plans for Palindrome. He needed a shitload of laboratory supplies to prepare for Phase Three, and all the flooding and road closures had fucked up the delivery schedule. There were shortages of cell-culture dishes, centrifuges, aerosol sprayers, and vaccine doses. Grant was starting to doubt that he could get everything ready for deployment in just forty-eight hours. But that's what he'd promised Keller, and the K-Man had no tolerance for failure.

And now, on top of all that, Grant had to worry about Derek Powell.

Until a few months ago, Powell was the ideal soldier. He was born and raised in Brooklyn, educated at West Point, and trained to be a warrior at the Army Ranger School in Georgia. He did three tours of duty in Afghanistan, leading Special Operations teams against the Taliban and Islamic State jihadis. By his third tour, though, the war wasn't going so well. The terrorists were taking over the country, and the Rangers were badly outnumbered and taking major losses. The U.S. Army desperately needed to give its soldiers an edge.

That's where Grant came in. He was a Special Ops veteran with decades of experience in all the Middle East shit shows, so he knew which skills the Rangers needed. Keller assigned him to work with Palindrome's scientists to find the right mix of genetic enhancements for the soldiers. Grant never completely understood the researchers' techniques—his policy was to leave the science to the scientists—but basically it involved a carefully designed molecule that could cut and paste the DNA inside a cell. The researchers produced viruses that contained the building blocks for this molecule, then injected the microbes into the Rangers. Then the viruses would invade the soldiers' cells and rejigger their chromosomes.

There was more to it than that, but Grant didn't have to know all the details. What he cared about were the results, and Phase One of the Palindrome Project was pretty damn successful. The scientists injected the viruses into a hundred volunteers from the Rangers' Third Battalion and put them all into a new unit under the command of Derek Powell, who'd also volunteered for the injections. And over the next three months, the unit's performance was outstanding. Their casualty rate plummeted, and their kill rate skyrocketed.

But it was a radical experiment, so there were bound to be problems. Some of the soldiers developed serious complications: skin lesions, seizures, internal bleeding. And a few Rangers began to exhibit some very peculiar behaviors. One man refused to eat anything but chewing gum. Another stopped talking and would communicate with the other soldiers only by Morse code. The symptoms were all over the map, because every man's DNA was different and the interactions between the redesigned genes were so complex. But the researchers assured Grant that they could fix the problems. It was a trial-and-error process, they said, just like any other scientific investigation.

Then, during a night raid on one of the Taliban villages, Powell broke away from his team and ran straight toward the enemy. It was a suicide move, completely insane. All alone, he sprinted a quarter mile under heavy fire and fought his way into the mud-walled compound where the jihadis were holed up. Then, just to make things worse, another Ranger team called in an air strike on the village, and a B-52 dropped a dozen five-hundred-pound bombs on the shit-pile. The next morning, they found a hundred charred bodies at the site, most of them dismembered or half-buried or fused together. The soldiers assumed that Powell's body was somewhere in the heap, but it was impossible to tell which corpse was his.

But no one actually saw Powell die. And now here he was, back in Brooklyn, running around with one of the scientists who'd turned him into Superman.

Grant finished his second cigarette and reached for a file on the table.

It was the Jenna Khan file, which was getting thicker by the hour as Grant's aides investigated the woman's background. Her employment and academic records were in the file, as well as half a dozen photos. She was pretty hot, actually. A sexy little Pakistani, as brown and curvy as a harem girl.

Until the night before, he'd never heard of her. She was just a name on a list, one of the 213 researchers working on Palindrome. None of the scientists at her level knew how the army was using their research—that information was restricted to the lab directors—so there was no need to monitor her for security reasons. There *was* one black mark on her record: ten months ago she'd refused to conduct an experiment testing the effects of the gene-editing molecule on samples of human brain cells. But that wasn't so unusual. Three other researchers at her lab had also objected to the experiment on moral grounds, and they'd all been dismissed. The Khan girl was kept on for practical reasons—she was an expert on the genetics of behavior, and her research on animals was yielding useful results. But when she finished her animal experiments six months later, she was fired too.

At that point, she fell off the government's radar, because everyone assumed there was no reason to worry about her. She'd signed a confidentiality agreement when she worked at the lab, and the Feds could arrest her if she revealed *anything* about Palindrome afterward. Her family was poor and vulnerable: Hamid Khan, her father, was a green-card holder who'd immigrated thirty-two years ago, but he'd never applied for citizenship, and after the crackdown on Muslim immigrants he lost his job at Flatbush Taxi Service. The mother was deceased—sudden cardiac arrest, twelve years ago—and Jenna's brother was severely handicapped, both physically and mentally. The Khans were in such bad financial shape that they couldn't even leave South Brooklyn after the riots in June, when the government established the Federal Service District and all the decent people got out of there.

But then Colonel Grant took the precaution of rounding up all the Palindrome researchers, and he quickly realized that he should've paid more attention to Jenna Khan. Grant's investigators were still trying to figure out her connection to Derek Powell, but in the meantime they'd discovered something even more surprising, and it involved Jenna's brother. Sitting on the table in front of Grant was a separate file on Raza Khan, a folder that was just as thick as his sister's. And now, even though the colonel had dozens of interrogators at his disposal, he was going to interview the Khans himself. He wanted to get a good look at Raza and try to understand why the Palindrome scientists had suddenly become so interested in him.

At noon on the dot, the heavy steel door swung open, and a pair of guards brought the prisoners into the interrogation room. Both of the Khans wore orange jumpsuits and were in restraints: Hamid's hands were cuffed behind his back, and Raza was strapped into a wheelchair. One of the guards sat Hamid down in the immovable chair that was across the table from Grant, while the other officer wheeled Raza to a spot next to his father. Then the guards left the room. Grant didn't want them listening in, and he didn't need their help anyway.

Hamid was nervous as hell. His balding head was slick with sweat. His nose was purple from the beatdown that the arresting officers had given him, and his cheeks twitched with anxiety. He was in his late fifties, short and pudgy and aging fast, a sad sack who'd graduated from a top university in Pakistan but couldn't find any work in America except driving a taxi. In other words, pathetic and uninteresting. Grant gave him a quick once-over, then concentrated on his son.

Raza leaned against the wheelchair's straps, his torso arched and his head tilted backward. His skin-and-bone arms hung limply at his sides, the stiff hands curved like hooks in his lap. The jumpsuit was much too big for him—the short sleeves came all the way down to his elbows, and the pants billowed like drapes around his legs. His face was the color of wet sand and shaped like a wedge. It narrowed sharply to his beak of a nose and his gaping mouth.

Grant shook his head. He couldn't believe the kid had survived for so long. According to Raza's file, his illness had paralyzed him at the age of thirteen, and now he was twenty-three. He hadn't walked or talked in ten years.

And yet Raza's eyes were *alive*. They surveyed the interrogation room, moving slowly and methodically from left to right. Then they came to a stop and focused on Grant. Raza's eyes locked on him, fierce and penetrating, their dark irises glittering under the room's fluorescent lights. It startled Grant, it was so intense. The boy's gaze was violent, almost frightening.

Grant turned away from the kid and frowned. *Jesus, what's wrong with me? I'm jumpy as hell.* He'd been working nonstop for so long, he was starting to get wacky. As soon as he was done with these two, he was going to lie down for a while.

He turned back to Hamid. Enough fucking around. Time to get down to business. "Mr. Khan, you know why you're here, right? Why we arrested you and your son and brought you to this detention facility?"

This was a standard opening line for any interrogation. Most suspects weren't too bright, and often they'd blurt out the truth if you intimated that you already knew it. But Hamid shook his head, quickly and decisively. "No, sir, I do not. I honestly believe that someone has made a mistake."

His English was formal and precise, with a trace of a British accent. A lot of educated Pakistanis sounded like that. But they usually started blubbering once you applied a little pressure.

"You have no idea at all, Mr. Khan?"

"Truly, I don't. I have a green card, and all my papers are in order. And both my daughter and son are American citizens. They were born in this country, and I could show you their birth certificates if—"

"Let's talk about your daughter for a minute. You know where Jenna is right now?"

The question threw him. He blinked a few times, clearly confused. "Well, isn't she in the women's section of this prison? All three of us were arrested at the same time, so I assumed she—"

"No, she's not here. She got away from the arresting officers and now she's on the run. And we have a strict policy about fugitives: we go after them hard. If your daughter doesn't turn herself in very soon, I'm going to order my men to take extreme measures. That means if they spot her running away from them, they'll shoot her on sight."

Hamid's eyes widened. "Please, sir, don't do that!" He half-rose from his seat and leaned across the table. "Why would you shoot her? She's done nothing wrong!"

"Are you sure about that?"

"Of course I'm sure! She's an exceptional girl. She graduated first in her class at Columbia and—"

"Did you know that Jenna was stealing experimental drugs from the lab where she worked? Drugs that she used to perform unauthorized treatments on your son?" Grant pointed at Raza but didn't look at him. He didn't want to get distracted again. "She was clever about it, so the lab director never discovered the thefts. But my men have begun a thorough investigation of your daughter, and they've found discrepan-cies in the requisition forms she filled out."

Hamid opened his mouth but said nothing. His face took on a dark look of despair. He sank back down to his seat and lowered his head. He stared at the floor. "Please. You have to understand. She was just trying to help her brother. Is it fair to punish her for that?"

"What exactly was she trying to do?"

Grant already knew the answer to this question—it was in the Raza Khan file—but he wanted to hear Hamid say it. The strategy here was to get the ball rolling. With any luck, one confession would lead to another.

"Raza's illness is a rare genetic disease." Hamid glanced at his son, then looked down at the floor again. "Before he became sick, he was a normal, happy boy. And very smart too, a genius at mathematics. But everything changed after he turned thirteen. His disease is so rare that no one had ever studied it in detail, but Jenna had a theory. She believed the problem was a faulty gene that was linked to the genes that control sexual devel-opment. That's why Raza's symptoms didn't appear until he approached puberty."

Grant nodded. "And Jenna thought she could fix his faulty gene? Using the drugs from her lab?"

"Yes, that was the goal. She said she'd custom-designed a drug that she thought would help Raza. And it did help him, at least at first. His breath-ing improved and he seemed more responsive. But then his condition got much worse, and Jenna stopped the treatment."

"Was anyone at the lab helping her?"

Hamid shook his head firmly. "No, definitely not. She didn't want to get anyone else in trouble. She knew it was wrong to steal from her em-ployer, but she was willing to do anything to cure her brother."

Now Grant was ready to spring a surprise on him. He opened the Jenna Khan file, pulled out a photograph, and held it up for Hamid to see. "What about this man? Have you ever seen him with Jenna?"

It was a picture of Derek Powell in camouflage fatigues. The photo was taken almost a year ago, before Powell became a Palindrome subject, but it was the most recent picture Grant could find. Hamid stared at it in-tently, furrowing his sweaty brow. Then he shook his head again. "No, I've never seen him. He looks like a soldier."

Grant studied Hamid carefully. The puzzled look on the guy's face seemed genuine. If Hamid was lying, he was doing a good job of hiding it. "Did Jenna have a boyfriend? Maybe someone you never met?"

Hamid shook his head a third time, but now he didn't seem so certain. "Jenna gave up on boyfriends. The last time she went on a date was months and months ago. She said she didn't have time for it—she worked twelve-hour days at the lab, sometimes even longer. And after she lost her job, she spent all her time looking for a new position. It became very difficult to look for work after they shut down the subway service to our neighborhood, but—"

"She told you she was looking for work, but isn't it possible that she was actually seeing somebody?" Grant held up the photo of Powell again. "Maybe she was meeting this guy somewhere?"

Hamid fell silent. He bit his lower lip as he thought it over, probably recalling his recent conversations with his daughter, wondering if there was anything he'd missed. Grant leaned back in his chair and gave the guy some time. For a moment he thought about his own kids, how they tried to hide *everything* from him, especially after their mother turned against him. He grimaced at the thought. *Forget those bastards. Don't waste another second on them. You got more important things to do.*

Then Raza broke the silence. The fucked-up cripple let out an ugly grunt, loud enough to echo against the room's bare walls. It was the kind of noise that an old, senile hag would make, bellowing her fury from her bed in the nursing home, unable to use words because she's forgotten how to speak English. But when Grant turned his head at the sound, the kid glared at him so furiously that there was no doubt he'd understood every word of the interview. He knew exactly what Grant was doing. His emaciated body didn't move an inch, but it seemed like he was looking right through Grant's skull. Raza stared at him in disgust, peering with contempt at his innermost thoughts.

Grant squeezed the armrests of his chair. His heart was pounding. All of a sudden, he was terrified.

Shit! Stop looking at me, you fucking freak!

At the same time, Hamid turned to his son. He leaned as far he could toward the wheelchair, straining against the handcuffs behind his back. He obviously wanted to put his arms around the boy. "It's all right, Raza. Everything's fine." His voice was softer now, less formal. "We'll be going home soon. I just need to clear up this mistake."

Grant took a deep breath, struggling to calm himself. The researchers were right: the kid was abnormal, different from everyone else in a very fucking fundamental way. They'd come to that conclusion after Grant's investigators showed them the evidence of Jenna's secret treatment of the boy, in particular the striking changes she'd made to his DNA. (She'd recorded the results of the genetic procedure on her laptop, which the FSU officers had found in her apartment.) But Grant could see the kid's strangeness without looking at his genes. The fucker was off the deep end. Totally gonzo.

Hamid muttered something to Raza, a couple of soothing words in another language, probably Urdu or Punjabi. Then he turned back to Grant. "I know my daughter very well, sir, and I can tell you with full confidence that she wasn't involved with this soldier. But if you still wish to speak with Jenna, I can try to help you find her, as long as you promise not to use any violence."

Grant was breathing a little easier by this point, coming back to normal. The terror subsided almost as quickly as it had arisen, and now he felt only humiliation and anger. He hated all of these Khans. He wanted to punish the whole family. "And how would you help us, Mr. Khan? Do you have some idea where Jenna might be?"

"No, unfortunately I don't." Hamid gave him an apologetic look. "But I'm her father, so I'll work harder than anyone else to make sure she comes home. I'll walk up and down the streets, calling her name. I'll print flyers with her picture on them and put them up everywhere." He tilted his head toward Raza. "But you'll have to release both of us from this prison before I can do all those things."

Grant smiled, marveling at the Pakistani's boldness. He really thought he could talk his way out of this. He didn't understand just how much things had changed. "No, that won't help. We're going to keep you right here until we find her." He pointed at Raza again without looking at him. "But we're going to move your son to a different building on the island, a medical facility. Our staff there will be able to give him better care."

Hamid jumped to his feet. His lips quivered in alarm. "I need to go with him to that facility. Raza becomes very agitated when he's left alone."

"He won't be alone. Some of the finest doctors in the world will be treating him. Trust me, they'll give him plenty of attention."

"No, you don't understand!" His voice rose in pitch. The guy was starting to blubber, just as Grant had predicted. "Raza needs me. He'll go out of his mind if I'm not there!"

Grant stood up, stepped around the table, and went to the door. He opened it and gestured at the pair of guards in the corridor. "The interview's over. Take Khan back to his cell, and take the kid to the Research Center."

Hamid turned around and stood between the guards and his son's wheelchair. *"Please! You can't do this!"*

The bigger of the two guards marched toward him. "Get out of the way. Now."

"It's not legal! It's—"

The guard socked him in the stomach. Hamid doubled over, gasping for breath, and the guard deftly grabbed his arm and dragged him out of the interrogation room.

The other guard took hold of the wheelchair and pushed Raza into the corridor, heading in the opposite direction.

Grant watched them go. He started to feel better as the guards moved off. There was something seriously wrong with that kid. Disturbingly wrong.

But that's why the boy was going to the Research Center. The scientists would do some tests on him, maybe extract a few tissue samples. One way or another, they'd figure it out.

NINE

Jenna woke up inside a tomb. She lay on the marble floor of a mausoleum in Green-Wood Cemetery, shivering in the darkness.

She wasn't dead. But her body hurt so much, she almost wished she were. Her leg muscles were sore from her hips to her ankles. Her feet ached and throbbed.

She sat up, lifting her head from her makeshift pillow, which she'd made by folding and bunching up her sweatpants. To her left, a gap between the mausoleum's iron doors let a slender shaft of sunlight into the bare room. Derek stood just inside the doors, his half-lit head turned toward the gap, looking outside, keeping watch. His hulking body stayed absolutely still, but his breath came in rasps. He sounded like Death itself, scraping its skeletal fingers against the tomb's stone walls.

All in all, they'd run at least ten miles the night before. After leaving Bay Parkway, they headed north through Bensonhurst, zigzagging along the side streets to avoid the police patrols. Derek carried Jenna most of the way, at first because she was in shock over what he did to the *New York Times* reporter, and later because she was simply too exhausted to go on. By 5 a.m. they reached Borough Park, a quieter neighborhood with less flooding and fewer cops. But the sky was already brightening, so Derek started to look for a place to hide. Jenna assumed he'd break into an abandoned building, but instead he dashed for the cemetery and boosted her over its spiked fence.

He carried her for another mile across the sprawling graveyard, which was thick with trees and looping pathways and hundred-year-old monuments. Just before sunrise he climbed a hill that was studded with gravestones and topped by a building that looked like a miniature Roman temple. It was only twelve feet wide and twenty feet long, but it had an impressive granite portico at the front, with a pair of fluted columns flanking the doors. Derek set Jenna down on the grass and tugged one of the heavy doors, which slowly creaked open. Then he pulled her into the mausoleum and told her to get some rest.

She wasn't sure how long she'd slept. Eight hours? Ten hours? But she could tell from the bright shaft of sunlight that the storm was over. She unfolded her sweatpants and pulled them up her sore legs, trying not to make a sound. She didn't want Derek to notice her, didn't want to deal with him at all. After a few seconds, though, he looked over his shoulder and pointed at the far wall of the mausoleum.

"There's food and water if you want it."

Then he turned back to the gap between the doors and resumed his watch.

Jenna would've preferred to refuse the offer, but she was too hungry. She rose unsteadily to her feet and stepped toward the wall at the back of the marble room. To her left and right were the final resting places of the family members who'd paid for this mausoleum. The stone coffins were stacked on top of one another, four of them on either side, each with a name and a pair of dates chiseled into it. The family's last name was Higgins, and most of them had died a century ago. On the far wall was a stained-glass window with the words VIRTUE AND IMMORTALITY etched into the yellowish pane. On the floor at the base of the wall were two plastic jugs of water and a box of protein bars.

She picked up one of the jugs and took a long drink. Then she unwrapped a protein bar, devoured it, and grabbed another. This was more evidence of Derek's meticulous planning. He'd come to this cemetery beforehand, maybe days ago, so he could break into this mausoleum and leave these supplies here. In addition to his superhuman fighting abilities, the guy was an excellent strategist. But he was also completely amoral.

When Jenna had studied behavioral genetics at the Rockefeller University lab, she'd identified several genes that triggered compassion and empathetic behavior. In Derek's case, it looked like all those genes had been turned off.

She thought of Keating again and remembered the sound of his skull shattering. Her stomach turned. She dropped the protein bar, unable to take another bite.

She couldn't do this. She couldn't just wait here until nightfall and then let Derek drag her across the city to the next stage of his meticulous plan, whatever that might be. At that very moment, Abbu and Raza were probably cowering in one of the FSU's jails, huddled in a filthy cell block with hundreds of detainees and a staff of brutal guards trained to fear and hate Muslims. The thought of it made Jenna frantic—she needed to start looking for her father and brother *right now*. She wanted to shove Derek aside and bolt out of the mausoleum, charging through the gap between the heavy iron doors.

But that would never work. If she was serious about escaping, she had to come up with a better plan. She had to rely on her wits and try to outsmart him. Luckily, in a battle of wits, Jenna had a chance. Although her genes weren't enhanced like Derek's, she could be pretty damn sneaky when she put her mind to it.

She stepped toward him. "Who are you looking for? Mourners? You think some descendant of the Higgins family is going to come here to pay his respects?"

He shook his head but didn't turn to look at her. "No mourners. After the big storm three months ago, Green-Wood closed its gates and stopped allowing visitors. But the cemetery isn't empty."

"What do you mean? Who else is here?"

He shrugged. "Gang kids, mostly. Sometimes they jump over the fence. You know, to get high and knock over the gravestones. And sometimes the cops chase them."

"Well, this isn't such a good place to hide then, is it?" She was trying to rattle him. "What if the cops come this way?"

"This is a good vantage point." He pointed at the gap between the mausoleum's doors. "If the cops show up, I'll see them coming a long way off. Hear them, too."

Jenna stepped closer and looked through the gap. In front of the Higgins mausoleum, the cemetery grounds sloped steeply downhill. There were several marble monuments scattered across the yellowing grass and a bronze statue of a Roman goddess holding her left hand in the air, but otherwise there was a clear view from the mausoleum to the cemetery's entrance, about half a mile away. In fact, she could see all the way west to the Brooklyn-Queens Expressway and New York Harbor.

She took a step backward. Derek was right, this was a good place to hide. It was much better than holing up in an abandoned building where they could be surrounded and trapped. Jenna was impressed by Derek's ingenuity, so impressed that she began to seriously question whether she could outsmart the guy. But even genetic engineering couldn't make him perfect. There was a weakness in him somewhere, a chink in his armor. She just needed to keep probing.

"So how did you know about this place? You know anyone buried in this cemetery?"

He didn't say anything at first. He just stood by the doors, looking outside, his lungs rattling in his chest. But after several seconds, he shook his head. "I grew up near here. In Flatbush."

This was a surprise. She and Derek were fellow Brooklynites. Her neighborhood and his were less than five miles apart. She wondered for a second which high school he went to. Although it was hard to tell how old Derek was—the gene-altering drugs had ravaged his body too much— she guessed he was about thirty, the same age as her.

Then he did something even more surprising. He looked over his shoulder at her and, for the first time, Jenna saw him smile. "I used to come here to catch turtles. Snapping turtles." He spoke with quiet awe, as if remembering a dream. "This cemetery has a pond that's full of them. Big fucking things."

He raised his hands and held them about two feet apart to show her how big the turtles were. Then his smile faded, and he turned away from her.

Jenna waited for him to say something else, but he didn't. He went back to peering through the gap between the doors. For a moment she felt a twinge of sympathy for the man. She'd just caught a glimpse of what Derek was like before the drugs and the genetic alterations, back when he was human. And she wanted to see it again.

"Do you still have family in Flatbush?" she asked.

He said nothing. He didn't nod or shake his head. But Jenna got the feeling that the answer was no.

"Listen to me, Derek. We need to talk about what happened to you. Did they give you injections when you were in the army?"

Still nothing. Even the rattling noises in his chest subsided. Maybe he was holding his breath.

"You want me to cure you, right? Well, I can't do a thing if you won't talk to me."

He finally turned around and looked at her. In the half-light, his face was a mottled wreck. Blood leaked from the corners of his eyes and trickled down his cheeks. "The doctors called the drug 'Crisper.' Like the drawer in your refrigerator where you put your lettuce. It made no sense at all."

Jenna nodded. "CRISPR is an acronym. It stands for Clustered Regularly Interspaced Short Palindromic Repeats."

He let out a snort. "Really? That's a fucking complicated name for it."

"It's a description of a special kind of genetic sequence. It was first discovered in the DNA of bacteria, actually." Jenna paused, wondering how much to say. It was probably best to keep it short and sweet. "Some bacteria have evolved a molecular tool for altering their own genetic code, to help them fight off other infectious microbes. And scientists realized they could use the same tool to change the genes of all kinds of species. Including humans."

"Jesus Christ. Palindromic Repeats." He let out another snort, but it sounded more bitter than amused. "I guess that's why they called it the Palindrome Project."

"When did you get the injections?"

Derek turned slightly so he could keep one eye on Jenna and still watch over the cemetery grounds. "It started last April. We were in Afghanistan, at our base in Kandahar. A hundred soldiers from Third Battalion volunteered for it. Including me."

"How many shots did they give you?"

"Dozens. In the legs, the arms, the chest." He tapped his torso, the ridges of muscle under his T-shirt. Then he raised a hand to his head and patted the black stubble on his scalp. "But the worst were the injections in the head. The doctors took us to the field hospital at our base and drilled a bunch of holes into our skulls."

Jenna nodded. The injections delivered viruses to Derek's muscle and nerve cells. The microbes invaded his cells just like ordinary flu viruses—they broke through the cell membranes and released their genetic material inside. But these particular viruses carried the genetic instructions for producing the CRISPR molecular complex, which had been designed to modify human DNA. The CRISPR complex latched on to all the targeted genes and cut pieces of them from Derek's chromosomes. The viruses also carried new, improved DNA sequences, which were inserted into the gaps.

"What happened afterward? When did you notice the effects?"

He let out a labored breath. "The first day was hell. It felt like my bones were cracking. Like all my insides were turning to mush. They hooked me up to an intravenous line and I lay on a cot all day and night. I was going in and out of consciousness, completely out of my mind." He frowned and shook his head. "But after twenty-four hours, I started to get better. And a day after that, I was ready for action. I was jacked, you know? I was dying to go back to the front lines. A week later, our platoon got ambushed while I was leading a patrol through the Sulaiman Mountains, and *boom* I turned into a fucking assassin. I started running up and down the mountainside, picking off the jihadis. I killed a dozen of them in five minutes."

Jenna wished she could take notes on this. Derek's symptoms were very similar to what she'd observed in her animal experiments. Starting two years ago, she'd injected CRISPR into hundreds of rats, flooding them with gene-editing molecules that were designed to enhance their intelligence and muscular coordination. In all her experiments, the rats were near death for the first twenty-four hours, and then they recovered from their illness and showed phenomenal improvement in the maze-running and pattern-recognition tests. Apparently, it took a day for the viruses to fully infect the body and deliver CRISPR to all the brain and muscle cells.

"What about the other soldiers who got the injections? Were the effects the same for them?"

Derek cocked his head. He thought it over for a few seconds before answering. "Well, that's the funny thing. Everyone's experience was a little different. Some guys got an amazing boost to their memory. Others became unbelievably good marksmen." He raised his hand and scratched the dead skin near the wound on his neck. His arm was trembling. "But the changes weren't always good. After a few weeks some guys got sick again, even worse than the sickness at the beginning. Except this time it wasn't just physical illness. A couple of my men went batshit. We had to put them in straitjackets and send them back home."

Again, Jenna thought of her animal studies. After a month, half of her rats started behaving strangely. After two months, most of them were dead. She tried treating them with different types of CRISPR molecules, altering different combinations of their genes. But the results were always the same.

What's more, she already knew that CRISPR was dangerous for humans too, because she'd tested the treatment—in secret—on her brother. She'd taken the risk because Raza's disease was slowly killing him, and his doctor said he had less than two years left. She had a good reason to be hopeful about treating him with CRISPR: Raza had only one flawed gene that needed to be fixed, so Jenna assumed the process would be simpler and safer than her animal experiments, which manipulated the hundreds of genes involved in brain development and intelligence. But after a few months of improvement, Raza started having fits of panic and anger, wordless tantrums so violent he almost bit off his tongue. The attempt to repair his flawed DNA had apparently mangled several other genes in his brain cells, causing harmful changes in mental activity and behavior. Jenna stopped the treatment at once.

That's why she'd objected to her lab's experiments on human brain tissue. She told the lab director, Dr. Tung, that they needed to do a lot more basic research before they could jump ahead to developing CRISPR treatments for people. But Tung ignored her concerns, and six months later he kicked her out of the lab. And now one of the victims of those treatments stood trembling in front of her.

"I was scared. All the men under my command were falling apart, and I knew it would happen to me too. Every night at our barracks I'd check myself for symptoms. I'd lie in my bunk and wonder if I was going insane." He looked down at the floor, folding his arms across his chest to stop them from shaking. "But after a few nights I stopped being scared and started getting angry. Because I realized that my real enemy wasn't the Taliban or Al-Qaeda or any of the other goddamn jihadis. My enemy was the U.S. Army. It was the people who'd done this crazy fucking experiment on me."

Jenna felt another twinge of sympathy for Derek. *It's not his fault. They turned him into a monster.* But then she thought of Keating again, and the memory froze her. Yes, the CRISPR injections might have distorted Derek's character. They might've altered his genes enough to maximize his aggressiveness and minimize his compassion. But could that excuse what he did?

She bit her lip. *Stay focused. Keep asking questions.*

"So what happened then? What did you do?"

He unfolded his arms and began rubbing his hands together. That didn't stop the trembling either. "I knew the army would never let me go. Because I was their guinea pig now, and that's all they cared about. They were gonna keep watching me and testing me until I was either dead or a whacked-out zombie. So I didn't have a choice. There was only one way out." He shrugged. "I had to pretend to kill myself."

"Wait a second. You faked your own death?"

"It wasn't that hard. In Afghanistan, there are lots of ways to get yourself killed. We were on a night raid in Zabul Province and I waited until our air-support team called in a strike on the village where the Taliban were. I ran into their compound just as the B-52 flew overhead, and I ran out of the village just before the bombs fell." He pointed at the ugly lesion on his neck. "I got some shrapnel injuries, nothing too serious, but afterward I noticed they weren't healing right. Then I started having breathing problems. The symptoms were weird, like the abnormal shit I'd seen in the other guys in my unit. And I knew it would get worse unless I did something about it."

"So you came back to America?"

"Yeah, that was easy too. Anyone with half a brain could sneak across the border between Afghanistan and Pakistan. Then I went to Karachi and paid a few bribes to get on a cargo ship that was headed for New York. Your family's from Karachi, right?"

Jenna paused before answering. She was so focused on Derek's story that she hadn't expected a question about herself. "How do you know that?"

"I know all about you. Once I got to New York, I did some digging. I knew Palindrome was a classified project, but I assumed the government would recruit the best scientists in the country, the big-time experts on DNA and all that stuff. So I went to the library and found a computer and got some of their names from the Web. Then I paid a visit to one of them and got him talking."

Now Jenna was alarmed. There were plenty of people at the Rockefeller lab whom she disliked, but there were others whom she cared about. "Who did you talk to?"

Derek shook his head. "It's probably better if I don't tell you."

"Why?" Dread churned inside her. "Did you bash his head in, like you did to the reporter?"

"He was the director of your lab. A jackass named Tung. And he *deserved* every damn thing I did to him." Derek raised his voice, making it echo against the mausoleum's walls. "Tung was just a useless bureaucrat. He admitted he didn't even understand the research. But he knew everything about the scientists in his lab, and he said you were the best. He said you were a genius at this kind of work, a fucking DNA magician. And he told me where to find you." He stared at her. His eyes were bloody slits. "So now we're gonna go to your lab and you're gonna work on a cure. You're gonna make a drug that'll reverse what those bastards did to me."

She felt no sympathy for Derek now. She could understand his desire to get back to normal, but he clearly didn't care about anything else. He was cold-blooded and cruel and willing to hurt anyone who got in his way. Although Jenna had never liked Dr. Tung, she was still appalled. "Well, if you did your homework, you'd know that I don't work for Rockefeller University anymore. And now that the FSU is after me, I can't even get close to the place. Rockefeller has a whole team of security guards to protect the labs that do government work. They'd arrest me in a second."

He kept glaring at her. "We're not going to Rockefeller University. A few weeks after they fired you, they moved all the Palindrome labs to a new location. They're on Rikers Island now."

"Well, that's even worse. It's the FSU headquarters. That place is like a fortress."

"You don't have to worry about the FSU. Or getting into the lab. I'll take care of all that."

"Bullshit." She glared right back at him. "I don't care how much they altered your genes, you still can't take on a whole army. And even if we managed to sneak inside the lab, do you realize how long it would take to extract tissue samples from you and sequence their DNA? And then figure out all the changes we need to reverse?"

"It doesn't matter." He swept his arm in a slicing arc, cutting her off. "Don't you see how sick I'm getting? We gotta do this tonight. There's no other option."

"Of course there are other options! Just think about it for a second. What about going to *The New York Times*?" She reached into the pocket of her sweatpants and pulled out the iPhone that Keating had given her. "We already have the video that their reporter took, the footage of the massacre. And we can also tell them about Palindrome. The project is an atrocity, just as horrible as the experiments that the Nazis did. If we reveal everything to the newspaper, then maybe it'll help you get the medical attention you need and—"

"Fuck that. The newspapers are useless. The government's gonna shut them down any day now." He pointed at her, and Jenna noticed that his arms weren't trembling anymore. "You don't get it. It's too late to save the world. All we can do is try to save ourselves."

"You're wrong." Jenna was seething. "We can still fight. I was a part of Palindrome, but now I'm gonna stop it. I'm gonna go to the *Times* and expose what the government is doing. And I'm gonna get my father and brother out of whatever fucking jail the FSU has sent them to."

"You can't. You'll never see them again. The Feds are gonna make them disappear."

It was too much. Jenna lost control. She no longer cared that Derek was a foot and a half taller than her and two hundred pounds heavier, or that he was a genetically enhanced killing machine. She let out a scream and charged at him, roaring across the stone room.

But she didn't slam into him. Halfway there, she heard a shout from outside the mausoleum.

"HEY! What the fuck's going on in there?"

Jenna stopped herself a couple of feet from Derek. Without a word, she stood next to him and peered through the gap between the mausoleum's doors. At first she saw no change from before: the same yellowing lawn sloping downhill, the same marble monuments looming over the dead grass. But then she looked directly ahead, at the bronze statue of the Roman goddess, and saw the barrel of a shotgun resting on the statue's shoulder.

Jenna looked a little closer at the monuments and saw that each one served as cover for a crouching gunman. Their pistols and rifles jutted from behind the marble blocks and pillars and obelisks, the muzzle of each gun pointed at the Higgins mausoleum. But the gunmen weren't cops. She caught a glimpse of the shotgun-toting man behind the bronze statue and saw a black-and-gold bandanna wrapped around his head. He cupped a hand around his mouth and shouted at them again.

"You're in our territory, *amigos*. You're trespassing."

TEN

Lieutenant Frazier was doing his patriotic duty. He stood guard at the only surviving wharf in storm-wrecked Brooklyn, herding dozens of illegals onto a Federal Service prison ship.

It was three o'clock on a warm, sunny afternoon. Superstorm Zelda had moved out to sea, and now the weather was perfect, not a cloud in the sky. There weren't even any puddles on the concrete wharf where Frazier's team had gathered the escapees from the South Brooklyn District. That's because Frazier and his men were far inland, miles from the ocean. The wharf was on the Gowanus Canal, a waterway that snaked between Carroll Gardens and Park Slope, a pair of higher-elevation neighborhoods that hadn't flooded.

The only problem was the stench. The canal's waters were reddish-purple and smelled like a mix of rotten eggs and shit. The Gowanus was basically a liquid waste dump, a hundred-foot-wide trench brimming with sewage and chemical sludge. But a few years ago the government did something smart: it built a floodgate at the mouth of the canal, a barrier to stop storm surges from streaming up the waterway and spreading the toxic muck. And the day before Zelda hit New York City, the FSU docked its prison ships in the calm basins behind the barrier.

They didn't look like prison ships, at least not from the outside. The one docked at the wharf looked like a Navy cargo boat, gray and plain. The illegals who boarded the ship had no idea that it was packed with detention cells until they went belowdecks. And Frazier had come up with a trick to speed up the process—he'd ordered his men to paint a big red cross on the hull and the words RESCUE/SUPPLY SHIP. His officers spread the news that a Red Cross ship was distributing free food and bottled water to the storm victims, and soon the scumbags came running from all over Brooklyn and crowded into the parking lot next to the wharf. They lined up on the gangway and shuffled onto the boat, dragging their feet, exhausted. Their clothes were wet and filthy. Half of them were barefoot.

Frazier smiled. His plan was working so well that he didn't even have to point his rifle at the bastards. In thirty minutes his officers processed more than a hundred illegals, including dozens who'd fled the district through the Bay Parkway checkpoint the night before. As Frazier scanned their faces, he kept a special lookout for the Somali woman in the bikini top, the addict who'd abandoned her son. She'd escaped punishment so far—he'd checked all the dead ragheads he'd shot at the fence, and her body wasn't there—but he planned to deliver his judgment on her very soon.

He was also planning a fitting punishment for Derek Powell. The FSU's reconnaissance team had launched its surveillance drones after the storm cleared, and now the small quadcopters hovered over every part of the city, pointing their cameras at the streets and parks and rooftops. Colonel Grant had promised to alert him as soon as they found any sign of the traitor. Frazier's Stryker vehicle idled in the corner of the parking lot, just a few yards from the wharf, ready to go at a moment's notice.

Parked next to the Stryker was a big white truck that Frazier's men were unloading. They were carrying boxes and pieces of machinery from the truck to the prison ship, which was going to cruise to Rikers Island once its detention cells were full. Apparently, the storm had flooded so many streets in Brooklyn that it was easier to send supplies to the FSU headquarters by boat. Frazier thought it was a little strange to put a team of law-enforcement officers on a resupply job, but when he'd asked Grant about it, the colonel had told him to shut his fucking mouth and follow orders.

Frazier suspected that the supplies were for Palindrome. Nothing else could make Grant so twitchy. The colonel seemed to be ramping up the project, maybe preparing a new kind of drug or recruiting a new group of volunteers. Whatever he was doing, it was agitating the hell out of him.

A pair of corporals stood inside the white truck, struggling to lift a bulky machine wrapped in sheets of protective plastic. It looked like an industrial-size fan, a massive thing with two-foot-long blades, big enough to blow a windstorm on a Hollywood movie set. Curious, Frazier marched toward the back of the truck. He was going to grab that huge fan and pick it up by himself and show those corporals exactly how pathetic they were. But before he got there, a New York Police Department patrol car came down the street and turned in to the parking lot.

The car stopped in the middle of the lot, and two NYPD officers stepped out. The driver was just a patrolman, a skinny kid in a dark blue uniform, but the other cop was a police captain, a balding, ruddy, middle-aged guy with a huge potbelly ballooning his white uniform shirt. While the patrolman stood at ease next to the car, the captain smiled and came toward Frazier. A couple of gold fillings glinted inside his mouth.

"Good afternoon, soldier." The guy looked him up and down, his eyes lingering for a moment on Frazier's assault rifle. Then he stuck out his right hand. "I'm Captain Bill Adams, commander of the 76th Precinct. How you doin' today? At least it's not raining anymore, right?"

Frazier shook the captain's hand but didn't smile back at him. The guy's behavior was suspicious. As a rule, the New York cops hated the FSU. They'd totally opposed the creation of the Federal Service Districts, and now there were constant turf battles between the NYPD and the Feds. So why was Captain Adams acting so friendly?

"I'm Lieutenant Rick Frazier, Federal Service. How can I help you?"

The captain glanced at the FSU ship and the dozens of slimeballs trying to get aboard. His eyes roved everywhere, taking it all in. "Listen, I was hoping you could do me a favor. The storm hit my precinct pretty hard. Everything south of the expressway is underwater, and I got two thousand people jammed into an emergency shelter in Carroll Gardens. We weren't prepared for so many people, so we don't have enough food for them all. And we can't get any more supplies from the other precincts, because they're in bad shape too." He paused, glancing at the ship again.

"So we could use a little charity, see? You think you could share some of your Red Cross packages with us?"

Frazier thought it over for a moment. He wasn't sure how to respond. "Uh, Captain? I think we have a misunderstanding."

"Look, I know you guys are overwhelmed too. But if I don't get some food to that shelter real soon, I'm gonna have a riot on my hands. Those people are gonna run through the streets and break into every supermarket and bodega in the area."

"But we don't have any food for you."

"Now come on, Lieutenant. You got a whole damn Red Cross ship here. You mean to tell me that you can't spare anything?"

"It's not real." Frazier took a step toward Captain Adams and lowered his voice so that none of the illegals could overhear him. "My men painted that red cross on the ship. We have no supplies, no food, no bottled water. We're just pretending to give it away so we can round up the scumbags."

Adams stared at him for a few seconds, blinking rapidly. "What the fuck? You're *pretending*?"

Frazier nodded. "Yeah, it's a trick to get them on the boat. We're doing everything we can to recapture the illegals who broke out of the district."

"You're kidding me, right?" The captain tilted his head. His face reddened. "Because this is such a shitty idea, I can't fucking believe it. You're trying to catch your fugitives by rounding up everyone who's hungry?"

"We'll process the detainees when we get them to Rikers. If some of them turn out to be citizens with clean records, we'll release them." Frazier edged closer to Adams and tried to give his voice a confidential, officer-to-officer tone. "We're dealing with some bad hombres here, Captain. Just as bad as the fuckers who blew themselves up in Times Square last month. Yeah, we're probably arresting some innocent people too, but there's no avoiding it. The most important thing is catching the terrorists. That should be our top priority, don't you think?"

It didn't work. Adams scowled and stepped backward. He raised a flabby arm and pointed at the crowd of scumbags on the wharf. "You think *they're* the terrorists?" He was shouting, furious. "You really think one of those poor bastards is a *suicide bomber*?"

The poor bastards turned their heads. They stopped shuffling up the gangway and stared at Adams. Frazier bounded toward the captain, stepping between him and the slimeballs, blocking their view of him. "Lower your voice, goddamn it!"

"Why should I? This is—"

"Because you're interfering with an authorized federal operation!"

"Is that what you call it? An operation?" Adams sneered and shook his head. "No, it's a fucking scam. And worse than that, it's unconstitutional. Maybe you can get away with it in your Federal Service Districts, but not in my precinct. I'm stopping it right now." He turned away from Frazier and pointed at the patrolman standing by the car. "Garcia! Come over here and help me disperse the crowd!"

Now Frazier was pissed. He followed Adams and Garcia toward the wharf, two steps behind the captain, staring with immense hatred at the back of his balding head. "You sack of shit! I'm warning you!"

Adams ignored him. He stopped at the foot of the gangway and addressed the scumbags and ragheads, raising his arms to get their attention. "Folks, I got some bad news. There's no free food on this boat. If you're looking for help, your best bet is to—"

Frazier launched his fist at the back of Adams's head. His knuckles cracked the captain's skull and rammed the splinters of fractured bone deep into his brain. The motherfucker fell forward, propelled by the momentum of the punch. But he was dead even before his face hit the concrete.

Officer Garcia stared at the captain's body for a horrified moment. Then he looked at Frazier and reached for the semiautomatic in his belt holster. But before his fingers could touch the gun, Frazier smashed his bloody fist into the patrolman's breastbone and crushed his heart. Garcia fell backward, sputtering and clawing at his chest.

Frazier watched the kid die. Then he raised his head and glared at the scumbags on the wharf. "Get on the fucking boat. *Now!*"

They ran up the gangway, shoving and elbowing each other.

But Frazier's men just stood there, staring. They clutched their assault rifles and kept their distance, arranged on the wharf in a rough semicircle around him. Frazier stared back at them, feeling nothing but contempt. They were imbeciles. Each one probably thought Frazier was going to kill him next.

He pointed at two of his officers, choosing them randomly. "Put the bodies in the patrol car. Then push the car into the canal."

The men rushed forward and started dragging the corpses toward the car. They might've been afraid of the repercussions from this act, but at the moment they were clearly *more* afraid of Frazier than anything else.

In all, about sixty people had witnessed the killings, so it was a little unrealistic to hope that Colonel Grant would never hear of them. But Frazier wasn't going to worry about it now.

Then his secure phone buzzed, and the call was from Grant himself. Frazier was astounded—*How did the colonel find out so fast?*—but when Grant came on the line, he started talking about something else.

"Lieutenant, our drones just picked up something unusual. Half an hour ago, they observed a group of about twenty civilians in Sunset Park. We ran the images through our facial-recognition program, and it identified most of them as members of the Latin Kings gang. They converged near the Brooklyn-Queens Expressway, then moved east and climbed over the fence surrounding Green-Wood Cemetery."

Frazier was confused. "Uh, yes sir, but what does this have to do with—"

"It looks like the Latin Kings are gearing up for a fight, but no other gangs are active in the area. So who are the Kings fighting? These guys are heavily armed, and not just with handguns. They're carrying shotguns and TEC-9s too."

"You think they're planning to start a riot?"

"In a cemetery? No, I don't think so. They're just a few miles north of Bay Parkway, so I'm getting the feeling that this involves Powell somehow. How fast can you get to Green-Wood?"

Frazier was already running toward the Stryker.

"I'll be there in ten minutes."

ELEVEN

"Listen up. I want to talk to the big black brother in there."

The man with the black-and-gold bandanna was shouting at them. His voice came from behind the statue of the Roman goddess, whose shoulder he was using to steady his shotgun. Jenna craned her neck, trying to get a better look at him through the gap between the mausoleum's doors, but all she could see below the bandanna were two black eyebrows. They arched like gull wings.

"I saw you at Bay Parkway, *amigo*. You're a crazy motherfucker, you know that? How many of those FSU cops did you shoot?"

Derek narrowed his bloody eyes. He stood a couple of feet to Jenna's left, squinting through the gap at the man with the bandanna and the other gunmen outside the mausoleum. His gaze flicked from left to right, resting briefly on all the monuments that the men crouched behind. Then he pulled his pistol out of the waistband of his jeans and leveled it.

Jenna knew he could easily take out the bandanna guy. Although the target was small—just the top of the guy's head—Derek's aim was exceptional. But he didn't fire. He just pointed the gun outside, holding it steady, the muscles in his arm tense and bulging.

Bandanna Man poked his head a little higher above the statue's shoulder. Now Jenna could see a pair of close-set eyes and a tattoo on the left side of his face. It was a crude drawing of a crown, with five sharp points on top.

"My *muchachos* have been watching you since last night. I told them to follow you and find out where you lived. Because you got some mad skills, brother. The Latin Kings could use a badass like you."

Derek didn't react, didn't move. Jenna leaned closer to him. "The Latin Kings?" she whispered. "That gang is still in this neighborhood?"

"Yeah. Bunch of stupid-ass punks." Derek blinked, and a tear of blood leaked from the corner of his eye. "Never liked them. They've been here since I was a kid."

The leader of the Latin Kings lifted his head a little more, exposing a pencil-thin mustache and a big toothy grin. "Hey, bro, you listening? I know you got a lady friend in there, and maybe I interrupted something you two were doing. But since you and your girlfriend are in my territory without permission, the least you could do is show me a little courtesy, right?"

Derek frowned. Another bloody tear trickled down the side of his nose. "I *am* showing you courtesy." He raised his voice just enough so that the Latin King could hear it. "I haven't killed you yet."

The gangbanger tilted his head back and laughed. Then he stepped to the side, giving up the protective cover of the statue. At the same time, he lowered his shotgun and laid it on the grass next to the goddess's feet. "Okay, how's this? I'm putting down my gun. I'm giving you proof of my good intentions." He spread his arms wide. He wore black pants, a bright gold T-shirt, and a necklace of black-and-gold beads. "So how about you let me come inside your crypt? We got some business to discuss, man. I think you'll find it very interesting."

"You can talk from right there." Derek leaned forward, thrusting the barrel of his pistol between the mausoleum's doors. "Go ahead. Say what you want to say."

The guy laughed again. It was an easy, natural laugh, not fake at all. Then he shook his head. "No, I want a *private* conversation." He took a step toward them. "Look, you can shoot me if you want. But then my *muchachos* are gonna fire back at you. Maybe they'll hit you and maybe they won't, but either way they're gonna make a lot of noise. And that'll get somebody's attention. The cops will hear it, those fucking FSU *pende-*

jos." He took another step forward. "Believe me, you don't want those cops to come up here, brother. They've been hunting all over the city for you."

He kept walking toward the mausoleum, slow and casual. Jenna thought for sure that Derek would start shooting, but he held his fire. She supposed it was a logical choice: the FSU was definitely a bigger danger than this black-and-gold gangbanger. He didn't even look threatening. He was grinning too much, as if he thought the whole confrontation was a joke.

And yet he had twenty well-armed men following his orders, so he was clearly more than a joker. As he came closer, Jenna felt both fear and hope inside her. *This is an opportunity. This guy can help me get away.*

Soon he stood right in front of the mausoleum. Derek opened the doors a little wider but kept his gun trained on the gangbanger. The guy stopped grinning and put a serious expression on his face, which was caramel-colored and surprisingly handsome, even with that awful crown tattoo. He was young but not a teenager, probably in his early twenties. Above his bandanna, spiky black hair sprouted from the top of his head.

"Yeah, this is better. Now I don't have to shout anymore. Let me introduce myself—I'm King Hector of the Almighty Latin King Nation."

Derek frowned again. "King Hector?"

"Well, my legal name is Hector Torres. But in our Nation, every man is a King." He raised his right hand and made a gang sign, bending his middle and ring fingers. "*Amor De Rey.* That's our motto in Spanish. It means 'King's Love.'"

"I'll take your word for it. What do you want from us?"

Hector ignored Derek's question and turned to Jenna instead. He dropped the gang sign and bowed slightly in her direction. "*Buenas tardes, chica.* You're very beautiful, you know that?"

Jenna rolled her eyes. Her hair was a tangled mess, her nightshirt was damp with sweat, and she smelled like a swamp. She wasn't in the mood for compliments. "And you're a bad liar."

"Hey, I'm polite. Nothing wrong with that. So why don't you be polite too and invite me inside?" He turned back to Derek and pointed at the gun in his hand. "Believe me, I won't try to jump you. I'm not stupid, man. I saw how fast you are. Shit, you're faster than a fucking cobra."

Derek kept him waiting for a few more seconds. Then he pushed one of the doors all the way open and let Hector inside the mausoleum. Jenna backed up toward the stained-glass window on the far wall, but Derek stayed close to the guy, ready to blow his brains out if he made a wrong move.

Hector turned his head this way and that, as if admiring the marble room. Then he focused on Derek. "I have to be honest with you, *amigo*. You don't look so good. Your eyes are bleeding."

"It's nothing. I can see you just fine." He raised his gun, pointing it at the Latin King's forehead.

Hector didn't look at the pistol. He was playing it cool, pretending not to notice it. "So what's your story, brother? Did you used to work for the FSU?"

Derek shook his head. "No. Why would you think that?"

"Because you're just like one of their cowboys. You know, big and fast and strong."

"Cowboys?"

"Yeah, *vaqueros*, badasses. It's a special kind of officer the FSU has, one for each district. I call them cowboys because that's what they look like when they're riding around in their armored trucks. The one in Brooklyn is a big white asshole with a buzz cut. He was there last night, at Bay Parkway, firing that machine gun at the crowd. Then he jumped out of the tower when you went after him with the Stryker."

Derek said nothing, but Jenna could guess what he was thinking. She remembered the man they saw above the elevated subway tracks, the ghostly figure jumping from the sentry tower. Azrael, the Angel of Death.

She stepped toward Hector. "You know that FSU officer? You've seen him before last night?"

"Yeah, almost every day for the past three months. That *vaquero* pays special attention to the Latino neighborhoods like Sunset Park. He thinks we're hiding all our illegal cousins under our beds and in our closets. I told my boys to keep an eye on him all the time, wherever he goes. Because he's bad fucking news."

Jenna nodded. "We saw what he did at Bay Parkway. How he shot all those people."

"That's nothing new for him. He's been killing people ever since he got here. He and his men bust into apartments in the middle of the night. They arrest women, kids, old people in wheelchairs. And if anyone complains, he shuts them up fast." Hector grimaced and shook his head. "Let me ask you a question. Where did your family come from? Are you an Arab or something?"

"My parents came from Pakistan, but I was born here. At Kings County Hospital."

"But the Feds still give you shit, right? They stop you on the street and ask for your ID and frisk you. They assume you're a terrorist, and that's fucked up. But wait till you hear *my* story." He slapped his palm against his chest, making it thump. "I was born here too. And my parents and grandparents were born here. My great-grandparents were immigrants, they came to New York seventy-five years ago. But they came from Puerto Rico, so they were already American."

Derek let out a grunt. He sounded impatient. "Is there a point to this story?"

"Come on, man, hear me out. This is a fucking injustice. When that candy-ass in the White House sent the FSU to New York, who do you think they came after first? Whose apartments did they bust into?" Hector's voice rose. His black-and-gold necklace swung back and forth. "They came after us—the Puerto Ricans, the Dominicans, the Mexicans. We were the main targets for all the raids and roundups. And you know what the cops said when we tried to tell them we were legal? They said, 'You all look the same to us. We can't tell you spics apart.'"

Hector was breathing hard, fuming, mad as hell. Derek, though, seemed unimpressed. He let out another impatient grunt, and Jenna suspected he was about to say something insulting. She cut him off before he could. "Hector, can we get back to that FSU officer you were talking about? Did you ever see him do anything physically extraordinary? Anything way beyond normal in terms of speed or strength?"

Hector nodded vigorously. "Yeah, I've seen it. One time, an old fat guy yelled at him in the street, called him a Nazi. Well, the cowboy grabbed him under the jaw and picked him up with one hand. Like this." He raised his hand and clasped his own neck, just below the jaw. "Then he shook the fat guy around until he broke his fucking neck. He *paralyzed* the guy. And the cowboy got away with it, because all the other cops backed him up. They said he was acting in self-defense. Fucking unbelievable."

"And you said there are others like him? Working for the FSU?"

"Yeah, there's another big asshole who leads the raids in the Federal Service District in the Bronx. I got a look at him last month when I went to a sit-down with the Latin Kings up there. And I hear there's one in the Newark District too."

Derek scowled, his impatience boiling over. He stretched his arm and brought his pistol a few inches closer to Hector's forehead. "I only care about one thing. What's the name of the asshole cowboy in Brooklyn?"

Hector held up his hands as if surrendering. "Sorry, brother. I don't know."

"Are you sure about that?" Derek closed the gap between them and pressed the gun against Hector's left temple. The pressure from the muzzle creased his crown tattoo. "Are you trying as hard as you can to remember?"

Hector seemed remarkably calm for someone with a gun to his head. His eyes drifted a bit to the left, but he managed a smile. "Don't shoot me, all right? There's a reason I can't remember his name, and that's because I never knew it. The FSU cops don't wear name tags or badge numbers like the New York cops do." He waited for a response, but Derek said nothing. So Hector kept talking, his hands still up in the air. "They say they don't wear name tags because they're an antiterrorism unit, and they don't want the terrorists to know their names. But that's bullshit. They keep their names secret because they're the fucking secret police."

Jenna waited a few more seconds, but Derek didn't lower his gun. He was weeping blood again, the red tears sliding down his cheeks. She started to worry that he'd do something stupid, maybe even shoot Hector, so she stepped toward Derek and got his attention. "You think this FSU officer might've been in the army? One of the soldiers in your unit?"

Derek nodded. Reluctantly, he withdrew his gun, pulling it away from Hector's temple. "Yeah. I just don't know which one. There were a dozen big white guys who volunteered for the injections. And they all had buzz cuts."

Jenna turned to Hector, who'd lowered his hands. "Let me ask you another question about that officer. Did you ever notice if he suffered from any side effects? Like what Derek has—bleeding eyes, mottled skin? Or anything else that looked unusual?"

Hector didn't answer right away. He turned his head slightly, his gaze shifting back and forth between Derek and Jenna. "Okay, now I get it. The army gave drugs to the soldiers? To turn them into *vaqueros*?" He pointed at Derek. "But the drugs fucked you up, right? And now you're pissed at the government?" Hector nodded, confirming his own guesses, his face jumpy and excited. Then he pointed at Jenna. "And you're part of it too, *chica*? You sound like you're a doctor or something. Like you know all about it."

Jenna frowned. She hadn't realized she'd revealed so much. Hector was smart, no doubt about it. But maybe that was a good thing. Maybe she could make an arrangement with him. "Hector, how many Latin Kings are there? Just the twenty who came with you? Or are there more?"

He grinned again. "Oh, a lot more. The *muchachos* I brought with me are just my personal bodyguards. We got five hundred Kings in Sunset Park and another seven hundred in East New York." He stuck out his chest, preening. "And I'm building alliances too. With the Crips in Flatbush, the Bloods in the Bronx, the Trinitarios in Manhattan. We even got a headquarters, at the Triborough Houses in East Harlem."

"Alliances? To do what?"

"What do you think? To fight the FSU." He raised his hand and made his gang sign again. "Before those *pendejos* came to New York, we were doing stupid shit, beefing with each other, breaking up into a million little sets. But now we're working together. We got a common enemy."

"Well, I want to join your alliance. I can fight too."

Derek turned his head and glared at her. His red tears came faster now, as if his raging heart was pumping them out. He kept his gun trained on Hector, and Jenna was very grateful that the gangbanger was there. If she and Derek had been alone, he definitely would've shot her, at least in a nonessential part of her anatomy. "You think I'm an idiot, Jenna? You think I don't know what you're doing?"

Hector held out his hands. "Hey, hey, calm down, brother."

Blood streamed from Derek's eyes. It sheeted down his cheeks and trickled into his mouth and dripped from his chin. He had two gaping wounds where his eyes should've been, but somehow he could still see Jenna, still glare at her with cold fury. "I know why you're being so friendly with this punk. You don't want to cure me. You're trying to get away from me."

Jenna steeled herself. Derek needed to know the truth. "Look, you're asking for the impossible. I *can't* cure you, at least not by myself. The damage to your DNA is too extensive. We're gonna need a whole lab and a team of researchers to fix it. But maybe Hector can help us with all that."

"*Hector?*" Derek's voice rose. The truth was enraging him. "How can *he* help?"

"It's like he said—we need to get everyone behind us and fight the FSU. First, we have to shut down Palindrome and free all the detainees. Then we have to get the government to take responsibility for treating you and all the other soldiers they experimented on. It won't be easy, but if we work together, we can—"

"*This scumbag won't help us!*" Derek thrust his gun again at Hector's head, pressing the muzzle against the black-and-gold bandanna. "*He just wants to use me! Just like the army did!*"

Hector winced. "No, brother, I—

"*Shut up! SHUT UP!*"

He was going to pull the trigger. Jenna was sure of it.

But before he could fire the gun, she heard the sound of glass breaking. Something crashed through the stained-glass window at the back of the mausoleum. It landed on the marble floor and bounced with a metallic clang. It looked like a hugely oversized bullet, about three inches long and two inches in diameter.

Derek lowered his pistol and charged toward her.

"*GRENADE!*"

TWELVE

Frazier pulled the trigger of the M320 launcher attached to his rifle. The grenade shot out of the muzzle and sped toward the mausoleum at two hundred miles per hour. But Frazier's eyesight was so good that he could clearly see the stubby projectile in flight, arcing over the dead grass and gravestones.

It was beautiful. And so was the sound of it smashing through the stained-glass window at the back of the tomb. But the best part was the anticipation. In exactly half a second the grenade would detonate on the mausoleum's floor and vaporize the motherfuckers inside.

Time slowed down for him, creeping almost to a halt. That was one of the effects of the injections: if Frazier put his mind to it, he could decelerate the flow of images streaming into his brain and study them like the frames of a film reel. He saw the stained-glass window shatter into a thousand shards, all of them falling in a brief, brilliant shower. He saw his soldiers advance from their positions, rising from behind the headstones they'd been using for cover. And he saw them aim their rifles at the punks from Sunset Park, the stupid kids with their gold-and-black necklaces and bandannas, crouched behind the monuments on the other side of the mausoleum.

Then the grenade exploded. A white-hot flash lit up the empty window, and a tenth of a second later Frazier heard and felt the blast. It hammered the mausoleum's stone walls, shaking the whole structure. The noise echoed across the cemetery, and a hundred birds scattered from the trees.

Frazier's joy was so intense, he closed his eyes to savor it. He imagined Powell dying, his huge body ripped apart. He pictured the Khan girl too, pulped inside her nightshirt, and that Latin King gangbanger drowning in his own blood. They deserved it, all three of them. Powell was a traitor, the worst kind of criminal. The others were accomplices, collateral damage.

And then, while his eyes were still closed, another image emerged from the darkness. He pictured a woman running through the woods of southern Missouri. It was a memory of something that had happened when Frazier was fourteen, a week after his little brother died. He saw himself with a hunting rifle in his hand, chasing a grown woman through the woods. The woman was short and fat and wore loose, green scrubs that snagged on the bushes as she tried to get away. She was the nurse from the emergency room, the one who'd refused to treat Andy.

But something was wrong. Someone was coughing.

Frazier opened his eyes. Black smoke billowed from the mausoleum's window. His soldiers were outflanking the Latin Kings, maneuvering behind the dumb punks and cutting them down. But beneath the noise of the gunfire and the still echoing explosion, he heard a man yelling in Spanish and a woman coughing and gasping.

It was impossible. The blast should've killed all of them. And yet somehow they'd survived. The sounds were coming from somewhere in front of the mausoleum, out of Frazier's view, but he could picture the three of them still alive, still breathing, and he could guess what had happened.

Fucking Powell! He's screwing me again!

Frazier raced across the grass. He wasn't going to lose another fight to that motherfucker. He was going to end it right now.

THIRTEEN

It happened so fast. In one instant, Derek came rushing toward Jenna, his right arm hooked around Hector, his left clamping around her waist; in the next, they hurtled through the doors and crashed face-first to the ground in front of the mausoleum. And in the instant after that, the grenade exploded.

The blast wave battered them. It whooshed over their prone bodies and pounded their skulls. But the mausoleum's doors had started to close behind them, and the thick iron slabs absorbed most of the blast. Bits of shrapnel rocketed through the gap between the doors—Jenna heard them whiz though the air—but they passed over the back of her head and struck the grass farther away. They would've killed her if she'd been standing up.

Ears ringing, Jenna lifted her face from the grass. The fall had knocked the wind out of her, and the air was hot and sulfurous. She struggled to breathe, hacking and wheezing.

Hector also lay facedown in the grass, four feet to her right. He raised his head and shook it, cursing in Spanish. Jenna didn't see Derek, though. He'd shoved her and Hector out of the mausoleum and saved their lives,

probably acting on pure instinct, his enhanced nerves and muscles spring-
ing into action. It was automatic, a genetically programmed reflex, which
explained why he'd saved Hector even though he hated the gangbanger.
But where the hell was Derek now? He wasn't anywhere nearby. He'd
vanished.

Then Jenna lifted her head a little more and looked over her shoulder.
Derek stood by the corner of the mausoleum, leaning against its granite
façade, half-hidden by one of the fluted columns. He held his pistol with
both hands, in ambush mode, waiting to shoot someone. And a moment
later, his target came sprinting around the corner, a big white FSU officer
with a blond buzz cut and an assault rifle.

It was the Angel of Death. Now Jenna saw him up close, in body armor
and a black uniform.

Derek stepped forward and pointed his gun at the man, but he didn't
fire. He hesitated for a fraction of a second, his bloody eyes narrowing.
He recognized his target. Shock and disgust contorted his face.

An instant later, he curled his lip and pulled the trigger. But the hesitation was enough to save the FSU officer. He skidded on the grass and
dodged out of the bullet's path. Then he spun around and ran for cover.

Derek took another step forward, arms outstretched, adjusting his aim.
He yelled "FRAZIER!" in a harsh commanding voice, like an army drill
sergeant yelling at one of his soldiers. Then he fired his gun three more
times.

All three shots missed. The cop named Frazier jinked wildly across the
grass, leaping and swerving like an acrobat, moving faster than Jenna's
eyes could follow. He zigzagged away from the mausoleum and dove
behind the massive pedestal of a stone obelisk. Within a second, though,
he reappeared at the edge of the pedestal and started firing his rifle. Derek
ducked for cover behind the bronze statue of the Roman goddess.

Hector crawled a few feet away and retrieved the shotgun he'd dropped
in the grass. Then he crept back to Jenna. "Follow me, *chica*! Stay low!"

That was all the encouragement she needed. She scrambled as fast
as she could on her hands and knees, trying to get away from the
battle. Derek and the Federal Service cowboy weren't the only gunmen
in the cemetery; there were another twenty FSU officers running past
the Higgins mausoleum, charging into a firefight with Hector's Latin
Kings. The cops looped to the north of the mausoleum, maneuvering

around the gangbangers to shoot them from behind. So Hector led Jenna in the opposite direction.

Bending low, they scuttled along the mausoleum's southern wall. The gunshots echoed everywhere, bouncing against the cemetery's hills and all the stone pillars and obelisks and monuments. The noises crackled in Jenna's ears, loud and terrifying, but she kept her head down and followed Hector. They passed the mausoleum and sprinted downhill past rows and rows of gravestones. Then Hector turned around and pulled her behind a monument that was big enough to shield both of them.

Jenna crouched beside the stone block, panting, desperately trying to catch her breath. But Hector was in better shape. He calmly opened his shotgun, checked the shells inside, then snapped it closed.

"You're on your own now, *chica*." He pointed farther downhill at an asphalt path that ran between the cemetery lots. "Keep running that way until you get to Hillside. You can't miss it, it's the biggest mausoleum in the cemetery. Then turn left and climb over the fence and get the fuck out of here."

"Wait, what about you? Where are you going?"

"I gotta go back there and help my *muchachos*." He looked over his shoulder. "The cops are chasing them and shooting them down. But I'm gonna sneak up behind them. Maybe I can even get a shot at the cowboy."

Jenna frowned. Hector didn't have a prayer. But she kept her doubts to herself. She owed the man. "Thanks for taking me this far."

"Hey, it's like I told you. I'm polite." He grinned at her again. Then he reached for his black-and-gold bead necklace, pulled it over his head, and offered it to her. "Take this, okay? If you show it to any Latin King, he'll know it's from me. And he'll do anything you ask him to."

She took the necklace and put it on, tucking it under her nightshirt. "I'll do that. Good luck, Hector."

He raised his right hand and did his gang sign again, but this time he brought his hand close to his face and kissed his outstretched thumb. "*Amor De Rey!*" Then he spun away from her and dashed uphill, heading back to the gun battle.

Jenna stayed crouched behind the monument for a few seconds, waiting to see if anyone fired at Hector. But no one did, so she guessed the coast was clear. She took a deep breath and continued running downhill.

In half a minute she reached the asphalt path and raced across another field of gravestones. This was the plainer, poorer section of the cemetery, the lots for people who couldn't afford mausoleums or obelisks. The grass was knee-high here, and the headstones were low and worn-down. Jenna had to keep her eyes on the ground, or else she'd trip over one of the grave markers and break her neck. She could still hear the battle, but the gunshots were dulled and muffled, like distant thunder.

After another minute, she stopped and dared to take a look behind her. There weren't many trees in this section, so she had a clear view of the cemetery grounds for hundreds of yards in every direction. To her relief, no one was following her. The graveyard she'd just crossed was empty and still. The tall grass gleamed in the afternoon sunlight.

Jenna laughed. Her relief turned into a stronger emotion, a euphoria that swelled inside her chest and spread all the way down to her toes. *She was free!* She wasn't anyone's prisoner now. She could make her own plans instead of following Derek's, and as she gazed across the empty graveyard she began to map out her strategy. Her first goal, of course, was to find her father and brother. And once they were safe, she would figure out a way to stop the Palindrome Project.

But then she saw a cloud of black smoke erupt at the far edge of the grassy field, a quarter mile away. A second later, she heard the explosion, which was just as powerful as the blast inside the Higgins mausoleum.

Then she spotted Derek. He raced past the black cloud, a giant figure in a gray T-shirt, like a football player on a high-intensity training run, doing wind sprints to get ready for the next big game. Another smoke cloud erupted several yards to his left, but he didn't flinch, didn't stumble. The Angel of Death was firing grenades at him, showering the field with explosions, but Derek didn't change course or slow down. He saw Jenna at the other end of the graveyard and headed straight for her.

She turned around and ran.

Hector was right about the Hillside Mausoleum. It was huge.

Jenna saw the back of the building as she came barreling down the hill, running faster than she'd ever run in her life. The mausoleum had been built into the steepest part of the slope; the front of the building rose five stories above the base of the hill, but only the top floor stood above the ground behind it. The building was long too, with newer sections extending the structure hundreds of feet to Jenna's left and right. It curved slightly to match the contour of the hill, like a bumper curving around the front of a car.

She looked to the left, trying to figure out the shortest route to the cemetery's fence, but she knew right away it wasn't short enough. Derek was only a hundred yards behind her. He had no gun in his hand—he must've run out of bullets—but he would definitely run her down before she could reach the fence. Or the cop named Frazier would blast her to smithereens. He was still firing his grenades at Derek, and the explosions were cratering the cemetery grounds.

Jenna's stomach clenched, but she kept running. Her only chance of escaping Derek was to go inside the Hillside Mausoleum and try to lose him. So she sped toward the back of the building, heading for its newest section. It was a modern structure, newer than almost everything else in the cemetery, and it was sheathed in glass like a greenhouse. She quickly surveyed the whole thing, wondering how she could break inside. Should she hurl a rock at one of the big glass panes? Or maybe throw herself at the glass? It might slice her to pieces, but at this point she was willing to risk it. She'd rather die than go back to being Derek's prisoner.

But she didn't have to break inside. There was a glass door at the back of the mausoleum, and to Jenna's surprise it wasn't locked. She swung it open and dashed into the building and started looking for a place to hide.

She found herself on the highest floor of an airy, empty atrium. There were glass panes overhead and at the front of the building too, giving her a panoramic view of the southern half of the cemetery. Gray tiles covered each floor of the atrium, and at its center was a free-standing stairway that went down to the building's lower levels. To Jenna's left and right were walls of polished gray marble, each divided into a grid of three-foot-wide squares. And each marble square was marked with a chiseled name and a pair of dates.

She was already nauseous from running so hard, but now she felt dizzy. Each square was a crypt, a sealed chamber for a casket. She was surrounded by hundreds of them. But she gritted her teeth and suppressed her queasiness. There was no time for it.

She craned her neck, looking for a way out of the atrium. There were too many windows here. She could see Derek through the glass behind her, charging toward the back of the mausoleum, less than fifty yards away.

Then she turned left and spotted a passageway leading to another part of the mausoleum. She rushed past more crypts and a planter full of silk flowers and a pair of empty armchairs intended for mourners. In a couple of seconds she entered an older section of the building that had fewer windows, thank God. This section had its own atrium and stairway, and Jenna hurtled down the steps, racing toward the lower floors. If she could find a good place to hide, she might be able to slip away from Derek. He didn't have an unlimited amount of time to look for her, because Officer Frazier was chasing *him*.

But before she could make it down to the fourth floor, she heard rapid footsteps echoing across the mausoleum. Derek was inside. He'd entered the building through the same door Jenna had used. He was just seconds behind her. Her plan was falling apart.

Then an enormous blast shook the building. The stairway vibrated under Jenna's feet, and she heard a cacophony of breaking glass, dozens of windows shattering at once and thousands of shards smashing against the marble. She crouched on the steps and covered her head, bracing herself for the lethal cascade.

But none of the shards rained down on her. She looked up and saw that the older section of the mausoleum was undamaged. Officer Frazier must've fired one of his grenades at the building, and luckily for her, it had struck the newer section, which she had just left and Derek had just entered.

Jenna raised her head and listened carefully. She waited to hear Derek's footsteps again, or maybe a groan of pain. But she heard nothing.

Is he hurt? Dead?

She told herself it didn't matter. Derek was a monster. He'd killed Keith the homeless guy and Keating the *Times* reporter, and he'd come very close to killing Hector too. He'd kidnapped Jenna and threatened to shoot her and stopped her from looking for her father and brother. He'd made it very clear that all he cared about was himself and that he would annihilate anyone who got in his way.

And yet Jenna couldn't help but think that she owed him something. Derek had rescued her from the FSU. And he'd saved her life *three times* over the past twenty-four hours. Although he had selfish reasons for keeping her alive, she still felt grateful. And now that he was hurt—and maybe dying—it seemed contemptible to desert him. She couldn't just run away and let him die.

Warily, she climbed back up to the top floor. This was probably the dumbest thing she'd ever done, but she couldn't stop herself. She approached the passageway and poked her head around the corner and peered at the section of the mausoleum where the grenade had exploded.

The blast had shattered all the windows at the back of the building and most of the overhead panes too. There were big piles of glass shards all over the tiled floor and the stairway. The biggest pile was at the other end of the passageway, next to the planter brimming with silk flowers. The shards in this pile were still sliding and settling, because Derek lay underneath them.

His eyes were closed, but he was still breathing. His lungs still made their awful rattle, now magnified by the emptiness of the mausoleum. But he didn't try to sit up or sweep the glass shards off his body. That was a bad sign.

Jenna took a step forward, just one. Maybe he was faking it. "Derek? Can you hear me?"

No response. A couple of shards slid off his chest and clinked against each other. Jenna took another step forward, then another, tiptoeing down the passageway. When she looked at Derek again, she saw a dark puddle spreading underneath him, creeping across the floor. He was bleeding to death.

"Derek!"

She ran the rest of the way toward him, the glass crunching under the sneakers he'd given her. A jagged shard the size of a notebook stuck out of his left side, just above the waistband of his pants. Blood gushed in pulses from the wound, in time with his heartbeat.

Jenna kicked some of the glass away from his body and knelt beside him. She knew she shouldn't try to pull the shard out of his waist, because that might make the bleeding worse, but should she apply pressure to the wound? Or would that joggle the piece of glass and cause more damage? She was confused, desperate. Although she'd studied genetics and brain physiology for years, she'd never had any training in first aid.

"*Derek!*" She yelled right into his face. "*What should I do?*"

He opened his bloody eyes. Smaller bits of glass were embedded in his scalp. His lips trembled, trying to form a word. It came out as a whisper. "Go."

"You had first-aid training in the army, right? You gotta tell me what—"

"*Go!*" The word boomed out of him now. Fresh trails of blood leaked from his eyes. *"Get out of here!"*

Jenna shook her head. "Are you crazy? You're gonna bleed to death unless—"

"Don't worry about me! I'll be all right!"

That was ridiculous. Derek was far from all right. The pool of blood underneath him was six feet wide. It soaked the knees of Jenna's sweatpants. She stopped arguing with him and tried to think, but it was like trying to grip the air. She clenched her hands in frustration and smacked them against her thighs.

Then she heard something behind her. The sound of glass crunching under someone's boots.

She jumped to her feet and spun around. Officer Frazier had snuck up behind them. He pointed his assault rifle at Derek, holding it with one hand, but his eyes were on her. He stretched his mouth into a broad, shit-eating grin.

"You little bitch."

He seemed amused. His eyes were bright blue and glittering. His face was sweaty and flushed, and his body armor was spotted with dirt and blood, but he wasn't breathing hard. He was enjoying himself.

Frazier leapt toward her, grabbed the collar of her nightshirt, and yanked her away from Derek. He did it all in one blindingly fast motion, so sudden that it felt like God Himself had hauled her across the floor. Now they stood by the wall, next to the marble crypts. He pulled her close, bunching her nightshirt in his fist. "You thought you were smarter than me, didn't you? You thought I was a stupid goddamn redneck and you were the smartest little bitch in the world."

He looked down at her, openmouthed, breathing on her. Jenna squirmed, trying to back away, but he yanked her even closer, forcing her to look at him. And that was the worst part, that's what made her tremble and panic. At first glance, Frazier's face looked normal, even handsome—strong chin, straight nose—but up close she saw that his skin was unnaturally smooth, like the skin of a balloon. It was unnerving, alien. Like Derek, he wasn't *homo sapiens* anymore. He belonged to a different species, a new kind of predator, designed to kill humans.

He tugged so hard on her nightshirt that it started to rip at the back. She had to do something fast, say something that would stop him. "Look, I know what happened to you. You were in the Palindrome test. They gave you injections, right?"

Frazier tilted his head and looked askance at her. "So you're still play-ing games? You still think I'm stupid?"

"They injected you with CRISPR to modify your genes." Jenna kept going, racing to make her point. "But the procedure was flawed. CRISPR made more changes to your DNA than anyone intended. Random changes that are messing up your metabolism and breaking down your body. So far, you haven't suffered as much damage as Derek has, but eventually those genetic changes will kill you."

His smile ebbed. Anger flared in his eyes. "You're lying. Just like you lied before." He lowered his inhuman face, bringing it within inches of Jenna's. "Remember how you lied to me? At the emergency room in Springfield?"

"Springfield? What—"

"You lied right through your teeth, you and all the other nurses at the hospital. You said it wasn't a medical emergency." Spittle flew from his mouth and pasted her cheeks. "And because it wasn't an emergency, you said we needed to pay up front. But you knew we couldn't pay. So we had to go back to the public hospital in Cassville instead."

Jenna shook her head, confused. *Pay up front? Public hospital in Cass-ville?* She had no idea what Frazier was talking about. But his anger was growing, his face reddening. He was losing touch with reality, and she needed to get through to him before he became unreachable.

"Just calm down and listen, okay? We have to work together and stop the Palindrome tests. Then maybe we can get the research labs to develop a treatment that'll reverse the changes to your DNA and—"

"Bitch! Don't you realize what you did?" He shouted into her face, so close and loud it made her cringe. "We had to drive forty miles to that damn hospital! And guess what happened to Andy along the way?"

He pulled his head back and waited for her to answer. But she was dizzy and scared and totally bewildered. "Andy? Who's Andy?"

"He was my brother, my little brother, only nine fucking years old. And you killed him!"

The sound of Frazier's voice suddenly changed. It became high-pitched and shrill, frantic and devastated. It was the voice of a frightened, furi-ous boy. It had somehow emerged from the man's past, a traumatic mem-ory revived by his genetically enhanced brain. And the change wasn't just in his voice—his face quivered like a boy's face and turned tantrum-red.

The horrible memories had pushed aside his adult consciousness. They'd taken over his body.

"Andy had an asthma attack in the backseat of our car! And we didn't have any inhalers or anything else, *because you wouldn't treat him!*"

Now Jenna was terrified. She'd assumed that CRISPR hadn't damaged Frazier as badly as it had hurt Derek, but she was wrong. The damage was in his brain. He was hallucinating like a schizophrenic. He saw Jenna as a villain from his past, some emergency-room nurse who'd played a role in the trauma he was reliving. He'd completely abandoned the real world and entered a nightmarish place that only he could see. And Jenna was at his mercy.

She needed to bring him back to the real world somehow, but he was so far gone. All she could do was try to shock him. Just scream at him as loud as she could.

"LISTEN TO ME! I'M NOT THE NURSE YOU'RE THINKING OF! AND THIS ISN'T AN EMERGENCY ROOM! THE YEAR IS 2023 AND WE'RE IN—"

Frazier let go of her nightshirt and grabbed her neck. He clamped his right hand around her throat, just below her jaw, and squeezed.

"Enough talking. I'm gonna kill you now."

She couldn't breathe. He'd closed her airway.

"How does it feel?" He looked into her eyes, studying them carefully. "Getting desperate yet? No? Well, wait a few seconds."

She felt the pressure building inside her. At first it was only mildly uncomfortable, a hot tension in her chest. But it got worse very quickly, and she started to twist and kick and flail. She clawed at Frazier's hand, trying to release his grip on her, but his fingers dug deeper into her throat. And all the while, he kept looking into her eyes, watching her struggle. His face was serious, full of grim satisfaction.

"Good, that's good. Your lips are turning blue. Now you're feeling it."

She was in full panic. She opened her mouth, gagging, straining for breath. Her head swam and her vision darkened. It felt like her eyes were bursting out of their sockets.

"Now you know how Andy felt. That's your punishment."

Jenna's world was going black. She couldn't see Frazier's face anymore. It was just a patch of darkness against the darker wall behind him. And she was dissolving into the darkness too, sinking into a vast black sea.

But then the darkness swelled. An immense wave rose from the sea, climbing hundreds of feet above the black surface. An instant later, it came crashing down, knocking her and Frazier to the floor. Jenna landed on her side, thumping her hip bone and ribs. Frazier let go of her neck and hit the floor several feet away.

The pressure was gone. Her airway opened.

I can breathe!

Jenna retched and sucked a mouthful of air into her lungs. The pain in her throat was excruciating, but she took in another breath, then another. She curled into the fetal position, gasping, helpless as a baby.

The pain slowly subsided and the darkness began to lift. After a couple of seconds, she could see the world again: the marble wall, the silk flowers, the glittering shards of glass. And she saw Derek and Officer Frazier wrestling on the floor, fighting for possession of Frazier's assault rifle.

Derek was on top. He was larger and heavier than Frazier, and although the jagged glass shard was still sunk deep into Derek's waist, he fought as if he wasn't injured at all. With one hand on the rifle's stock and the other on the barrel, he pushed the weapon down toward Frazier's neck. He was the immense black wave Jenna had seen in her delirium, an unnatural force strengthened by genetic enhancements, so biologically superior that even a grisly gut wound couldn't stop him. Derek had caught Frazier by surprise and overpowered the maniac. He'd saved her life once again.

But she wasn't out of danger yet. Frazier gripped the rifle with both hands, keeping the barrel a few inches above his throat. At the same time, he bucked and writhed under Derek, doing everything he could to throw him off. Blood pulsed from the wound in Derek's side and coated the edges of the glass shard and streamed to the floor. He was weakening. Frazier was getting a better grip on the rifle, getting ready to tear it out of Derek's hands.

Jenna's head was still swimming, but she managed to sit up and stagger to her feet. She had to do something to help Derek. Maybe kick Frazier in the ribs. Or stomp on his skull. But as she stepped toward the two men, the mausoleum seemed to whirl around her. She doubled over and retched again. She was still shaky from her near-asphyxiation. Her legs trembled so hard, she could barely stand.

After a few seconds, she straightened up and took another step toward them. But Derek turned his head to the side and glared at her. "*Goddamn it! I told you to go!*"

With Derek distracted, Frazier took the opportunity to knee him in the groin. Derek winced but stayed on top of Frazier. He leaned all his weight on the rifle, trying mightily to bring it down.

Jenna felt so woozy. She could barely look at the men, much less join their fight. And yet she couldn't leave either. She stood there, wobbling, the floor tilting underneath her. "Derek . . . I . . ."

"I'll find you! Just go! The other officers are coming!"

Those last five words broke her trance. Alarmed, she raised her head and peered through the mausoleum's broken windows. She didn't see any FSU men running across the cemetery grounds, but Derek was right: they would be coming, very soon. And Jenna couldn't let the FSU arrest her again. She had to find Abbu and Raza. That was the most important thing.

Swaying, she turned away from him and lurched toward the stairway.

FOURTEEN

Lieutenant Frazier snarled at the man above him. It was his stepfather. It was his shithead uncle, the one who used to poke him with a lit cigarette. It was his third-grade gym teacher, the pervert who'd told all the boys in his class to pull down their shorts for a "health inspection."

The bastard pushed down on the rifle. Frazier pushed back, bracing his shoulders and elbows against the floor, but the rifle's barrel inched downward, edging toward his throat. The bastard's face was directly above him, less than a foot away, and it changed shape every second, its features shifting and transforming. It was like a fucking slide show, like the presentation the FSU gave to its officers to familiarize them with the most-wanted criminals and terrorists. But the faces he saw above him now didn't come from a mug-shot book or a government database. They came from Frazier's memories, from the darkest corners of his brain.

Then the bastard drew his head back and whipped it forward, slamming his forehead into the bridge of Frazier's nose. Pain shot through him like a lightning bolt, flashing inside his skull. But when Frazier opened his eyes and looked up again, he noticed something different. The bastard trying to kill him was *black*. So he couldn't be Frazier's stepfather or gym teacher or anyone else from Cassville, which was the white-trash capital of southern Missouri. Frazier rejected all the fucked-up pictures from his memory, flinging them aside so he could see the real face beneath.

It was Derek Powell. His old commander.

Frazier snarled again, louder and angrier. He hated Powell more than any of the others. Just a year ago, Frazier had practically worshipped the guy, mostly because Powell was the only officer in the army who wasn't a complete fucking asshole. Instead of acting like everyone else and treating Frazier like a moron, Powell told him he was smart enough to join the Rangers. When Frazier made it into the Ranger regiment, Powell got him assigned to the best platoon in the Third Battalion, and they served together in all the Afghan hot spots: Kandahar, Ghazni, Lashkar Gah, Jalalabad. And when the army offered a $10,000 bonus to anyone who signed up for Palindrome, they both volunteered.

But a few months later, it all went to hell. Powell started spreading rumors, talking shit about the battalion commanders. He said they'd made a secret deal with some Washington dickhead, who'd turned the Rangers into a bunch of fucking guinea pigs because he wanted elite soldiers for a new police agency. And then Powell went nuts and got himself blown up, but Frazier had always suspected it was a trick, and now he knew for sure. Powell had gone over to the other side. He'd joined forces with America's enemies—the illegals and ragheads and wetbacks and terrorists—and that was the worst fucking crime of all.

Now Frazier had a focus for his rage. Powell and the Khan bitch were traitors. They wanted to take everything away from him—his pride in his country, all the beliefs he grew up with. But Frazier wasn't going to let them get away with it. He was smarter than they thought. The Khan bitch had already left the mausoleum, but he could stop Powell. He knew exactly what to do.

And a moment later, he did it. He took his right hand off the rifle's stock, letting it drop to the floor, and thrust his left arm upward to raise the gun's barrel. These simultaneous actions tilted the rifle to a forty-five-degree angle. And because Powell was holding the gun so tightly, he rolled onto his left side, where the glass shard was lodged. The shard's outer edge jammed against the tiled floor, and its sharp inner point plunged deeper into Powell.

The traitor screamed. Frazier pressed his advantage and rolled on top of Powell, using his body weight to ram the glass shard farther into the bastard's abdomen. Then he wrenched the rifle out of Powell's hands and scrambled to his feet.

Frazier backed up a couple of yards and pointed the gun at the traitor. Powell lay on his back and convulsed, his arms and legs thwacking the floor. Blood erupted from his side in a fountain, spraying the names and dates carved into the marble wall.

Frazier grinned. He stood there for a little while, watching Powell writhe, enjoying every second of it. But this time he didn't close his eyes to savor the moment. He was anxious to kill the bastard. He wouldn't relax until the traitor was dead.

He aimed the rifle at Powell's black skull.

"Frazier! Lower that fucking gun!"

It was Colonel Grant. And he didn't look happy.

FIFTEEN

Vance raced across the West Wing. POTUS was howling again.

Luckily, the Oval Office was right down the hall. The Secret Service agents saw Vance coming and opened the office's door. After he stepped inside, the agents swiftly closed the door behind him.

The President of the United States wasn't behind his desk. He lay on his side on the big beige sofa in the middle of the room. He'd taken off his jacket but not his tie, which hung over the edge of the sofa cushion. His eyes were closed and his mouth was open, and for a horrified second Vance wondered if he was still breathing. But then POTUS rolled his head on the cushion and opened his mouth wider and let out another ugly howl.

Vance winced. He bent over the couch. "Mr. President! Wake up!"

He kept rolling his head but didn't open his eyes. He'd ruined all the hard work that his hairdresser had done that morning. His yellow coiffure mashed against the arm of the sofa. Loose strands of hair lay matted to the upholstery.

Vance bent lower and shook the president's shoulder. "*Stop howling!* Everyone in the building can hear you."

That got his attention. He opened his eyes and looked around the office, suddenly frantic. "What time is it?"

Vance looked at his watch. "It's seven o'clock."

"In the morning?"

"No, in the evening." He pointed at the flat-screen TV mounted on the wall. "You said you were going to watch the news for a while."

The president covered his face with both hands. At first it looked like he was rubbing his eyes, but then he let out a soft, muffled sob. POTUS was crying. "Oh God . . . oh God."

Vance felt a twinge of dread in his stomach. He knew what was coming. "Look, let's not—"

"I dreamed about her again . . . I saw my little girl."

He was talking about Princess. His daughter. Vance's wife.

"First she was young . . . so young, just a baby . . . and then she was grown up. She was in her wedding dress, Vance."

This happened after every one of his howling fits. The president wanted to talk about his dreams of his daughter. But Vance *didn't* want to talk about it, so he said nothing.

"She was so beautiful . . . but I knew it wasn't real . . . and that's why I screamed . . . it hurt so much, I couldn't help it."

Vance braced himself for more. Sometimes there was a third part to the dream. Sometimes POTUS relived the moment right after the explosion, when he shoved all the Secret Service agents out of his way and knelt beside her body.

But this time, thank God, the president stopped talking. He ran out of words and just sobbed. His torso shook so much that the sofa creaked underneath him.

The dreams and the howling fits had started a few weeks ago. They were the latest symptoms of his illness, which the White House doctors had diagnosed last year. The fits usually happened late at night, after he'd fallen asleep in front of the television. The worst part of it, at least from Vance's point of view, was that the president wouldn't let any of his aides or assistants help him when he got like this. He distrusted the entire White House staff, right down to the secretaries and janitors. His wife had abandoned him, and his sons were useless, so the whole burden of taking care of him had fallen to Vance, who was completely unsuited for it. He'd become a babysitter for his father-in-law, and that definitely wasn't what he'd signed up for.

He waited half a minute or so, hoping the president's crying jag would pass. But if anything, the sobs became louder and more insistent. Vance decided to act as if it wasn't happening. That helped sometimes. "You have to be more careful about when you fall asleep. There are still plenty of officials in the White House at this hour, and you don't want them to hear—"

"You mean reporters?" He took his hands off his face and sat up. Tears were still dripping down his cheeks, but now his eyes were frightened and darting. "Did any of those fucking reporters in the briefing room hear me?"

Vance shook his head. "No, we banned reporters from the West Wing two years ago. Remember?"

"Right, right. That was a smart move." The president nodded vigorously, agreeing with himself, but he was only pretending to remember the West Wing ban. Long-term memory loss was another symptom of his illness, and it was getting worse. "Those reporters are a bunch of fucking liars. We should throw the worst ones in jail to teach them a lesson. And we should put them in the same jail cells as the illegals they love so much. Then they'd see what those thugs are really like, right?"

"Yes, that's a good idea. But the press corps isn't our main concern right now." Vance tilted his head to the left, in the direction of the offices on the westernmost edge of the West Wing. "The vice president is still in his office tonight. He's spending more hours on the job lately. Which is a little suspicious, in my opinion."

The president scowled, scrunching his face and bringing his yellow eyebrows together. "Don't worry about him. He's a moron. He's probably kneeling behind his desk again. Praying to God for a pair of balls."

Vance frowned. His father-in-law's political instincts had deteriorated along with everything else. The vice president was the biggest danger to the administration, by far. Bigger than the press and the Democrats and all the federal judges put together. "There's a reason why the veep is spending more time in the White House these days. He's watching you. He disguises his ambition well, but he wants your job."

The president's face got angrier and uglier. He narrowed his eyes to slits and pursed his lips. "That idiot? That fucking Sunday-school teacher? He'll *never* be president. I mean, look at all the polls. His numbers are pathetic." He wrinkled his nose in disgust. "That's why we have to change the Constitution, Vance. If I don't get a third term, the country's gonna go right back to the Democrats next year. And then they'll start a whole new round of investigations, and I don't have to tell you how bad that'll be."

Vance shook his head, exasperated. It was so difficult to explain things to POTUS, even the most basic issues. "The veep knows he's unpopular, so he's looking at the alternatives. If he can prove you're unfit for office, he'll become president right away. Then he'd be the incumbent in next year's election, and that's always a huge advantage."

"Jesus fucking Christ! I'm not letting that dope take over!"

"You may not have a choice. The vice president has the authority to seize your position if he can convince the cabinet and Congress that you're crazy. That's in the Constitution too, the 25th Amendment. And if the veep hears one of your screaming fits and is clever enough to make a recording of it, that would give him a very convincing piece of evidence."

This seemed to get through to him. The president closed his mouth and lowered his head and looked down at the big oval rug beneath the sofa. The bluster drained out of his face, leaving it pale and deflated. His jowls sagged below his jawline. "Shit. You think that's what he did? You think that prick is recording me?"

Vance shrugged. "I don't know. Maybe not yet. But we have to take precautions. We have make sure this doesn't happen again, understand?"

The president kept looking down at the rug, which had the Great Seal of the United States woven into the fabric. He ran a hand through his disheveled hair, making it even more of a mess. "Christ, I don't believe this. I just wanted to take a fucking nap. I lay down and closed my eyes for a second, just a second. And then . . ." He raised his head. There were tears in his eyes again. "What the hell's wrong with me? I used to be so tough. I never had any of these problems before."

Vance sighed. He didn't have the patience to go through all the explanations again. The president's illness was a type of frontotemporal dementia, a disease that slowly destroyed the brain, similar to Alzheimer's but with more effects on behavior and emotions. It was caused by a rare genetic flaw that disrupted a crucial brain protein, and there was no effective treatment. The White House doctors had explained all these details to the president, but the information had never really sunk into his mind. He'd refused to accept the bad news, which meant that Vance had to repeat it to him over and over. Better to change the subject.

"How about some dinner? That might take your mind off your problems. I could ask the stewards to bring you a cheeseburger? Or maybe a taco bowl?"

"Goddamn it!" The president rose from the sofa and pointed at him. "You were supposed to fix this, Vance! You said if you had enough money for the genetics research, you could come up with a cure!"

"Okay, calm down. Your voice is getting loud again, and you don't want—"

"I gave you billions and billions of dollars! I transferred money from all over the budget to *your* department. So where's the fucking cure? What the hell did you do with all that money?"

The president stood in front of him, almost nose to nose, red-faced and glowering. Despite his illness and all his infirmities, he could still be brutally intimidating. And when he got into a rage, he forgot all the distinctions between his friends and his enemies. In fact, he directed his most vicious contempt at his friends, because he was convinced that they'd all betrayed him.

"Answer me, Vance! You said you'd have a cure by now. So are you a liar, or are you fucking incompetent?"

At that moment Vance hated the president more than he hated anyone else on earth. But unlike POTUS, Vance knew how to keep those feelings to himself.

"I've told you before, the CRISPR treatment isn't ready yet. The results from the initial experiments were promising, but there were some very serious side effects. We can't give you the injections until we're sure they're safe."

"I don't care about the side effects!" The president pointed at himself. "I mean, look what's happening to me! How could the side effects be any worse than this?"

"You won't have to wait that much longer. We're about to start a new phase of the experiment, and in just a few weeks we'll have some more results."

"A few weeks? Are you nuts? I'll be dead by then! I'll be under the fucking ground!"

Vance wished he had a gun. He wouldn't shoot the president. No, that would be stupid. But if Vance had a gun right now, he'd cock it and hold it against the president's forehead. He wouldn't pull the trigger, but he'd threaten to, just to get the narcissistic asshole to shut up.

He was still daydreaming about this plan when he heard a knock on the door to the Oval Office.

"Uh, Mr. President? Mr. Keller?" The voice on the other side of the door belonged to one of the Secret Service agents. "Can I talk to you for a minute?"

Vance looked over his shoulder, alarmed. The Secret Service men were under strict orders not to disturb them during the president's mental-health crises. The agents could make an exception to the rule only in the event of a national emergency —a major terrorist attack, an earthquake, a nuclear war, and so on. Which meant that something very bad had just happened.

Vance strode toward the door and opened it. The pair of Secret Service men stood in the corridor, looking nervous. Standing just behind them was the vice president.

Under ordinary circumstances, the veep was the blandest man in Washington. He was usually dull and dim and slow, his face vacant and colorless under his neat thatch of white hair. But now his brow was furrowed and his lips were pulled back from his teeth. As soon as he saw Vance in the doorway, he elbowed past the Secret Service agents.

"I need to see the president." His voice was firm. There was even some emotion in it. "Right now."

Vance gave him a cordial smile. "What's wrong? You look upset."

He nodded. "I *am* upset. And I have every right to be." He craned his neck, trying to look over Vance's shoulder and peer into the Oval Office. "Where's the president?"

Luckily, POTUS had retreated to the adjoining room, where he ate most of his meals. That gave Vance the freedom to invent a good excuse. "He's in the middle of a phone call. With the prime minister of Japan. I'm afraid it's going to be a fairly long conversation. Can you come back later? Or maybe wait until tomorrow?"

The vice president shook his head emphatically. "No. Tell him to get off the phone."

This was shocking. The veep was a stickler about rules and courtesy, so for him this behavior was totally outrageous. Vance grew worried. "Listen, maybe we should go to my office and try to—"

"No, I want to talk to the president. About the Palindrome Project."

He said those last two words very loudly, probably louder than they'd ever been spoken. Vance grimaced as they echoed down the corridor, making the Secret Service agents prick up their ears and stand a little straighter. The vice president wasn't supposed to know about Palindrome.

He nodded again when he saw Vance's reaction. "Yes, I know about it. I received a letter this afternoon from the attorney general's office, delivered by messenger. And then I turned on my television and learned that the attorney general had resigned and left Washington without even holding a press conference. That's a strange coincidence, don't you think?"

Vance kept his face blank, but his stomach was churning. The AG had played a clever trick. He must've written the letter to the vice president in advance and arranged for someone to deliver it if he got arrested. Evidently, the attorney general had hoped that the veep would go ballistic and make enough trouble to bring down the administration. Then the vice president, out of gratitude, would free the AG from federal prison.

And everything was proceeding according to the AG's plan. The veep's colorless face had turned as pink as a pencil eraser. "Here's the thing that really ticks me off, Vance. You're going against God. It's right there in the book of Genesis, chapter one, verse twenty-seven: 'God created man in his own image.' And no man has the right to change that, either through genetics or anything else."

Vance had to think fast. The vice president was openly discussing Palindrome in the West Wing corridor, so what was to stop him from revealing the existence of the project to *The New York Times* or *The Washington Post*? And if he got the religious conservatives riled up over this issue, the Republicans in Congress might finally find their backbones and turn against the president. So the situation was dire. It demanded an immediate, forceful, decisive response.

"Okay, I hear you loud and clear. I'll go get the president. Just wait here for a moment."

Vance turned around and marched into the Presidential Dining Room.

POTUS sat in a chair at the head of the long table, covering his face with both hands again. When he heard Vance come into the room, he lowered one hand, revealing the left side of his quivering mouth and a wet, frightened eye.

"Did he go away, Vance?"

"Shut up and listen. You're going to do exactly as I say."

SIXTEEN

Jenna hid in Prospect Park until nightfall. She sat under the trees on Lookout Hill and waited until the last rays of twilight flickered through the foliage.

It was a miracle she'd made it this far. After she left Green-Wood Cemetery, she was an easy target for the FSU's surveillance network. There were security cameras at every intersection in the neighborhood, and a whole fleet of quadcopter drones buzzed overhead. She heard a clatter of running feet as she raced toward Prospect Avenue, and she assumed it was a squad of men in black uniforms. The noise was very close, just around the next street corner.

But they weren't FSU officers. It was a crowd of civilians running toward a supermarket. Someone had shattered the market's glass doors, and people were coming out of the store with armloads of bread and milk and cereal boxes. There were so many looters in the street that it was easy for Jenna to lose herself in the crowd. She sprinted another three blocks and reached the edge of Prospect Park, which was even bigger than Green-Wood and full of hills. After climbing over a wrought-iron fence, she dashed up Lookout Hill, one of the park's densely wooded sections, and dove under the cover of the hundred-year-old trees. She could still hear the drones buzzing overhead, but their cameras couldn't see her through the thick canopy of leaves.

Was her escape really a miracle, though? Or was it a matter of luck and geography, not divine intervention? Jenna wasn't a good Muslim anymore—she'd stopped following the Islamic rules twelve years ago, after her mother died—and science was a much stronger force in her life than religion was. And yet, as a scientist, she always tried to be open-minded. Although there was no convincing scientific evidence for God or miracles, she couldn't disprove their existence either. So as she rested on the hilltop, she recited a prayer of thanks, the second prayer she'd said in the past twenty-four hours, after a whole decade of disbelief: *Praise be to Allah, lord of the heavens and lord of the earth, lord and cherisher of all the worlds.*

Jenna knew Prospect Park well. When she was a girl, she came here often with her parents and Raza, sometimes to visit the zoo, sometimes to feed the ducks in the lake. She'd always felt comfortable here, and right now it was probably the safest place in all of Brooklyn. Although mobs of looters and rioters were tearing through the nearby neighborhoods—she could hear the screams and sirens and car alarms—no one but Jenna was on Lookout Hill this evening. It helped that the woods were still soaked from the storm the night before.

After sunset, she sat for another half hour on the damp ground. She was waiting for the sky to get fully dark, but she was also using the time to make her plans. She wasn't sure where the FSU had taken Abbu and Raza, but the most likely place was Rikers Island. The Feds had rounded up thousands of New Yorkers over the past three months, and Rikers was the only jail big enough to hold that many detainees. Jenna couldn't go near the island, though, without getting arrested herself. And for the same reason, she couldn't go to the federal courts to challenge the detentions.

What she needed was an ally, an advocate. If she could get a powerful lawyer or government official to draw attention to the illegal treatment of her father and brother, then maybe the FSU could be forced to release them. But Jenna had no money for a lawyer, and she didn't know anyone in the government. She was a nobody, a nonentity, a penniless, friendless, unemployed fugitive.

She wasn't completely empty-handed, though. She reached into her pocket and pulled out the iPhone that the *New York Times* reporter had handed her. She couldn't access the video stored on the phone—Keating hadn't revealed his password—but she remembered the instructions he'd given. He'd told her to deliver it to a woman named Tamara, most likely a fellow reporter or editor at the *Times*, who lived at 168 Prospect Park West.

That was the best option. First of all, it was the right thing to do. The world needed to know about the massacre at Bay Parkway. Second, if *The New York Times* revealed the video of the bloodbath, plus the details of the Palindrome experiments, then the FSU might be pressured to release *all* their detainees. The newspaper was the perfect ally for Jenna. And the apartment buildings on Prospect Park West were right across the street from the park, only half a mile from where she was hiding.

Soon the sky turned black. The power was still out all across Brooklyn, and the woods on Lookout Hill grew prehistorically dark, as pitch-black as they were two thousand years ago. Jenna stood up and groped her way down the hill. She stretched her arms in front of her and reached for tree trunks in the darkness. She stumbled over loose stones and patches of mud. She couldn't see more than a few yards ahead, so she guided herself by sound rather than sight, heading with trepidation toward the noisy crowds of rioters.

She hiked under the trees for the next twenty minutes. Then she reached the low stone wall at the western end of the park and crouched behind it. The moon was rising behind her, illuminating the blacked-out neighborhood. When she peeked over the wall, she could see the apartment buildings across the street, most of them stately and elegant and four stories tall. Park Slope was one of the nicest parts of Brooklyn, where a two-bedroom apartment could cost a million dollars and most of the residents were doctors, lawyers, or bankers. But the rich folks weren't on the street tonight. They were in their expensive apartments, huddled behind locked doors, while the refugees from the storm walked up and down Prospect Park West.

They weren't rioters, not really. They were ordinary men and women, old people and teenagers, even some toddlers trailing after their parents. They'd looted supermarkets and bodegas, but only because they were hungry. They ate the stolen food as they walked down the street, ripping open packages of cold cuts and bags of tortilla chips, guzzling bottles of water and Coke and beer. The storm had ravaged so much of Brooklyn that it seemed like half the population was newly homeless. They couldn't go back to their flooded neighborhoods, so they milled across Park Slope, adrift and exhausted.

All at once, though, the mob started running. At first Jenna thought the FSU was chasing them, but there were no officers or armored Strykers in sight. The refugees shouted at one another and converged at the intersection of Prospect Park West and 13th Street. Then they ran farther west, stampeding toward the commercial strip on Eighth Avenue. Someone must've spread the news that another store was being looted. Within minutes, the whole crowd hustled off. The street in front of Jenna was deserted.

She looked left and right to confirm there weren't any cops nearby. Then she climbed over the stone wall and raced across the street and took cover in the doorway of one of the apartment buildings. Because the streetlights were out, she had to squint to read the address number above the door: 176. She was close. She headed north, scurrying toward the next doorway down the street. That building was Number 174. She kept going.

The funny thing was that Jenna had once dreamed of living in this neighborhood. Two years ago she became friends with another researcher at her lab, a biochemist named David Weinberg. He lived in Park Slope, half a mile from here, in an apartment his parents had bought for him. Jenna started dating David, even though he wasn't Pakistani or even Muslim. (He was Jewish!) It was a bit daring of her, but her father didn't mind—he really liked David—and after a year she started thinking seriously about marrying him. But she worried about leaving Raza. Although her father could care for her brother without her help, Jenna had always handled the nighttime duties: reading books to Raza, singing lullabies, doing everything she could to help him go to sleep. He clearly loved this nightly ritual, and so did Jenna. She couldn't bear the thought of giving it up.

For months, she agonized over the decision. In the end, though, all that emotional turmoil was for nothing. Last winter, David broke up with her. He gave her a lame excuse—"we're growing apart"—but Jenna suspected it had something to do with her troubles at work. She'd become a pariah at the lab after she'd objected to the human testing of CRISPR, and David didn't want to be associated with her. He was ambitious and angling for the lab director's job, and their relationship was hurting his chances. So he dumped her, which ended Jenna's dream of living in Park Slope. But she wasn't heartbroken. David had turned out to be a jerk, and she was glad she'd seen his true colors before it was too late. Counting her bless-ings, she decided to swear off men for a while.

Now she crossed 12th Street and dashed toward the entrance of a large brick building that took up half the block. This was Number 168. On the right side of the doorway was an intercom panel with about twenty but-tons, each marked with a name tag printed in Gothic lettering. Next to Apartment 3A was the name Tamara Carter.

Jenna pressed the button. No answer. She pressed it again. Still noth-ing. Getting desperate, she leaned on the button until her index finger started to hurt. Then she remembered: if the power is out, the intercom won't work.

Chagrined, she rubbed her finger until the pain went away. *Well, that was stupid.*

After some thought, she stepped away from the building's entrance and backed up until she stood near the curb. Then she looked up at the windows on the third floor. The shades were drawn and the curtains were pulled shut, but behind them she saw soft, wavering lights, probably from candles. Most of the building's residents seemed to be at home. It was just a matter of getting Tamara's attention.

She looked to her left and right again. She felt nervous and exposed. Now that every cop in Brooklyn was looking for her, the last thing she wanted to do was draw attention to herself. But she didn't have a choice. She drew in a deep breath.

"*Tamara? Tamara Carter?*"

Jenna's voice echoed against the brick façade. She thought she saw a shadow move behind one of the curtains on the third floor, but nothing else happened. Clearly, she needed to get louder.

"*TAMARA! I'M A FRIEND OF KEATING! WE NEED TO TALK!*"

A third-floor window opened. Jenna couldn't see who was behind it, but she heard a woman's voice, sharp and wary.

"What is it? Who are you?"

"Please, can I come up to your apartment? I saw Keating last night, the reporter from your newspaper." She refrained from mentioning what had happened to him. She couldn't shout that kind of news from the sidewalk. "He asked me to give you something."

The street fell silent. Then the woman on the third floor said, "Wait a minute," and closed the window.

Thirty seconds later, the building's door opened. A tall black woman in jeans and a tank top stood in the doorway. She was slender and very beautiful, with hair so close-cropped it looked like a light shadow on her scalp. In her left hand she held a flashlight, and in her right was a revolver, which she pointed at Jenna's chest.

"Come over here. Where I can see you."

Tamara didn't seem frightened. Her voice was calm and she held the gun steady. And strangely enough, Jenna wasn't frightened either. So many people had pointed guns at her in the past twenty-four hours that she was getting used to it.

Jenna approached the doorway, moving slowly and raising her hands above her head. She tried to look Tamara in the eye, but she couldn't see the woman's face so well because the flashlight was blinding her. "I'm so sorry about bothering you like this. My name is Jenna Khan and I—"

"Get inside." Tamara backed up, but didn't lower her gun. She retreated to the foot of the building's stairs as Jenna stepped through the doorway. At the same time, she trained her flashlight on Jenna's sneakers and sweatpants, which were caked with mud. "Jesus Christ. Did you sleep in the park?"

Jenna shook her head. She kept her hands in the air. "No, but I was hiding there. The Federal Service cops are after me. But I swear, I haven't done anything wrong."

"Where did you see Allen? No one at the *Times* knows where he is. Are the cops after him too?"

Her voice rose when she said "Allen," which Jenna guessed was Keating's first name. Tamara's composure was cracking a bit, showing how scared she really was. Jenna panicked for a moment, unsure how to say this.

"I saw him at Bay Parkway, at one of the checkpoints for the South Brooklyn District. The cops, they . . . they hurt him very badly."

"Hurt him? What did they did do? Did they beat him?"

"I didn't see it happen, but yeah, it looked like they beat him up bad. I only saw him afterward, and he gave me his phone because he'd shot some video of—"

"Just say it. Is he dead?"

Jenna couldn't speak. But she nodded.

Tamara lowered the revolver. She lowered the flashlight too, shining it on the floor, and for the first time Jenna got a good look at her face. She wore deep purple lipstick and a bright gold nose ring. Her eyelashes were long and thick, and her eyes were gorgeous. And they were filling with tears.

Jenna dropped her arms to her sides. She wanted to say something else, maybe add a few words of explanation, but Keating's death was so horrible that she couldn't think of anything that would console Tamara. So the two women just stared at each other.

Finally, Jenna broke the silence. "I'm . . . I'm so sorry. Are you also a reporter for the *Times*? Or an editor?"

Tamara shook her head. "No. I work for the city. For the New York City mayor's office." She uncocked her revolver and tucked it into the waistband of her jeans. "Come upstairs. I'll get you some clean clothes."

She turned around and started climbing the apartment building's stairway. After a moment of hesitation, Jenna followed her. "So you know Allen how . . . ?"

Tamara didn't say anything until she reached the second floor. Then she looked over her shoulder at Jenna.

"He was my boyfriend."

Jenna asked if she could use the shower, and Tamara said yes. It was a good idea for two reasons, the first being that Jenna stank to high heaven. But more important, she sensed that Tamara needed some time alone. The poor woman was struggling. She just barely managed to hold it together while she handed Jenna a towel and led her to the bathroom and lit a candle on the windowsill. But as Jenna stepped into the shower and turned the faucet handle, she heard a low, anguished wail coming from the other side of the bathroom door.

The water in the shower wasn't hot—the blackout must've shut down the building's water heater—but Jenna didn't care. It was a pleasure just to wash the dirt and sweat off her skin. She watched the dissolved filth stream down her legs and pool around her feet and funnel into the drain. After a few minutes, she began to shiver, partly because the water was so cold and partly because she'd been so tense and frightened for so long. She'd finally reached a safe haven, a place where she could let down her guard for a little while, and now she was overcome by all the worry and distress she hadn't allowed herself to feel before. She turned off the water and started crying. She reached for the towel and buried her face in it.

Jenna wept into the towel until she stopped shivering. Then she dried herself off and stepped out of the shower. She noticed that Tamara had taken away her grimy sweatpants and nightshirt and laid out some clean clothes for her on the bathroom countertop. The jeans were too long, but they fit her nicely once she rolled up the cuffs. And the T-shirt—black and seamless, with a scoop neckline—was actually quite attractive. Tamara, apparently, had a sense of style. She was one of those hip, fashionable New York women whom Jenna had always envied from afar.

But right now she didn't envy what Tamara was going through. In fact, Jenna felt guilty for crying in the shower. Yes, her fear and anxiety were terrible, but Tamara's grief had to be worse.

Jenna stalled for another five minutes. She picked up the bead necklace that Hector had given her and put it back on. She adjusted the necklace and looked at herself in the mirror above the sink. Then she left the bathroom and walked back to the apartment's tastefully decorated living room, which overlooked Prospect Park West.

Tamara sat on a beautiful blue couch in the middle of the room. In front of her was an equally beautiful mahogany table, on which stood a tall, flickering candle in a crystal holder. Spoiling the picture, though, were Jenna's soiled sweatpants, which lay on a pile of old newspapers on the floor. And in Tamara's right hand was Keating's iPhone, which she'd removed from the pocket of the sweatpants.

She was watching the video of the massacre. She held the phone close to her face, just a couple of inches from her nose, but the sound of gunfire was clearly audible across the room. Jenna's stomach twisted when she heard it. She remembered the rattle of the machine gun in the sentry tower, the people running and screaming and dropping into the floodwaters. She froze on the living-room carpet, feeling the terror all over again.

After a minute or so, the screams subsided, but the rattling gunfire grew even more intense. Jenna guessed the video had reached the point where Derek commandeered the Stryker vehicle and started firing back at Frazier. It amazed her now that Keating had been able to record the whole thing, even as he lay dying on the floor of the sentry tower. And Jenna saw the same amazement on Tamara's face as she watched the video. Her purple lips parted and she gaped at the footage. She took a deep breath and whispered, "Allen. Jesus Christ."

Then the gunfire ceased and the video ended. After several seconds, Tamara raised her head and looked Jenna in the eye. "Thank you for bringing this. It means a lot to me, just knowing what Allen was trying to do."

Jenna felt awkward. She didn't know what to say. "Yes, it was very brave. I haven't watched the video—I didn't know the password for his phone—but it sounds like he . . . like he recorded everything that happened on . . ." Her voice trailed off. She couldn't talk about it. "I'm sorry. I'm just glad you knew the password. Because everyone needs to see this."

Tamara nodded and somehow managed to smile. She was obviously hurting, but she was also pretty tough. "There's a funny story about that password. A few weeks ago Allen changed it to 'Tammy' because he knew how much I hated that nickname. We weren't dating for very long, only since last June. But I had high hopes for that boy." She raised her hand to her face and wiped her eyes. Then she turned off the power on the iPhone and rested it on her lap. "So where were *you* when all this shooting was going on?"

Tamara gave her a brave look, and that made Jenna brave too. She stepped forward and sat down in an armchair on the other side of the coffee table. "I was in the armored vehicle with Derek. He's the guy who fired back at the FSU cop in the sentry tower. You saw that cop in the video, right? The one who murdered all those people?"

"Yeah, the cop who jumped out of the tower at the end. That's one scary motherfucker." Tamara shook her head. "I sure as hell hope he broke his neck when he jumped."

Jenna frowned. "No, he didn't. He's enhanced. He's a former Special Forces soldier who received a gene-editing therapy. It's part of an experiment called Palindrome. I know about it because I used to work at a genetics lab that was involved in the project."

Tamara's reaction was surprising. She didn't cock her head or narrow her eyes. She didn't look at Jenna in astonishment or disbelief. She simply nodded. "Okay. Now I think I know who that motherfucker is. His name is Lieutenant Rick Frazier, right?"

"What? How do you know that?"

"I told you, I work in the mayor's office. And I see all the reports the mayor gets." Tamara shrugged. "The New York Police Department has its own intelligence division. Those are cops who usually gather information about terrorist plots, that kind of thing. But since the FSU came to town, the intelligence division has been watching the Feds, monitoring their abuses, all the brutality against innocent civilians in Brooklyn. And Frazier is definitely the worst."

Jenna was dumbstruck. "You mean you already know what he's done during the immigration raids? The beatings?"

"Yeah, we were collecting evidence, hoping to get enough to file charges against him. We've also received reports of abusive FSU officers in the other Federal Service Districts. Judging from their behavior, the NYPD suspected the leaders of the federal squads were jacked up on steroids or some other kind of performance-enhancing drug."

"So why isn't this in the news? Why didn't Allen put it in the *Times*?"

The question seemed to agitate Tamara. She leaned forward, perching on the edge of the couch cushions. "Believe me, he tried. But his editors wouldn't run the story. They were getting pressure from the newspaper's owners." She bent over the coffee table and pointed at the old newspapers on the floor. "The owners of the *Times* are scared shitless, because no one's on their side anymore. The president hates them, and so do all the new judges on the Supreme Court. So now the *Times* won't print *anything* unless they have irrefutable evidence." She picked up the iPhone from her lap and waved it in the air. "That's why Allen went to Bay Parkway. He was trying to get video of what the FSU is doing, photographic evidence that no one could dispute."

Tamara was breathing hard. She looked distraught and disgusted. Scowling, she slipped Keating's phone into the pocket of her jeans.

Jenna gave her some time, letting her seethe. But all the while she kept her eyes on the iPhone, which poked out of Tamara's pocket. Allen Keating had been right: the video was the key. It would redeem the sacrifice he'd made.

After waiting a few more seconds, Jenna pointed at the phone. "So are you going to show that video to the *Times*? That's what Allen would've wanted, right?"

Tamara thought it over for a moment. Then she shook her head. "Allen was an optimist. The situation is worse than he thought. You know what would happen if I showed this video to one of Allen's editors at the *Times*? The guy would call the newspaper's publisher, and the publisher would alert the FSU. Then the cops would show up here and arrest both of us. Because the newspaper's owners would rather cooperate with the government than lose their whole business."

"Then why don't we put it up on the Web ourselves? We can upload the video on YouTube, maybe one of their activist channels. We can also publicize the information about Palindrome, put it on Facebook and some other sites."

"No, that would be just as dangerous. The Feds use all kinds of software to monitor the internet. They'd take down the video in minutes, and then they'd figure out where it came from."

Jenna was getting frustrated. "Well, what the hell should we do? We can't let the FSU get away with this. They also arrested my father and brother, you know. My brother is paralyzed and can't even move his arms, but they threw him down and put handcuffs on him anyway."

"Jesus."

"Yes, it's disgusting. And horrible and evil. And I want them to pay for it."

Tamara grimaced, wrinkling the bridge of her nose. Clearly, she was disgusted too. "Don't worry. They're gonna pay. No doubt about that." She'd lowered her voice, making it deep and forbidding. Then she rose from the couch and stepped around the coffee table. "Come on. My car is parked on the street. It's a big SUV, so it should be able to get through the flooded areas."

Now that Tamara stood in front of her, Jenna could see the revolver still tucked into the woman's jeans. She felt a pang of dread as she stared at it. They were about to leave the safe haven. "Wait, where are we going?"

"To Manhattan. Gracie Mansion." Tamara tugged her shirt down so that the black fabric covered the handle of her gun. "We're gonna talk to the mayor."

SEVENTEEN

Colonel Grant sat in the tiered observers' gallery of the operating theater, looking down at the surgical team. Behind the big sheet of glass that separated the gallery from the operating room, three surgeons, two anesthesiologists, and six nurses were hard at work. They were all trying to save Derek Powell's life.

Grant looked at his watch. The operation had started at six o'clock in the evening and now it was almost ten. At first, the doctors had been optimistic about Powell's chances. Although he'd lost a lot of blood, the paramedics were able to stabilize him at Green-Wood Cemetery and load him into the FSU's medevac helicopter. But soon after he arrived at the Research Center on Rikers Island, Powell had a seizure and went into cardiac arrest. They had to shock him with the defibrillator half a dozen times to get his heart going again. The anesthesiologists yelled at each other and the nurses scrambled around the room and the surgeons cut into Powell's chest and abdomen. They split open his torso, revealing the soupy red mess inside.

Grant watched it all through the glass. He was no medical expert, but he could see that things were going to hell. Powell was dying.

But was that such a catastrophe? Until seventeen hours ago, Grant had thought Powell had died in Afghanistan. And it wasn't like they were losing an American hero. The guy was a deserter and a traitor. He'd single-handedly destroyed the Bay Parkway checkpoint and killed a dozen FSU officers. Worst of all, he was a threat to Palindrome. Why did he run off with that geneticist, the Pakistani bitch who was still on the loose? He and the Khan girl must've been planning to sabotage the project, maybe because they didn't like how the research had turned out. It was vindictiveness, pure and simple. Death was too good for someone like that.

And yet . . . and yet . . .

Personally, Grant had always liked Powell. He'd noticed the young soldier for the first time seven years ago, when Powell was a lieutenant fresh out of West Point and Grant was still the commander of the Army Rangers' Third Battalion. Lieutenant Powell had excelled at the Ranger selection program, showing extraordinary combat skills and endurance. His performance was equally remarkable after he went to Afghanistan and led his platoon into battle against the Taliban. Powell was tough as nails, but he also had a brain. And he had the warrior spirit, always ready for action.

Six years later, when Grant was working for the White House and trying to recruit test subjects for the Palindrome Project, he wasn't surprised when Powell—now a captain—became one of the first volunteers. The injections turned him into an even better soldier, smarter at training his men and more skilled at killing the enemy. Grant was so impressed, in fact, that during one of his visits to Afghanistan he took Captain Powell aside and had a long conversation with him about Palindrome and all the amazing things it made possible. He even told Powell about the New America Initiative, Keller's plan to reestablish law and order in the country. The K-Man had promised to put Grant in charge of the effort, and the colonel was going to need several outstanding officers to serve under him. He'd hoped that Powell would become one of his deputies, part of the team that would make America great again.

Now Grant couldn't believe how badly he'd misjudged the man. Frowning, he stared at the surgical team on the other side of the glass and forced himself to look at the doctors cutting into Powell's body. Then Grant heard a door open and turned his head.

A young man in a white lab coat entered the gallery and headed toward him. He was one of the Palindrome scientists, a lab director at the

Rikers Island Research Center. He had short black hair and wore a red T-shirt under his lab coat, which made him look a little ridiculous. More than half of the Palindrome researchers were either Asian or Jewish, and this guy belonged to the latter category. He was smart and dedicated, and Grant had promoted him to the director position a few weeks ago when a spot opened up. But soon after promoting the guy, Grant discovered how annoying he could be. He was too intense. He talked a mile a minute.

His name was David Weinberg.

He approached Grant and leaned over his chair. "Uh, Colonel? Can I talk to you for a second?"

"You're already talking to me. What do you want?"

Weinberg nodded. He was so eager to start yapping, he didn't take offense. "Well, I just wanted to give you an update from the molecular genetics team. The operation on Powell has given us the opportunity to collect samples of his body tissues." He pointed superfluously at the operating room. "Over the past three hours, we've analyzed the DNA from the samples and compared them with the records we have for this test subject. And the results have been intriguing. His body is changing in ways that none of us anticipated. Most of the changes are maladaptive, but a few are—"

"Slow down, Weinberg." Grant raised a hand. "I'm not one of your professors. Talk in plain English."

The guy nodded again. He actually smiled. Weinberg was so damn excited about his discovery that nothing short of a bullet to the brain would stop him from talking about it. "Okay, I'll go slow. CRISPR changes the genes, right? Those are the sections of DNA that tell the body how to make its proteins. But genes aren't the whole story. They actually take up less than two percent of the space on the chromosomes." Weinberg's voice was slower than before but just as annoying. He sounded like a third-grade teacher. "The sequences *between* the genes used to be called junk DNA, because scientists thought they were useless. But now we know that these sequences can interact with the genes, turning them on and off."

This was why Grant usually avoided talking to the scientists. It took them forever to get to the point. "Can we get back to Powell? Just tell me what's going on with him."

"Sure, sure. The basic problem is that CRISPR isn't as reliable as we'd assumed. Powell's treatment was supposed to change only the targeted genes in his DNA, but some of the CRISPR molecules hit the wrong targets. They made unexpected changes to Powell's junk DNA, which disrupted the normal functioning of hundreds of other genes. That's why Powell started exhibiting such a wide range of symptoms—the bleeding eyes, the respiratory difficulties, the discoloration of his skin." Weinberg pointed again at the operating table. "That's also why the doctors are having such a hard time treating him. His biochemistry is completely abnormal. Sedatives and painkillers and other drugs don't have the usual effects on his body."

Despite the gobbledygook, Grant got the gist of it. Wincing, he turned back to the operating room and stared at Powell's split torso and exposed organs. The sight was horrible enough, but now Grant realized that Powell might not be fully sedated. He might be feeling every second of this torture.

Grant was furious. He stood up and jabbed his index finger at Weinberg, poking him right in the middle of his red shirt. "Let me see if I can summarize what you're saying. You geniuses thought you knew what you were doing, but you weren't as smart as you thought you were. In other words, you fucked up. Does that sum it up, more or less?"

Weinberg was at a loss for words, probably for the first time in his life. With an expression of pain and surprise on his face, he gawked at the finger pressed against his breastbone. He looked like a hurt five-year-old. "Colonel, we warned you about the risks of human trials. Remember all the debates we had about this last year? But you ordered us to go ahead anyway, and so you can't blame us now for—"

"You know what? I made a mistake." He pressed harder against Weinberg's chest. "I should've insisted that you assholes test the drugs on yourselves first. If I'd done that, I'm pretty sure you would've been more careful."

Weinberg stepped backward. He retreated halfway across the gallery. The guy had taken Grant's threat seriously, and now he looked terrified.

Like most of the Palindrome researchers, Weinberg was afraid of the thing they'd created. Specifically, the scientists were afraid of being accidentally infected by the virus that carried the gene-altering treatment. The fear was overblown, ridiculously exaggerated. Because the virus was blood-borne—delivered by injection to the patient's brain and muscle tissues—infection required blood-to-blood contact. What's more, everyone at the Research Center had received vaccinations against the specific type of virus used in the CRISPR treatments. The vaccine caused the body's immune system to produce antibodies; if the researchers were accidentally exposed to the virus, their antibodies would kill it before it could invade their cells and alter their genes.

And yet the scientists were still afraid. It was irrational, but they couldn't help it. Their fear had its own logic.

Grant approached Weinberg. The colonel was good at exploiting fear. It was one of his talents. "Maybe that's what we should do in Phase Three. Test the new virus and the new CRISPR treatment on the scientists first. We just got a shipment of vaccine for the Phase Three virus, but maybe we should put a hold on vaccinating the research staff. What do you think?"

Weinberg held his hands out in front of him like a traffic cop, as if to stop Grant from coming any closer. "Look, there's no need to get upset. I can fix the problem with Powell. I have an idea."

Reluctantly, Grant nodded. He was still angry. "Okay. I'm listening."

"Now that we've thoroughly analyzed Powell's DNA, we can make more changes to it, alterations designed to help him survive. I only need a couple of hours to formulate a new CRISPR treatment for him." Weinberg's voice was speeding up again. "We can give him the injections tonight, and the effects should start to kick in by tomorrow. It's our best hope for keeping him alive."

Weinberg looked at Grant, anxious to see his reaction. But Grant kept him waiting. To be honest, he wasn't sure what to do. His gut instinct was to simply let Powell die. The poor bastard had suffered enough.

On the other hand, the Palindrome Project was more important than the fate of any one man. Powell had volunteered for the experiment, and the scientific tests weren't over yet. He could still contribute to their goal, their great task. The results from Powell's next test would further their efforts to strengthen the country. Very soon they would bring forth a new generation of Americans, tougher and more loyal and inherently better than most of the sorry specimens who now infested the nation. The potential was tremendous. It justified any sacrifice.

Grant folded his arms across his chest. "Go ahead. Develop the new treatment for Powell. But keep me informed. I want progress reports from your team every six hours."

Weinberg was visibly relieved. He took a deep breath and steadied himself by propping his hand against the wall. "Thank you, Colonel. We won't let you down."

"And one more thing. I want you to accelerate the tests you're conducting on Raza Khan."

That name had an immediate effect on Weinberg. He swallowed hard, his face blanching. Ever since this afternoon, he'd been performing a battery of diagnostic tests on the Khan freak, but he clearly wasn't comfortable with the assignment. And Grant knew why: until a year ago, Weinberg had been screwing Jenna Khan, the freak's sister. They'd kept the relationship secret because they were coworkers at the time, but Grant had uncovered the secret during his investigation of the Khan bitch.

Grant enjoyed watching the researcher's discomfort. He stepped closer. "I want an explanation for the unusual results of the boy's brain scans. Your reports so far have been worthless, pure shit. You obviously don't have a clue."

Weinberg backed up against the wall. "Colonel, I . . . I've been trying to . . ."

Grant's phone rang. He grimaced and reached for it, digging into his pocket. If it was anyone but Keller, he was going to tell them to fuck off. But it was the K-Man. His name flashed on the phone's screen. And when Grant answered the call, he heard Keller's voice against a background of booming, thumping noise that he recognized right away, mostly because he'd spent so many years in the army. It was the sound of a helicopter in flight.

"We need to speed up our plans, Colonel. I just left the White House, and I'm on my way to New York." The helicopter engines roared, almost drowning him out. "In an hour I'll arrive at Rikers Island. And I'm bringing the vice president."

EIGHTEEN

Jenna tensed in the passenger seat of the SUV as Tamara drove toward the police checkpoint on Tillary Street. This was the entrance to the approach road to the Brooklyn Bridge, so security was tight. A dozen New York City cops and two dozen Federal Service officers were inspecting the cars and trucks headed for Manhattan, shining their flashlights into the faces of all the drivers and passengers.

Jenna's stomach roiled. She had a bad feeling about this. She glanced at Tamara, then looked over her shoulder to see if they could make a U-turn. "This looks bad. We should turn around."

But Tamara didn't seem worried. She eased off the gas pedal of the big Chevy Suburban and steered toward the line of cars farthest to the right. "Nah, it's not so bad tonight. I've seen backups here that are a hundred times worse. You should see it on Monday mornings, it's un-fucking-believable."

"I'm not talking about the traffic." Jenna pointed at the officers who were examining the cars a hundred yards ahead. "I'm talking about the cops. The FSU is looking for me. Those officers probably have flyers with my picture on them."

"Well, that's why I pulled all the way to the right side of the street. At this checkpoint, the New York cops work the right side and the FSU assholes work the left." She tapped the steering wheel, clicking a long fingernail against the rim. "They hate each other so much, they have to keep the whole street between them."

Jenna looked closer at the police officers up ahead, who were illuminated by huge floodlights powered by rumbling generators. It was true—the FSU men in black uniforms were checking the cars in the left two lanes, while the cops in blue uniforms were checking the cars on the right. But she was still wary. "Don't you think they're sharing information? The FSU must send its list of fugitives to the NYPD. So the New York cops are probably looking for me too."

Tamara reached over to the passenger seat and gave Jenna's arm a squeeze. "Relax, sister. I'm with the mayor's office, remember? That gives me some pull with the men and women in blue. Watch this."

She leaned forward and threw a switch below the dashboard. The light bar mounted on the SUV's roof began flashing its blue and red LEDs. Then Tamara steered around the car ahead of them, veering into the shoulder on the right side of the road. She pulled up to a pair of New York cops at the checkpoint, a young patrolman and a middle-aged woman with short dreadlocks under her officer's cap. Tamara rolled down the driver-side window and waved at the older officer. "Hey, Lizzie. Working overtime?"

The officer rolled her eyes and stepped toward the SUV. "I don't want to even talk about it. I've been on duty for three shifts now, all because of the fucking storm. I'm so tired, I can barely stand up."

"I'm going uptown to see the mayor. You want me to ask him to send some more officers here?"

Lizzie frowned. "Yeah, tell him I need a hundred more people. And tell him they have to be good at kicking ass, because I want them to knock the shit out of those FSU motherfuckers across the street."

"I'll see what I can do. Take care." Tamara rolled up her window. Then Lizzie and the patrolman waved them through the checkpoint.

Jenna breathed a sigh of relief. The cops hadn't even glanced at her. "Wow. That was impressive."

Tamara shook her head. "It's insane. Look what the Feds have done to us. We have to sneak around our own damn city." She hit the gas, and the SUV raced ahead. "This can't go on. It just can't."

Traffic was light because of the big jam behind them, and in less than a minute they were halfway across the Brooklyn Bridge. It looked like the storm hadn't done much damage to the bridge, which was so sturdy and rock-solid that it could probably withstand a dozen hurricanes in a row. But as Jenna peered out the SUV's windows at the East River below, she could see the devastated shorelines on both sides. The full moon was directly overhead, and its light spattered on the flooded streets and darkened buildings.

Behind them, on the Brooklyn side of the river, the park below the bridge was underwater. Ahead, on the Manhattan side, the South Street Seaport was a flooded ruin, and so was the housing project to the north. The lights were out all over Lower Manhattan, and the empty skyscrapers stood on the southern tip of the island like a row of tombstones. Towering above them all was One World Trade Center, the tallest and darkest building, its spire a black needle against the moonlit sky.

The bridge's roadway ran high above the swamped city, but as Tamara sped into Manhattan they gradually descended to street level. She shook her head again and pointed straight ahead. "You see City Hall over there? They had to evacuate it when the storm hit. They never had to do that before." She plowed into a deep puddle, and the water fantailed behind the car. "The storms are coming every month now, you notice? And they keep getting worse."

At City Hall, Tamara turned right and drove north on Centre Street. The floodwaters had drained from the traffic lanes, but there were few vehicles on the road aside from the police cars and ambulances. On the sidewalks, though, were hundreds of homeless people. They took shelter in doorways and lay on park benches and huddled on the street corners. Jenna guessed that most of them had fled their apartments when the storm surge hit Lower Manhattan and flooded their buildings. Now the victims were wandering down Broadway and Centre Street, trying to find a dry place to spend their first full night outside. Many of them seemed to be heading north, toward the higher-elevation neighborhoods.

Jenna winced as she stared at them. She wasn't the only one in trouble, not by a long shot. "My God, look at all the homeless. How many buildings were flooded here?"

Tamara let out a whistle. "Oh man. Hundreds. Maybe even thousands. All of Battery Park City is underwater. And the housing projects along the East River."

Jenna shook her head, getting angry. "You know, my father predicted this. He worked as a taxi driver after he came to America, but in Pakistan he studied geology at the University of Karachi. So he knew about the greenhouse effect and global warming. He used to talk all the time about how much the climate was going to change in the next few years."

"Yeah, my professors in college used to talk about it too." Tamara shrugged behind the steering wheel. "But who cares about the truth, right?"

"It made my father so mad. He would read the newspaper every morning during breakfast and point to the articles about hurricanes and wildfires and drought. And he would say, 'You see? It's killing the country. It's destroying the cities and costing trillions of dollars.'" Jenna's eyes stung. It hurt to think about Abbu. "And he said it would only get worse. He said America would become like Pakistan, with terrorists everywhere and criminals running the government."

"Your father was right. Things are going to hell. But I wouldn't give up just yet." Tamara glanced at her, taking her eyes off the road for a second. "A disaster can also be an opportunity. Sometimes things have to get really bad before people get desperate enough to change. So there's still hope."

"What about the mayor? Is he desperate enough to do something?"

Tamara didn't answer right away. For several seconds she just stared at the dark street ahead. Then she nodded. "I think he'll do the right thing. But he'll need some convincing. The big problem with Mayor DeMarco is that he's afraid to stand up to the Feds. Someone's gotta put some spine into him."

She gripped the steering wheel firmly, her veins bulging from the backs of her hands. This middle-of-the-night meeting with the mayor was a gamble, and Tamara was clearly nervous about it. But Jenna felt a surge of conviction. She was sick and tired of running. She was ready to fight.

Soon they came to Canal Street, the heart of Manhattan's Chinatown. This area was usually bustling with tourists and locals, but now it was dark and deserted, all the restaurants and souvenir shops locked up tight. Then they sped into Soho and the East Village, which were equally empty. The only lights came from the emergency vehicles and the candles flickering in the windows of the tenement buildings. But as they approached 14th Street, Jenna noticed that the sky to the north was glowing. It brightened as they raced up Park Avenue, and when they reached

20th Street she saw the glare of streetlights just ahead. Power had been restored above 26th Street. They reentered the familiar radiance of New York City.

Tamara hit the brakes, and the SUV slowed down. Traffic was heavier on this stretch of Park Avenue, and most of the vehicles were police cars. Jenna saw cops on the sidewalks too, both FSU and NYPD. They were rounding up the homeless people here, stopping them from going any farther north. Dozens of detainees lay facedown on the sidewalk, their hands cuffed behind their backs. Jenna remembered her own arrest the night before, and she thought again of Abbu and Raza. She clenched her hands in anger, her fingernails digging into her palms.

After a few minutes they crossed 57th Street and drove into the Upper East Side. The grand apartment buildings on Park Avenue blazed with electric light, every window illuminated. The sidewalks below were guarded by men in uniforms, but most were neither FSU nor NYPD officers; they were private security guards, hired by the rich East Siders to protect their enclave. There were even more guards north of 86th Street, and up ahead Jenna saw a barricade that had been constructed across Park Avenue, a high wall made of sheet metal and plywood. On the other side of the wall, fires were burning. Flames leapt from the rooftops of the housing projects a mile farther uptown.

Jenna pointed ahead. "What's that? Riots?"

"I don't know." Tamara craned her neck and squinted at the barricade and the fires. Then she made a right turn on 88th Street. "There was flooding in East Harlem too. And some of the housing projects up there are in terrible shape. When fires start in those buildings, they can get out of control pretty quick."

They drove for another two minutes, passing churches and barbershops and pizzerias, all locked and shuttered. Then they reached a park that sat on a ridge between East End Avenue and the East River, a strip of greenery protected by seawalls and its elevation above the water. There was a driveway that led into the park, and at the top of the driveway was an old-fashioned, two-story mansion, shining under dozens of security lights. Jenna recognized it right away: Gracie Mansion, the official residence of New York City's mayors.

Tamara pulled the SUV up to the gate, which was manned by half a dozen New York cops. These officers looked a lot more intimidating than the ones at the Brooklyn Bridge. The biggest cop, a thick-necked, broad-shouldered bruiser, stepped toward the driver-side door as Tamara rolled down her window. He aimed his flashlight at her face.

"What are you doing here, Ms. Carter?" His voice was strained, unfriendly. "No one told us you were coming tonight."

"Sorry, Frank. It's a special meeting. Not on the mayor's schedule."

Instead of replying, the cop named Frank pointed his flashlight at Jenna. He kept the beam on her for several seconds, studying her face. She felt a strong urge to open her door and bolt out of the car, or at the very least turn away from the flashlight, but she resisted it. She kept her face blank.

Finally, he shifted the flashlight back to Tamara. "Who's your friend? She's not on the staff. I've never seen her before."

"She requested a meeting with the mayor, and I approved it. Frank, is something wrong? Why are you giving me such a hard time?"

He let out an unhappy grunt. Then he lowered the flashlight. "Yeah, there's something wrong. Didn't you see all the fires? There's a huge crowd of pissed-off people just ten blocks uptown. They're torching everything that's not too waterlogged to burn. And if they decide to come this way, there's nothing we can do to stop them. We'd need at least a thousand officers to scare them off."

Tamara scowled. "Then why are you making me wait here? Let me in so I can try to do something about it."

Frank let out another grunt. But after a couple of seconds he stepped away from the Suburban and opened the gate.

Tamara raced the last ten yards, skidding the SUV to a halt outside the mansion. Then she and Jenna jumped out of the car and hurried up the steps to the front door.

Mayor Bob DeMarco was pacing across the mansion's library. He shouted into an iPhone as he loped to and fro, taking enormous strides past all the antique furniture in the room, the nineteenth-century bookcases and armchairs and settees. He was so involved in his phone conversation that he didn't even look up when Jenna and Tamara stepped through the doorway.

"Okay . . . let's just . . . listen, I just want to ask you one . . . what exactly do we know for sure?"

Jenna was struck by how big and ungainly he was. DeMarco was almost six and a half feet tall, with exceptionally long arms and legs. His head was also long—it was about the size and shape of a loaf of white bread—and it was topped with thinning gray hair. He was in his early sixties and still in good shape, but his cheeks were sunken and his brow corrugated with fatigue. He looked frazzled and exhausted. There were sweat stains under the arms of his white button-down shirt.

He nodded while listening to the caller on his iPhone. After several seconds he noticed Tamara standing by one of the bookcases and mouthed the words "police commissoner" to her. Then he turned around and continued pacing. He didn't acknowledge Jenna at all.

"So . . . so let me see if I understand. You have a probable homicide of Captain Adams, the precinct commander. And his driver too, Officer Garcia. And you've heard a rumor that . . . okay, okay, a report from a trusted source . . . that an FSU commander might've committed the . . . how did you say it happened? The guy punched the captain in the head?"

DeMarco grimaced and pulled the phone away from his ear. The police commissioner was yelling so loudly on the other end of the line that Jenna could hear him from across the room. The guy was cursing at the top of his lungs, saying something about a goddamn patrol car that had been dumped into the shit-stinking Gowanus Canal. The mayor kept nodding and trying to ask questions, but he couldn't get a word in. After a while, he slapped his hand to his forehead and tugged his wispy hair. Clearly, he wasn't enjoying his job right now.

The commissioner finally stopped yelling, and DeMarco jumped in. "Listen, Steve, I'll do everything I can. I'll call the District Attorney and make sure he puts his best prosecutors on the case. But in the meantime we have an emergency situation in East Harlem. I know your officers are furious about this rumor . . . I mean, this trusted report . . . but you need to convince them to help us out here . . . no, I can't promise that the FSU won't . . . no, I don't have any control over their . . . listen, this is a direct order, okay? Send two hundred officers to East 96th Street. And make sure they're equipped with riot gear. Right *now,* understand?"

The mayor ended the call. He pocketed his phone and wiped the sweat off his brow. Then he loped across the room at full speed, heading straight for Tamara. "I need your help with this, Carter. The police department is going nuts." He stopped right in front of her and bent forward at the waist, looming over her like the tallest guy in a subway car. "You're friendly with some of the precinct commanders, right? You think you can talk some sense into them?"

Tamara held up her hands. "Okay, slow down. What—"

"The cops are freaking out because one of their captains is missing, and there's a rumor going around that the FSU killed him. The story is completely insane, but it's spreading on the police department grapevine, and they all believe it." DeMarco was getting agitated. He waved his long arms up and down and sprayed saliva as he talked. "Two thousand officers have already called in sick for the midnight-to-eight shift. They're refusing to work in the areas where the FSU is operating. And that's a big problem, because the Feds are all over the damn city now."

"Bob, take a deep breath. I've got some more bad news for you." She pointed at Jenna. "This is Dr. Jenna Khan. She's a scientist, a geneticist. She used to work at a lab that did research for the FSU."

DeMarco turned to Jenna and looked at her for the first time. He extended his hand, but his expression was wary. "I'll be honest with you, Dr. Khan. I've already had enough bad news for one night."

Jenna stepped forward. "I'm sorry, Mr. Mayor, but this is worse than everything else you've heard." She shook his hand, which was twice the size of her own. "I was involved in a classified federal project called Palindrome. Have you heard of it?"

"No, but that's not surprising. The Feds tell me nothing. We're not on very good terms nowadays."

"I was working on a new genetic-engineering technique. It was supposed to be used for treating diseases. But the FSU had different plans."

The mayor let go of her hand. He seemed uncertain about whether he should take her seriously. "Genetic engineering?"

She nodded. "After I left the project, the other researchers applied the technique to altering human DNA, specifically the genes that control intelligence and reflexes and agility. They tested the treatment on Special Forces soldiers in Afghanistan, and now some of those soldiers are working for the FSU."

DeMarco opened his mouth but didn't say anything. It looked like someone had just gouged a hole in his loaf-like head. He gaped at Jenna, bewildered.

She decided to press on. "Over the past twenty-four hours I've observed two of the test subjects. Both have genetic enhancements that have radically improved their combat skills, but they're also suffering from unforeseen side effects. One of the subjects is an FSU lieutenant whose brain has been damaged by the genetic alterations. Basically, the treatment has turned him into a psychopath. Last night, he fired a machine gun at a crowd on Bay Parkway and murdered at least a hundred people."

Tamara edged closer and caught the mayor's eye. "We have video evidence of the massacre. You know Allen Keating, the *Times* reporter? He shot the video with his phone before . . ." Her voice quavered, but she shook her head and brought it under control. ". . . before he died. That motherfucking FSU officer killed him. He beat Allen senseless."

This piece of news snapped DeMarco out of his trance. "Oh God. Isn't he the reporter you've been dating?" He stretched an arm toward Tamara and clasped her shoulder. "He's dead?"

She shrugged his hand off. She was too angry to talk about it.

Jenna came to her aid. "The lieutenant's name is Frazier. He almost killed me too. His mind is breaking down and his consciousness is destabilizing. But until his brain ceases to function, he's going to keep on killing."

"Wait a second." The mayor swayed for a moment, unsteady on his feet. "You said *Frazier*?"

"Yes, Lieutenant Rick Frazier. Apparently, the police department's intelligence division has been monitoring him for the past few months because of his abusive behavior."

"Jesus." The mayor turned away from her and lurched to the left, as if he'd suddenly lost his balance. He leaned against one of the bookcases and took a couple of deep breaths. Then he slowly stood up straight, resting a hand against the wall to steady himself. "That's his name. Frazier. That's who the cops are spreading rumors about."

Jenna stepped toward him. "You mean the rumors you mentioned before? About the police captain?"

"The cops are saying a guy named Frazier killed Captain Adams. With a single punch to the head."

"Well, he's definitely capable of doing that. And the Feds are letting him run wild all over Brooklyn."

"Jesus Christ. This is a fucking nightmare." DeMarco lowered his head and stared at the carpet.

Tamara came forward and glared at the mayor. She twisted her purple lips in disgust. "Is that all you can say? 'This is a nightmare?' That's your whole reaction?"

The mayor didn't look at her. "No, of course not. But what can we do? How can we—"

"It's time, Bob. You need to call the president and tell him to get his fucking Gestapo out of our city!"

DeMarco raised his head. His eyes were wide, and sweat dripped from his brow. It was strange to see such a large man get so frightened. "That won't work. The president will just refuse. And he has the law on his side, the goddamn Federal Service Act. Congress passed it and the Supreme Court upheld it, so now the FSU has legal immunity. I can't do a thing."

"Ignore the law! Close the roads going to the FSU headquarters on Rikers Island. Cut off their power and water and gas." Tamara confronted him, tilting her head back so she could look right into his face. "The FSU won't be able to operate here if they have no food or water. They'll have to send their officers back to Texas or Georgia or wherever the hell they came from."

He frowned. "So you want me to use the NYPD to set up a blockade around Rikers?"

"After hearing those rumors, the New York cops would be happy to do it."

"And what if the FSU tries to reopen the roads? What if the Feds start shooting at our cops?"

"Then we shoot back!"

DeMarco shook his head. "Do you realize what you're saying? You're talking about starting a civil war!" He shouted those last few words, which echoed against the walls of the library. The mayor's face was flushed and frantic. He was terrified.

And in the silence that followed, Jenna heard a roar outside. It was a pounding, juddering mechanical noise that grew very loud very fast, so loud that it rattled the glass in the library's windows. Then she heard the sound of rapid footsteps banging against the mansion's old floors, and a moment later she saw the thick-necked police officer named Frank, the cop who'd stopped Tamara's car at the security gate. He rushed into the room, wide-eyed and breathless.

"Mr. Mayor! Helicopters are landing on East End Avenue! The Feds are right outside!" Frank pointed out the window. "We're under attack!"

NINETEEN

A dozen Special Forces helicopters thundered over the East River. Colonel Grant watched them from the FSU's heliport, located on the roof of the tallest building on Rikers Island.

He peered through a pair of infrared binoculars that showed the glowing heat signatures of the helicopter engines against the night sky. Halfway up the river, near the northern tip of Roosevelt Island, the squadron split into two smaller groups that flew in opposite directions. Thanks to the phone call from Keller an hour ago, Grant knew where each group was headed. Six of the choppers dove toward the mayor's residence in Manhattan. The other six zoomed toward Rikers.

Grant felt a stirring in his chest. It was like what he'd felt twenty years ago when he was a gung-ho army lieutenant on his first tour in Afghanistan. The same quickening of his pulse, the same fierce adrenaline rush in his veins. He hadn't felt it in so long that he'd almost forgotten how intoxicating it was. *God, I love this. The battle is starting right here, right now! We're gonna clean up New York and then the rest of the country. And I'm gonna command all our forces, the warriors of the New America Initiative. That's what Keller promised.*

After a while Grant lowered his binoculars and took in a lungful of the brackish night air. Standing next to him on the rooftop was Lieutenant Frazier, who wore his black FSU uniform but wasn't carrying his assault rifle. Keller had told Grant to bring "your best man" to the heliport, and Frazier was the obvious choice. He'd come to Rikers with Grant after they captured Derek Powell at Green-Wood Cemetery, and though Frazier had been acting a little weird since then—pestering the doctors at the Research Center, repeatedly asking them about Powell's condition—the lieutenant's loyalty was beyond question. If Grant ordered him to jump off the Empire State Building, Frazier would do it in a heartbeat.

Keller had also instructed Grant to make room in the jail complex for more detainees. The Special Forces team might not capture the mayor alive—DeMarco had NYPD bodyguards, and they would definitely resist his arrest—but if the soldiers managed to get him to Rikers in one piece, Grant planned to spend the rest of the night interrogating him. For seven years, the New York City government had obstructed the White House, fighting its efforts to deport illegals and potential terrorists. Now, though, Grant would remove those obstructions. He was going to persuade DeMarco, by any means necessary, to cough up the names of all the uncooperative city officials.

Then there was the huge task of placing New York under martial law. First, they needed to take control of the city's infrastructure—the streets, sewers, water pipes, and power lines. Next, they had to appoint FSU officers to take over the fire department, the housing authority, the criminal court, and the board of education. They also had to review the loyalties of the New York police force to determine which officers could be transferred to the FSU and which needed to be fired. It would be an enormous undertaking, but Grant was looking forward to it. He enjoyed the challenge of a big job, as long as he was in charge.

But all those duties could wait until tomorrow. Right now, Grant needed to handle the vice president's visit.

The colonel raised his binoculars again to look at the closer group of helicopters, which were less than a mile away. After several seconds, five of the choppers veered south toward LaGuardia Airport, where the Special Forces would take over the control tower and secure the airfield for military use. The sixth chopper proceeded alone to Rikers Island, heading straight for the heliport. Grant recognized its silhouette—it was a VH-60N, a Black Hawk specially modified for transporting the government's highest officials. When it was carrying the vice president, it was designated with the call sign "Marine Two."

Soon the helicopter touched down on the rooftop. The crew powered down the engines and lowered the boarding steps at the front of the chopper. Then Vance Keller came out of the aircraft and approached Grant. The K-Man pointed to the side, signaling that he wanted to speak in private for a moment, so Grant stepped a few yards away from Lieutenant Frazier.

Keller definitely wasn't happy. His face looked ashen under the light of the full moon, his broad forehead shining above a pair of dark eye sockets. He leaned close to Grant to prevent anyone from overhearing them, and for a second Grant thought of vampires. The K-Man's teeth were within biting distance of Grant's neck.

"Is everything ready?" Keller's voice was low and grim. "You carried out all my instructions?"

Grant nodded. "Everything's good, sir."

"The prisoners are in the interrogation rooms? And you've performed the vaccinations?"

"Absolutely. We've prepared a nice little tour for the veep. Entertaining and informative."

"This has to go smoothly. We can't afford any mistakes." He beetled his brows. His eyes glinted within their dark sockets. "If we screw up now, the whole show is over. We'll lose everything and go to prison, quite possibly the execution chamber. You understand?"

"We won't screw up. This is too important." Grant felt the stirring in his chest again. "We hold the future of America in our hands, sir."

Keller attempted to smile, not very successfully. "Yes, we do. All right, here comes the vice president." He stepped away from Grant and faced the helicopter.

First, half a dozen Secret Service agents in gray suits came down the boarding steps. They surveyed the heliport, turning their heads left and right and paying particularly close attention to Lieutenant Frazier. Then one of them muttered something into his headset, and a moment later the vice president emerged from the chopper.

The veep wore a navy-blue suit with an American flag pin on the lapel. He stared straight ahead, unsmiling, as he came down the steps and walked across the roof, flanked by his Secret Service men. His thin white hair flounced in the breeze.

Grant had met him a couple of times before at the White House, and the veep had struck him as one of the most boring human beings on the planet, but now he seemed different—wary, jumpy, all his nerves on high alert. He'd stumbled upon a very dangerous secret, and he wasn't sure what to do next. He could've gone public with the news, revealing what he knew to Congress or the press, but that would've gone against the grain of his nature. So instead he'd demanded to see the Palindrome Project in person. He'd ordered Keller to arrange a VIP inspection of the Rikers Island headquarters, and the K-Man had complied. For the first time in seven years, the vice president had done something ballsy. He'd started to act like a man who might someday become president.

He stopped in front of Grant and Keller, but his eyes were on Frazier. Because the lieutenant was six inches taller than everyone else on the rooftop, he was kind of hard to miss. The veep pointed at the center of Frazier's enormous chest. "Who's this? A bodyguard?"

Frazier had been ordered not to say a single goddamn word, so he just stood there, blank-faced. Grant stepped forward and smiled at the vice president. "That's correct, sir. Lieutenant Frazier usually does security work for me, but tonight he's going to help us with the inspection tour. He's been with Palindrome since the early days of Phase One."

The veep frowned. "Phase One? That's when the treatment was tested on the Special Forces soldiers?"

The attorney general had clearly revealed everything he knew about Palindrome in his letter to the vice president, including some of the details of Phases One and Two. Luckily, though, the AG had known nothing about Phase Three, so neither did the veep. Grant kept smiling. "Yes, and Phase Two involves bringing the most successful test subjects to the Federal Service Unit, where we can closely evaluate their performance. Lieutenant Frazier is one of the stars of the experiment, and he can vividly demonstrate the project's potential benefits."

This information failed to set the veep's mind at ease. In fact, it seemed to have the opposite effect on him and his Secret Service men. The agents tensed, and their hands moved a bit closer to the guns hidden in the holsters under their gray jackets. The vice president knew about the enhanced combat skills of the Palindrome subjects, and he'd obviously warned his bodyguards about it.

Grant stopped grinning. This wasn't going well. He hated all this diplomatic bullshit.

The K-Man, though, was good at it. He caught the veep's eye and gave him a sympathetic look. "Don't worry, the lieutenant is unarmed. If it'll make you feel more comfortable, your men are free to pat him down."

The vice president thought it over for a second, then nodded at his agents. Two of them stepped toward Frazier, who obligingly spread his arms wide. He remained silent and kept his face blank as the agents frisked him. It was an impressive show of restraint on his part, but Grant wasn't surprised. The lieutenant was good at following orders.

When the agents were done, they nodded at the veep and returned to their positions beside him. The vice president turned back to Keller. "Thank you for your consideration, Vance. We're ready to start now."

"Then please come this way." The K-Man strode ahead, leading the veep and his entourage toward the building's rooftop entrance. At first, Grant and Frazier followed them at a distance, but this arrangement clearly upset the Secret Service—the agents kept looking over their shoulders—so Grant nudged Frazier forward until they marched right behind Keller.

The Research Center was just below the heliport. It occupied the whole building, providing enough space for all the researchers who'd been relocated from Rockefeller University, the Salk Institute, the Cold Spring Harbor Lab, and the Scripps Institute. In less than a minute Keller led the veep to the airlock, which isolated the laboratories and prevented any stray microbes from escaping. A technician in a white coat helped them open and close the airlock doors, and then the K-Man guided the vice president to the animal-testing lab on the ninth floor. Keller had given Grant a rough idea of how the inspection would go, but most of the details were unimportant. The only crucial part of the operation would come at the very end.

The animal lab was packed with cages and smelled like a menagerie. One room had dozens of rhesus monkeys; the next contained hundreds of rabbits; the next held thousands of mice. Keller pointed at the cages and began to describe the CRISPR method for making changes to DNA. Because the vice president had no scientific background, the K-Man kept his explanations simple and nontechnical and consistently upbeat, always emphasizing the positive. As a matter of fact, he was a terrific guide. If he hadn't gone into politics, he could've led tours at the San Diego Zoo.

"What I want to emphasize is that we didn't rush the scientific process. We did experiments on animals for three whole years. We developed a unique CRISPR treatment for each species, then injected the animals with viruses that triggered the genetic changes. We evaluated the safety of each change and carefully examined what happened when we altered several genes at the same time." He pointed at an elaborate rat maze with dozens of twists and turns. "But animal testing couldn't answer all of our questions. Although human DNA is very similar to monkey or chimp DNA, there *are* important differences, especially in the genes that govern brain development and intelligence. So to fully explore the effectiveness of the CRISPR treatment for humans, we had to begin human testing. It was the only way."

The vice president stopped in front of a cage full of albino rats. He stared for a few seconds at the red-eyed, pink-eared creatures, which had huddled in the corner of the cage for warmth. Then he turned back to Keller. "Did you ever consider whether the experiments were immoral?"

The K-Man was unperturbed. "Yes, we did. If CRISPR can cure a genetic disease, it would be immoral *not* to investigate it, don't you think?"

"Don't play games with me, Vance." The veep raised a finger and shook it at Keller, like an angry schoolteacher. "You don't really care about diseases."

"I assure you, the experiments we've done will help doctors develop treatments for cancer, heart disease, and dozens of other—"

"Sure, that's a good cover story. But your main purpose here isn't curing people. It's upgrading them. It's tinkering with their God-given bodies and turning them into something unnatural and unholy."

The vice president raised his voice so loud that it agitated the rats in the cage behind him. They broke from their huddle and skittered across the cage bedding, running in frantic circles. The Secret Service agents seemed to get nervous too. They sidled across the lab and positioned themselves around the veep, each man ready to take a bullet for him. But the K-man stayed calm. He nodded respectfully, acting as if the vice president had just made a logical argument and not a lunatic rant.

"I understand your concerns. Believe me, under ordinary circumstances we wouldn't have even considered taking these steps. But the CRISPR technology is like the proverbial 'genie in a bottle.' Now that scientists know how to easily manipulate DNA, it's very hard to stop them from using the technique. Once the genie is out of the bottle, how can you stuff him back inside?"

The veep shook his head. "It's not so hard to stop. You simply pass a law that makes it illegal to tamper with God's design."

"Yes, a well-enforced law might halt the research in this country. But what about the geneticists in China and Russia and Iran and North Korea? They're all studying and developing CRISPR. The CIA has received reports of gene-editing tests recently performed on soldiers in the Russian army and intelligence officers in China. If we don't do the same, their Special Forces will have a huge advantage over ours. They'll be stronger, faster, and deadlier. We can't allow that to happen."

Grant had to bite his cheek to stop himself from chuckling. He had plenty of friends in the CIA, and he saw all their intelligence reports. There was no evidence whatsoever that Russia or China was using CRISPR to create super-soldiers. But the K-Man was a master of bullshit, and the vice president wasn't clever enough to see through it.

The veep went silent, and some of the religious fervor drained from his face. After a few seconds, though, he scowled and shook his head again. "I still don't like it. We shouldn't stoop to their level. We shouldn't have to resort to the same evil methods that our godless enemies are using."

Keller stepped toward him. "Would it make a difference if I could show you how much good this technology is already doing? If I could give you strong, solid proof that CRISPR is saving American lives?"

The vice president folded his arms across his chest. "I don't know if it would make a difference. But I'm not closed-minded. I'm here to see everything."

The K-Man smiled. "Please follow me."

He led the veep and his Secret Service men out of the animal labs. They marched down the hall, then took the elevator to the fourth floor. Then they entered the behavioral research lab, where the human subjects of the Palindrome tests were caged.

Colonel Grant was far from squeamish. He'd never felt any discomfort about performing medical experiments on prisoners. That was because the prisoners chosen for the CRISPR treatments were the worst of the worst, the foulest pieces of human garbage. They were terrorists captured in Syria and Yemen and Afghanistan, mass murderers who'd killed hundreds of American soldiers and civilians. If anything, the experiments were too gentle. Grant would've been happier if the treatments had required electric shocks and amputations.

But as he stepped into the behavioral research lab with the vice president's entourage, Grant's stomach tightened so violently that he almost doubled over. It felt like he'd just been kicked in the balls. He stopped in his tracks and clutched his midsection. He had to clench his teeth to stop himself from crying out.

Frazier stopped too and gave him a questioning look. Grant grimaced and muttered, "Must've been something I ate." With a tremendous effort, he stepped forward and continued walking down the corridor.

The pain didn't go away, though. It kept grinding inside him, tearing up his guts, intensifying with every step he took. Soon they reached the part of the floor where two corridors intersected, and Grant felt something even worse, a jolt of inexplicable fear that made him catch his breath. The veep and the Secret Service agents marched past him and turned right, following Keller toward the interrogation rooms, but Grant stopped again and turned his head to the left. His eyes were drawn to one of the doors on that side of the corridor, about ten feet away.

It didn't look like much. It was just a plain white door with the number 17 written on it in black numerals. But in Grant's mind, it was the entrance to hell. It was the source of all his fear and pain, which seemed to stream down the corridor like invisible radiation. The waves of agony passed right through the walls and converged on him, spearing his heart.

He knew what was behind that door. It led to one of the monitoring rooms for the test subjects who required constant observation and study. The prisoner inside the room was Raza Khan.

Frazier gave him another look of concern. "Uh, sir?" He bent over so he could whisper in Grant's ear. "Don't you think we should—"

The door suddenly opened. Grant's panic was so fierce, he lost his balance. He thought he saw Raza burst out of the room, his paralyzed arms and legs now revived and powerful, his fingers transformed into razor-sharp claws.

Grant shut his eyes and started to fall. But Frazier caught him, gripping both his arms, and held him upright. "Sir?" His voice was still a whisper, but now very urgent. "What's wrong?"

Then Grant heard another voice, louder and higher-pitched than Frazier's and a hundred times more annoying. "Colonel, you have to see this! It's astonishing!"

Grant opened his eyes. The person standing in the doorway of Room 17 wasn't Raza Khan, thank God. It was David Weinberg, the lab director whom he'd yelled at a couple of hours ago. In his right hand he held a long sheet of graph paper with dozens of jagged lines scrawled across it.

"Look at this EEG!" Weinberg grinned like a maniac. "From the Khan boy!"

Grant's first impulse was to tell Weinberg to get back to his fucking job, but the guy was practically dancing with excitement, and the sight was so disturbing that Grant couldn't say a word. Weinberg rushed toward him, waving the sheet of graph paper.

"It started happening as soon as we attached the electrodes to him! I've never seen this kind of electrical activity in the brain, not even during the worst epileptic seizures!" He spread the paper with the EEG results right in front of Grant's nose. "See how the neural oscillations are aligned? This is generalized activity involving the whole brain, and yet it's all intricately coordinated!"

Grant stared for a moment at all the jagged lines spiking up and down. He didn't see anything astonishing there. What he saw instead was a picture of his own anger, violently sharp and very fucking generalized. All his fear turned to fury. He wanted to rip Weinberg's head off for interrupting the VIP inspection they'd planned so carefully.

But Grant was still too shaky from his panic attack, so he turned to Frazier instead. "Lieutenant, get this asshole out of my sight."

"With pleasure, sir."

Frazier grabbed the collar of Weinberg's lab coat and dragged him back to Room 17. He shoved the bewildered scientist into the room and slammed the door shut. Then he returned to Grant and rested a hand on his shoulder. "We better catch up to the others," he whispered. "Keller looks pissed."

The K-Man glared at them from the far end of the corridor, where he stood in front of a heavy steel door. The vice president and his Secret Service agents had turned around too, their faces taut with suspicion and impatience.

Grant hurried toward them, tottering a bit but doing his best to hide his unsteadiness. He breathed a little easier as he put some distance between himself and Room 17. His anger ebbed and the pain in his stomach faded to a dull ache. By the time he reached the veep's entourage, he was able to smile and flatter and lie again.

"My apologies, gentlemen. Our researchers are very enthusiastic about their work." Grant stepped past Keller and the vice president and slid his security card through the card reader on the wall. The steel door opened, and Grant led the visitors inside. "Please move all the way to the back so everyone can fit. And watch your step, please, it's dark."

They filed into a room that was fifteen feet long but only five feet wide. The space was entirely bare, no furniture of any kind. Up ahead, at the far end of the narrow room, was another steel door; to their right was a blank wall, and to their left was a thick black curtain. Grant and Keller went to the far end, while Frazier came in last and closed the door behind him, plunging the room into total darkness. Then Grant flipped a switch on the wall, and an electric motor began to pull the black curtain to the side.

"As you may have guessed, we're in an observation room. The interrogation room is on the other side of the one-way mirror." Grant pointed at the big sheet of half-silvered glass that was exposed as the curtain retracted. In contrast to the observation room, the interrogation room was brightly lit, enabling them to see it clearly through the glass. "The prisoner is Ahmed Yasin, whose name you may recognize from several reports written by our colleagues at the CIA."

Ahmed sat cross-legged on the floor of the interrogation room, ignoring the chairs and table that had been provided for him. He was a stick figure in an orange jumpsuit, skeletally thin because he'd refused to eat or drink for the past two months and had to be force-fed all his meals. The guards had shaved off his hair and beard, and his naked skull resembled a peach that had sat on the shelf for too long. His scalp and face were mottled with bruises, some fresh and purple, some older and yellowing. His hands were cuffed behind his back and his legs were shackled, and yet he looked like he was eager for another battle with the guards. He glowered at the one-way mirror, snarling at the glass, even though all he could see was his own reflection.

Grant pointed at him. "Until a year ago, Ahmed was a driver and courier working for Hassan Mohammed, the leader of Al-Qaeda's operations in Yemen. The CIA had heard that Hassan was planning an attack against U.S. airliners, so when they captured Ahmed last year they tried like hell to get information out of him, in particular the exact whereabouts of his boss. They subjected him to six months of enhanced interrogation, but it was a waste of time. Ahmed didn't tell them a thing. He's a true believer."

The vice president took a step backward and bit his lower lip. He seemed to be frightened and mesmerized by the sight of the terrorist. The Secret Service agents also seemed uneasy. They coughed and cleared their throats and shifted anxiously in the darkness. But Keller and Frazier just stood there, looking unfazed and slightly bored. They'd seen all this before.

Grant moved his hand to another switch on the wall, a dimmer switch. "Then the CIA sent Ahmed to Rikers and my interrogators had a go at him. But we didn't have any luck either. In fact, Ahmed's resistance only grew worse. Here, let me show you what this bastard is really like." He turned the dimmer switch clockwise, slowly turning on the overhead lights in the observation room. "I'm equalizing the light levels in the two rooms. Now Ahmed will be able to see us."

As the lights came on above them, the optics of the one-way mirror changed. Half of the light from the overheads reflected off the glass, and half passed through it, which meant that the mirror wasn't one-way anymore. Grant could still see Ahmed, but he could also see the reflections of everyone in the observation room, their translucent figures superimposed over his view of the interrogation room. And Ahmed could see the same thing on the other side of the mirror, his own reflection sharing the glass with the American infidels he despised.

Ahmed's reaction was instantaneous. He scrambled to his feet and threw himself at the mirror. Because of his restraints, he couldn't punch or kick the glass, so instead he slammed his forehead against it. He swung his head forward and back, banging it against the hardened pane and moving his lips all the while. Grant flipped another switch that turned on the audio feed from the interrogation room, and then they could hear Ahmed's voice coming from the overhead speakers. He was screaming curses in Arabic.

After a few seconds, Grant turned off the audio and stepped forward. He stopped right in front of the mirror, less than a yard from the raving prisoner, and gave him the finger. Then he turned around and looked at the vice president. "This, in a nutshell, is the threat we're facing. Millions of people hate America with an undying passion. How do we fight this kind of enemy?"

The veep was so horrified, it looked like he was having trouble breathing. He swallowed hard, and the air whistled out of his throat. For a long while he said nothing and just stared at Ahmed, whose eyebrows were bleeding from the repeated blows against the glass. Then the vice president pressed his lips together firmly and turned back to Grant. "Our administration has a clear-cut strategy for fighting terrorism. We've reinforced our borders to stop the terrorists from getting into America. And we've launched military operations around the world to thin the ranks of our enemies and deprive them of any secure base of operations."

This sounded suspiciously formal, like a line from a campaign speech. Grant nodded but didn't say anything. Keller was the better person to discuss policy issues, and after a moment the K-Man stepped forward and faced the vice president.

"You know as well as I do that our strategy isn't working. There are more terrorists than ever in Africa and the Middle East. And their internet propaganda has inspired hundreds of American citizens to take up their cause."

The veep shook his head. "No one said it would be easy. But we're making progress."

"No, we're not. Trust me, I'm in charge of all our antiterrorism initiatives, and I've seen all the classified reports. The more troops we send to Yemen and Afghanistan and Somalia, the more we turn the people of those countries against us." Keller pointed at Ahmed, who now leaned against the mirror, exhausted, pressing his battered forehead to the blood-smeared glass. "Every day, we're creating more terrorists like this one. It's a failing plan. We have to try something new."

The veep's face reddened. He opened his mouth, but he was so flustered that it took him a couple of seconds to get the words out. "So is this monster behind the glass part of your new plan?" He glanced at Ahmed, then quickly turned away. "Did you change his genes too? If so, I'm disappointed, Vance, because it doesn't look like you've improved him very much."

Keller gave him a patient smile. "No, we didn't change his genes. Whenever we test a new idea, we need to have a control subject who *doesn't* receive the experimental treatment. That gives us a baseline we can use to make comparisons. Ahmed Yasin is the control subject for this experiment. We didn't do anything to him." The K-Man turned to Grant. "Colonel, can you show us the test subject who *did* receive the treatment?"

Grant headed for the steel door at the far end of the room. He used his security card again to unlock the door, then held it open for the others.

"You're going into another observation room that's identical to this one. Please be careful."

He repeated the same steps as before. The vice president and his Secret Service men filed into the room, stumbling in the dark and coughing nervously. Once everyone was inside, Grant flipped the switch that pulled back the black curtain. Just like before, they saw an interrogation room through the one-way mirror, with a metal table and two chairs bolted to the floor. But there were *two* people in this room, a prisoner in an orange jumpsuit and a guard in a black uniform, both sitting on the chairs. And on the table between them was a feast: a large bowl of yellow rice, a platter heaped with roast chicken, a pile of pita bread, a ceramic teapot and two cups.

The prisoner in this room wasn't handcuffed or shackled. He was heavyset but apparently in good health, with a long, full beard hanging from his face and a crisp, white turban wrapped around his head. He was eating the chicken and rice with gusto and talking animatedly with the guard, an FSU officer who used to work as an interpreter for the army. Grant hit the switch that turned on the audio feed, and although the two men were talking in Arabic, the tone of their conversation was clear. They were chatting and laughing, having a great time.

Grant turned off the audio, then pointed at the prisoner. "That man is Hassan Mohammed—the terrorist who used to be Ahmed's boss, the leader of Al-Qaeda in Yemen. The CIA captured him by accident four months ago when his new driver took a wrong turn and they cruised right into the agency's drone base. The agents interrogated him just as hard as they did Ahmed, and once again they failed to get anything out of him. But then they sent Hassan to us, and we injected him with a new CRISPR treatment. We call it the Serenity sequence."

Grant paused to let Keller continue the story. This was the final stop of their VIP inspection tour, and now they were gearing up for the climax. The K-Man stepped close to the vice president and grasped his elbow. "Our animal studies laid the groundwork for this particular treatment. There's a long history of genetic manipulation of domestic animals to make them tame. For thousands of years, farmers selectively bred their cows and horses and dogs, using trial-and-error breeding techniques to eventually produce animals that were less troublesome and more obedient. Our researchers identified the genetic changes associated with tameness, the specific DNA sequences that make docile animals different from their wild cousins. Then we devised a CRISPR treatment that could make the same changes to human DNA."

The veep was speechless. His face had turned bright pink and his forehead glistened with sweat. He tried to say something, but his Adam's apple bobbed and his whole body trembled. He raised one of his quivering hands to massage his throat, kneading the loose skin under his jaw. "I . . . I don't . . . I can't . . ."

"This is the solid proof I was talking about. CRISPR turned this terrorist into a cooperative informant, eager to help us. And thanks to the information he provided, the Air Force was able to destroy seven Al-Qaeda camps in Yemen and eliminate almost all their leaders. It was one of the greatest victories *ever* in the War on Terror." Keller pointed at the jovial Hassan, who was shoveling a spoonful of rice into his mouth. "What's more, we can repeat this success. We can inject the same treatment into all the suspected terrorists in our custody. And now that Phase Three is almost ready, we'll have a more effective way to deliver the CRISPR molecules to their intended recipients. We'll be able to pacify an entire village at once. Maybe even the entire Middle East."

The K-Man waited for the vice president to say something, but all the veep could do was open his mouth wide and let out a strangled croak. At the same time, three of his Secret Service agents collapsed. They started convulsing on the floor of the observation room, foam dribbling from the corners of their mouths. The other three agents finally realized what was going on, but they were too feverish and weak to respond fast enough. Before they could pull their guns from their holsters, Frazier lunged across the room and bashed their heads in.

Now all the Secret Service men lay on the floor, either dead or dying. The vice president was the only visitor left standing, and that was only because Keller held him up by his elbow. The veep was twitching and jerking, clutching his throat, spitting up mucus and blood. But the K-Man held him close, as if they were lovers.

"You see, we developed a new virus for carrying the CRISPR treatment. It's an airborne virus that enters your body when you breathe it in. Because it doesn't need to be injected, it can spread the genetic changes much more quickly and efficiently. But we weren't sure how fast it would work, so we set up this test." He gently lowered the veep to the floor and knelt beside him. "For the purpose of the test, we designed a CRISPR molecule that kills lung tissue. When the virus infects a lung cell, the molecule makes genetic changes that dissolve the cell's membrane. The researchers prepared trillions of these airborne viruses, and I released a vial of them into the cabin of our helicopter after we left the White House. Of course, I vaccinated myself against the virus first. And I made sure that Colonel Grant and his colleagues received the vaccine too."

The vice president died while the K-Man was talking to him. Keller frowned at the corpse, then stood up and checked his watch. Then he looked at Grant. "It's seven minutes to midnight. And I released the virus at ten-forty-two."

Grant did the calculation in his head. "One hour and eleven minutes. Not bad. But chemical weapons can kill faster."

Frazier left the room to get seven body bags. In the meantime, Keller lifted his right foot and closed the veep's gaping mouth by tapping the corpse's chin with the toe of his shoe. "The goal of Phase Three isn't mass murder, Colonel. When we use this virus again, it will be carrying a much different treatment."

Grant nodded. He knew what their goal was.

TWENTY

A burst of gunfire shattered the windows of Gracie Mansion's library. Jenna grabbed Tamara's arm and yanked her down to the carpet.

Frank the cop did the same thing for the mayor, pulling him down to the floor and out of the line of fire. Then, lying faceup, Frank drew his pistol and aimed at the beautiful Tiffany chandelier hanging from the ceiling. His shot obliterated the bowl of colored glass and the lightbulbs within, and the library went dark. Now it would be harder for the soldiers outside to target them.

Jenna should've been terrified, but she wasn't. Over the past twenty-four hours she'd gotten a crash course in surviving police shoot-outs, and she'd learned the importance of keeping calm and staying low. She listened carefully to the battle outside the mansion: the thumping of the helicopters, the shouts of the soldiers, the sputtering gunshots. The Federal officers who'd leapt from the choppers were exchanging fire with the New York cops in front of the building. Their bullets smashed the windowpanes and strafed the library, whizzing across the room just a couple of feet above Jenna and Tamara. They were still too exposed. They needed to move away from the windows and find better cover.

Tamara lay on her stomach next to a bookcase. She'd removed her revolver from the waistband of her jeans and pointed it at one of the shattered windows, but the gun shook in her hands. Jenna crawled closer to her. "Tamara! Does this place have a basement?"

She didn't respond. Her teeth chattered and her eyes stayed on the window, which still had a couple of unbroken panes. She'd probably never fired a gun before. Or been shot at either.

Jenna touched her arm, which was tense and trembling. "Listen to me, okay? We can't stay here. Is there a basement in this building?"

Keeping her eyes on the window, Tamara nodded. "There's a staff office down there." She jerked her head to the left. "The stairs are that way, past the dining room."

Jenna turned to Frank, who also lay on his stomach, pointing his gun at one of the windows. The mayor cringed beside him on the carpet, curling his lanky frame into a ball. Jenna whistled to get their attention. "Come on! We're going to the office downstairs!"

Then she scrambled out of the library. After a moment of hesitation, the others followed.

More gunfire pummeled the mansion as Jenna crawled on her hands and knees across the dining room. She winced at the noise but didn't slow down. This was a bad situation, but it wasn't any worse than the shootout at Green-Wood Cemetery or the massacre at Bay Parkway or the firefight outside her apartment building in Brighton Beach. She had a chance of surviving it if she didn't lose her head, so she kept her focus on reaching the stairway. Tamara crawled behind her, and Frank brought up the rear, practically dragging DeMarco across the floor. They were going along with her plan because it made sense, she guessed. Or maybe because they were petrified and couldn't think of anything better.

Soon she found the steps and hurried down to the basement. There were no windows here, so Jenna felt safe enough to stand up. The others stood up too and ran behind her down the corridor. Within seconds they reached a large windowless office, with a desk, a conference table, an antique chair, and a pair of file cabinets. Once they were all inside, Frank closed the heavy fireproof door and locked its dead bolt. Then he shoved both of the file cabinets behind it for good measure. They could still hear the helicopters outside the mansion and the jarring gunfire, but the noises were muffled.

Jenna got the feeling that DeMarco rarely used this office. The file cabinets were dusty, and the conference table was crowded with out-dated computers and fax machines and even a couple of manual typewriters. The mayor's main office was in City Hall, where all the top officials worked, and he probably used this room only if an emergency came up late at night and he needed a private place to make a phone call. On the desk was an old-fashioned speakerphone with a lot of black buttons, but when Jenna picked up the receiver she didn't hear a dial tone. The soldiers must've already cut the mansion's telephone and cable lines.

DeMarco leaned against one of the file cabinets, panting and heaving. Tamara stood next to him, still holding her revolver but pointing it at the floor. Both of them were in bad shape, and Frank looked shell-shocked too. He put his gun back in its holster and wiped the sweat from his forehead. Then he grabbed his police radio from his belt and pressed the TALK button.

"This is Sergeant Frank O'Connor at Gracie Post." He shouted into the radio's mouthpiece. "Ten-thirteen, ten-thirteen, we need immediate assistance. Any unit, please respond!"

He took his finger off the button, and a burst of loud static came out of the radio's speaker. Frank waited several seconds, but there was no response. So he tried again.

"Repeat, this is O'Connor at Gracie. We got a Level Four emergency here. Can anyone hear me?"

Again, there was no response except the blast of static. By this point, Tamara and DeMarco had pulled out their cell phones, but it was clear from their expressions that neither one could get a signal. And Jenna knew why. It was Physics 101, the basic laws of electromagnetics. She'd studied the subject during her freshman year at Columbia.

"The Feds are jamming us." Jenna pointed at the ceiling. "One of their helicopters must have a transmitter that's broadcasting radio noise. The noise is louder than our radio transmissions, so it's blocking them."

The mayor stared at her. He cocked his long head and narrowed his eyes, and at first Jenna thought he was giving her a look of disbelief. But then he curled his lip and bared his teeth, and Jenna realized he was enraged. He moved away from the file cabinets and confronted her. "Did you know this was going to happen? Because it's pretty damn suspicious. First you show up here to tell me about genetic experiments and super-soldiers, and five minutes later the fucking army starts shooting at us."

Tamara stepped between them and got in DeMarco's face. "You're being ridiculous, okay? I brought Jenna here. She had nothing to do with this attack."

"She worked in their labs, didn't she? The FSU's genetics project?" DeMarco pointed at Jenna, stretching his long right arm over Tamara's shoulder. "That's what started this mess, right?"

"But she's not with them anymore. She didn't—"

"She and the other scientists, they're all to blame. They helped the Feds do their illegal experiments, and now the administration thinks they can get away with anything. They think they can shut up everyone they don't like and take over everything they don't already control."

Jenna shook her head. "I opposed the experiments on humans. Believe me, Mr. Mayor, I had no idea they would do this."

"Yeah, that's what the Nazis said. 'We had no idea where all those trains full of Jews were going. We thought they were taking a long vacation or something.'"

"Bob, that's *enough*!" Tamara placed a hand on the mayor's chest and actually shoved him backward. "We don't have time to fight each other. We need to figure out a plan."

DeMarco retreated until he leaned against the file cabinets again. He scowled at Tamara, hard and bitter. "A plan? Are you serious? The mansion is surrounded and we can't call anyone for help. In five minutes the FSU men are gonna storm into the building and start checking all the rooms. How the fuck is a *plan* gonna help us?"

Tamara looked at the mayor with surprise and disgust. Sergeant Frank O'Connor didn't seem very happy either, and Jenna was dazed. She turned away from the others and went to the other side of the office, moving slowly and stiffly. She stopped beside the conference table and looked down at all the electronic junk heaped on top of it. She could see her reflection in the blank screen of one of the old computers.

Although she didn't want to admit it, there was some truth in what DeMarco had said. She *was* partly responsible for Palindrome. Even in the early days of the project she could've guessed where it was headed, and she should've tried to stop it. She should've ignored all the confidentiality agreements she'd signed and called *The New York Times* and CNN and her congressman's office. She should've warned them all about what the researchers in her lab were doing.

To her shame, though, the idea of stopping Palindrome had never even occurred to her. She'd been too busy designing experiments and analyzing the results. She'd hoped the research would help Raza—at least at the beginning, before his CRISPR treatment failed—but to be honest, helping her brother had never been her primary motivation. From the start, the driving force for Jenna had been sheer scientific greed. She'd wanted to explore and comprehend *everything*. She couldn't stand the thought that Nature was keeping secrets from her, maybe because she was so angry at Nature for killing her mother and crippling her brother. So she'd devoted her life to extracting those secrets. It was a special kind of revenge. Nothing else mattered.

It made her sick to think about it. She grimaced at her reflection on the dead screen. She wanted to smash the thing.

Instead, she forced herself to stare at something else. She looked past the old computers and spotted an even older piece of equipment at the far end of the table. It was a rectangular console, as big as a suitcase, with knobs and switches on the front and a couple of six-inch speakers. It looked like it dated from the 1940s, a vintage radio for calling ships at sea or cargo planes headed for the war in Europe. It was so old, it might've belonged to Fiorello La Guardia, the New York mayor whom they named the lousy airport after.

But Jenna noticed something surprising about this radio. Its electrical cord was plugged into the wall, and so was its antenna cable. Another cable ran from the radio to an old-fashioned microphone mounted on a desk stand.

She bent closer to it and studied its switches. Then she flicked one of them, and a blast of static came out of the radio's speakers. She quickly found the dial for volume and lowered it.

"Goddamn it!" DeMarco stomped toward her. "What the hell are you doing now?"

Jenna ignored him and turned to Tamara. "This radio still works. And it's connected to an external antenna. Which probably goes up to the mansion's roof."

Tamara shrugged. "But what's the point? Radios are useless. Didn't you say the Feds were jamming us?"

"We don't know how powerful their jammer is. Its noise is definitely loud enough to block signals from cell phones and handheld radios. But this radio is different. It runs on AC current instead of batteries." Jenna pointed at the electrical cord and the antenna cable. "It can send a lot more power up to that antenna."

"That old thing?" Tamara gave the radio a skeptical look. "Jesus, it's *ancient*."

"Doesn't matter. If the antenna is large and mounted high up on the roof, the transmitted signal will be a lot stronger. Maybe strong enough to cut through the noise."

That got Sergeant O'Connor's attention. He bent over the table to give the radio a closer look. "You know, my dad used to have a ham radio like this one. It was powerful as hell. He used to talk to people in Africa and Australia with it." Frank started adjusting one of the dials. "Okay, I'm setting the frequency to the police department channel. Give me that mic."

Jenna reached for the desk-stand microphone. But as she handed it to Frank, she heard an unwelcome noise coming from the corridor outside the office. It was the clomping of boots, two pairs of them. A moment later, someone banged a fist against the office's locked door. "Open up!"

The mayor jumped at the noise, and Tamara aimed her revolver at the door. But Frank calmly flipped the switch on the microphone and held it under his nose. "This is Sergeant O'Connor at Gracie Post! Ten-thirteen, ten-thirteen, we need immediate assistance!"

"*Hey!*" The soldier banged against the door again. "*I hear you in there! Open up NOW!*"

"Any unit, please respond! The Feds have attacked Gracie Mansion, and the mayor's life is in danger!"

There was no response. But then Jenna remembered that she'd turned down the radio's volume a minute ago, so she reached for the dial and turned it back up. Then a voice rose above the static and blared from the speakers: "O'Connor, this is Dispatch at the One-Nine Precinct. Can you hear me?"

Frank let out a whoop. "I hear you, One-Nine. And I'm hoping like hell you can send some patrol cars to Gracie Mansion, because we're in a fuck-load of trouble here."

"We just sent six cars to the riot on East Ninety-sixth Street. Is that what you're talking about?"

"Negative, this is different. The FSU landed helicopters outside the mansion a few minutes ago and assaulted the mayor's security detail. There was heavy gunfire and multiple casualties. Now the Feds have cornered the rest of us in an office in the basement." Frank paused, and the soldiers in the corridor banged the door so hard that the file cabinets shook behind it. "DeMarco is here, standing right next to me, and he'll be in plenty of trouble if the Feds get to him. I'm guessing they'll either arrest him or shoot him."

The room fell silent. The mayor turned pale and backed up against the wall. Even the FSU men outside the office stopped their banging. After five long seconds, the dispatcher for the 19th Precinct finally responded: "O'Connor, I'm contacting headquarters. We have to inform Commissioner Hayes about this."

"Sure, great, but in the meantime you gotta send some cops to help us!"

"Look, first I have to—"

The dispatcher's voice was drowned out by a loud metallic clang, followed by three more clangs in quick succession. Jenna turned toward the noise and saw a silvery glint at the edge of the office's door. The soldiers in the corridor had wedged the sharp end of a long steel tool between the door and the doorjamb. With each metallic clang, they hammered the tool a little farther into the gap. They were prying the door open.

"No more time!" Jenna rushed at Frank and grabbed the microphone from him. Then she turned to Tamara and DeMarco. "You have to send out a message!"

The mayor didn't react. His eyes were fixed on the clanging door, his face frozen in horror. The crisis had paralyzed him, and now he was useless. But Tamara stood firm. She stepped over to the conference table and stared at the mic in Jenna's hands. "What kind of message?"

Jenna pointed at DeMarco. "The Feds are gonna arrest him. There's no way we can stop that. But we can stop the FSU from taking over the city." She offered the microphone to Tamara, holding it out as far as its cord would allow. "The mayor should send a message to the police commissioner, a final order to all the officers in the department. He should order them to resist the takeover."

Tamara nodded. It was civil war. Now there was no way around it.

Three more clangs echoed across the room. The soldiers pounded their steel tool deeper into the gap between the door and the jamb. Then they pivoted the tool and used it as a lever, wrenching the door's edge. The gap widened. The dead bolt began to pull away from the jamb.

"Bob, get over here!" Tamara glared at DeMarco. "You know what you have to do!"

The mayor didn't budge. He just stood there with his back against the wall, staring at the failing dead bolt. After a couple of seconds, his knees buckled and he slid down to the carpet.

"*Jesus Christ, Bob! If you don't—*"

The steel door groaned, and the dead bolt suddenly tore away from the jamb. The door started to swing open, but a moment later it hit the file cabinets with a thud. One of the soldiers in the corridor yelled "Shit!"

Tamara turned away from the mayor. She gave her revolver to Jenna, practically shoving it into her hands, and grabbed the microphone. "*This is Tamara Carter, senior advisor to the mayor. I have an urgent message from Mayor DeMarco to all the officers in the New York Police Department. The FSU has attacked Gracie Mansion and is about to arrest the mayor and his staff. This is an unconstitutional—*"

The soldiers on the other side of the door hurled themselves against it. The door slammed into the file cabinets again, hitting them so hard this time that they tilted and fell over. As the cabinets toppled, Sergeant O'Connor raced toward the mayor and stood in front of him, shielding his crumpled body. Frank raised his pistol and pointed it at the half-open door. "Stay where you are, assholes! You better not step inside!"

"*This is an unconstitutional attack by the federal government, so all New York police officers are duty-bound to oppose it.*" Tamara bent over the microphone. It was shaking in her hands, but her voice was loud and clear. "*DO NOT turn over your weapons to the FSU. Repeat, DO NOT surrender your service weapons or vehicles to the federal authorities. You must honor your oath to protect New York City by resisting this unlawful takeover!*"

Then the pair of FSU officers charged into the room and started shooting.

Jenna threw herself to the floor, but the soldiers didn't aim their assault rifles at her. As soon as they ran into the office, they fired at Sergeant Frank O'Connor. He fell back against the mayor as the bullets hit him, his body jerking grotesquely. But somehow he managed to fire his pistol three times, and the third shot hit one of the Federal Service officers in the face.

The soldier collapsed, tipping forward. His partner hesitated for a moment, then unleashed another barrage at O'Connor, firing at least a dozen more bullets. Half of them struck the sergeant and half struck the man he'd tried to shield.

Frank stopped writhing. He was dead, and so was the mayor. Their corpses sprawled in the corner of the office, Frank's body draped over DeMarco's. So much blood ran from their wounds that the carpet couldn't absorb it all. It puddled under their bodies and spread across the floor.

Tamara stared at them, horrified, but only for a fraction of a second. Furrowing her brow, she bent over the microphone again. *"Mayor De-Marco has just been assassinated! Federal officers shot him dead, in cold blood, right in front of my eyes! They—"*

Jenna saw it all happen, looking up from the floor. The FSU officer spun around and pointed his assault rifle at Tamara. He braced the rifle's stock against his shoulder and started shooting.

At the exact same moment, Jenna fired the revolver at him.

The noise was deafening. Jenna dropped the gun and closed her eyes and waited for the soldier to shoot her too. But the gunfire stopped and the room fell silent. There were no sounds at all, and no more bullets streaking overhead. There was only a strong, metallic odor in the air, the scent of fresh blood.

When Jenna opened her eyes, she saw both FSU officers lying on the carpet, facedown and motionless. She'd shot the second one between his eyes. There was a big, gory wound at the top of his head, where the bullet had exited.

Tamara lay on her back a few feet away. Although she wasn't dead yet, she clearly wouldn't live much longer. The gunfire had torn three holes in the front of her tank top, and the blood had darkened her jeans from her waistband down to her crotch. Her eyes had rolled up into her sockets and she was shivering all over, fighting the pain from her wounds and the shock from blood loss. But her hands remained clamped around the microphone. The vintage radio was ruined—the bullets had smashed its rectangular case and antique workings—but Tamara didn't seem to notice. She looked like she was struggling to find the words for another message.

Jenna crawled over to her. Blood gushed from Tamara's chest and stomach. There was nothing Jenna could do to save her, but she gripped Tamara's shoulder and squeezed it tight, just to let her know that someone was there. And Tamara felt it. She instantly dropped the microphone and clutched Jenna's arm instead.

"Allen . . . oh Jesus . . . just get out of here!"

She looked right at Jenna but didn't see her. Her voice was a halting, frantic whisper.

"Take your phone . . . and go out the service door . . . go on, Allen!"

Tamara shut her eyes tight, obviously in agony. She arched her back and flailed her legs against the floor and let out a scream. She was raving, out of her mind, seeing her dead boyfriend beside her. But after a moment she opened her eyes and reached for the iPhone in her pocket. She clawed at the thing until she got a good grip on it, and then she thrust it at Jenna.

"Go down the hall . . . past the storage closets . . . run like hell, you hear?"

Jenna took the phone. It didn't matter that Tamara thought she was someone else. The important thing was to honor her last request. Jenna silently made a promise: she was going to escape Gracie Mansion and deliver Allen Keating's video to someone who could make it public. She wanted it broadcast across the whole country. In this war, their best weapon was outrage, so she was going to make sure that *everyone* saw it.

"I'll do what you want, okay? Just relax." Jenna slipped the phone into her own pocket. "I'll do all of it. I swear."

Tamara shut her eyes again and lay still. Her breath rattled in her throat, but at least she wasn't writhing anymore. She'd done her final duty. The war would go on without her.

The muffled noise of more gunfire came through the mansion's walls. Jenna heard footsteps on the floor above, probably Federal Service officers running from one part of the building to another. The battle outside Gracie Mansion had resumed. Maybe the New York Police Department had responded to Tamara's distress call and dispatched reinforcements to the scene. At least that's what Jenna hoped. She had no chance at all of escaping the mansion unless something else distracted the FSU men.

Jenna picked up the revolver from where she'd dropped it. Then she bolted out of the room and ran down the basement corridor.

She followed Tamara's directions. She raced down the hall, dashing past a long row of closet doors, each marked with a brass number. But her mind was in so much turmoil that she couldn't focus on why the doors were numbered, or anything else for that matter. Jenna carried a horrible new fact on her conscience: just two minutes ago, she'd shot someone to death. She'd killed a human being.

She never got a good look at the soldier's face. She'd glimpsed it when she aimed her revolver at the FSU officer, but that fleeting sight was strictly for the purpose of targeting, and it hadn't stuck in her memory. Now she couldn't recall what his eyes or nose or hair looked like. The only thing she remembered was that the officer was young. Probably in his early twenties.

But that fact alone was enough to make her nauseous. She stumbled down the hallway and had to stop next to one of the closet doors. *My God. He was barely out of his teens. His whole future ahead of him. And I took it all away.*

Jenna leaned against the door, dizzy and sweating. She took a deep breath and tried to clear her head. She'd shot the boy in self-defense. The soldiers had killed everyone else in the room, and they would've killed her too if she hadn't acted. So why was her head spinning so badly now? And why, when she tried to picture the boy she'd killed, did she see Raza's face instead?

Then she heard footsteps again, the boots of the Federal Service officers. They were closer now. More FSU men had come down to the mansion's basement, at least half a dozen by the sound of it. A moment later, the men started shouting. They'd discovered the bodies in the office.

Jenna fought down her nausea and forced herself to keep moving down the corridor. She turned left and right, looking for the service door that Tamara had mentioned. She needed to find it before the soldiers reached this part of the basement.

She finally saw it at the far end of the hallway, beyond all the numbered closets. This door was taller and wider than the others and completely blank, no identifying number or label. But when she gripped the brass doorknob, it turned. She stepped into a dark room and swiftly closed the door behind her.

She stood in a vestibule, five feet wide and ten feet long. It was the mansion's service entrance, for bringing furniture and appliances into the building without messing up the beautiful parlors upstairs. The walls were unfinished plywood, and the only light came from a glowing red EXIT sign. Below the sign was another door, locked from the inside by an antique dead bolt. Jenna rushed toward it and gripped the bolt, which slid open with a rusty squeal.

At the same time, she heard the soldiers march into the hallway she'd just left. One of them shouted an order at the others. There was a flurry of banging and shuffling as they searched the closets.

Frantic, Jenna cracked open the service door and peered outside. The door was underneath the mansion's porch, so the darkness here was very deep. She couldn't see much outside, but the noises were everywhere:

helicopters hovering, a megaphone blaring, and gunshots echoing across the neighborhood. And beneath it all was the sound of a large, angry crowd, hundreds of voices yelling and chanting and cursing.

She opened the door a little farther and glimpsed the leading edge of the mob, less than fifty feet away. Although there was a security fence around Gracie Mansion, people were streaming through a jagged gap in the barrier, which must've been blasted open by the FSU assault team when they'd attacked the mayor's residence. It looked like the rioters had marched down from East Harlem and converged on the mansion, expecting to confront the mayor, but instead they'd run straight into the Federal Service men who'd taken over the building. One of the officers was shouting into the megaphone, probably from one of the mansion's upper-story windows.

"Go back! Turn around and leave the area IMMEDIATELY!"

Jenna opened the door all the way and stepped outside. She had to stoop to avoid banging her head against the boards of the porch, but she was glad to be underneath it. She was safe here, hidden in the shadows. Just ten yards ahead, the mansion's security lights illuminated the driveway in front of the building, which was packed with shirtless young men. Most of them had wrapped bandannas around their faces, concealing everything but their eyes, and quite a few carried bricks or chunks of concrete. They seemed unimpressed by the FSU officer with the megaphone. Instead of turning back, they edged closer to the mansion's entrance.

"I said GO BACK! This is your FINAL WARNING! We're authorized to use DEADLY FORCE!"

One of the shirtless men yelled something in Spanish, and then the whole crowd surged forward. In the same instant, Jenna heard a shout behind her. She looked over her shoulder at the vestibule and saw an FSU officer rush into it from the corridor. He was another kid barely out of his teens, cradling an assault rifle. He headed straight for her. "Hey, you! Stop right there!"

The revolver was in Jenna's hand, but she couldn't bring herself to shoot the boy. Instead, she threw the gun at him as hard as she could. Then she raced out of the shadow of the porch and into the crowd.

TWENTY-ONE

Lieutenant Frazier stood at attention in his commander's office, nervous as hell. He needed to ask Colonel Grant a question, and he was very worried about how the colonel would answer.

Grant was making him wait. The colonel sat behind his desk, on the phone with the secretary of defense, who'd called just a few seconds after Frazier stepped into the office. So now Frazier had to stand there in front of the desk while Grant lied about the situation in New York City. The defense secretary had been Grant's commander at one time, but their roles were reversed after the colonel started working at the White House, and now Grant clearly enjoyed bossing around his old boss.

"General, this isn't a request. This is an order. I received it two minutes ago from Keller, and he got it directly from the president." Grant leaned back in his chair and smiled. "You need to send three more helicopter squadrons to New York and put them under the Federal Service Unit's control. And we want you to transport an infantry brigade to Rikers Island within the next twelve hours. Is that understood?"

The colonel paused for about ten seconds, letting the SecDef get a few words in. Then he interrupted, raising his voice by several decibels. "No,

I don't want any National Guardsmen. I want active-duty military units. The public disturbances in New York have reached crisis levels, and we need a combat-ready response team. In other words, the best soldiers you have."

Grant paused again, but not for long. This time, he interrupted the SecDef immediately. "No, it isn't rash. Federal law allows us to deploy active-duty troops to respond to an insurrection, and that's what we're facing in Manhattan tonight. Thousands of armed criminals are marching through the streets of East Harlem, and the local police can't stop them." Grant raised his voice another notch. "And here's something else you should know. The vice president flew to New York earlier this evening to talk with the mayor about the crisis, but we lost radio contact with the veep and his security team after they arrived at Gracie Mansion. It's possible that the rioters have reached the mayor's residence and assaulted the authorities there."

His smile broadened as he listened to the SecDef's response, which must've been very stunned and apologetic. After ten more seconds, Grant leaned forward in his chair. "Very good, General. You have your orders. Please contact my office immediately if you run into any problems."

Grant hung up the phone, then looked at Frazier. He was still smiling. "As you can see, we've come up with a cover story. You know, to explain what happened to the vice president and his Secret Service agents. They were killed, along with the mayor, when the rioters from East Harlem attacked Gracie Mansion." He gave Frazier a conspiratorial wink. "Not bad, huh? Now everyone in Congress will be screaming for blood. They'll let out a cheer when we put New York under martial law."

Frazier tried to look happy about it, but he couldn't muster much enthusiasm. To tell the truth, he didn't care about the vice president or the secretary of defense or any of the fucked-up political games that Colonel Grant liked to play. Frazier cared about the important things: duty, honor, loyalty, and above all, justice. He saw himself as a crusader, an instrument of justice, delivering swift punishment to everyone who'd ever fucked with him. He'd started this crusade back in Cassville, when he was just a teenager; before he left his hometown and joined the army, he beat the shit out of his drunk stepdad and his cocksucker uncle. He pulped the town's perverted gym teacher too, putting him in the hospital. And in Afghanistan he did much worse to hundreds of deserving ragheads.

Now it was Powell's turn.

"Sir, what's Powell's condition? Is he going to live?"

Grant stopped grinning. He let out a long breath and rolled his eyes. "You've already asked me that question three times tonight, Lieutenant."

"I'm very sorry, sir. But a couple of hours ago you said the operation on Powell was touch and go, and so I wondered if anything has changed since then."

"Nothing's changed. He's still on the operating table." The colonel waved his hand to the left, in the direction of the Research Center's operating theater. "That asshole Weinberg injected him with a new CRISPR treatment, and he thinks Powell will make it. But the other doctors aren't so optimistic."

"Why?"

"Powell's hanging on by a thread, and they think he'll die before the new genetic changes can take effect. They say he has only a twenty percent chance of survival. Maybe even less."

Frazier nodded. This was good news. In all likelihood, he wouldn't have to worry about Powell. The traitor would die a slow, painful death, and justice would be served.

But what if he beat the odds?

"Sir, what's the plan if Powell lives?"

Grant frowned. All his good cheer was gone. "What do you want me to do, Frazier? Court-martial him? Put him in front of a firing squad?"

"He deserted his unit in Afghanistan. He sabotaged the FSU's operations and destroyed our Bay Parkway checkpoint. And he killed twelve of my men."

"Yes, yes, I know all that. But he's still part of the Palindrome experiment, and he can still give us useful results. If he lives, we might learn how to improve the treatment."

This was the answer Frazier had been afraid of. He didn't like it one bit. Keeping Powell alive was a truly shitty idea. "What about security, sir? If Powell recovers, he'll be a threat to everyone at this facility."

"We've already prepared for that. The new CRISPR treatment for Powell includes the insertion of the Serenity sequence into his DNA. You know, the same genetic change we did to Hassan Mohammed, the Al-Qaeda fucker in the interrogation room. The treatment pacified the shit out of that raghead, so it should make Powell more obedient too."

"But what if it doesn't work?"

"Lieutenant? Just drop it. If Powell survives, we'll take the necessary precautions and increase the security of the labs. We have bigger things to worry about right now." Grant stared at him hard. "Speaking of which, I want you to go see Weinberg. That asshole won't stop bothering me."

The sudden change of subject flustered Frazier. He felt confused and disappointed. "See Weinberg? About what?"

The colonel lowered his head and focused on one of the papers on his desk. It looked like a memo of some kind. "Remember how Weinberg interrupted the inspection tour for the veep? Well, it's the same damn thing. He wants to tell me something about Raza Khan, the crippled kid, but I don't have the time to listen to his bullshit."

"So you want *me* to talk to him?"

Grant nodded without looking up. "You've seen the Jenna Khan file, so you already know the relevant facts about her brother. Just listen to what Weinberg has to say about him and then write it all down for me in a report. I'll take a look at it when I get a chance. It's more efficient that way."

Frazier didn't buy it. First of all, Grant had never asked him to be his goddamn secretary before. Second, the colonel was so obsessive about Palindrome that it was completely out of character for him to dodge a conversation about it. And third, Frazier remembered what had happened to Grant when Weinberg interrupted the inspection tour an hour ago. The colonel had started acting jittery and frantic, like a cornered animal. Something had terrified him, and it was connected to that crippled freak, that fucking Raza Khan.

Grant picked up a pen and held it over the memo, but his hand shook so badly that he couldn't write anything. Just thinking about the cripple had scared the hell out of him. After a few seconds he raised his head and scowled. "What the fuck are you waiting for? Go talk to Weinberg. He's in Room Seventeen."

Frazier nodded and walked out of the office. He was going to take care of the problem for Grant. He intended to find out what that Khan freak was doing to the colonel. And then Frazier was going to put an end to it. Permanently.

Room 17 was on the same corridor as the operating theater where the doctors were working on Derek Powell. Frazier marched down the hall, looking straight ahead, intending to go directly to his meeting with Dr. Weinberg. But at the last moment he stopped, just ten feet short of his destination, and opened the door to the operating theater instead.

He stepped into the gallery, which was like an auditorium where the seats curved around the glass-walled operating room. But Frazier was the only spectator to this operation. On the other side of the glass, a dozen doctors and nurses bent over the enormous body on the table. In the narrow gaps between their surgical gowns and caps, Frazier could see Powell's split-open torso, its flesh peeled back to expose his lungs and intestines.

Frazier moved across the gallery, trying to get a good look at Powell's face, but it was hard to see anything with all the doctors scurrying around the table and blocking his view. Frazier got a glimpse of the operating room's monitors, though, and he liked what he saw. Powell's heart rate was weak and his blood pressure barely detectable. His vital signs were close to flatlining.

I hope you're suffering, Powell. I hope you burn in hell.

Frazier propped his fists against the glass. He wished he could break into the operating room and deliver the fatal blow himself. All he needed to do was shatter the glass and shove the doctors aside. Then he'd thrust his hands into the incision they'd made and rip out the traitor's heart.

But no. That would mean violating Colonel Grant's orders. If Frazier did that, he'd be a traitor too. He'd be just as bad as Powell.

So he lowered his arms and stepped backward, moving away from the glass. He would let nature take its course and kill Powell slowly. Room 17 was right next door, so maybe Frazier would hear it happen. When Powell's vitals flatlined, maybe the high-pitched buzz of the monitors would penetrate the walls.

Frazier left the gallery and went back to the corridor. He took two big strides, then opened the door to Weinberg's laboratory.

Like the interrogation rooms and the operating theater, Room 17 was divided into two sections that were separated by a big window, a sheet of glass five feet high and eight feet across. Frazier stepped into the observers' section, a smallish space crowded with computer screens and laser printers. Dr. Weinberg sat in the middle of all the hardware and stared at one of the screens, which displayed a dozen white horizontal lines, all jiggling in elaborate patterns. Weinberg was studying their movements so carefully that he didn't hear Frazier enter the room. The guy just sat there, frozen, his eyes fixed on the screen. Annoyed, Frazier was about to yell at the asshole to get his attention, but then he noticed something disturbing on the other side of the glass.

Raza Khan sprawled in a wheelchair in the patients' section of the lab. His body was twisted and tiny, a stunted figure inside a prisoner's orange jumpsuit. His head had been shaved, and a tangled mane of silver wires ran between his skull and a large, boxy machine behind his wheelchair. Each wire was attached to an electrode pasted to the kid's bare scalp.

Frazier recognized the equipment, because the Palindrome researchers had used it on him too. It was an EEG—an electroencephalograph—a machine that records the brain's electrical activity. The scientists had attached Frazier to the machine before and after each round of CRISPR injections to find out if the treatments were boosting his brainpower. But the EEG hooked up to Raza Khan seemed more advanced than the ones Frazier had seen before. The electrodes covered every square centimeter of the boy's skull. They were so thickly clustered, they looked like a swarm of silver bees.

This sight, though, wasn't the most disturbing one in the laboratory. There was another patient connected to the EEG, an old, dumpy man sitting on a stool to the left of Raza's wheelchair. His nearly bald scalp was covered with electrodes too, and his face was badly bruised, but Frazier recognized him from a picture in the Jenna Khan file. It was Hamid Khan, Raza's and Jenna's father.

Hamid wasn't supposed to be here. He'd been assigned to the General Detention Facility on the other side of Rikers Island, so his presence in the Research Center was a cause for concern. But the truly alarming thing about him was that he wore a pair of khakis and a blue polo shirt. Someone had given him street clothes to wear instead of his prison jumpsuit.

Frazier shook his head. This was un-fucking-believable.

"Hey, Weinberg!" He stomped toward the asshole and grabbed his shoulder. "What the fuck is going on here?"

The guy didn't respond. He just kept staring at the lines on his computer screen. Frazier had to spin the asshole's chair around and get in his face. "Hey, I'm talking to you! Why did you bring the cripple's father to the lab? And where the hell did he get those clothes?"

Weinberg looked at him blankly. His eyes were unfocused, and his skin was very pale. "You're Lieutenant Rick Frazier, Palindrome Subject Number Twenty-Three."

Frazier wanted to slap him. "Answer the question, shithead! Why is Hamid Khan here?"

"I'm analyzing the cognitive abilities of his son, Raza Khan. Raza was never officially a subject of the Palindrome tests, but Dr. Jenna Khan developed an unauthorized CRISPR treatment for him in an attempt to cure his genetic disorder."

Weinberg spoke in a weird monotone, slow and emotionless. He sounded exhausted and almost robotic, which was probably the result of spending way too many hours in the laboratory. But Frazier didn't care how tired the guy was. He wanted an explanation, and so far he wasn't getting it. He tightened his grip on Weinberg's shoulder.

"Listen to me! Did you request Hamid's transfer from the General Detention Facility?"

Weinberg nodded. "I needed him to participate in a new test I devised."

"A test? What the fuck are you talking about?"

"Jenna Khan's treatment of her brother was very different from all the other Palindrome therapies. It was intended to repair the flawed gene that had caused his paralysis, but it unexpectedly changed many other genes involved in the nervous system. In particular, it altered the genes that control the transmission of signals in the brain. And those altered genes have become much more active in the past twenty-four hours, most likely because they were triggered by the boy's intense fear and stress." He pointed at the jagged lines at the top of his computer screen. "These are the brain waves from Raza's frontal lobe. Notice how powerful and coordinated they are. Now look at this." He pointed at another set of lines at the bottom of the screen. "These are Hamid's brain waves. You see how Raza's oscillations mimic his father's?"

Frazier stared at the lines, but he couldn't make any sense of them. And it was a waste of time anyway. Weinberg was just trying to distract him. Frazier leaned his weight on the bastard's shoulder, pinning him to his chair. "Goddamn it! I don't give a fuck about his brain waves! Who authorized you to transfer Hamid and bring him here? It wasn't Colonel Grant, was it?"

Surprisingly, Weinberg didn't yelp or whimper. Even though Frazier was applying enough pressure to dislocate the guy's arm, he didn't seem afraid or even the least bit upset. He kept his eyes on the computer screen, almost in a trance, as if the jiggling lines had hypnotized him. "No one authorized me. I did it because Raza asked me to."

"What?" Frazier was so irritated, he started shaking the guy. He shoved him backward, and the chair nearly tipped over. "That freak can't even talk!"

Despite the rough treatment, Weinberg's face stayed blank. Very slowly, he raised his arm toward the big window and pointed at the crippled kid in the wheelchair. "He's learned to communicate without words. Go see for yourself."

Frazier let go of Weinberg's shoulder. Enough with the shaking—he was going to pound the crazy fucker's skull. But as Frazier cocked his fist and took aim, he glimpsed a flash of movement out of the corner of his eye. He looked through the window at the other section of the lab and saw Hamid Khan wave at him. The old man smiled, and the electrodes on his head gleamed under the room's fluorescent lights.

This was too much. Frazier forgot about Weinberg and moved toward the sheet of glass. To the left of the window was a door that connected the lab's two sections, and luckily it was unlocked. Frazier flung the door open and strode into the patients' section, stopping in front of Hamid and his freakish kid.

They looked ridiculous, the dumpy Pakistani and the cripple wearing identical caps of electrodes, with all the wires running back to the boxy machine behind them. Frazier's mind took a sudden leap, and he thought of the beauty salon in Cassville where his grandmother used to get her hair done, all the old ladies sitting in a row, each with a domed hair dryer over her head. That's what the electrode caps looked like, silver domes for withered biddies with dead white hair. But Frazier clenched his teeth and shook his head, and the memory dissolved. This was no time for distractions. He needed to keep his mind on a tight leash, keep it focused.

He pointed at Hamid. "Who gave you those clothes?"

The old man smiled again. It wasn't a pleased or amused smile. He was just doing it to be polite. "Dr. Weinberg gave me these pants and this shirt. But please, sir, don't be angry with him. It's not his fault that he broke the rules."

"And why the hell did he give them to you?" Frazier bent over him. "Why do you need to wear street clothes for a fucking EEG test?"

"You're right, I don't need them for this test. I'll need them afterward. In a few minutes, Dr. Weinberg is going to help me leave this jail. He said we'll have a better chance of getting past the guards if I'm not wearing a prisoner's uniform."

Hamid's voice never rose or quavered. He made his confession in a casual, offhand way, still smiling politely. Frazier looked over his shoulder at Weinberg, who'd gone back to staring at his computer screen. "Jesus Christ! He's planning to help you escape?"

"Yes, sir. But as I said, it's not Dr. Weinberg's fault." Hamid pointed at his son. "Raza is telling him what to do."

Frazier stood up straight and forced himself to look at the cripple. The kid hadn't moved an inch in the past five minutes. His bony torso leaned against the armrest of his wheelchair, his back arched and his clawlike hands resting in his lap. His head hung backward at a painfully sharp angle, and his mouth was open so wide that Frazier could see all the way down to his tonsils. The only sign of life was in his eyes, which stared back at Frazier, tracking him carefully. But other than that, the kid was a vegetable.

Frazier turned back to Hamid. "I got some news for you, raghead. Your boy ain't giving instructions to anyone. He's a few cans short of a six-pack, if you know what I mean."

Hamid stopped smiling. At least he knew when he was being insulted. "Raza is already very angry at you. And you're making it worse."

"Oh yeah? That's too bad." Now it was Frazier's turn to smile. He leaned over the wheelchair and reached for the thick mane of wires extending from the electrodes on Raza's head. "But hey, I think I see what the problem is. These wires are probably bothering him. It's time to disconnect, don't you think?"

Hamid jumped to his feet so suddenly that several of the electrodes popped off his scalp. "Raza was right about you. He said you were evil."

Frazier grabbed Raza's wires. There were at least a hundred of them, but with a little effort he was able to curl his fingers around the entire bunch. "Okay, you've had your fun, old man. Now you're gonna go back to your cell in General Detention. And we're gonna throw Weinberg into a cell too and find another researcher to study your creepy kid."

"Raza! I give you my permission." Hamid turned away from Frazier and looked down at his son. "Do whatever you want with him."

Frazier chuckled. He tightened his grip on the bunch of wires and prepared to yank them off the cripple's head. "All right, kid, this might hurt a bit. Just—"

Then everything went black.

Frazier woke up on a bench on the Coney Island boardwalk. It was a warm spring afternoon, with pale green buds on the trees and sunlight sparkling on the Atlantic. It was too early in the season for swimming, but a few dozen people lay on the beach, sunning themselves on towels and chaise lounges. A bigger crowd strolled down the boardwalk, some walking east, others going west. Young mothers pushed strollers, elderly folks shuffled along with the help of canes and nurses, and rowdy groups of teenagers shouted at one another and drank from bottles wrapped in brown-paper bags.

At first Frazier thought his brain had shifted again and he was reliving another memory—not from his childhood this time, but a more recent memory, from the period after the FSU assigned him to New York City. But he grew less certain as he gazed at the scene around him. He'd come to New York only three months ago, so he'd never seen Coney Island in the spring. Also, this neighborhood was nothing like the ruined district that Frazier had patrolled with the FSU. The boardwalk here was still intact, the beach had plenty of sand, and the roller coasters and Tilt-a-Whirls in the amusement park were still running. This was Coney Island before the superstorms, before global warming accelerated and sea levels rose and dozens of hurricanes ravaged the East Coast. It was a memory from at least a decade ago, when the problems were just starting to get serious.

Frazier got up from the bench and looked around. He turned toward the ocean and noticed a family on the beach nearby, sitting on a big, red blanket spread across the sand, about twenty feet from the boardwalk. They were having a picnic, eating hummus and pita bread and olives from Tupperware containers arranged on the blanket. He realized with a start that this was the Khan family, or at least a younger version of it. He was immersed in one of *their* memories instead of his own. It had somehow wormed its way into Frazier's skull and taken over his mind.

Hamid Khan reclined on the beach blanket, looking ten years younger than the man Frazier had seen in the laboratory. He had a full head of dark hair and a sturdy, athletic physique. His wife was a small, slender woman dressed in conservative but stylish clothes—a brown kaftan over black leggings, and a beige hijab over her head. Jenna was a college girl in jeans and a light sweater, with her own hijab covering her hair, a bright blue one. She sat cross-legged on the blanket with her nose deep in a book, a massive textbook titled *Principles of Biochemistry*.

And Raza ran in circles around the blanket, a black-haired boy of nine or ten, in sandy shorts and a SpongeBob T-shirt. He had all the energy and mania of a kid his age, constantly picking up rocks and sticks from the sand and throwing them as far as he could across the beach. He had no symptoms yet from his genetic disorder, not even a limp. He laughed and teased Jenna every time he ran past, calling her "baji," which was probably the Pakistani word for "sister." And occasionally he'd grab a piece of pita bread from the picnic spread and stuff it into his mouth.

But there *was* one unusual thing about Raza. The boy's face seemed blurry. No matter how hard Frazier stared at him, it never came into focus. What's more, this was the only part of the whole memory of Coney Island that wasn't sharp and clear. After thinking it over, Frazier concluded that this memory must be Raza's. His face was blurry because it's impossible to remember your own face in any detail.

Frazier felt a twinge of discomfort. One of Raza's memories had invaded his mind, and Hamid had warned that the kid was angry at him. The beach seemed to darken, even though the sun was still high above and there wasn't a cloud in the sky. Something bad was coming. This scene wouldn't end well.

After a while Raza knelt on the sand and dug out a larger rock, a smooth black stone about the size of a softball. It was so heavy he had to use both hands to pick it up. First, he tried rolling the stone like a bowling ball, but that was clearly disappointing. It rolled only a couple of feet on the sand before coming to a stop. Then he cupped the stone in one hand and held it against the crook of his neck, as if he were in an Olympic shot put competition. He must've seen a shot-putter on TV, because he did a pretty good imitation of the throw, spinning around three times before flinging the stone. And it hurtled pretty far through the air, clearly a lot farther than the boy had thought it would, arcing fifteen feet above the sand. It landed in the shadows under the boardwalk, directly below the spot where Frazier stood.

Someone cried out beneath the boards. A moment later, a tall, skinny teenager raced out of the shadows and onto the beach, hopping on one foot and grimacing in pain. He was an older kid, maybe eighteen or nineteen. His hair was long and blond and greasy, his forehead spotted with zits. He wore a black T-shirt with a white skull printed on the front, and he had a rattlesnake tattoo running down his arm. In his right hand he held a large bottle wrapped in a brown-paper bag. Several ounces of malt liquor spilled out of it as he hopped around on the sand.

"Shit!" He bent over to look at his injured foot, which was inside an old sneaker, and almost lost his balance. "Who the fuck threw that rock?"

Two other grungy teenagers emerged from under the boardwalk, both of them laughing and pointing at Skull Guy. At the same time, Raza ran to his father. Hamid stood up and wrapped his arms around his son, who buried his face in Hamid's shirt. "I'm sorry!" Raza bawled, his voice muffled. "I'm sorry, I'm sorry, I'm sorry!"

The injured teen heard the boy and glared at him and Hamid. "Hey! Is that kid the one who did it?" He limped across the sand toward the Khan family. "Did he throw that rock?"

Hamid nodded. "Yes, I'm so sorry, it was my son. But he didn't mean to hit you."

"What the fuck? He threw that thing right at me!"

"But it's very dark under the boardwalk. He didn't see you and your friends there." Hamid patted Raza's back but kept his eyes on the teenager. "Is there anything we can do? Are you badly hurt?"

Skull Guy swayed on his feet. He looked more drunk than injured, but he put an outraged look on his face. "What the hell do you think? Of course I'm fucking hurt! Did you see the size of that motherfucking rock?"

Hamid winced at the language, but refrained from objecting. He pointed at Mrs. Khan instead. "My wife is a nurse. Why don't you let her examine your foot? She could tell you whether you need to go to the emergency room."

Mrs. Khan stood up, slowly and tentatively, obviously a bit scared. Skull Guy gave her a once-over and scowled. "Nah, no way. I don't want her examining me. She looks like a fucking terrorist." He grinned and turned to his two drunk buddies. "Right? Am I right? Look at her and the other bitch. They're like a couple of Jihadi Janes. They probably got suicide bombs under their heebie jabbies."

His friends laughed and stepped closer to the Khans. Jenna tossed her book aside and leapt to her feet. "That's enough! We said we're sorry. Now go away!"

Skull Guy cocked his head and came toward her. He stepped on their beach blanket and knocked over one of the Tupperware containers. "What was that? You think you can kick us off the beach now?" He pointed at himself and his friends. "That's a little ass-backwards, don't you think? I mean, *we're* the Americans here, and you're just a bunch of shit-eating camel-fuckers. You think you can come here and order us around in our own damn country?"

Hamid handed Raza to Mrs. Khan, then stepped between Jenna and the blond punk. "Please, we don't want any trouble. We're very sorry about this accident and—"

"It wasn't a fucking accident!" Skull Guy raised his voice and flung his arms up. The bottle was still in his right hand, and malt liquor sloshed all over the blanket. "Your cocksucking little brat threw the rock right at me!"

"Stop it!" Hamid went toe-to-toe with the punk. Although Skull Guy was taller, Hamid definitely outweighed him. "I won't tolerate this kind of foul talk anymore! This is no way to speak in front of women and children. You should be ashamed of yourself!"

The punk took a drunken step backward. Hamid had intimidated him, but the teenager covered it up by grinning. He turned to his friends for support, and they stepped forward, one to the left of the blanket and one to the right. Then Skull Guy pointed at Jenna. "Hey, bitch, what's under your heebie jabbie? If we take it off and see what's under there, does that give us the right to fuck you? Isn't that how your religion works?"

Hamid lunged at him, but the punk backed up again, jumping out of reach. At the same time, Skull Guy gave a hand signal to his friends. "Take 'em off!"

His companions rushed toward the Khans. One of them grabbed Mrs. Khan's hijab and the other yanked off Jenna's. Then they ran off with the headscarves, whooping and hollering across the beach.

It happened so fast that neither woman could stop them. Jenna and her mother just stood on the soiled blanket, stunned and appalled, while the teenagers ran toward the ocean, the hijabs trailing behind them and flapping in the breeze. Hamid didn't react either, which surprised Frazier. The man grimaced, but he didn't run after the punks or even shout at them. After a couple of seconds he bent over and started packing away the Tupperware containers, preparing to leave the beach.

He'd obviously decided that confronting the teens would be futile. It would just bring him down to their level. Better to simply collect his belongings and go home. That was the best way to preserve his dignity.

For Raza, though, things like dignity were unimportant. He saw the teenage boys attack his mother and sister, and he responded instinctively. He charged toward Skull Guy, stopped in front of the greasy bastard, and stomped on his injured foot.

The punk howled. At the same time, he swung the malt-liquor bottle downward and smacked it into Raza's head.

Frazier heard the thunk of glass against bone. Raza staggered and lurched backward, looking even wobblier than the drunk teenager. Then the boy collapsed on the sand.

Jenna screamed, "NO!" Hamid dropped all the Tupperware and leapt over the blanket, hurtling toward his son.

Skull Guy stood there for a moment, looking down at the fallen boy at his feet. Then he raised his head and saw Jenna and Hamid rushing toward him. He took off like a shot, his heels kicking up sand as he sprinted across the beach. The other punks saw the danger too and followed right behind him, letting go of the hijabs as they dashed toward the boardwalk. The headscarves floated on the breeze for a few seconds, then fluttered to the ground.

Jenna and Hamid knelt on either side of Raza. To Frazier's relief, the boy sat up and raised his hand to his head. He let out a piercing scream, but that was all right—he was alive, he was conscious, he was going to be okay. But then the boy pointed his other hand over Jenna's shoulder, and she turned around. Twenty feet behind her, Mrs. Khan lay facedown on the sand.

At the same moment, Frazier felt an immense surge of terror. It seemed to rise from the Atlantic and sweep across Coney Island, flooding every inch of the remembered landscape and drowning Frazier's mind as well. The fear was paralyzing, suffocating, worse than anything he'd ever felt, even when Andy died. And it was accompanied by a voice that boomed across the ocean, a voice he'd never heard before but recognized nonetheless: *She had a heart condition, an arrhythmia, but no one thought it was serious. Then she saw me collapse on the beach and her heart just stopped. I was the first one to notice what happened to her.*

Now Frazier knew why Raza had put this scene in his head. He'd wanted Frazier to feel the worst agony in the world, so he'd flooded his mind with these thoughts and images. It was Raza's most devastating weapon, this memory of his mother's death.

The torture went on for so long, it might as well have been eternal. Frazier felt like he'd been writhing since the beginning of time. In reality, though, it lasted only thirty minutes.

Frazier woke up on the floor of Room 17. He scrambled to his feet and looked around, scanning both sections of the room. Hamid Khan and Dr. David Weinberg were gone. Raza was still there, still in his wheelchair, his head tilted back at the same painful angle, but when Frazier came toward him, the kid's eyes didn't move. They were cloudy, glazed over.

The freak was dead.

TWENTY-TWO

Jenna dove into the crowd surging toward Gracie Mansion. A second later, the FSU officers on the mansion's upper floors opened fire on the rioters.

Pandemonium erupted all around her. Gunshots boomed and echoed, people threw themselves to the ground, men with bandannas masking their faces toppled backward and lay still. Some of the rioters turned around and fled, and some raced for shelter under the mansion's porch, where Jenna had just emerged from the service entrance. But most of them just stood there in front of the building, too scared to move, making them easy targets. The Federal Service officers slaughtered them, firing hundreds of rounds from their assault rifles.

Jenna kept her head down and ran. She'd been in the same murderous situation the night before, at Bay Parkway, and she'd learned something important from that experience: although she couldn't outrun a bullet, she could minimize her time in the killing zone. In this case, the zone was the driveway in front of the mansion, so she raced away from it as fast as she could, heading for the security fence that surrounded the building.

The rioters were packed shoulder to shoulder here, but Jenna lowered her head and charged through the crowd. Gunfire streaked from the mansion behind her, the bullets zinging from the windows to the driveway, and dozens of people fell to her left and right, but she didn't stop, didn't even slow down. A tall man in a Knicks jersey sank to the ground in front of her, struck by a bullet that took off the top of his skull, but she leapt right over him and bounded toward the fence.

The FSU officers had blown up a section of the fence when they'd attacked the mansion, and now the terrified rioters tried to escape through the gap. They rushed toward it and climbed over the charred wood and metal, shoving and trampling each other in their desperation. The mansion's floodlights, though, illuminated the right side of the gap, and that's where the FSU sharpshooters concentrated their fire. They mowed down so many of the rioters that their bodies covered the wreckage of the fence. It became a ridge of corpses.

But the terrified people kept coming. They converged on the gap and scrambled over the dead and dying.

Jenna veered away from them and dashed toward the other side of the gap. This side was darker because a nearby tree blocked the floodlights. She carefully picked her way through the darkness, clambering over a couple of splintered planks and a tangle of twisted steel beams that used to be fence posts. Then she jumped down from the wreckage and ran toward the streetlights on East End Avenue.

In seconds she reached 88th Street and sprinted down the block, trying to put as much distance as possible between herself and the riot. But as she approached the next intersection she saw an even larger crowd streaming down York Avenue. Hundreds of people ran through the street and vandalized the parked cars, smashing their windshields with bricks and tire irons. Hundreds more thronged the sidewalks and shattered the windows of the stores and apartment buildings. They tore down the buildings' awnings and busted open their doors and ripped the uniforms off the doormen who didn't run away fast enough. Millions of glass shards littered the pavement, each gleaming in the moonlight.

Jenna stopped for a moment and tried to figure out the safest escape route. The rioters had whipped themselves into a frenzy, furious and chaotic. They laughed and shrieked as they demolished the bus shelters and looted the boutiques and jewelry stores. The destruction was mindlessly random, because the mob attacked everything in its path. Nothing was safe.

She decided to keep running west on 88th Street, hoping to skirt the worst of the violence. But there were crowds marching down First, Second, and Third Avenues too, and an enormous bonfire raged at the corner of 88th and Lexington. The entire population of New York City seemed to be on the move tonight, all the men and women and children from Harlem and the Bronx descending on the rich, privileged neighborhoods of Manhattan. The New York police had retreated farther south, and the private security guards had abandoned their posts in front of the luxury high-rises and townhouses. At the heart of the bonfire was the blackened chassis of a police patrol car, apparently left behind by the retreating cops.

There was an old stone church on the street corner, and Jenna ducked under one of its archways and hid within the shadows. She leaned against the locked door, panting, confused, and watched the rioters hurl things into the bonfire—garbage they'd dumped from cans, side mirrors they'd ripped off the parked cars, armfuls of clothing they'd just looted from the stores. The mob was angry but also ecstatic, ferocious and mesmerized. The rioters hardly knew what to do with themselves now that they'd invaded the Upper East Side, so they did everything at once. They raged and laughed, brawled and clowned, snarled and celebrated. It was anarchic, incomprehensible.

But no, that wasn't exactly true. Jenna was an expert on the genetics of behavior, and she understood the power of violent emotion. And over the past twenty-four hours, she'd gained some personal insight into the malignant effects of systemic persecution—or, to put it in nonscientific terms, she'd gotten an up close look at how America fucks over its black and brown people. The Jenna Khan who hid in the church doorway on Lexington Avenue was very different from the naïve young woman she'd been before the Federal Service officers burst into her family's apartment. She knew more about suffering now. She was starting to grasp the mindset of the desperate, because now she was desperate too.

Jenna took a deep breath. She couldn't stay here. If she wanted to help Abbu and Raza, she had to keep moving. She dashed away from the church and ran west another block on 88th Street.

At the next corner, she saw the biggest crowd yet. A horde of thousands trooped down Park Avenue, overrunning the northbound and southbound traffic lanes as well as the median strip of grass between them. The rioters swarmed around the grand apartment buildings on the avenue and shattered all their ground-floor windows. They stormed into the buildings' courtyards and ransacked their lobbies, smashing chandeliers and mirrors and concierge desks. And they climbed to the upper floors and banged on the doors of the penthouse apartments, terrifying the corporate lawyers and financiers who'd paid millions and millions of dollars to live there.

Jenna crouched behind a battered Mercedes near the corner and looked up and down the avenue. She could see silhouettes in the windows of the fancy apartment buildings, the rich and famous gazing anxiously at the riot below. A window opened on the top floor of the building across the street, and an elderly man poked his head out, his glasses and bald scalp reflecting the moonlight. At first Jenna thought he was so petrified that he was going to jump, but when she looked closer she saw that his lips were moving. Although she had no chance of hearing him—the mob on Park Avenue was way too loud—she felt certain that the old man was calling for help.

Then something else caught her eye. A bright light appeared in the night sky all the way to the south, just above the massive MetLife Building that stood astride Park Avenue. The light was spectacularly radiant, twice as bright as any star, and coming closer. After a few seconds Jenna realized it was actually a string of lights, half a dozen in all. They were moving in a line, speeding uptown, flying less than a hundred feet above Manhattan's skyscrapers.

They were helicopters. A moment later Jenna could hear them. She assumed they were military aircraft, designed to transport soldiers to battlefields, probably the same kind of helicopters that had carried the FSU assault team to Gracie Mansion.

She reached into her pocket and pulled out Allen Keating's iPhone. Then she typed in the password—"Tammy," or 82669 on the phone's keypad—and tapped the camera icon. It looked like the FSU was going to land its helicopters on Park Avenue, and Jenna planned to record whatever happened next. Because the avenue sloped downward to the south, she had an excellent view of the crowd of rioters, which extended at least a quarter mile ahead. If any of the soldiers fired on the mob, she was going to get video of it.

Soon the helicopter at the head of the line swooped over the roof of the MetLife Building. It descended into a man-made canyon, flanked by the Midtown skyscrapers on either side of Park Avenue, and then zipped uptown at a blistering speed, just fifty feet above the median strip. The other choppers followed close behind, their rotors thumping the air. Jenna expected the helicopters to slow down and land on the traffic lanes, or at least hover above the avenue to allow the soldiers to jump out, but instead the aircraft accelerated. They raced past 60th Street, then 70th, then 80th, looming ever larger on the iPhone's screen.

Then the helicopters flew over the mob and opened fire.

Each chopper had four machine guns, mounted on stubby racks on either side of the aircraft, and all of them spat tracer rounds at the crowd. It was like a scene from a war movie, the glowing bullets streaking down from the helicopters in a thunderous shower, but now the ammunition wasn't aimed at the Vietnamese jungles or the Iraqi deserts or the Afghan mountains. The soldiers were firing on American citizens. Jenna's hands shook as she held the iPhone and watched the killing machines zoom across its screen.

The avenue was so densely packed that nearly every bullet struck at least one of the rioters. They fell in long lines that matched the paths of the helicopters, leaving trails of corpses that ran down the street. Each chopper killed dozens, and together they slaughtered hundreds. And once the helicopters flew past the mob, they climbed into the night sky and made wide banking U-turns, returning to the airspace over Midtown so they could descend to Park Avenue and strafe the crowd again.

At first, most of the survivors cowered on the pavement, staring in shock at all the dead bodies around them. But when they saw the helicopters make those U-turns and fly south to Midtown, they staggered to their feet and started running in the opposite direction. Although no one gave them any orders, the rioters moved north in frantic synchrony, like a herd chased by wolves. They abandoned their invasion of the Upper East Side and retreated uptown, stampeding back to East Harlem. Screaming in fear, they hurried past Jenna's hiding place on 88th Street, where she recorded video of their retreat and all the bodies they had to step over.

The helicopters swooped down again into the man-made canyon and this time they concentrated their fire on the tail end of the fleeing crowd. They cut down the wounded and the stragglers, shooting hundreds in the back. The rioters in the thick of the mob redoubled their speed, knocking down and trampling the people in front of them. The smarter ones fled down the side streets, and half a dozen dove behind the same Mercedes that Jenna was using for cover. In response, one of the helicopters shifted course and aimed its guns at the corner of Park and 88th.

Jenna dropped the iPhone and scrambled under the car. She flattened herself on the asphalt and slid beneath the chassis, snagging the back of her shirt on the exhaust pipe. Then the Mercedes clanked and shuddered as the large-caliber bullets pounded its hood.

She heard a shriek, very close, but the noise of the machine guns drowned out everything else. Jenna closed her eyes and covered her ears, but she could still hear the guns blasting. It was hideous, unbearable. She was losing control, going mad, going batshit crazy. Desperate, she started counting in her head, slow and silent. She tried to shut out all the horrible noises by focusing on the numbers in her mind.

She counted to ten. Then to twenty.

Then she took her hands off her ears and opened her eyes. The gunfire had stopped. The helicopters had flown off. The bullets had punctured one of the car's tires, but Jenna was unhurt. She gave herself a few more seconds to catch her breath. Then she slid out from under the Mercedes.

Most of the crowd had already fled past 88th Street. She looked uptown and saw the rioters sprinting north, but the avenue behind them was littered with bodies. It was like the pictures she'd seen of the killing fields in Cambodia, where the corpses covered the ground like a ghastly carpet. Within twenty yards of Jenna there were at least fifty bodies sprawled on the pavement, all of them torn and scythed by the machine guns. Even worse, the helicopters were climbing into the sky again, getting into position for another strafing run. Their strategy was to chase the mob back to East Harlem, and it was working. When Jenna looked south, she saw a convoy of armored vehicles on Park Avenue, a second wave of FSU troops barreling uptown to finish the job.

She didn't have much time, but she took a couple of seconds to consider her options. If she went north or south on Park Avenue, the FSU would get her. There were helicopters to the east too, chasing the rioters up Lexington and Third Avenue. But to the west, the sky was empty and the streets deserted. And Central Park was less than a quarter mile away.

Jenna bent over, picked up the iPhone from the pavement, and stuffed it into her pocket. Then she turned away from the killing fields and ran west.

She raced into Central Park and dashed under the trees near the reservoir. She could still hear the FSU helicopters firing their guns in the distance, so she was glad to find a place where no one could spot her from the air. But soon she realized she should've gone somewhere else.

Thousands of rioters had already streamed into the park from the surrounding neighborhoods. Many of them had just escaped from the helicopter assault, and they wandered in a daze across the moonlit jogging paths and softball fields. But others gathered in feral groups and rampaged through the park, attacking anyone who was lost or alone. As Jenna hurried along one of the gravel pathways she saw brawls and beatdowns and even uglier things in the shadows. She heard screams and whimpers and hysterical weeping. The riots had unleashed the worst impulses in everyone. The strong were preying on the weak.

Jenna broke into a run. She was horrified, but not surprised. It was a sad rule of human behavior: violence breeds more violence. It was written so indelibly in our DNA, Jenna doubted that even CRISPR could erase it.

She found another pathway and veered north of the reservoir, trying to avoid contact with anyone else in the park. After a couple of minutes, though, she heard a clatter of footsteps and looked over her shoulder. Four men crashed through the bushes and started jogging on the path behind her, about thirty feet back. She couldn't see their faces in the darkness, but they were big, burly guys in jerseys and basketball shorts, and they all carried beer bottles. One of them laughed and pointed at Jenna.

"Hey, girl. Wanna party?"

She faced forward and ran faster. But the men sped up too, keeping pace with her. They laughed louder.

"Why are you running, baby? Come on, slow down. We're not gonna hurt you."

The men sped up a little more and started to catch up to her. Soon they were only twenty feet behind, close enough that Jenna could hear them breathing. She was panting, already breathless, but her pursuers weren't winded. She couldn't stay ahead of them much longer.

Panicking, she left the path and bounded down a wooded hill. She zig-zagged between the trees and bushes, feeling her way through the dark, trying like hell not to trip on the rocks and tree roots. But the men stayed right behind her, whooping and thrashing as they followed her down-hill. She had no doubt about their intentions—they planned to rape her—and she felt a new surge of horror, as thick and heavy as the darkness. She bolted out of the shadows and ran toward a grassy field that glowed in the moonlight.

A group of men stood in the field, at least a dozen of them. Jenna couldn't see their faces either, but she raced toward them anyway. They couldn't be any worse than the men behind her. But as she got closer, she noticed that these men were armed. Instead of beer bottles, they held switchblades and baseball bats. They turned their heads toward Jenna as she approached, and then the biggest man in the group stepped away from the others and pulled a pistol from the waistband of his pants.

The four men behind Jenna gave up the chase when they saw the gun. They dropped their bottles and ran headlong in four different directions.

Jenna wanted to run too, but she stood her ground. She stepped right up to the gunman and gave him a careful once-over. He was tall, at least six-foot-four, and wore a shiny tracksuit and a baseball cap. She could barely see his eyes because the brim of his cap blocked the moonlight, but she got the feeling that he was studying her just as carefully. To be specific, he seemed to be staring at her chest.

After a few seconds, he pointed at her. "Where did you get that?"

Jenna realized her mistake. He wasn't staring at her chest. His eyes were fixed on her bead necklace.

She squinted at him. It was hard to tell in the darkness, but it looked like the guy's tracksuit was black-and-gold. She gripped her necklace and lifted it to eye level. "Hector Torres gave this to me. You know him?"

"*Amor de Rey!*" The guy raised his hand and made the Latin Kings gang sign. "I'm one of Hector's enforcers. What can I do for you, *chica*?"

TWENTY-THREE

By the time Vance Keller arrived at Citi Field, twenty thousand people had been waiting in the stadium for almost an hour. They were here this afternoon to see the president, who'd come to New York to celebrate his decision to place the city under martial law.

Vance's helicopter touched down in the parking lot outside the stadium, which was in the borough of Queens, not far from Rikers Island. Citi Field was the home of the New York Mets, but the baseball season had been suspended after Superstorm Zelda hit the East Coast. The Federal Service Unit had taken over the stadium and chartered two hundred buses to deliver the president's supporters to the rally. Most of them had come from upstate New York and central Pennsylvania, rural counties that were full of Republicans. Colonel Grant had arranged military escorts for the buses so they could safely travel through Manhattan and the Bronx and the other areas that had been overrun in the riots the night before.

A team of FSU officers saluted Vance as he stepped out of the helicopter. He nodded and followed them across the parking lot, feeling upbeat and energized. It was a gorgeous September day, warm and cloudless, seventy-five degrees at noontime. There was a slightly unpleasant smell in the air, the odor of the fires still burning in Harlem and sending plumes of smoke eastward. But other than that, the weather was perfect.

As Vance and his escorts approached the stadium, he heard a rumbling overhead. Looking up, he saw a Number 7 train on the elevated tracks a hundred yards away. It pulled in to the Citi Field station, and another thousand supporters emerged from the train cars, accompanied by several dozen men in black uniforms. The FSU had seized control of New York's subway lines, as well as its water, sewer, sanitation, and power systems. Federal officers patrolled the streets and operated checkpoints at the bridges and tunnels. Normal deliveries of food and fuel had resumed, and loyal citizens were returning to work. Meanwhile, the rioters and criminals had retreated to their slums, defeated. They'd seen the deadly might of the U.S. Army, and they wouldn't challenge it again anytime soon.

There was a crowd outside the stadium's main entrance, but it was quiet and orderly. The latecomers stood in line in front of the metal detectors, waiting for the FSU men to frisk them and check their bags. At the end of the line, some of the people had turned around to watch the helicopter land, and they pointed at Vance as he came near. He and his security team headed for the VIP entrance, but he got close enough to the crowd that he could hear them shouting. They broke into applause. They were cheering him. Most of them were overweight, he noticed, and all of them were white.

"Yo, Vance! Way to go, man!"

"That's right! Give 'em hell, Vance! Lock 'em all up!"

"Yeah, waste those motherfuckers! Send 'em back where they came from!"

Reluctantly, he stopped and waved at the crowd and winced when they cheered even louder. He hated this part of the job. He couldn't stand to look at them. They were so ugly and needy, so criminally stupid. This was why Vance usually stayed in the background and worked behind the scenes. Unlike his father-in-law, he got no pleasure from performing for these idiots.

What's more, he didn't trust them, especially the New Yorkers who'd taken the subway to the stadium. The president never had many fans in New York City, and the number had surely plunged after the helicopter assault the night before. Vance suspected that a large fraction of the people at Citi Field—maybe a quarter, maybe even a third—were really political opponents of the president. They were just pretending to be his supporters until they went inside the stadium and POTUS came onstage. Then they'd start booing and hissing and doing everything they could to disrupt his speech. The same thing had happened at nearly every rally during the reelection campaign; in fact, the protests in 2020 were so predictable that the president had actually looked forward to them. He used to taunt the protesters and encourage the rest of the crowd to attack them. It was all part of the show.

Vance winced again. He didn't like thinking about the reelection campaign. It triggered too many bad memories. Even now, as he waved at the idiots in front of the stadium, he felt a stab of horror in his stomach. For the ten thousandth time, he remembered what happened to Princess.

And along with the memories came the self-recrimination and second-guessing. He'd made so many mistakes. There were the obvious ones, of course: the policy failures that allowed a teenager to become radicalized by the internet, the security lapses that enabled the brainwashed kid to smuggle a suicide vest into the arena where Princess was speaking. But the more painful errors were Vance's personal misjudgments. He should've never let his wife go on the campaign trail. He should've resigned from the White House staff and convinced her to do the same. They should've escaped Washington while they still had the chance.

He stopped waving at the crowd but didn't lower his hand. He was sick with regret. He stood there in the parking lot for so long that one of the FSU officers edged toward him. "Sir? Shouldn't we, uh, get going?"

Vance nodded. He turned away from the crowd and marched briskly to the stadium's VIP entrance.

He couldn't change the past, but he could change the future. Today's rally was going to be different from all the others. Vance was glad that so many of his opponents were in the stadium this afternoon—they would prove the effectiveness of his strategy and the righteousness of his cause. He was going to finish the task of reconciliation that his wife had started.

He and his entourage passed through the gate and walked into the stadium's entrance hall, a grand rotunda with escalators and curved stairways going up to the Promenade Level and skyboxes. Hundreds of people were packed into this space, their progress slowed by all the security barriers and checkpoints. The air in the rotunda was stuffy and humid, despite all the newly installed ceiling fans whirring overhead, and Vance felt greatly relieved when he saw Colonel Grant standing in front of a glass door marked PRIVATE. The colonel opened the door for Vance, and the two men walked down a hushed, carpeted corridor, followed by half a dozen FSU bodyguards.

Grant gestured over his shoulder at the rotunda they'd just left. "Sorry about all the commotion back there, sir. I had to make a few last-minute adjustments, and things got a little hectic."

Vance looked at him carefully. "But is everything ready? Are we good to go?"

The colonel nodded. "Yes, sir, we got everything done in time. There shouldn't be any problems."

He sounded confident, no doubt about that, but Vance was skeptical. Was Grant blowing smoke at him, covering up something? Over the past twelve hours they'd suffered a couple of setbacks that had delayed the deployment of Phase Three. Grant claimed that the difficulties were totally unanticipated and that nothing could've been done to prevent them. But Vance was starting to wonder.

"Colonel, what's the situation with the New York police? How many of them have turned in their service guns?"

Grant didn't flinch. He looked straight at Vance as they marched down the hall. "We're continuing to have trouble with that, sir." He lowered his voice. "So far, only four thousand of the thirty-six thousand uniformed officers have surrendered their weapons. Most of the police vehicles are also unaccounted for, the NYPD's patrol cars and helicopters and harbor boats."

Vance halted in the middle of the corridor. He wanted to make it clear how distressing this piece of news was. "How did this happen? Didn't you send your teams to the precinct stations to collect the guns and vehicles?"

Grant halted too, and so did the bodyguards. The colonel gave his men a hand signal, instructing them to step back a few paces to keep them from eavesdropping. Then he turned back to Vance. "We sent teams to all seventy-seven of the precincts this morning. All but five of the station houses were empty, cleared out. No officers manning the desks, no guns in the weapons lockers, no patrol cars in the parking lots."

Vance grimaced. It was worse than he'd thought. "So is this an organized mutiny? Have the leaders of the police department instructed their officers not to cooperate with us?"

Grant nodded. "That seems to be the case. The police commissioner, Steven Hayes, is missing. So are most of the deputy commissioners and bureau chiefs. Do you remember what I told you last night, about the radio transmission that the army intelligence officers intercepted?"

"The signal from Gracie Mansion?"

"Yeah, that one. Apparently, it was transmitted at the same moment that the assault team broke into the mayor's office. The audio includes the gunshots that killed DeMarco, and some of the screaming too. Our jammers couldn't block the signal because it was a lot stronger than we expected." Grant's face seemed to harden. "It obviously had a big effect on the NYPD rank and file. And as you know, there was already friction between the New York cops and the FSU."

Vance clenched his teeth. His cheek twitched and jaw muscles quivered. He needed to calm down and think clearly. He silently chanted his mantra, reciting the words in his head: *I can't change the past, but I can change the future. I can't change the past, but I can change the future.* Then he pointed at Grant. "Well, where are the cops now? It's hard to believe that thirty thousand officers just disappeared. You must have an idea where some of them are hiding, yes?"

The colonel nodded again. "Some are lying low. They're in their homes, waiting for instructions, maybe with patrol cars hidden in their garages. But it looks like most of the officers have gathered at a handful of police facilities that were chosen because they're easy to defend. We sent drones to those sites, and the surveillance video shows that the cops are digging in. They're fortifying the places against attack."

"Where are they?"

"The biggest is Floyd Bennett Field in Brooklyn. That's the base for the police department's Aviation Unit and Emergency Service Unit, so they already have a lot of weaponry and ammunition stockpiled there. Another group of officers has gone to Rodman's Neck, the NYPD's training facility and firing range in the Bronx. And a bunch of them have holed up at the department's counterterrorism headquarters on Randalls Island, just a few miles from here."

Vance tried to picture the tactical situation, the geography of the enemy's forces. The New York cops knew they were up against the power of the U.S. Army, so they'd selected positions on islands and peninsulas on the outskirts of the city. They were well-trained and disciplined, and they had enough guns to put up a good fight. But the military would still defeat them. It was just a matter of properly allocating the government's resources.

"Colonel, I want you to request more soldiers from the Pentagon. More helicopters and armored units, and a brigade of Marines too. We need to quash this rebellion at once."

"I agree with you, sir. But I'm getting some, uh, resistance from the Department of Defense."

"Resistance?"

"Several generals on the Joint Chiefs of Staff have objected to the use of their troops to put down the riots. They're particularly concerned about the body counts from the helicopter assault last night in Manhattan."

"Which generals? I want names."

"Well, the loudest objector seems to be General Miller, the army chief of staff. He's been arguing with the joint chairman and the Marine Corps commandant, trying to convince them to challenge the White House. And the situation will definitely get worse once we order them to fight the NYPD."

Vance shook his head. He was starting to get angry. "This is outrageous. The president is their commander in chief. Any general who refuses to carry out the president's orders should be court-martialed."

Grant glanced at the FSU bodyguards, who were pretending not to hear the conversation. Then he stepped closer to Vance and bent toward his ear. "Again, sir, I agree with you, a hundred percent. But I spent twenty years in the army, most of the time working for those Pentagon bastards, so I know how stubborn they are."

"Stubborn? More like insubordinate!"

"Yes, sir, exactly. But I think the best strategy right now is to hold off on the military operations and focus on Palindrome. We've worked so long and hard on this project, and it's so close to success now. And if Phase Three is successful, it'll solve a whole lot of our other problems. You see what I'm saying, sir?"

Vance did. Despite his anger, he knew Colonel Grant was right. He closed his eyes and took a deep breath and repeated the calming words in his head: *I can change the future, I can change the future.* But when he opened his eyes, he was still angry. The feeling was too strong to be dissipated by mantras or deep breathing. To get his anger out of his system, he needed to focus it on somebody. And Grant was the only target in sight.

He glared at the colonel. "I see your point. And for the sake of your own survival, Colonel, you better pray that Palindrome succeeds. Lately, your performance has been less than inspiring."

Grant took a step backward. "What do you mean?"

"I'm referring to the defection of Dr. Weinberg. And the escape of one of your prisoners." Vance raised his voice. He wanted the bodyguards to hear this. "I have my own informants in the intelligence agencies, and they told me about your urgent radio messages after the escape last night. You haven't found them yet, have you? Neither David Weinberg nor Hamid Khan?"

The colonel widened his eyes and opened his mouth. He looked genuinely surprised. "Sir, I wasn't trying to hide anything from you. Yes, it was a disturbing incident, but it hasn't really affected Palindrome in any way."

"It's affected my opinion of your competence. You better not make any more mistakes, Colonel."

With that, Vance strode past Grant and marched down the corridor. The bodyguards followed him, but the colonel just stood there, clearly stunned and embarrassed. That's good, Vance thought. Grant had been getting too cocky. Maybe this would remind him who was in charge.

Half a minute later, Vance stepped through a doorway under a sign saying NEW YORK METS CLUBHOUSE. This was usually the baseball team's locker room, but the Secret Service had turned it into a base of operations for today's presidential address. The agents had set up a command post next to the row of players' lockers, which were more like fancy dressing alcoves, with baseball caps on the shelves and Mets uniforms on the hangers. At the center of the room were two tables, one loaded with communications and surveillance equipment, the other with an assortment of guns. About thirty Secret Service agents surrounded the tables and equipped themselves with radios and binoculars and sniper rifles, preparing for their assignments.

There were soldiers in the room too: infantry grunts in body armor, Special Operations men disguised in civilian clothes, high-ranking generals in their dress uniforms. In fact, Vance spotted General Miller, the doughy, gray-haired army chief whom Grant had complained about.

Miller and several other generals stood behind the secretary of defense, who was shaking hands with the president.

POTUS looked good. He looked remarkable, actually. He wore his standard outfit—red tie, white shirt, dark blue suit—but he seemed much less bloated than usual. His face had a healthy color, neither too pale nor too pumpkin-like, and he grinned with delight at the dour defense secretary. The president looked at least ten years younger than he had the day before, but Vance knew that his father-in-law's medical condition hadn't really improved. His doctors had injected him with a specially crafted mix of stimulants, designed to give him an energy boost that would last for an hour or two. Over the past year, these injections had become standard procedure. The president got one before each of his public appearances.

After shaking hands with the SecDef, POTUS made his way to the other generals and shook hands with them too, laughing and slapping each one on the back. Then he spotted Vance across the room and gave him a big, sweeping wave.

"Look who's here!" The president's voice was loud and hearty. "Vance, come on over and say hello to these generals! They're terrific!"

Vance shook his head and held up his index finger. This was the signal he'd devised to tell the president that they needed to talk in private.

Luckily, POTUS recognized the signal. He turned away from the generals and stepped toward Vance. The president was still grinning, flying high on his cloud of amphetamines. "Hey, did you hear the news? We got a huge crowd waiting out there, at least forty thousand people. It's tremendous!"

"We need to talk about your speech. And about those generals." Vance pointed at the men in dress uniforms. "They're not as terrific as you think."

During the president's speeches, Vance always stood on the left side of the stage, about thirty feet from his father-in-law. That way, he could watch POTUS and his audience at the same time and monitor the interactions between them. Right now the president was still waving at the crowd, pacing back and forth across the stage so he could point and smile at the people in each of the stadium's seating sections. Predictably, the crowd was going bonkers. The president's favorite song, "We Are the Champions," blared from Citi Field's loudspeakers.

The stage had been erected on what was usually the stadium's center field. Behind the podium was a giant video screen that displayed fifty-foot-high images of the president for the benefit of the people in the nosebleed seats. Immediately below the stage was a security buffer, a ten-foot-wide strip occupied only by Secret Service agents, and on the far side of the buffer was a Plexiglas barrier that held back the crowd. A few thousand people stood on the field, swarming over the tarp-covered baseball diamond, but the majority of the attendees sat in the stadium's tiered levels, filling about half of Citi Field's seats. The total attendance, according to the Secret Service, was 21,502, but the president had convinced himself that the actual number was twice as much. That was also predictable. On the subject of crowd size, he had a vivid imagination.

He kept waving at his supporters. Many of them wore bright red T-shirts left over from the 2020 reelection campaign, and they held up signs that had been distributed at the stadium's entrance, big red posters with the word VICTORY written in blocky white letters. Every few seconds the president would point at one of the signs and give a thumbs-up to the crowd, and the people would scream louder and hop up and down. He was in no hurry to begin his speech. He liked this part of the event the best, because his supporters were giving him pure adulation, unconnected to any political ideology. They were promising to love him forever, no matter what he said or did.

Behind the president, underneath the jumbo video screen, were the standard decorations. Fifty American flags stood at the back of the stage, lined up from left to right, and above them stretched a red-white-and-blue banner bearing the slogan from the 2020 campaign: KEEP AMERICA GREAT! Standing in front of the flags was a long row of generals and admirals, including all seven members of the Joint Chiefs of Staff and a dozen of their deputies. They'd taken a break from their jobs at the Pentagon so they could serve as a patriotic backdrop for the rally. Military men were good at standing at attention, even for hours. Unlike civilians, they wouldn't yawn if they got bored.

Standing beside Vance on the sidelines was Major Michael Weston, Colonel Grant's chief deputy at the FSU, a large, humorless soldier. He wore a radio headset that allowed him to communicate with all the FSU officers and Secret Service agents posted in the various sections of the stadium. His job was to give updates to Vance and relay any warnings from his men. Major Weston was less resourceful than Colonel Grant but more deferential and efficient, and that's what Vance needed right now. This event was more than just another political rally. It was the crux of Vance's plan, the linchpin of all his years of effort.

The president was still warming up the crowd. He held up both hands and gave a double thumbs-up to his supporters, who responded with the loudest cheers yet. At the same time, Major Weston nudged Vance.

"I just got an alert, sir." Weston leaned close and spoke in an undertone, even though the noise in the stadium was earsplitting and there was absolutely no chance of anyone overhearing them. "One of my plainclothes officers on the field level noticed something suspicious. Look to the far right, about fifty feet from the stage."

Vance looked in that direction but didn't see anything unusual. The field was jammed with cheering supporters and jiggling VICTORY signs. The right side of the crowd seemed identical to the left side and the middle. "I don't see anything."

"There's a bunch of young people, college-age kids, all wearing red campaign shirts. Their leader seems to be that tall guy with the scruffy beard and the blond hair." Weston tilted his head and tried to point with his chin. "See him?"

Vance squinted. After a few seconds he spotted Mr. Scruffy Beard, who looked seriously unkempt and undernourished. He was surrounded by a dozen hippie-dippie types, mostly long-haired unshaven boys and short-haired unattractive girls. Although they wore the red campaign shirts and carried VICTORY signs like everyone else, they seemed less enthusiastic than all the people around them. They didn't jump or wave their signs every time the president turned their way.

"Yes, I see." Vance turned back to Weston. "How close is your officer?"

"He's right behind them. He thinks they're wearing T-shirts under their campaign shirts, probably with some kind of protest message written on them. And he thinks one of the girls has a banner wrapped around her midsection. Wrapped tight, like a corset, under her shirt. That's how she smuggled it into the stadium."

"And we're assuming they'll cause a disruption at some point?"

"Yeah, they're probably waiting for the right moment, after the crowd quiets down. Then they'll strip off their red shirts and unfurl their banner." The major grimaced. "My officer is asking for instructions. He wants to know if he should call in a team to deal with the problem."

Vance shook his head. Arresting the protesters would spoil his plan.

He preferred to do nothing now except observe them. This strategy had no downside, because the president had banned all unfriendly journalists from the rally. There was no chance that any protest would be televised. "Leave them alone. I want to see what happens."

"Yes, sir." Weston obediently turned around and muttered the orders into his headset.

Finally, the president stopped waving and headed for the lectern at the center of the stage. "We Are the Champions" faded to silence, but the crowd kept roaring. POTUS stepped behind the lectern, spread his arms wide, and beamed like a happy child, taking it all in. Then he leaned toward the microphone.

"Thank you, everybody. Thank you so much." His voice boomed across the stadium, louder than a jet engine. "It's great to be back in my hometown, the incredible, beautiful city of New York."

The crowd erupted, bellowing their approval, even though most of the people in the stadium didn't live anywhere near New York City. Also, it was a little odd that the president was praising New York just twelve hours after his armed forces strafed Park Avenue. Vance looked at Mr. Scruffy Beard and his hippie-dippie companions, expecting to see some kind of outraged reaction to this comment. But they just stood there, plainly nervous, their heads turning this way and that.

The president waited for the cheering to die down, then leaned toward the mic again. "And what about his crowd, huh? We got more than fifty thousand people here today, which I believe is a record for this stadium. You know, when I was a kid the Beatles came to this stadium to give a concert, and everyone said that was the biggest concert in history. But we have even more people here now than the Beatles had." He nodded vigorously, confirming his own statement. "What do you think of that? We're bigger than the Beatles!"

He'd just made at least three factual errors, but his supporters didn't care. They erupted again, cheering mostly for themselves now. Vance smiled at their eagerness, their simple devotion. He'd done the right thing by choosing a baseball field for this rally. These people supported the president in the same way they cheered on their favorite sports teams. It was a matter of identifying with something big and exciting and glorious. They'd joined one of the sides in the eternal battle of us versus them, and they were going to stick with that side even if it killed them.

The president smiled and nodded for a few more seconds. Then he lowered his head and abruptly changed his expression. He closed his mouth and narrowed his eyes and beetled his eyebrows. The change was magnified on the giant video screen behind him, which turned his face into a twenty-foot-high totem, somber and ominous. "Okay, we need to get serious for a minute. I came to New York today because we have a very big problem in this country. And I think you know what the problem is, right? The corrupt Democrats are doing everything they can to sabotage our efforts. They're a bunch of liars and crooks and obstructionists. You wouldn't believe how much damage and misery they've caused."

He frowned and shook his head, looking deeply disappointed. His supporters murmured their assent, quieter now.

"We've seen some of that horrible damage right here in New York. The Democrats have devastated this city. Instead of deporting the illegal aliens like they should've done, they put out a big, friendly welcome mat for them! And you can guess what happened then, right? The illegals stole all the good jobs from American citizens, and the murderers and rapists ran wild in the streets. Look what happened just last night in Manhattan. Did everyone see the riots on television last night? Did you see what those people did to the stores and apartment buildings?"

The president waited out the chorus of agreement from the crowd. Then he shook his head again. "It made me sick to my stomach. Those people are animals. But I have something even more upsetting to tell you. I'm very sorry to have to say this, but my advisors have just confirmed the facts beyond any doubt." He paused and narrowed his eyes even more, turning them into furious slits. "Last night, the vice president went to Gracie Mansion, the home of New York's mayor, to discuss the security situation. And during that meeting, the rioters attacked the mansion. Those animals killed the mayor *and* the vice president."

Twenty thousand people gasped. They all inhaled at once, and their cries echoed across the stadium. Although Colonel Grant had started spreading the cover story the night before, and the officials in the Pentagon and the Secret Service and the FBI had already digested the news, this was the first public announcement of the deaths. The president pressed his lips together, trying his best to look grim and incensed. He knew the truth about the veep's death—Vance had given him a rough outline of it, excluding a few of the gory details—but he was good at revising the truth to suit his own needs. Now he played the role of the grief-stricken leader, the man who would acknowledge the nation's anguish and use it as a springboard for decisive action.

"I want to say a few words about our late vice president. I truly loved that man. From the moment I met him, I knew he was a true patriot, a God-fearing American hero. His deep Christian faith was an inspiration to us all. And I'm gonna tell you a secret: I was planning to support him in next year's presidential election. Although I love my job very much and wish I could stay in the White House for at least another term, I would've gladly handed it over to a man like him. He was one of the very few people in the country who could be trusted with the position."

Citi Field had gone silent. The stadium was so quiet, Vance could hear the sniffling and weeping of the more emotional supporters in the crowd. He sensed they were restraining themselves in deference to the president. In their hearts, the people wanted to rage and wail, but they were so desperate for guidance and consolation that they bit their lips and stifled their cries. They hushed themselves so they could listen to their leader. They wanted to hear every word.

"I don't have as much to say about Mayor DeMarco. I didn't know him so well, and I don't want to say anything negative about him at a time like this. But I think everyone will agree that the Democratic leaders of New York failed miserably. They created the horrible situation we saw on television last night. And it's my responsibility as president to protect the American people. So you know what I did?" He paused again for dramatic effect. "I fired those failing Democrats. I put New York under martial law, and I sent our terrific army to the city to restore order. And our soldiers did a tremendous job." He turned and pointed at the generals behind him. "So let's give a big hand to our men in uniform. They're the best, right?"

The applause was thunderous. It was so loud that the stage shivered under Vance's feet. He looked again at Mr. Scruffy Beard and the other disguised hippies, thinking they might choose this moment to take off their red campaign shirts. Presumably, the president's opponents wanted to demonstrate against martial law, and this would be the ideal time to stage their protest, while the rest of the crowd was congratulating the generals. But the malcontents did nothing. Their faces were blank. They looked uncertain, intimidated.

Meanwhile, the president reached for the microphone on his lectern. It was a wireless mic, so he was able to remove it from its stand and take it with him as he stepped away from the lectern and walked across the stage. He headed for the row of military men, but kept his eyes on the crowd. "Now I have to warn you, folks: The battle is just beginning. We're gonna need more soldiers to keep the peace in New York. We have to get this country back on the right path, and that means I'm gonna order more military operations over the next few days. I've already asked Congress to hold a special session later this afternoon. And I'm counting on the full cooperation of everyone at the Pentagon too." He turned toward his generals, looking half at them and half at the crowd. "So are you with me, guys? Are you gonna do your duty and follow my orders?"

The generals didn't say anything at first. Although they were all smart, competent officers with decades of experience under their belts, they'd never been asked to affirm their loyalty in a public arena like this, so they had no protocol for how to respond. After a couple of seconds the men turned their heads ever so slightly toward the highest-ranking general among them, the chairman of the Joint Chiefs of Staff, who was tall and brawny and completely bald. He exchanged a nervous look with the other officers, communicating without words. Then he stepped forward and saluted the president.

"Yes, sir! We'll follow your orders!" The joint chairman's voice was deep and booming, clearly audible to most of the crowd, even though he didn't have a microphone. "We're proud to serve under your command!"

The president nodded, but he didn't seem fully satisfied with the response. His blond eyebrows still hung grimly over his narrowed eyes. He stepped closer to the joint chairman. "And what happens if one of your deputies doesn't like my orders? What will you do if there's insubordination in your ranks?"

There was another brief pause. Vance looked up at the jumbo video screen and noticed that the joint chairman's bald scalp was sweating under his officer's cap. "We will respect the chain of command, sir. Anyone who doesn't follow orders will be relieved of his duties."

"That's good. I'm glad to hear it." The president nodded again. Then he stepped a couple of yards to the left and pointed at another general farther down the row, a pale, pudgy officer with gray hair. It was General Miller, the army chief of staff. "Because this officer here has been insubordinate. He refused to follow my orders to send more troops to New York City!"

Murmurs of surprise spread across the stadium. They gathered force as the thousands of supporters stared at the pair of men on the video screen, the president fuming and reddening as he pointed at Miller, who opened his mouth in shock. POTUS was doing an excellent job, following all the instructions Vance had given him and adding a few nice touches of his own. He was a natural-born actor. Even with a degenerative illness ravaging his mind and body, he could still deliver a convincing performance, as long as he was injected with enough amphetamines beforehand.

The president leaned toward General Miller and poked him in the chest. His finger jabbed one of the medals pinned to Miller's uniform. "This man objects to using army brigades to fight the rioters and insurrectionists. He doesn't care about all the Americans who were killed in the riots, including our wonderful vice president. Instead, he sympathizes with the criminals and illegal aliens who rampaged through our streets last night!"

Miller shook his head. "That's not true! I—"

"He's a fake general! He's not protecting America. He's siding with our enemies!" POTUS stepped to the right, pulling the microphone away from General Miller to prevent anyone from hearing his denials. Then the president turned back to the joint chairman. "I want you to arrest General Miller *immediately*. Remove him from his command and replace him with someone who will fight for America!"

Now the crowd roared so ferociously, the whole stadium shuddered. Although Citi Field was only half full, the president's supporters generated enough sheer volume to make up for all the vacant seats. They threw their hearts and lungs and souls into the effort, twenty thousand people screaming as one. At first it was just noise, just a storm of voices, without any meaning or message. But after a while it coalesced into a three-word chant, a deafening waltz that blasted out of the stadium and reverberated over the borough of Queens.

Vance listened carefully. The chant was so loud and throbbing, it was hard to understand the words. Was it "Four More Years, Four More Years"? Is that what the crowd was saying?

No, that wasn't it.

"LOCK HIM UP! LOCK HIM UP! LOCK HIM UP! LOCK HIM UP!"

The jumbo video screen showed the president, General Miller, and the chairman of the Joint Chiefs, arranged in a tense triangle. POTUS was still pointing at Miller and staring at the joint chairman, waiting for an answer. Miller turned his head to the left and right, trying to appeal to the generals standing beside him, but the other officers avoided eye contact. The joint chairman also refused to look at him; instead, he looked in the opposite direction and gave a hand signal to someone offstage. A few seconds later, a pair of military policemen marched over to General Miller. Each MP grabbed one of Miller's arms, and they led him away.

The crowd stopped chanting and started applauding. Twenty thousand supporters cheered and hooted and clapped until their palms were red and stinging. Vance looked one more time at Mr. Scruffy Beard and his friends, wondering if this was the moment when the protesters would finally cry foul. He waited for them to rip off their campaign shirts and unfurl their banner and denounce this latest abuse of power, this public purging of the dissenter who'd opposed the president. It was their best chance to get noticed and make a statement. Maybe one of them would shoot video of the protest and try to upload it onto Facebook or YouTube.

But the hippies didn't do any of those things. They didn't seem angry or anguished or outraged. In fact, they were indistinguishable from the rest of the crowd. They were clapping too.

Vance made sure that the president's speech didn't go on too much longer. After half an hour POTUS started to tire, and his voice grew hoarse as the stimulating effects of the amphetamine injection faded. He repeated himself a few times and scowled at the teleprompter and made a couple of ugly throat-clearing noises. So Vance gave his father-in-law the wrap-it-up signal, and the president stepped away from the lectern. He waved at the crowd again, and they cheered him off the stage.

Major Weston left too and went looking for Colonel Grant. But Vance remained on the stage while all the supporters filed out of Citi Field. Most of them returned to their chartered buses, which revved up for the long trip back to upstate New York and central Pennsylvania, but several thousand made their way to the subway station and rode the Number 7 train back to their homes in the city. Vance marveled over the fact such a large group of New York City residents had come to the rally, and not one of them had tried to disrupt the president's speech. It seemed like a statistical impossibility. He couldn't remember the last time they'd staged an event that was so trouble-free.

Once the crowd was gone—it took almost an hour for everyone to exit the stadium—Vance climbed down from the stage and walked across the tarp-covered baseball field, which was littered with discarded VICTORY signs. He headed for the section where Mr. Scruffy Beard had stood, and after several minutes he found what he was looking for: the banner that the hippies had smuggled into Citi Field. They'd abandoned it on the ground, folded and hidden beneath one of the signs. Vance picked up the banner and unfurled it. Painted on the long strip of white cloth in neon-blue letters were the words WE ARE BETTER THAN THIS.

He was still studying it when Grant appeared. The colonel grinned as he hurried across the field. His mood had improved dramatically since Vance had last seen him. "Good news, sir! We have preliminary results from the blood tests. The research team did the analysis in record time."

Vance dropped the banner. He'd ordered Grant's team to randomly select a hundred people from the crowd and get blood and tissue samples from them at the stadium's medical station. "And?"

"All the samples tested positive for the virus. Everyone was infected."

Vance turned his head and gazed at Citi Field's entrance hall, the rotunda that everyone at the rally had passed through on the way to their seats. Early that morning, Grant's research team had installed aerosol sprayers and fans on the rotunda's ceiling. The equipment was designed to spread the airborne virus to the crowd. Thanks to the unique features of this engineered microbe, they'd achieved a transmission rate of nearly 100 percent, infecting everyone except Vance, Grant, and all the other top officials who'd been vaccinated.

But infection was only the first step. Vance looked Grant in the eye. "What about the DNA tests?"

Grant's smile grew wider. "We found genetic changes in most of the tissue samples. And the changes were more advanced in the people who'd arrived earliest at the stadium. Within an hour the virus started producing CRISPR molecules inside the cells of the infected people and inserting the Serenity sequence into their DNA."

Vance smiled back at the colonel. This explained why no one in the crowd had disrupted the president's speech, not even the people who'd brought the protest banner. The virus had seeped into their brains and

remodeled their cells. It had altered their neurotransmitters and recep-
tors, making subtle tweaks to the biochemistry that governed their behavior. They were the same genetic changes that had tamed Al-Qaeda
terrorist Hassan Mohammed, but now they'd pacified twenty thousand
people at once.

This is revolutionary. Vance trembled, full of awe and triumph. *This is
going to change the world. A golden age of harmony is at hand.*

"And all the people who attended the rally are now actively infectious?"

Grant nodded. "That's right. Now they'll go home and spread the
virus to all their friends and families. And the genetic changes will
spread with it."

Vance shook his head in wonder. Phase Three had begun.

TWENTY-FOUR

Frazier was humiliated. Although he'd made plenty of mistakes during his years in the army and the Federal Service, he'd never been jailed before. Now he sat in one of the Research Center's detention cells, where they usually kept the prisoners that the Palindrome researchers were experimenting on. And the worst part was, he deserved it. He'd fucked up royally.

Thirteen hours ago, at 2 a.m., he'd emerged from Room 17 and raised the alarm, informing his fellow FSU officers that Raza Khan was dead and his father Hamid had escaped, apparently with the help of Dr. David Weinberg. Frazier alerted the guards at the Rikers gate and ordered them to stop Weinberg, but the guards reported that the scientist had left the jail complex in his car fifteen minutes before, accompanied by an older man whom he'd identified as one of his research colleagues. When the officers asked Frazier why he hadn't tried to stop the escapees before they left Room 17, he told them the truth: he'd blacked out while questioning Weinberg and Hamid, and by the time he'd regained consciousness, Raza was dead and the fugitives were long gone.

Needless to say, no one believed him. After a heated discussion, Frazier's fellow officers led him to the detention cell.

The first round of questioning took place ten minutes later in Frazier's cell, and it was relatively brief. The interrogators—a pair of FSU officers who worked in a different division of the agency—asked Frazier if either Weinberg or Hamid Khan was armed. "Not to my knowledge," he answered. Then they asked if he knew where the escapees were headed. He replied that he had no idea. Then they asked the most important question, the one that had been on their minds all along: why did he black out? Did Weinberg and Khan overpower him? And if so, how the hell did those two measly creatures manage to subdue a genetically enhanced soldier?

Frazier had no answer. Or rather, he had an answer, but he couldn't say it. It was just too fucking bizarre.

The interrogators left his cell, and then the doctors came in. It looked like they were willing to at least consider the possibility that he'd really lost consciousness. So they poked and prodded him and took samples of his blood and piss and skin, probably for DNA testing. Then they left him alone, and he napped on the cell's bunk for a couple of hours. Shortly after dawn, though, the interrogators returned and asked him the same questions, this time with greater hostility and skepticism. Frazier was tempted to tell them the whole story, including all the strange details he still didn't understand—the confrontation with Raza, the sudden immersion in the kid's memories, the picnic on Coney Island Beach that ended so horribly. But he kept his mouth shut. Better to seem uncooperative than to make them think he'd gone crazy.

There were two more rounds of questioning, one in the late morning and one in the early afternoon. Then, at 3 p.m., Colonel Grant himself stepped into Frazier's cell. The two FSU interrogators came in with him, but after a few seconds he ordered them to wait outside in the corridor. Once they were out of earshot, Grant stepped toward Frazier's bunk and pointed at him. The colonel's face was hard and unforgiving.

"Get on your feet, Lieutenant."

Frazier rose from his bunk. This was his last chance. If he didn't say something now, they were going to lock him up forever. "Sir? There's something you should know. Something I haven't mentioned yet to anyone."

"All right, spit it out."

Frazier nodded. "It was that freak, Raza Khan. He's the reason why I blacked out."

Grant stepped closer. The look on his face was dead serious. "You're saying the cripple did it? Before he died on us?"

"I know it sounds crazy, sir, but that kid did something to me. He got into my head and started screwing around with my thoughts. I swear, it was like fucking telepathy. He couldn't move his body, but he could do things with his mind." Frazier tapped his own temple for emphasis. "I'm telling you, sir, the freak planned the whole thing. He was trying to help his dad escape, so he messed with my head and Weinberg's head too. That's why Weinberg started acting and talking like he was hypnotized. Somehow the kid figured out how to manipulate him."

The colonel said nothing at first. He just stared at Frazier, tilting his head up so he could look him in the eye. *Now I'm fucked*, Frazier thought. *Instead of putting me in prison, they're gonna ship me off to the nuthouse.*

But after a few seconds, Grant stretched his arm toward Frazier and clasped his shoulder. "You're right, Lieutenant. That's exactly what happened."

Frazier was so surprised, he couldn't tell if Grant was serious or not. Maybe the colonel was making fun of him. "So . . . you don't think I'm crazy?"

Grant shook his head. "Not at all. But if I were you, I wouldn't tell anyone else about it. You and I are the only people who witnessed this . . . this phenomenon." He frowned. "The freak tried to get inside my head too. You saw what he did to me."

"You mean, during the inspection tour last night? When we passed Room Seventeen?"

"That was the worst attack. The effect got stronger when I was near him. It almost drove me out of my fucking mind."

Frazier recalled something else from the night before. "Before I blacked out, Weinberg showed me the freak's brain waves. He said the CRISPR treatment had changed the way the kid's mind worked."

The colonel reached into his pocket and pulled out a folded sheet of paper. "Yeah, Weinberg was studying the electrical activity in Raza's brain, and he detected a big spike in the intensity of the signals." Grant unfolded the paper, which was a copy of the EEG results that Frazier had seen the night before. "We found this printout in Room Seventeen after Weinberg and Hamid ran off. I won't pretend to understand all this shit, but I can tell you what my staff researchers said when they examined the thing. Apparently, the signals in Raza Khan's head were hundreds of times more powerful than a normal brain wave. They were strong enough to extend beyond the kid's skull and generate electromagnetic fields in the surrounding area. Kind of like a biological radio, see?"

Frazier stared at the jagged lines on the EEG printout. Now that he knew what they meant, the curves and twists looked sinister. "So he sent out his thoughts like radio signals? That's how they got into my head?"

"They went right through your skull and interfered with your own signals. And the freak tried to do the same thing to me." Grant scowled at the sheet of paper in his hand. "It was a nasty fucking trick, and with practice the kid got better at it. Once he was confident enough, he must've pumped up his brain to maximum volume so he could hypnotize Weinberg and get him to free Hamid. And when you came into Room Seventeen, the freak revved up his brain again so he could knock you out. But he must've pushed himself too far and blown a fuse or something. We're doing an autopsy on him right now to see what happened."

"Jesus." Frazier couldn't help but be impressed. "He sacrificed himself."

"I wouldn't get too sentimental about it." Grant lifted his head and aimed his scowl at Frazier. Then he refolded the printout and stuck it back in his pocket. "I, for one, am very fucking glad the freak is dead. Now we just have to clean up the mess he made. Weinberg knows everything about Palindrome, so we need to track down that asshole and drag him back here. That'll be your job, Lieutenant."

Frazier pointed at himself. "You mean I'm cleared for duty? I can go back to work?"

"Yeah, you're good to go. Sorry to keep you locked up for so long, but we needed to test your DNA, and then I had to go to Queens to get Phase Three started. Believe me, you're lucky you missed that shit show. That fucking Vance Keller is worse than all the Khans put together."

"Sir, what's the status of the search for Weinberg? Where have you looked so far?"

Grant spread his arms wide. "We sent his picture to every Federal Service team in the city, but no one's spotted him yet. The problem is, he could be hiding in a million places, and we don't have the manpower to look everywhere. Because the New York cops won't cooperate with us, the FSU has to keep the peace in the whole goddamn city, and that leaves us pretty stretched."

Frazier stared at the floor and thought it over for a moment. "Well, we can make a guess about Weinberg at least. Raza did a real number on that guy's brain. The kid hypnotized the shit out of him, so there's a chance that Weinberg is still following the instructions the freak gave him last night. And one of those instructions was probably *Take my dad to Jenna*. So if we can find her, we'll also find Weinberg and Hamid." He raised his head and looked at Grant. "But we don't know where Jenna is either, do we?"

"No, we don't. But I know someone who might give us a clue to her whereabouts." Grant stuck out his thumb and pointed it behind him. "And he's right here in the maximum-security wing."

"Who?"

"Your old commander, Derek Powell. He survived."

It took Frazier a while to get over his dismay. He'd seen Powell on the operating table the night before, his torso split open, his heart failing, his vital signs flatlining. Frazier had convinced himself that the man would die and justice would be served. So the news of Powell's survival hit him hard. It shattered his belief in a righteous universe. Frazier thought of the checkpoint at Bay Parkway, the truck crashing through the fence, the dead boy floating in the floodwaters. It was all Powell's fault. How could he be allowed to get away with it?

And Colonel Grant told Frazier something else that made the news even worse. After Powell regained consciousness an hour ago—the doctors had moved his gurney to a detention cell—he'd refused to talk to the FSU interrogators. They'd made threats and promises, even offering to pardon Powell if he cooperated, but he wouldn't say a word. When Grant paid a visit to the cell and approached Powell's bedside, the bastard just closed his eyes and turned away.

The colonel hadn't given up, though. He wanted Frazier to try talking to the traitor. It didn't seem logical—why would Powell open up to the man who'd nearly killed him? But an order was an order, and Frazier was a loyal soldier. He saluted Grant, marched out of his detention cell, and headed for Powell's.

The doctors had moved some medical equipment into the traitor's cell, as well as an extra-large gurney. The bed was more than seven feet long from head to foot, and yet it was barely large enough to hold Powell. His wrists and ankles had been cuffed to the bed rails, and thick belts had been strapped across his thighs and chest to keep him down on the mattress. As an extra precaution, two FSU officers armed with handguns stood by the door, ready to cut down Powell if he tried to break free of his restraints. Frazier eyed the bed and the officers, double-checking all the security measures until he was satisfied. Then he took a good look at his former commander.

Powell was alive, but just barely. His giant body lay on the bed like a mound of black earth, half covered by a tentlike hospital gown. His arms and legs, heavy and limp, poked out from under the gown's blue fabric, which rose and fell ever so slightly as he breathed. His face looked deflated, the skin hanging loose over his skull, his eyes closed and his mouth open, his scalp covered with thin black stubble. All in all, he seemed exposed and helpless, and Frazier felt a rush of satisfaction at the sight. This was worse than death, he thought. This was utter defeat.

But as Frazier stepped closer to the bed, he noticed several changes that told a different story. Frazier's memory was so good that he could recall exactly what Powell looked like yesterday afternoon, when they'd fought on the glass-strewn floor of the mausoleum, and he remembered seeing an ulcerous lesion on the side of Powell's neck. The lesion was closed now and almost healed. Powell's skin also looked healthier—the pale patches on his face were shrinking—and his lungs didn't rattle anymore when he inhaled. And a few seconds later, when the giant finally opened his eyes, Frazier saw that they weren't bloodshot at all. Powell looked right at him, calm and cool.

Frazier tensed. His former commander had been given a new CRISPR injection designed to repair the genetic damage caused by the earlier treatments. That's why his eyes had stopped bleeding and his lungs had stopped rattling. Although Powell was still recovering from his wounds right now, very soon he would grow stronger than ever. That made him a danger to everyone on Rikers Island, no matter how many belts and handcuffs tied him down.

Wary, Frazier stopped in his tracks. He glared at Powell, but at the same time he stayed more than five feet away from the hospital bed. "Well, well.

It looks like the doctors patched you up. It probably wasn't easy putting you back together after the shit-kicking I gave you yesterday."

Powell didn't react. He just stared at Frazier in that cool, indifferent way, as if he was watching a TV ad for car insurance. He seemed completely uninterested.

Frazier glanced again at the FSU officers at the door, his backup. Then he turned back to Powell. "If it was up to me, I would've let you bleed out. I don't have a lot of sympathy for deserters. Especially when they take sides with the enemy. Only the most fucked-up kind of cocksucker would do something like that."

Powell's eyes glazed over. If he were actually watching TV, he would've changed channels by now. Frazier realized that this strategy wasn't working—he couldn't prod Powell into conversation by insulting him. The situation called for a little more creativity.

After a few seconds, Frazier tried something else. "You know what pisses me off the most? I used to respect you. I used to think you were the bravest goddamn soldier in the U.S. Army." He pointed at Powell. "Remember the ambush at the start of our last tour, about a week after we flew into Afghanistan? When the jihadis surrounded us at that shitty outpost in Marjah?" He paused, hoping for some kind of response, but Powell said nothing. "We had no air support, no armor, no heavy guns. And this was months before we got the Palindrome shots. But you weren't worried. You even seemed happy about it. You remember what you said to the platoon?"

Still no reaction from Powell. He just kept staring.

"Okay, I'll remind you. You said, 'Drop your cocks and grab your socks, boys. It's showtime.' And we put on a show, all right. We didn't give a shit if we lived or died. We just followed your lead and killed every last one of those towel-heads." Frazier raised his voice. He was getting hot and angry. "And that's the problem, see? Because you're different now. Just six months ago, you were a war hero, and now you're a fucking traitor. You turned against your country and started knocking boots with burqa bitches like Jenna Khan. And I can't understand it. What got into you, Powell? What the fuck happened?"

Frazier was out of breath by the time he finished. He'd worked himself up, getting more furious by the second, and now he was shaking. And it wasn't because Powell had betrayed his country, America the Beautiful,

Home of the Brave. No, this was personal. Powell had betrayed *him*. He'd tossed Frazier aside like a piece of garbage.

But even as Frazier trembled with rage, he saw the change in Powell's expression. The man narrowed his eyes. He seemed to be irritated by something Frazier had said. "I didn't touch Jenna. I never touched her."

His voice was surprisingly loud. Frazier felt the urge to step farther away from the hospital bed, but he stood his ground. He needed to keep Powell talking. "What were you doing with her then? Why did you help her escape from the arresting officers?"

Powell frowned. He probably regretted opening his mouth, but now that he'd started talking he couldn't stop. "I thought she could cure me."

"Cure you?"

"She worked on Palindrome. She was one of the scientists. From what I could tell, she was the smartest one." He shrugged, moving his shoulders as much as his restraints would allow. "So I thought she'd be the best person to fix me."

Frazier was confused. "Wait a second. When did you find out about her? Back when we were in Afghanistan?"

"No. All I knew then was that something was wrong with me. And the army wasn't interested in fixing it. They just wanted to study us, and they swept all their mistakes under the rug." Powell raised his head off his pillow and looked Frazier in the eye. "You remember Colson? And Spinelli?"

Frazier nodded. They were two of the Palindrome subjects in their platoon who had to be shipped back home. Probably to a VA hospital, given their mental condition. But both those guys were pretty screwed-up to begin with, even before they got the injections. "Look, we all knew there were risks. That's why they offered the ten-thousand-dollar bonus for volunteering. But what you did? Deserting the battlefield? That was just wrong. You put yourself above everyone else. It was cowardly."

At first Frazier worried that he'd gone too far. He thought Powell would get enraged and try to lunge at him, despite the belt across his chest and the handcuffs on his wrists. But Powell didn't try to break free. He looked at Frazier for a few more seconds, furrowing his brow, clearly struggling with his emotions. Then his head sank back to the pillow, and the look of defeat reappeared on his face. "Yeah, I messed up. The whole thing was a disaster."

Frazier didn't know what to say. He hadn't expected Powell to give up so easily. "You should've trusted Colonel Grant. You should've talked to him as soon as you started having problems. Grant's a reasonable man. I mean, just look at how he's treated you in the past twenty-four hours. He saved your life and got you a brand-new CRISPR treatment to fix all your symptoms."

"You're right. I was stupid." Powell closed his eyes. "Jenna couldn't cure me. She said she couldn't do it alone, but I don't think she even wanted to." He took a deep breath and slowly let it out. "She only cared about her father and brother. She couldn't wait to get away from me."

He fell silent and took another deep breath. It looked like he was tired of talking and wanted to go back to sleep.

Frazier was disappointed. His former commander seemed so listless and beaten. He didn't sound like a soldier anymore; he sounded more like a homeless guy, a sad, decrepit bum, someone who'd given up on everything. In a way, this change in his personality was even more disorienting than his desertion and rebellion. It was a bigger step away from his true character.

But there was a reason for the change, Frazier remembered, a biological explanation. The new CRISPR treatment was at work inside his body, inserting the Serenity sequence into Powell's DNA. Within the cells of his brain, the CRISPR molecules were making the same genetic changes that had calmed the leader of the Yemeni terrorists, the fat Al-Qaeda asshole in the interrogation room. The new sequence was curbing Powell's rebelliousness and restraining his aggression. It was pacifying him.

Or at least that's what Frazier assumed was happening. He couldn't be sure about Powell's transformation until he put it to the test. He stepped closer to the gurney and leaned over the man. "Powell? It's not too late to make this right. There's still a chance for you to help Colonel Grant and the Palindrome Project. And if you help us out, I'm sure the colonel will take that into account when he's deciding the appropriate punishment for your actions."

Powell kept his eyes closed. He turned his head on the pillow, as if shaking off a bad dream. "Help? I can't help you. I'm no good. I'm useless."

"Listen carefully. We have to find Jenna Khan. We think she's associating with another Palindrome defector, and we need to arrest both of them before they interfere with the project. Do you know where Jenna is?"

Powell lay still. For a moment Frazier wondered whether he'd slipped back into unconsciousness. But after several seconds the man shook his head. "No. I have no idea."

"Don't lie to me, Powell. I was there in the mausoleum when you told Jenna to run off. You said, 'I'll find you.' That means you knew where she was going. Did you make plans to meet her somewhere?"

Powell shook his head again, still keeping his eyes closed. "We didn't make any plans. I told you, she wants nothing to do with me."

Frazier bent lower over the bed. His face was less than a foot from Powell's. "Think harder, Captain. This is your last chance. You can spend the rest of your life in a prison cell, kept alive only because the scientists want to study you, or you can try to win your way back into honorable service, doing your part to defend your country." He bent even closer to Powell and lowered his voice to a grim whisper. "You were with Jenna Khan for a whole night and day, so you must've spent at least some of that time talking with her. Did she mention any places where she thought she could hide or get help? Any place at all?"

Powell opened his eyes. He seemed startled and uneasy, as if he'd just remembered something. "There was an address. That newspaper reporter gave her an address." He looked straight at Frazier. "It happened in the sentry tower on Bay Parkway. Right after the shootings two nights ago."

Frazier's heart started thudding. "A reporter? Was his name Keating?"

Powell nodded on his pillow. "Yeah, that's it. He wanted her to deliver his iPhone to someone named Tamara. Because the phone had video of the shootings."

"What was the address?"

Powell didn't have to struggle to recall it. The CRISPR injections had enhanced his memory too. "It was 168 Prospect Park West."

Frazier smiled. The address was in Brooklyn, not far from Green-Wood Cemetery. It would take him only fifteen minutes to reach it by helicopter.

"Thank you, Powell. That's very helpful." Frazier was thinking ahead, already planning the raid, deciding how many officers he'd need. "I'm sure Colonel Grant will be pleased when he—"

"And there's something else. Hector Torres. The Latin King." Powell lifted his head and tried to sit up, straining against the belt across his chest. His eyes were fervent and angry now. "We met him at the cemetery, and that fucker started coming on to Jenna. He was in the shoot-out with your men afterward, and I don't know if he survived or escaped. But if he did, I bet he went after her."

This piece of information was also interesting, but not as useful as the address. Frazier needed something more specific. "Hector Torres? He's a leader of the gang?"

"He said he was building an alliance of all the gangs in the city. And he even told us where their headquarters was." Powell's cheek twitched. "The Triborough Houses. In East Harlem."

TWENTY-FIVE

A nineteen-year-old Latin King named Carlos Vilomar was showing Jenna how he'd put the iPhone videos on the internet. He and Jenna sat in front of a computer in Carlos's grandmother's apartment, which was in a housing project on East 124th Street. The Latin Kings had lived up to the promise Hector Torres had made: They'd done everything Jenna had asked, and more.

The apartment was apparently one of the gang's meeting places. Every night the young men gathered in the living room to eat and talk and play video games while Carlos's grandmother puttered in the kitchen and her bedroom. The Latin Kings had brought Jenna here after their encounter in Central Park the night before, and she'd crashed on the living-room sofa, but now it was late in the afternoon and she was alone with Carlos. He was the most tech-savvy member of the gang, so the others had assigned him to help Jenna upload the videos. They sat side by side on the couch, staring at the screen of a laptop propped on the coffee table.

Jenna liked Carlos. He was short and skinny and wore a Simpsons T-shirt that made him look a few years younger than his age, but he was also terrifically smart and bursting with energy. He waved his hands in front of the laptop's screen as he explained how he'd used Tor—The Onion Router—to hide his internet activity from the federal government. He kept brushing his long black hair from his eyes, and after a while Jenna suspected he was crushing on her. Or maybe, because he was nerdy and inexperienced, he was simply thrilled to have a chance to talk to a woman. Either way, it was sweet and flattering, a pleasant distraction. It helped Jenna forget—at least for a few minutes—all the horrendous things she'd seen the night before.

Carlos pointed at the screen, which displayed a page of gibberish, thousands of random characters packed together in a dense block that seemed to go on forever. "Okay, the first step is encryption. When I upload a video using Tor, the software encrypts my data and makes it unreadable, see? Then it sends the file to a randomly selected computer in the Tor network. Then that computer sends it to another machine in the network, also randomly selected. And then *that* machine sends the file to a third computer."

Jenna nodded, enjoying his explanation. Carlos was Dominican—he'd said his grandmother had brought him to the United States when he was a baby—but he spoke English without a trace of an accent. He was so clever, Jenna couldn't understand why he was with the Latin Kings. He should've been in college.

"That's how Tor hides your identity, see? The video file bounces around the layers of the network, and all the steps in its random journey are hidden, encrypted. By the time it comes out of the network and goes to YouTube or Facebook, no one can tell where it came from." Carlos cupped his right hand, as if he were holding a ball, and moved it in zigzags, as if he were bouncing it around. "They call it The Onion Router because of all the layers of security. I used it to upload your videos to dozens of websites, and it was totally anonymous. Pretty cool, right?"

She nodded again, smiling. Now Jenna realized why she liked Carlos so much: He reminded her of Raza. Ten years ago, her brother had been the smartest kid in his middle school. He won chess tournaments and spelling bees and was the star of the math team. Then his illness worsened and they'd had to pull him out of school, but Jenna sensed that his mind still churned with intelligence even after he became unable to talk or write or use the computer. That's why she'd tried so hard to cure him.

If she could've fixed Raza's genetic flaws, he would've regained his abilities. He would've become like Carlos, a young man full of energy and cleverness.

Jenna leaned across the sofa and nudged him. "What about the text file I gave you, the one titled Palindrome? Did you put that up on the websites too?"

"Yeah, I packaged all the files together." Carlos reached for the laptop's touch pad, did a Google search, and clicked on one of the links. "After I uploaded them, the government ordered YouTube and some of the other websites to take down the videos, but lots of people started sharing the files as soon as they went up, so they're everywhere now. They've gone viral, see?"

Jenna looked over his shoulder at the laptop's screen, which displayed the home page of a conspiracy-theory website called TruthIsNotFree.com. The page had links to both videos—the massacre in Brooklyn and the helicopter assault in Manhattan—as well as the text file containing everything Jenna knew about the Palindrome Project. She'd spent hours writing it all down, detailing her own research on CRISPR and what she'd learned from Derek Powell about the human experiments. Now she wanted to see how the text looked on the laptop, but Carlos clicked on one of the other files instead. The screen went black, and after a few seconds a video began to play.

It was the one Jenna shot on Park Avenue the night before, the footage of the helicopters. Once again she saw the aircraft swoop over the street and speed toward the crowd of rioters. Her throat tightened, and she felt a hot rush of adrenaline. Leaning forward, she stabbed the touch pad and stopped the video.

"Sorry, Carlos." She could barely speak. "Seeing it once was enough for me."

His face reddened. He gave her an apologetic look and closed the laptop. "Yeah, sure. I understand." He edged away from her, shifting his weight on the sofa cushions. He seemed less confident now that he didn't have a computer screen to point at. "But you did the right thing, you know? Everyone else was running away, but you stood there and pointed the phone at the sky. That was really brave."

They were both silent for a while. Jenna could hear the boy's grandmother cleaning plates in the kitchen. They'd shared an early dinner not too long ago, chicken and rice and plantains, and now Jenna was rested and her stomach was full. But she was also at a loss. She'd kept her promise to Tamara and broadcast the videos, but she had no idea what kind of impact they would have. Would the evidence of the massacres and the Palindrome experiments trigger protests across the country? And would the public outrage be strong enough to topple the FSU, or at least force them to release their thousands of detainees? That had been Jenna's intention, and now she was hopeful and desperate at the same time. If this plan didn't work, she didn't know what else to do. She couldn't think of another way to help her father and brother.

She turned back to Carlos. "So what kinds of reactions are we getting?"

He started to reopen the laptop, but he resisted the impulse. "Well, there are a lot of angry posts on Twitter and Facebook and the comments sections of the websites. People are blaming the army for the shootings, blaming the president. But, uh, some of the comments are just ridiculous."

"What do you mean?"

Carlos seemed reluctant to answer. "Okay, this is crazy, but some people are saying the videos were faked. They're saying they can prove it was all done with camera tricks and computer graphics. And because of that possibility, the major news sites like CNN won't run the videos or say anything about the experiments. It's kind of fucked up."

Jenna shook her head. She couldn't believe it. "I didn't fake anything! I'm telling the truth!"

Carlos edged farther away, retreating to the other end of the couch. It looked like he was reconsidering his crush on her. "No, no, I believe you. But people are stupid, you know? And there are so many lies out there."

She rose to her feet and stormed across the living room. She was furious. She was so pissed off, she wanted to scream.

Jenna stopped at the far end of the room, next to the apartment's front door, and looked down at the carpet. She'd always known that the world was full of liars, but she'd never been their target before. It was vile, infuriating, frustrating beyond belief. And she suspected that at least a few of those liars worked for the White House. It was one of their favorite tactics, using deliberate falsehoods to discredit their enemies. They'd done it so often, on so many issues, that no one could recognize the truth anymore.

Carlos gazed at her nervously from across the room. At first Jenna was too incensed to talk to him, but after a while she calmed down. She took a deep breath and started toward him, hoping to resume their conversation. But then the apartment's front door swung open behind her, and Hector Torres stepped inside.

He smiled, his dark eyes gleaming under the crown tattoo on his sweaty forehead. The leader of the Almighty Latin King Nation wore a black T-shirt and a gold bandanna. *"Buenas tardes, chica.* It's good to see you again."

Jenna smiled back at him. But before she could say anything, Carlos jumped off the sofa and bounded toward them. He raised his right hand and made the Latin King sign, bending his middle and ring fingers. *"Amor de Rey,* King Hector!" He had an awed look on his face. "I did everything you ordered. The iPhone videos are on the Web."

Hector made the gang sign too. *"Amor de Rey,* Carlos. I knew I could count on you." Then he turned back to Jenna. "I was worried about you. There were so many FSU *pendejos* in that cemetery. But it looks like you got out of there without a scratch. You're more beautiful than ever."

Jenna shook her head. "Let's not start with that again, okay? We need to talk about the Feds. And make a plan."

"Yes, yes, we have many things to discuss. But first I have a gift for you."

"Hector, I don't want—"

"Please, *chica.*" He winked at her. "You'll like this gift. I promise."

Hector stepped back to the door, held it open, and waved at someone standing in the corridor outside the apartment. A moment later, a balding man in khakis and a polo shirt came inside.

It was her father.

For the first half minute Jenna didn't say a word. She just hugged him. She held him tight.

His rib cage quivered under his shirt. Abbu was crying. He jutted his chin over her shoulder and buried his face in her hair, but she could still hear his muffled sobs. He smelled like sweat. He looked exhausted.

Hector and Carlos gave them some privacy. The two Latin Kings left the living room and joined Carlos's grandmother in the kitchen. The old woman had finished doing the dishes, and now the loudest sound in the apartment was the ticking of the clock that hung on the wall above the couch. The clock was shaped like a sunflower. Its hour and minute hands pointed at the petals.

Finally, Jenna pulled back and looked into her father's eyes. The question was burning inside her. It couldn't wait. "Where's Raza?"

He didn't answer. He tried to speak, but his lips only trembled. His silence terrified her.

"What's wrong?" Her voice rose high and sharp. "Is he okay?"

"I . . . I don't know." Tears seeped down his cheeks. "We had to leave him behind . . . at Rikers."

"He's still in the prison?" She tightened her grip on his shoulders. "Abbu, what happened? Why did they let you out of jail, but not Raza?"

"Jenna, please. I need to sit down."

He leaned against her, close to collapse. She quickly led him to the sofa, then sat down beside him. "I'm so sorry! Do you want a glass of water? Or maybe something to eat?"

"No, not yet. Let me rest a moment." Abbu leaned back against the cushions. He took a few deep breaths, and after a while he managed to smile. "Yes, that's better. I was walking for hours. We left the car in Queens, and then we had to take a very long route here, to get around all the checkpoints."

Jenna rested her hand on his shoulder. "It's all right. You're safe now."

He stopped smiling. "No, I'm afraid not. The FSU didn't let me out of jail. I escaped."

She almost laughed. She assumed he was joking. "Come on. You're kidding, right?"

"One of the scientists at the complex helped me get out. It was your old boyfriend, Jenna. David Weinberg."

She let go of Abbu's shoulder. The surprise left her breathless. She'd known that David had continued to work on Palindrome after she was fired from the project, and she'd also known that the labs had relocated to Rikers Island. But she hadn't expected her father to meet him there. "Wait, how did this happen? You saw David? You ran into him at the jail?"

"He was assigned to study Raza. Specifically, your treatment for Raza's illness. The scientists at Rikers found out what you did, and it made them curious, because it wasn't like any of the genetic treatments they'd worked on." Abbu raised his hand and touched his balding head. "Dr. Weinberg attached electrodes to Raza's head and measured his brain waves. And he did the same thing to me."

This was an even more disturbing surprise. Jenna couldn't understand it. "How . . . how could David do that? Didn't he recognize you and Raza?"

"Yes, he knew who we were. But that didn't stop him from studying us. He followed the orders they gave him."

"I don't get it. David agreed to examine and test you, and then he helped you escape? It doesn't make sense."

"Jenna, I need to tell you something." Abbu reached toward her and clasped both of her hands in his own. "It's upsetting, but you need to hear it. Something bad happened to Raza when you gave him that genetic treatment. You changed his genes in a new way, something no one else had ever done, and it made him different. It wasn't obvious at first, but after the arrest he got so scared from being in prison and separated from me. That's when he learned to use the new abilities you gave him."

She shook her head. "No, that's ridiculous. I didn't give Raza anything. All I did was try to repair one gene, the one that caused his illness. And even that didn't work. I just made his symptoms worse."

"You did more than that. I know you didn't intend it, but Dr. Weinberg said your CRISPR treatment rewired Raza's brain. It changed other genes that affect the nervous system, and those changes made his thoughts more intense, more electrically powerful. So powerful they could enter someone else's head."

Now she did laugh. She couldn't help it. "Sorry, I—"

"I'm serious." He frowned and squeezed her hands. "I heard Raza's thoughts. Nothing came out of his mouth, but I heard him just the same. When we were in Room Seventeen, he told me to find you. He said, 'Find my *baji* and tell her I'm okay.'"

Jenna composed herself and put a sober expression on her face. "All right, let me explain why that's impossible. The power of a neural signal in the brain is less than a billionth of a watt. The electrical activity is so weak, you have to put the electrodes right on the scalp to detect it. And billions of signals are flowing through the brain all at once. Even if you could detect them from a distance, you could never untangle one thought from all the others."

"You're right, I don't understand the science. But I heard Raza talking to me inside my head. I'm telling you, I heard him clear as day."

Jenna gave him a sympathetic look. "Listen, the mind is very suggestible. When people are under stress, they sometimes imagine hearing voices, and it can seem very real."

"I didn't imagine it!" He raised his voice, frustrated. "And neither did Weinberg. Raza put his thoughts into Weinberg's head and forced him to do things. Like helping me escape. Raza ordered him to do it. Your brother stayed behind because he knew a cripple couldn't get past the guards, but he made the escape plan for me, and he got Weinberg to carry it out."

She shook her head again. "No, there's a more reasonable explanation. Maybe David was planning all along to help you, but he had to keep it secret from the other researchers at Rikers. So he waited for the right moment."

"Then how do you explain what happened to the soldier? When that thug tried to stop us, Raza knocked him out cold! And he did it with his mind! He didn't need to lift a finger!"

Jenna stared at her father. In all likelihood, he was just too tired to think straight. He'd been through hell, and now he was delirious. What he needed was a good night's sleep. Then he'd come back to normal.

She decided to change the subject. "Abbu, where's David now?"

He let go of her hands and looked out the window. The late-afternoon light was slanting down 124th Street, shining on all the buildings in the housing project and on the girders of the Triborough Bridge to the east. Her father pointed in that direction. "Weinberg went to Randalls Island. You know, the island under the bridge, where all the baseball fields are."

"Why did he go there?"

Abbu shrugged. "I don't know. We walked together as far as 103rd Street, and then Weinberg said I could find you at the Triborough Houses, a mile farther north. And then he walked across the bridge at 103rd, that footbridge to Randalls, which doesn't have a checkpoint because it's only for pedestrians. That was at least an hour ago." He stretched his arms above his head and yawned. "It took me a long time to find you here. I asked everyone in front of the building if they knew where you were, and finally that young man with the bandanna told me to follow him."

"Well, it's almost six o'clock now. Do you want to—"

"What did you say?" He looked at her, alarmed, his eyes wide open. "Almost six?"

Jenna nodded, pointing at the sunflower clock on the wall. "Is something wrong? You look worried."

He stared at the clock, as if in disbelief. "God, I didn't realize it was so late!" He got up from the couch, banging his knees against the coffee table. "We have to get out of here!"

"Why? What's going on?" Jenna stood up too, her legs trembling.

Abbu grabbed her elbow and started pulling her across the living room. "That was one of Raza's instructions! He said we had to leave the building by six. No later!"

She stopped, digging the heels of her sneakers into the living-room carpet. "You heard Raza say this? Inside your head?"

"Please, Jenna!" He got a better grip on her arm and tried to drag her toward the apartment's front door. "The soldiers are coming!"

Carlos dashed out of the kitchen to see what the trouble was. Hector followed at a more leisurely pace and grinned as he approached Jenna's father. *"Señor,* where are you going? You just got here."

Abbu turned toward the Latin Kings and pointed out the window. "The FSU is going to raid the building! They'll be here any minute!"

Hector kept grinning. "Calm down, *Señor.* I always take precautions. Two of my friends are on the rooftop, keeping an eye on everything. They'll warn us if any *Federales* come near."

Abbu shook his head. "No, we're going!" He looked over his shoulder at Jenna. "Just trust me, okay? Can you do that? Please?"

She glanced at Hector and Carlos, then turned back to her father. He was acting like a madman, feverish and unhinged. She wanted to tell him to go back to the couch and relax, maybe lie down for a few hours. But Abbu's gaze was so desperate. He was pleading with her, begging to be believed. And because he was her father, Jenna was willing to at least pretend to believe him. She owed him that much.

She took his hand and headed for the apartment's door. "All right, where do you want to go?"

"Just away from here. Far away." He ran ahead, opened the door, and stepped into the corridor. "We'll figure out the rest later."

Hector and Carlos followed them out of the apartment. It was on the building's ground floor, so within fifteen seconds all of them marched down the corridor and rushed through the lobby. Abbu hesitated for a moment after they stepped outside, and then he started walking south. He pulled Jenna along, striding across the playground that lay in the shadows of the housing project's buildings.

Hector caught up to them and walked beside Jenna. He was still grinning. "I admire you, *chica.* You have great respect for your father, and that's very rare. But we're not in any danger right now. Here, I'll prove it to you."

He turned around to face the building they'd just exited and looked up at its roof, sixteen stories above them. Then he inserted his thumb and middle finger into his mouth and let out a piercing whistle. *"Hey, Luis! Manuel! I need a status report! Do you see any—"*

Jenna heard the crack of a gunshot, distant but unmistakable. She looked up and saw a boy in a black-and-gold tracksuit on the roof, running with his head down. A moment later, another gunshot resounded overhead, and the boy staggered toward the southern end of the rooftop. Reeling and lurching, he banged into the low parapet at the edge of the roof and tumbled over it.

In horror, Jenna watched him plummet sixteen stories down.

Then she heard the rumble of armored vehicles speeding toward them.

TWENTY-SIX

Frazier shot the lookouts himself. He took aim from a sniper's nest he'd improvised on the Triborough Bridge, at the top of a steel-gray bridge tower that rose two hundred feet above the Harlem River. From there, Frazier had an excellent view of the northern half of the housing project, including the roof of the apartment building where the Latin Kings were.

Both of the gangbangers on the roof wore gold bandannas. They were five hundred yards away, and the wind was strong at this height, but Frazier's enhanced eyesight made the targeting easy. First he picked off the taller boy, the one in the tank top. The other gangbanger started to run, heading for the building's stairway, but Frazier lined up his rifle's telescopic sight with the bandanna. The bullet drilled into the punk's skull, and he took a swan dive off the roof.

Then Frazier shouted, "Go!" into his radio, and the assault began. Three Stryker vehicles barreled down the bridge's exit ramp and veered left toward the Triborough Houses.

He smiled. The operation was going well. There were a few missteps at the start; an hour ago, when Frazier's team raided the apartment on Prospect Park West, they'd found no one at home. But they did find Jenna

Khan's nightshirt in a laundry basket, proving she'd been there. And when they put out an alert for the apartment's occupant, Tamara Carter, they learned she was a mayoral aide who'd been killed at Gracie Mansion the night before. If Jenna had gone into Manhattan with Tamara, she could've rendezvoused with her friends in the Latin Kings, whose headquarters was relatively close to the mansion. And maybe her father and Weinberg were there too. It was far from a sure thing, but Frazier felt it was worth checking out.

Now he looked down at the Triborough Houses and watched the Strykers jump the curb and pull up in front of the apartment building. Half of the FSU officers rushed into the building's lobby while the other half fanned out across the housing project, chasing the drug dealers who'd started running from the assault team. Frazier assumed that if the Latin Kings were harboring the escapees, they'd be in one of the gang's apartments, and he also assumed they'd put up a fight. But the FSU had more and better guns. If they got into a shoot-out, it would be over soon.

As Frazier eyeballed the fleeing drug dealers, though, he spotted a group of Latin Kings sprinting across a playground. It looked like several gangbangers had gathered in a protective cluster around their leader, a tall, skinny punk in a black T-shirt. Running alongside him were two smaller figures: a balding, brown-skinned man in a polo shirt and a pretty, short-haired woman in jeans.

They were Hamid and Jenna Khan. There was no sign of Weinberg, but he probably wasn't far.

Frazier raised his rifle, but the Khans ran behind another of the project's buildings before he could take a shot. They were headed south, and that was bad for targeting—his line of sight to that part of the project was blocked, there were too many buildings in the way. But Frazier didn't get upset. This time the Khan bitch had no hope of escaping him. And he'd rather take her alive anyway.

He slung his rifle over his shoulder and left the sniper's nest. Moving quickly, he climbed down the access ladder to the bridge's roadway, where another Stryker was idling. He didn't want to miss this.

TWENTY-SEVEN

Jenna had only one thought: Save Abbu. Now that she'd finally found her father, she didn't intend to lose him again.

She gripped his arm above the elbow as they ran across the housing project, racing down an asphalt pathway between the identical redbrick apartment buildings. Hector ran beside them and shouted orders in Spanish to half a dozen Latin Kings, who'd flocked around him like Secret Service agents, each man willing to take a bullet for his commander. Carlos ran ahead of the pack, leading them past a playground and a community garden, and more gangbangers emerged from the lobbies of the project's buildings. There was a minimum of panic, and each Latin King seemed to know what to do. Jenna got the feeling that they'd practiced this escape plan, readying themselves for the day when the Feds would attack.

Then the FSU officers opened fire behind them, and the orderly plan fell apart.

The bullets struck two of the teenagers running to Jenna's left. Both were big, brawny kids in sleeveless gold shirts, but they fell instantly and slid across the asphalt. The bullets also hit an old woman standing by the garden fence and a toddler skipping through the playground. Windows shattered on the ground floors of the buildings around them, and screams rose from all over the project. But the soldiers behind them kept firing.

Hector leapt forward and nudged Carlos to the right. "That way!" Without breaking stride, he pointed at another playground up ahead. Then he looked over his shoulder. "*Vámanos, muchachos*! Fast as you can!"

They swerved to the right, but the next round of bullets struck down two more Latin Kings. One was the tall boy in the tracksuit who'd rescued Jenna in Central Park. The bullet plunged into his back and exploded out of his chest. Blood splattered on the pathway in front of him, and he collapsed face-first into the mess.

Jenna stumbled and almost lost her balance, overcome by the screaming and gore. But she stayed on her feet and squeezed her father's arm and pulled him toward the second playground, which was larger than the one they'd just passed. All the kids and parents had already fled the sandbox and the jungle gym, but a couple of old men in gym shorts stood on the handball court, looking stupefied. They'd dropped the ball they'd been playing with a few seconds ago, and now it rolled across the court and bounced against the high concrete wall behind them.

Hector waved his arms at them. "*Señores*! Don't just stand there! Take cover!"

After a moment of paralysis, the old men scurried around the edge of the wall and dove behind it. Jenna followed them, dragging her father, who dropped to his knees as soon as he was safely behind cover. Hector and Carlos and the other Latin Kings skidded to a halt beside them, breathing hard and clutching their chests. The FSU fired another fusillade at them, but the bullets slammed into the wall. They pocked the concrete slab but couldn't penetrate it.

Hector stepped toward Jenna and her dad. "Are you all right, *chica*? *Señor*? You can rest here for a moment, okay?"

Jenna glared at him. "We can't rest. The soldiers are coming!"

"Don't worry. My boys will slow them down." He raised his arm and pointed at the upper floors of the apartment buildings. "Watch."

She looked up. Several windows were open on the fifteenth and sixteenth floors of the project's buildings. Hector slipped two fingers into his mouth, just like he'd done a minute ago, and let out another whistle, which was a signal to his men in those apartments. All at once, they pointed their handguns out the windows and fired on the FSU officers below.

Jenna couldn't see the soldiers—the wall was in the way, and she didn't dare peek around its edge—but she heard them yelling and running for cover. It was like the night of her arrest, when her neighbors in Brighton Beach took potshots at the officers in the street, but this was a hundred times worse. The soldiers fired back at the Latin Kings in the apartments, shattering dozens of windows. Then Jenna heard the rumble of the armored vehicles again, and the gunfire got louder. The FSU men inside the Strykers aimed the vehicles' machine guns at the apartments. The bullets blasted the redbrick buildings, and powdery cascades of debris rained down.

Hector leaned toward Jenna, bringing his lips close to her ear so she could hear him over the noise. "Now the *Federales* are busy, so we can slip away. Come on."

He placed a hand on her back and turned her around. Just fifty feet from the handball court was East 120th Street, the southern edge of the Triborough Houses. It was a relatively wide crosstown street, with three traffic lanes and a line of cars parked by the curb. Carlos had already run ahead and opened the driver-side door of a dirty gray Kia. It was a beater of a car, scraped and dented and at least ten years old. Jenna pointed at the thing. "That's our getaway car?"

Hector led her and her father toward the Kia. "Beggars can't be choosers, *princesa*. Get in the backseat with your *papi* and keep your heads down, okay?"

Jenna got in the car and pulled Abbu into the seat beside her. He was gasping and wheezing, scared out of his mind. She patted his knee, trying to calm him, and helped him put on his seat belt.

Meanwhile, Hector jumped into the front passenger seat and looked at Carlos, who'd just started the engine. "Let's roll, *amigo*. Turn around and go to Second Avenue. We'll head downtown to 110th and then—"

A familiar rumble interrupted him. Hector looked over his shoulder and stared through the car's rear window at a fast-approaching Stryker. The armored vehicle charged down Second Avenue, then slowed to make a left turn on 120th Street. It was only a hundred yards behind.

"Change of plans!" Hector pointed forward. "Go to First Avenue!"

Carlos pulled away from the curb and gunned the Kia's engine. The rear tires squealed, and in four and a half seconds they reached the corner of 120th and First. But another Stryker was dead ahead, and a third was two blocks to the north, racing down First Avenue. Carlos hit the brakes and turned to Hector. "What do I do?"

"Turn right!" Hector's eyes gleamed. To Jenna's surprise, he didn't look worried. His face was mad, ecstatic. "Just do it!"

They had no choice. Carlos peeled out and turned south on First Avenue, even though it put them against the one-way traffic. He jammed his palm against the Kia's horn, blaring a warning. The oncoming cars swerved out of the Kia's path, careening to the left and right.

Hector let out a whoop. "That's it, Carlos! Cruise right on through. Show them who's boss!"

Jenna stretched one arm in front of Abbu to brace him and reached toward Carlos with the other. "Stop, you're gonna kill us! Turn right at the next corner!"

But when they reached the intersection of First Avenue and 119th, they saw more Strykers. The armored vehicles barreled down Second Avenue to the west and Pleasant Avenue to the east, keeping pace with them on both sides. The only option was to keep driving south against the traffic. There were four lanes on First Avenue, giving Carlos some room to maneuver, but it was still a suicidal ride. Jenna stared in horror at the taxis and trucks up ahead, which blared their own horns as they sped closer.

For fifteen blocks, Carlos dodged the oncoming vehicles, which skidded and fishtailed and sideswiped each other as they steered around the Kia. But the Stryker chasing them down First Avenue simply knocked the cars aside and accelerated down the street, coming closer every second. And then, as they approached 105th Street, Jenna spotted an armored vehicle up ahead. One of the Strykers had looped around to cut off their escape. It was just two blocks away and closing in fast.

Jenna turned away from the windshield and looked at her father. He hadn't said a word since the raid began. He just sat there, terrified, staring straight ahead. She wanted to reassure him, to say something hopeful and comforting before the soldiers stopped their car and arrested them, but she was just as frightened as he was. It would be better if the FSU killed them, she thought. Better if the soldiers opened fire on the Kia and slaughtered them all. Although her father had said little about Rikers, Jenna suspected it had become a concentration camp. *What happened to you there, Abbu? What did they do to you and Raza?*

She shook her head, angry and desperate. But then Jenna remembered something else her father had said. He'd mentioned it ten minutes ago, back in Carlos's grandmother's apartment.

Something about a bridge.

"Carlos, turn left! *Left!*"

The boy reacted at once, steering the Kia so sharply that it almost spun out of control. They sped east on 105th Street, which dead-ended a block away.

Hector turned around in his seat and scowled at her. "Why'd you do that?" He pointed at the concrete barrier at the end of the street. "Now we're trapped!"

Jenna ignored him. She kept her eyes on Carlos. "Stop the car right here!"

He stopped the Kia about twenty feet from the dead end. On the other side of the barrier was the FDR Drive, and beyond the highway was the Harlem River. To the right was another housing project full of redbrick apartment buildings, and extending east from the project was a slender steel walkway that arched over the highway and the river. It was the 103rd Street pedestrian bridge, the one her father had mentioned, which led to Randalls Island.

Jenna opened the Kia's rear door, stepped to the curb, and pulled Abbu out of the backseat. "Come on!"

Hector was furious. He opened his own door and rushed toward her. "Where do you think you're going?"

"There's no checkpoint on the footbridge." She pointed at the walkway, which was painted an awful shade of green. "We can get out of Manhattan and go to Randalls."

"And what then? We'll be trapped there too."

Hector seemed ready to keep arguing, but Carlos cut him off. The kid jumped out of the Kia and grabbed Hector's arm. "Please, let's go!" He looked down the street at the convoy of Stryker vehicles hurtling toward them. "They're coming!"

Jenna dashed toward the footbridge, running as fast as she could while pulling her father along. Hector and Carlos followed them, sprinting on the sidewalk that ran between the barrier and the apartment buildings. Luckily, the path was too narrow for the Strykers, which halted on the street behind the Kia. But a moment later, the soldiers poured out of the armored vehicles and came after them.

There was a concrete ramp sloping up to the bridge, and in less than a minute Jenna was dragging Abbu up the incline. He kept looking over his shoulder at the officers in black uniforms, who jogged in neat rows on the sidewalk, cradling their assault rifles. They were less than a hundred yards behind, but they didn't raise their guns. Someone had clearly ordered them to hold their fire and capture the fugitives alive. As Jenna stared at the soldiers she glimpsed a tall FSU officer marching behind them and shouting something into his radio. He had a thick, muscled neck and a blond buzz cut.

It was Lieutenant Frazier. Azrael, the Angel of Death, hadn't forgotten her.

She faced forward and ran faster, yanking her father's arm. Hector and Carlos sped up too, and soon they dashed onto the footbridge that stretched over the Harlem River. The walkway was only ten feet wide and flanked on either side by a six-foot-high fence, presumably to stop would-be suicides from jumping off the bridge. The borough of Queens was to Jenna's right and the Bronx to her left, but she peered straight ahead at Randalls, the smallish island in the middle of the river, a patchwork of baseball fields and municipal facilities. *Where do we go now? Is there a place we can hide?* There was a psychiatric hospital on the island, and a sewage-treatment plant too, but how the hell could they hide in a place like that? *Shit! What do we do?*

Then Jenna saw something that extinguished all hope. On the closest part of Randalls Island were at least a hundred officers in helmets and body armor. They swarmed toward the foot of the pedestrian bridge and raced up the narrow walkway, running three abreast. They ran just as fast as the soldiers on the Manhattan side, and they were just as heavily armed. Each carried an assault rifle and several clips of ammunition.

Jenna stopped in her tracks. Her father collapsed on the walkway and vomited. Hector and Carlos stopped beside her and looked in all directions, staring in disbelief. They stood at the midpoint of the bridge, and the soldiers charged at them from both sides. The men from the Strykers were fifty yards behind them, and the officers from Randalls were fifty yards ahead. Within ten seconds, they would meet in the middle and it would all be over.

To Jenna's dismay, Hector grinned. "Want to go for a swim?" He pointed at the anti-suicide fence running along the walkway. "We can climb over that thing. And this bridge, it's not as high as the Triborough. Only fifty feet above the water, it looks like."

She shook her head. She might survive the jump, but her father wouldn't. And she wasn't going to leave him behind.

Instead, she turned to the officers rushing toward them from Randalls. Maybe their commander was less of a monster than Frazier. One of the soldiers at the front of the column waved his arms at them and shouted, *"Get down!"* He wanted them to lie on their stomachs so his men could cuff them.

Or maybe not. Jenna started to have second thoughts about their intentions. On closer inspection, she noticed something different about the officers coming from Randalls: Under their body armor, their uniforms weren't black.

They were dark blue. The NYPD color.

Jenna flattened herself on top of her father. An instant later, Hector and Carlos threw themselves down and lay prone on the walkway. At the same time, the New York cops raised their assault rifles. They didn't point their guns at Jenna or Abbu or Hector or Carlos. They aimed at the FSU officers on the other side of the bridge.

Then the cops opened fire.

TWENTY-EIGHT

Vance had to lie to Congress. He told the leaders of the House and Senate that the president was staying in New York to oversee the military operations there.

But the truth was, the president was dying.

The relapse happened just an hour after his speech at Citi Field. He and Vance were in the backseat of the presidential limousine, en route to the airport, when POTUS started slurring his words. The amphetamine injection he'd received before the speech had suppressed the symptoms of his dementia, but they returned with a vengeance as soon as the drug wore off. Within minutes he could barely talk or swallow. Then he had a coughing fit that grew loud and violent. His face turned an obscene shade of orange, and strings of saliva hung from his chin.

The Secret Service agents stopped the presidential motorcade. They halted the armored limos on the shoulder of Grand Central Parkway and transferred the president to the convoy's ambulance. This infuriated him. He thrashed and screamed as the agents strapped him to the gurney.

Vance went into the ambulance with him and ordered the Secret Service to change their itinerary. The president was too ill to fly back to

Washington. They couldn't take him to any of the hospitals in Manhattan either, because the doctors and nurses there might gossip about his condition. So the motorcade headed for Rikers Island. The FSU's Medical Research Center was the best place for him anyway.

The Research Center's doctors managed to stabilize the president, and after a couple of hours they allowed Vance to visit him in the intensive care unit. POTUS lay in a hospital bed raised to a forty-five-degree angle to ease his breathing. A plastic tube ran under his nose, and a mechanical ventilator pumped air into his nostrils. The doctors had given him sedatives too, enough to quell his agitation but still allow him to stay awake. Although the president's eyes were closed, he grimaced and muttered and seemed to be conscious. That was fortunate, because he needed to take care of some important business this evening.

Vance sat down in a chair beside the bed. The ICU was full of medical equipment, but there were no other patients in the room and only one nurse, who was preparing the president's dinner and keeping an eye on the heart-rate monitor. Vance asked her to leave the room for a moment so he could talk privately with the president, and after a moment of hesitation she stepped outside. Then he tapped his father-in-law's shoulder, which was barely covered by the loose hospital gown.

"Hello? Are you with me?"

He nodded but kept his eyes closed. His face had paled to dull pink, the color of a Band-Aid.

Vance pulled one of the folded documents out of the inside pocket of his suit jacket. "How are you doing? Do you feel well enough to talk?"

He grimaced again, pressing his lips together. "I'm fine, Vance. What do you want?"

The president's voice was quiet and raspy, but each word was dense with anger. The man was difficult even under the best of circumstances, even when everything was going his way. But when things went wrong, he was a horror show, and today his life had fallen apart. According to the doctors, he'd entered the end stage of frontotemporal dementia. The damage had spread to his brain's motor cortex, affecting his ability to speak and swallow. In a matter of weeks, it would shut down his whole body.

Vance steeled himself. He needed to focus on the next step. He unfolded the document in his hands, a letter printed on White House stationery. "Well, there's an urgent matter we need to discuss. The Federal

Service Unit is facing more problems in New York. Rogue officers from the city's police department have attacked and overwhelmed the FSU teams stationed on Randalls Island. It's a major setback."

The president didn't react. He didn't even open his eyes. Vance had expected his father-in-law to get enraged at this piece of news, but instead he seemed bored. "Is that it?"

"Please, this is serious. The New York police have become an army of insurgents. They took over the checkpoints on the Triborough Bridge and murdered dozens of FSU officers in a shoot-out on the 103rd Street footbridge. The cops killed every federal agent on that bridge except their commander, a lieutenant named Frazier. And he survived only because he jumped into the Harlem River."

The president opened his eyes and rolled them. "Jesus, why are you bothering me with this? Just take care of it."

Vance sighed. He felt like he was already running the federal government, and all he'd received for his efforts was aggravation. When Phase Three of Palindrome had begun, he'd assumed the Serenity sequence would squelch all opposition to the government, but the virus carrying that snippet of DNA wasn't spreading as quickly as he'd hoped. In particular, it hadn't spread to the traitorous New York police officers, because they had no contact with the people already infected. Vance had asked his researchers if they could use helicopters to disperse the virus over Randalls Island, but they dismissed the idea. Apparently, the aerosol sprayers worked much better in indoor spaces—like the rotunda at Citi Field—than outdoors. And Randalls was an especially windy place, making it difficult to deliver an airborne virus there.

But Vance's biggest problem was communicating all this to the president. *Keep things simple*, he thought. *It's like talking to a child.* "Here's why I need your help. The police officers on Randalls have plenty of weapons because the NYPD's counterterrorism unit is based there. And because they're on an island, they can fortify the place and defend it effectively with barricades on all the bridges. The only good military option is to launch an air strike against Randalls and destroy their headquarters. And the generals on the Joint Chiefs won't like the idea of bombing a New York police station."

"But they'll do it." The president shrugged, moving his shoulders against his pillow. "They saw what happened to General Miller at the rally. I showed them what I do to people who try to screw me."

"That's not enough. You need to give the generals the order in writing." Vance held up the letter he'd printed, which still required the president's signature. "This is addressed to the chairman of the Joint Chiefs, but we'll send it to all the other generals and field commanders too. It's an ironclad document. It gives them absolutely no choice except to follow your orders."

POTUS frowned. He'd always hated the day-to-day details of the presidency. They bewildered and frustrated him. "I can't believe this. I'm sick as a fucking dog, and you're pestering me with paperwork." He grabbed the letter from Vance, who also handed him a pen. "Do you even realize what I went through today? Almost choking to death? You know how horrible that was?"

Vance nodded. "Yes, it was horrible."

"I can't go on like this." He scribbled his signature on the letter, then threw it back at Vance. He was getting agitated again. "I'm not gonna lie here and turn into a fucking vegetable. I'd rather die than let that happen."

"Believe me, I understand what—"

"No, you don't understand!" He sat up in bed and clawed at his breathing tube. It looked like he was trying to rip it off. "I swear to fucking God, I'd rather kill myself!"

Vance leaned over the bed and reached for the man's hands. He gently grasped them in his own and set them back down on the mattress. He felt a surge of revulsion—he hated touching his father-in-law—but he didn't let it show. This was the crucial part of their conversation, and it needed to go perfectly. "You're right, this can't continue. It's time to take a risk." Vance let go of him. "I think you should try the treatment. The gene-altering procedure that we've developed for your condition."

The president stared. He seemed confused and surprised. "I thought you said it wasn't safe. That's what you've been telling me for months."

"I won't lie to you. It's an experimental treatment, and that means it's risky. But the Palindrome researchers have made great progress in the past few weeks. They've learned how to prevent most of the complications and control the side effects. So now I think we're at the point where the risks of doing the procedure are less than the risks of *not* doing it."

The president kept staring. He was a cagey man, not easily fooled. But he was also desperate. He feared his disease so much and wanted a cure so badly. "All right. When can we start?"

"Your condition's worsening quickly now, so there's no time to lose. We can give you the first round of injections tonight."

Again, POTUS looked surprised. "Tonight? You mean, right now?"

"Everything's ready to go. The scientists have prepared a CRISPR molecule that's designed to treat your type of dementia. It'll snip out the inherited mutations in your progranulin gene and replace them with the correct DNA sequences. Then your cells will produce a normal amount of the progranulin protein and your—"

"Okay, enough with the mumbo jumbo. Just tell me one thing—do I have a fucking prayer?"

"Yes." Vance gave him an ardent look, meant to convey utter confidence. "I think it'll work."

The president managed to smile. It was a grim sort of smile, tainted with skepticism, but there was also some hope in it. He was putting his trust in CRISPR. He was willing to give it a chance. "All right, let's do it. Give me the shots." He gripped the sleeve of his hospital gown and started rolling it up.

Vance shook his head. "No, it's not that kind of injection. The cells we need to repair are in your brain. The doctors will have to shave your scalp and drill several holes in your skull."

The president let go of the sleeve and raised his hand in a protective reflex. He touched his head, and an expression of doubt crossed his face. But it lasted only a moment. "Yeah, okay, I can handle that. I'll do whatever I need to do."

"Good. You're making the right decision." Vance reached into the pocket of his jacket again and pulled out the second folded document. "You just have to sign one more letter, and then we'll take you to the Center's operating room."

"Seriously? More paperwork?" He scowled. "It can't wait until afterward?"

"I'm afraid not." Vance unfolded the document and showed it to the president. "It's a letter to Congress. At your request, they're meeting in a special session this evening. And they're waiting for you to submit this nomination so they can vote on it tonight."

The president took the letter and squinted at it. He usually disliked reading official papers—he didn't have the patience—but this one was short and sweet, just a single sentence:

> *To the Congress of the United States:*
> Pursuant to the provisions of Section 2 of the Twenty-fifth Amendment to the Constitution, I hereby nominate Vance C. Keller of Washington, D.C., to be the Vice President of the United States.
>
> *September 13, 2023*

His eyes narrowed as he read the letter. Then he dropped it in his lap and looked up. "Well, well. This is a surprise."

"It shouldn't be." Vance put a casual look on his face. He'd rehearsed this moment in his mind, so he knew exactly what to say. "The Constitution gives you the authority to nominate a vice president. You need to install a suitable replacement for our dear departed hero, that God-fearing Christian patriot."

"And you assumed I'd want to nominate *you*?" The president cocked his head at a jaunty angle, but his voice was furious. "I guess you felt pretty certain about the choice, huh? So certain that you didn't even bother to ask for my opinion?"

"Just think about it logically. Take it step-by-step." Vance folded his arms across his chest, as calm and patient as a schoolteacher. "You and I have done many great things for this country, but some of our methods were unconventional. And if those methods ever came to light, our enemies would accuse us of terrible crimes. But we're in this bind together, so I can trust you to keep everything secret, and you can trust me. Why bring in a vice president who might betray us, like the old veep almost did?"

The president didn't buy it. If anything, he grew angrier. His eyebrows tilted over his narrowed eyes like accent marks. "That's bullshit. No matter who becomes the vice president, we don't have to tell him a thing. The only reason why that stupid Jesus freak became a problem is because you screwed up. You let him figure out what was going on with Palindrome. You totally fucked up the whole situation."

Vance sighed again. He needed to try a different argument. "Okay, there's another factor to consider. As I mentioned a minute ago, the treatment for your illness is risky. I think it's a risk worth taking, but there's a chance that—"

"A chance that I'll die? Is that what you're worried about?"

"Yes, in part, but—"

"Because you'll be in deep shit if I die and someone else becomes president, right? So this nomination is all about protecting *you*, isn't it?"

Vance shook his head. "It's not just about me. There's also a chance that the treatment will incapacitate you in some way. You might feel addled or stupefied while the CRISPR molecules are repairing your brain cells. In all likelihood, the problem would only last a few days or weeks, but it might be severe enough to prevent you from doing your job during that time. And if that happens and there's no vice president in place to temporarily assume your duties, the Speaker of the House becomes president. Did you know that?"

The president said nothing. He clearly hadn't thought of this possibility.

Vance was making progress. He pointed at the unsigned letter. "Do you see now why it's important to take care of this nomination? Important for both of us?"

POTUS still didn't say anything. Instead, he started coughing. He raised his hand to his mouth and coughed into his palm several times, explosively loud. He seemed to be trying to expel something from his throat, without much success. After a few seconds he doubled over on the bed and hawked a wad of phlegm across the room. But he kept on coughing. His eyes widened in fear and his face turned red. Saliva spilled down his chin and soaked the front of his hospital gown.

Vance stood up, alarmed. Luckily, the nurse waiting in the corridor heard the hacking noises and rushed back into the room. She nudged Vance aside, leaned over the bed, and slapped the president between the shoulder blades. Another wad of phlegm flew out of his mouth, and his coughing fit subsided. He caught his breath and fell back against his pillow, exhausted, his mouth gaping.

The nurse grabbed a Kleenex and wiped his chin. At the same time, she turned her head sideways and shot an angry look at Vance. "What happened? Did you make him upset?" Without waiting for an answer, she turned back to the president. "It's all right, sir. Everything's going to be all right."

POTUS stared at the ceiling for a while, too weak to move. Then he took a deep labored breath and looked down at his lap. The nomination letter and the pen had slid off him and lay on the bedsheet. With trembling hands, he picked them up and scrawled his signature on the letter.

"Here. Take it." He spoke in a whisper, barely audible. The letter flapped in his hand as he gave it to Vance. "Tell the doctors . . . I'm ready . . . for the injections."

The president wasn't angry anymore. Not in the least. There was nothing but fear on his face now. His lips quivered. His eyes were wet and pleading.

Vance refolded the signed letters and put them back in his pocket, allowing himself a satisfied smile. Everything had gone according to plan. The president had shown some resistance at first, but Vance had known all along that POTUS would surrender. His acquiescence was a direct result of the steps Vance had taken at Citi Field—the aerosol sprayers installed in the stadium's rotunda, the airborne virus that infected the crowd, and most crucially, the selective vaccinations. Although Vance and Colonel Grant had been vaccinated to stop the gene-altering virus, POTUS hadn't been. At the last minute, Vance had replaced the president's vaccine with a placebo.

The virus had subdued him. His edge was gone, the fierce inborn mulishness that had made him so infuriatingly successful. It simply wasn't in his DNA anymore.

In its place was the Serenity sequence.

TWENTY-NINE

The New York police saved Jenna's life—and more important, her father's—so she should've been grateful. But she quickly discovered that the cops on Randalls Island weren't a whole lot better than the officers in the FSU.

The trouble started on the footbridge, just seconds after the shoot-out. The New York cops got the jump on the Federal Service officers and killed most of them before the FSU men could fire back. Jenna didn't see much of the firefight—she lay facedown, on top of her father, on the bridge's walkway—but she heard the bullets whistling overhead. Then the cops ran past her and Abbu, leaping over their prone bodies, and chased the surviving Feds across the bridge. But a few NYPD officers stayed behind and pointed their assault rifles at Jenna and Hector and Carlos. One cop planted his boot on Jenna's back and pressed his rifle's muzzle against her head.

It was crude, cruel, humiliating. The New York cops were acting like assholes. Then it got worse.

The cops cuffed them. And marched them at gunpoint across Randalls

Island. The police officers led them to an old brick building that sat in the shadow of the Triborough Bridge. Jenna had driven past this building many times—it was near the highway junction where the taxis and trucks from Manhattan merged with the traffic from Queens and the Bronx—but she'd never realized what was inside. When the cops guided her and Abbu into the lobby, she noticed a logo painted on the wall, depicting a bald eagle and the New York City skyline, encircled by the words COUNTERTERRORISM BUREAU. Then they stepped into a command center full of high-tech video screens and a long row of gun lockers, each packed with assault rifles and ammunition clips.

Now Jenna understood. This building was home to an elite police squadron, a paramilitary counterterrorism unit. Because it was full of military-grade weapons, the New York officers had chosen it as a headquarters for their rebellion against the FSU. Using those weapons, the cops had forced the federal agents off Randalls and seized control of a major transportation hub at the heart of the city. It was a big victory for the NYPD and an embarrassing defeat for the Feds. But unfortunately for Jenna, the New York cops didn't seem to realize that she and Hector were on their side. And when she tried to tell the cops who she was, they ordered her to shut her fucking mouth.

The police officers took them downstairs to the basement and led them into a windowless interrogation room. They pushed Jenna and her father to the left side of the room and Hector and Carlos to the right. In between them was a gray steel table, massive and sturdy and surrounded by chairs. Four of them were empty, but the two chairs at the far end of the table were occupied by a couple of men in civilian clothes.

Jenna recognized the older, gray-haired man first. It was Steven Hayes, the New York City police commissioner. She'd seen his picture many times in the newspaper, always wearing a dapper suit and tie at press conferences and swearing-in ceremonies. Now, though, his tie was missing and his suit badly wrinkled, as if he'd slept in it for the past couple of nights. His face was drawn and furrowed, his eyes red-rimmed and half-closed. The change in his appearance was alarming. He looked like he'd aged twenty years since his last press conference.

But the other man at the end of the table alarmed Jenna even more. He'd changed so drastically that it took her much longer to recognize him, even though she knew him a lot better than she knew the police commissioner. Her breath caught in her throat.

"David?"

He didn't respond. Her old boyfriend stared straight ahead at the doorway she'd just walked through. He wore a red T-shirt and a loose-fitting lab coat that was slightly gray because it hadn't been washed in a long while. His hair was a mess, his face was covered with black stubble, and his nose was swollen and purple. But what disturbed Jenna the most were his eyes. There was no life in them at all.

"David, what's wrong?" She stepped toward him. "What happened to you?"

The cop behind Jenna grabbed her arm and pulled her back. But the police commissioner gave the man a hand signal, and he let go. Then Commissioner Hayes looked at her. "You can sit down, Dr. Khan. Your father too." He pointed at the empty chairs, then turned to Hector and Carlos. "All of you, please sit down."

Jenna frowned. She didn't trust this man. "What's going on? Why did you arrest us?"

The commissioner shook his head. "You're not under arrest. My men were just being careful. We needed to check our records and confirm who you were." He gave another signal to the cops behind them. "Officers, you can remove their cuffs now."

The cops took off the handcuffs, then stepped back and stood guard by the door. Jenna put her arm around her father, who was practically falling asleep on his feet, and guided him to one of the chairs. As soon as she lowered him into the seat, he tilted his head back and closed his eyes. Then she sat down beside him.

Meanwhile, the two Latin Kings sat on the other side of the table. Carlos was jumpy, turning his head this way and that, but Hector grinned and looked straight at the commissioner. "*Señor* Hayes, I've seen you before on the TV news. It's a pleasure to meet you."

Hayes didn't smile back at him. "I know you too, Mr. Torres. The detectives at the Gang Division have been monitoring your organization for some time."

"Well, thank you. I'm flattered." Hector leaned back in his chair. "It was very kind of you to send your officers to the footbridge to rescue us. But I'm curious about the timing. How did you know we were coming?"

"That's one of the things I'd like to discuss." The commissioner pointed at David, who was still staring straight ahead, silent and motionless. "This is Dr. David Weinberg. He arrived at this station a few hours ago and asked to see me. My detectives talked to him first, and he told them a very strange story."

Jenna leaned across the table and glared at Hayes. "How did he get the broken nose? Did your detectives do that to him?"

The commissioner shifted in his seat, clearly uncomfortable. "Yes, I apologize for that. Our officers have been under a lot of stress since martial law was declared. Because Dr. Weinberg's story was so hard to believe, the detectives questioned him intensively, and I'm afraid they got a little overzealous. But—"

"*Overzealous?*" Jenna rose from her chair. Her hands were shaking. "You knocked the shit out of him! Look at him, he's punch-drunk! You beat him so hard, he's half-comatose!"

Hayes shook his head. "No, that's not the detectives' fault. He's been like that ever since he got here. Like he's in shock or in a trance. He won't talk unless you ask him a direct question. Here, watch this." He turned to David and raised his voice. "Dr. Weinberg, do you recognize any of the people sitting at the table?"

David nodded, very slowly. "Yes."

"What are their names? And how do you know them?"

He turned his head toward Jenna and her father but didn't make eye contact. "They are Jenna and Hamid Khan." His voice was flat and emotionless. "Dr. Jenna Khan and I were coworkers at the Molecular Genetics Laboratory until she lost her job six months ago. Hamid Khan is her father. I encountered him at the Federal Service detention facility on Rikers Island and helped him escape from the jail."

"And how did you manage this escape?"

David reached into the pocket of his lab coat and pulled out a security card with his picture on it. "I used this to get Hamid out of the Research Center." Moving stiffly and mechanically, he put the card back in his pocket. "Then, at the security gate on the Rikers Island Bridge, I convinced the guards that he was a fellow scientist."

The commissioner pointed at David again. "You see? At first, my detectives thought he was just a nutcase. But then he told us so much about the FSU and the research they're doing at Rikers, and we realized he was serious. He's the one who told us that you were coming to the 103rd Street footbridge and that the Feds would be chasing you. He was right about everything."

Jenna couldn't stand it. She had her own questions for David, and she couldn't wait anymore. So she pushed her chair back, stepped around the table, and bent over him. She got right in his face. "What about Raza? Where is he? You left him behind?"

David nodded again, just as slowly as before. "It would've been impossible to take your brother out of the jail complex. But he gave me instructions. He told me what we needed to do."

This last sentence was just as disturbing as David's trancelike demeanor. Like Abbu, he was making the absurd claim that Raza had communicated with him. Either the delusion was spreading, or there was some truth to it. Jenna found this very hard to believe, but as a scientist, she had no choice except to keep an open mind. "And what did Raza say?"

"He said it was up to us to stop the Federal Service Unit. We need to shut down Phase Three of the Palindrome Project. The FSU is deploying a dangerous bioweapon against its enemies."

She stared at him. David was one of Palindrome's chief researchers. Unlike Jenna, he'd done all the experiments he'd been ordered to do, and he'd moved up to the supervisory ranks of the laboratory, so he was in a position to know the details of the classified project. But she was still skeptical. "A bioweapon? Using CRISPR?"

"We engineered an airborne virus that could deliver the CRISPR treatment. And we targeted a different DNA region, a section called Tame-1."

Jenna's throat tightened. She was familiar with that particular strip of DNA. She'd studied it in her experiments on the genetics of animal behavior. Tame-1 contained many of the genes that determine whether an animal is wild or domesticated, aggressive or tame. And most of those genes were also present in human DNA. "You identified the variant sequences that cause tameness? And you put those sequences in the airborne virus?"

David nodded a third time. "I helped prepare the first large-scale test of the bioweapon, which was released at Citi Field earlier today. Now the FSU will disperse the virus in airports, train stations, and other enclosed structures where the microbe can be transmitted to large numbers of people."

She backed away from him. It was disorienting, listening to David talk in such a calm, robotic voice about a plan to genetically pacify the population. Jenna almost laughed out of sheer dismay. *My God! Those arrogant idiots! What the hell were they thinking?*

Shaking her head, she retreated to her chair. Then she looked at the police commissioner. "Yeah, your detectives were right. David's shell-shocked or something, but he's on the level. He's not making this up."

"So it's really possible?" Commissioner Hayes seemed distressed and disappointed. He'd clearly hoped that Jenna would ease his fears and dismiss David's wild claims. "The Feds can do something like that? Release a virus that can warp people's minds?"

Jenna shrugged. "I wouldn't put it past them. Nothing they do surprises me anymore." She propped her elbows on the table and rubbed her forehead with both hands. She suddenly felt very tired. "If you're planning another battle with the FSU, you better do it soon. Once this virus gets around, it'll be hard to find anyone brave enough to join you."

Hector swiveled his head and gave her a sharp look. "Let me tell you something, *chica*. No fucking virus is gonna stop me. And the same goes for all the Latin Kings." He glanced at Carlos and raised his right hand to make the gang sign. *"Amor de Rey!"*

Carlos made the gang sign too. *"Amor de Rey!"*

Hector turned to Commissioner Hayes. *"Señor*, I'd like to offer our help. The Almighty Latin King Nation wants revenge on the *Federales* for murdering our brothers and sisters. And you want revenge for the assassination of your mayor. So we have a common enemy, yes?"

The commissioner frowned. Obviously, he had a deep-rooted distaste for gangbangers. "Mr. Torres, we don't want revenge. We just want to defend our city. The president's administration is endangering the lives of our citizens and trampling on their constitutional rights. So we're going to stop them."

Hector nodded vigorously. "I agree with you, *Señor*, with all my heart. And I'm asking you to let the Latin Kings join the fight. I have hundreds of men under my command, spread across the whole city. And with one phone call I can get in touch with the Bloods, the Crips, and the Trinitarios too." He reached into his pocket and pulled out a burner phone, one of the cheap, disposable models you could buy at a drugstore or bodega. "There must be something we can do to help. Do you have a plan of some kind? How are you going to fight the FSU?"

Hayes kept frowning for a few more seconds. But then he nodded. "I don't like you, Mr. Torres, but I'm not stupid. I'm squaring off against the most powerful military force in the world, so I'll take every bit of help I can get." He glanced at David, who'd reverted to blank-faced silence. "During our interrogation of Dr. Weinberg, he gave us some useful information about the FSU headquarters on Rikers. He drew maps for us, showing the locations of all the laboratories and detention centers and guard posts. So yes, we have a plan."

Now Hector looked concerned. He raised his hand to his chin and rubbed it. "You're going to attack Rikers? *Madre de Dios*, that's risky. Why attack the place where they're strongest?"

The commissioner glanced at David again. "According to Dr. Weinberg, that's where they're keeping the vaccine against this airborne virus. He says the FSU has stored thousands of vials of the stuff in their Research Center. If the virus is really as bad as he claims it is, then we're gonna need that vaccine."

Hector tapped his finger against his lips, deep in thought. "Okay, that makes sense. But I still don't see how you can pull it off. I did some time at Rikers back when it was a city jail, so I know the place pretty well. The only way to get there is that long bridge from Queens, and it's a choke point. If the FSU puts barricades on the bridge, you'll never get past them."

"We're well aware of the difficulties." The commissioner seemed annoyed. He clearly didn't like having his tactics questioned.

"What about sending your assault teams there by boat? The police department has plenty of boats for patrolling the harbor, right? I've seen some of them at your marina in Sunset Park."

After hesitating for a moment, Hayes nodded. "Yes, that's an option we're considering. Our Harbor Unit also has a marina here on Randalls, just west of this station. It's our repair facility, but we have several boats there that are ready to go."

Hector grinned, delighted. "All right, good! But an attack by sea is risky too. You need to draw the *Federales* away from the island's perimeter before the operation begins. If they see you coming, they'll sink your boats and kill your assault teams before they can even land."

Jenna watched Hector and Hayes, fascinated by their back-and-forth. The commissioner cocked his head, mulling it over, taking Hector seriously now. He seemed to have developed a grudging respect for the gangbanger. "We've been thinking about that too, staging a diversionary attack before the main assault on the island. We could send several counterterrorism teams to the Queens side of the Rikers Island Bridge and fire on the security gate there. Then the FSU would have to pull its officers away from the island perimeter so it could reinforce the soldiers on the bridge."

Hector leaned forward and pointed at Hayes. "And that's where the Latin Kings can help you, *Señor*! My *muchachos* should be the first ones to attack the bridge. We'll fire on the security gate, then retreat to the streets on the Queens side and wait for the FSU *pendejos* to come after us." He waved his hands over the table, growing more excited as he outlined the plan. "After they start chasing us through the streets, you can send in your counterterrorism officers and slaughter the *Federales* behind us. The FSU will have to put even more soldiers on the bridge, and the perimeter will be undefended. Then you can land your harbor boats anywhere on the island."

Hector's excitement was infectious. The police commissioner nodded and even smiled a little. Carlos smiled too and sat upright in his chair, eager to get started. Jenna also felt it, the hope and exhilaration, although she worried about what would happen to Raza during the attack. She needed to tell the commissioner about her brother and make sure that the police officers did everything they could to protect him.

But before she could mention Raza, she heard a distant whistling noise. It came from outside, from above the roof of the police station.

Jenna looked up. All she could see was the ceiling of the interrogation room, but in her gut she knew that something was plunging toward them. She grabbed her father and shoved him under the steel table. Whatever it was, it was coming down fast.

Then the room exploded.

THIRTY

Colonel Grant watched the air strike from the rooftop of the FSU's Research Center. Because it was the tallest building on Rikers, Grant had an excellent view of the explosions on Randalls Island, just a mile to the west.

Through his binoculars he saw the cruise missile hit the police station. It streaked down at a steep angle, then detonated against the station's roof. A brilliant orange fireball rose from the building, and chunks of masonry flew in all directions. The ball of fire and debris expanded so quickly that in a moment it engulfed the station, hiding what was left of the building. A thick column of smoke rose from the site and climbed into the sky above the Triborough Bridge.

It took five seconds for the blast wave to rush across the East River, and then Grant heard the explosion echo against the buildings on Rikers. At the same instant he felt a smaller explosion inside his chest, a burst of joy and triumph. He'd just obliterated his enemies—the New York police, the Khan bitch, that asshole Weinberg. They'd tried to fuck him over, but they'd failed. Now they were nothing but smoke.

After another second he shifted his binoculars to the south and focused on the squadron of Black Hawk helicopters racing toward the blast site. Because the target was so close to a critical highway junction and bridge, Grant had devised a strategy that would minimize the collateral damage. He'd ordered the army to launch just one cruise missile—a precision-guided Tomahawk—to destroy the police station and decapitate the NYPD leadership. Then the Black Hawks would mow down the New York officers at the bridge checkpoints, as well as any survivors from the cruise-missile strike. Right on schedule, the choppers dove toward the Triborough and fired their Gatling guns at the fleeing cops below.

Grant squinted behind the binocs, trying to get a better view. It was just past sunset and the sky was darkening. A bank of thick gray clouds had moved in from the southeast, and a strong wind whipped over the rooftop. Unbelievably, the meteorologists were predicting that another superstorm would hit New York by 10 p.m., less than forty-eight hours after the last one had blown through. By then, though, the battle against the NYPD would be long over. The army had also attacked the police strongholds at Floyd Bennett Field and Rodman's Neck, targeting the cops' arsenals and airfield. Very soon, the colonel would report the good news to Keller: *Our enemies are dead, and nothing else stands in our way.*

Then the war would spread. Grant would finally get the reward he deserved, the leadership of the New America Initiative, Keller's plan to remake and revitalize the country. And Colonel Grant would lead his warriors to the next battlegrounds: Chicago, Los Angeles, Philadelphia, Washington . . .

But as he watched the Black Hawks, he felt a tap on his shoulder. He'd gotten so engrossed in the battle that he hadn't heard anyone approaching. Alarmed, he lowered the binoculars and spun around.

It was Keller. He stood there like a scarecrow, the back of his suit jacket billowing in the wind, his pants flapping around his skeletal legs. His eyes reflected the dimming twilight, but the rest of his face was dark and cadaverous. "What are you doing up here, Colonel?"

There was a note of accusation in his voice, which confused the hell out of Grant. It should've been perfectly obvious what he was doing—the smoke was still rising from Randalls Island and the helicopters were still strafing the survivors. It was all plainly visible. "Uh, I'm observing the air strike, sir." Grant pointed at the island, even though that hardly seemed necessary. "As far as I can see, everything's going well. The Tomahawk scored a direct hit."

"Please, this is unnecessary. Several Pentagon aides are already monitoring the battle for me. You're not using your time wisely, Colonel."

Grant frowned. He was pissed. He'd done everything the K-Man had asked—tracked down the fugitives, found the Khan bitch, cornered them all at Randalls, and convinced the generals to launch the air strike—and it still wasn't enough. "I had a free moment, sir, so I thought I'd come up here. But if you have another assignment for me, I'd be happy to take it on."

"As a matter of fact, I do." Keller reached into the pocket of his jacket and pulled out a secure phone. Then he turned it on and held it in front of Grant's nose. "This was reported by the Washington bureau of the Associated Press ten minutes ago."

A news bulletin was displayed on the phone's screen: CONGRESS CONFIRMS KELLER AS VICE PRESIDENT IN EMERGENCY SESSION.

Grant had expected this, but not quite so soon. "Well, that was fast."

Keller nodded. "I did some arm-twisting over the phone. Made deals with several of the congressmen, offered a few favors. And I hinted that the president was ill, which added to the urgency." He put the phone back in his pocket. "So now it's time to take the next step."

He gave the colonel an expectant look and waited for him to respond. But Grant kept his mouth shut. Now that their project had reached the final stage, he was starting to question whether he could go through with this step. He was a loyal soldier, but he had his limits.

The K-Man sighed. He looked disappointed. "We've discussed this subject before, Colonel. Do you recall what I said?"

"Look, sir, I—"

"You need to prove your loyalty. We're about to start a new chapter in our country's history, and I plan to make you my second-in-command. But first I have to know if you're fully committed to the cause. Are you bold enough to do what's necessary, Colonel?"

Without waiting for a reply, Keller reached into the pocket of his jacket again, and this time he pulled out a syringe. Its tip was capped with a protective cover, and the clear plastic tube was filled with a yellowish fluid.

The K-Man held the thing in his palm. "The president is alone in a recovery room on the fourth floor. A few minutes ago, the doctors administered the first round of CRISPR injections. They also put him under sedation so he could get some rest before the next round. All you need to do is give him one more shot while he's sleeping." He extended his hand and offered the syringe to Grant. "I obtained this from one of my contacts at the CIA. The poison is slow-acting—it won't kill him until three or four hours after the injection. Better still, it's untraceable. Everyone will assume that he died from the gene therapy treatment. And I'll make sure the autopsy confirms it."

Grant stared at the syringe but didn't take it. He didn't like this plan. "You don't need me for this. You should get one of the doctors to give the injection, then eliminate the man afterward. That would be cleaner."

Keller nodded again. "Yes, perhaps. But there would still be a loose end." He raised his voice so Grant could hear it above the whistling of the wind. "Sometime in the future, Colonel, you might be tempted to turn against me. For whatever reason, you might choose to reveal the truth about the president's death. And I have to make sure that never happens." He stretched his arm a little farther and raised the syringe to eye level. "That's why we're going to do this together. I'm giving you the order, and you're going to carry it out. This arrangement will ensure that you'll never reveal our secret. It's a logical solution, don't you think?"

Grant stood there, frozen. The sounds of distant gunfire had stopped, meaning that the battle for Randalls Island was won, but he didn't turn around to look. He kept his eyes on the syringe in Keller's hand. The last rays of twilight had faded, and now the K-Man's face was utterly dark.

"Don't be a coward, Colonel. Be the man you were meant to be."

Grant stiffened, furious. If he'd had a gun on him at that moment, he would've shot the cadaverous bastard. He would've blown Keller's brains out, even if it meant going to the execution chamber for killing the new vice president.

But the colonel was unarmed, and after a couple of seconds he stopped glaring at Keller. His anger faded like the twilight, and in its wake he felt a cold certainty. *The K-Man is setting me up. If anything goes wrong, he's gonna pin the assassination on me. So I need to come up with a plan to protect myself. I have to make sure that someone else becomes the fall guy.*

He grabbed the syringe from Keller and slipped it into his own pocket. Then he left the rooftop and headed downstairs to the Research Center.

Grant's head started to ache as he hurried down the stairway. His stomach hurt too, and a hot acidic bubble formed inside his gullet and rose to his throat. After he left the stairs he got dizzy and stumbled in the fourth-floor corridor, but luckily no one was there to see it. Then the pain got worse and he doubled over.

It's nerves, he thought. *The pressure is getting to me. Which is fucking understandable, given the circumstances.* Plus, he'd hardly slept or eaten over the past two days. It was enough to make anyone dizzy.

But there was something else that disturbed him. The pain in his guts had a familiar edge. It was the same agony he'd felt the night before when he'd walked past Room 17. Although Grant was on the other side of the building now, more than two hundred feet from that room, the feeling was just as intense as the first time, just as excruciating. It made him drop to his knees and press his forehead to the floor.

He clutched his belly and retched. The pain cut through him like a knife, but the fear was even worse. *Jesus Christ! The freak is dead! How is this fucking possible?*

He took a deep breath and tried to clear his head. Yes, he reassured himself, Raza Khan was deceased. Grant had seen the corpse and super-vised the autopsy. The kid's brain was in a jar now, and the rest of his body had been incinerated in the Rikers Island power plant. So, unless the freak was tormenting him from beyond the grave, something else was causing the pain in his stomach. Nervousness, sleeplessness, hunger, whatever.

Or maybe the freak had damaged him somehow. Maybe the injuries were permanent, and Grant was going to feel this torture for the rest of his life.

He shook his head. *It won't stop me. I'm stronger than this.* Leaning against the wall for support, he got back on his feet. Then he slowly made his way down the corridor.

Grant walked another fifty feet or so, then turned left and went down another hallway. Then he stepped into the infirmary, where the Research Center's doctors treated the medical complications caused by the experimental CRISPR treatments. As Grant had expected, Lieutenant Frazier was there, running on a treadmill while one of the doctors jotted notes on a clipboard. Frazier had broken a couple of ribs when he'd escaped from the fiasco at the 103rd Street footbridge, but it looked like he'd already recovered from his injuries. Thanks to his altered DNA, he healed very quickly, which was a useful trait for soldiers and FSU officers.

Frazier turned his head as Grant approached the treadmill. Grinning, he stepped off the machine and saluted. "Colonel! Have you heard the news? The air strikes crushed the NYPD! We kicked their asses!"

Grant swayed on his feet, still dizzy, but managed to stay upright. "Yeah, yeah, I saw." He turned to the doctor, a dumpy bald guy with thick glasses. "Listen, could you go somewhere else for a while? I need to talk to the lieutenant."

The doctor scuttled off. Frazier looked at Grant with concern. "Sir? Are you okay? You look kind of shaky."

Grant scowled. To carry out his plan, he had to get tough on Frazier. He needed to apply some psychological pressure. "You're worried about me, Lieutenant? You think I need some help?"

Frazier shook his head. "No, sir. I just noticed that you seem—"

"*You're* the one who needs help, Frazier. You're a fucking one-man disaster. What the hell happened at the footbridge today?"

The lieutenant stopped grinning. He took a step backward. "I explained everything in my report, sir. I don't know how—"

"You ran right into an ambush. How many of our officers died because of your stupidity?"

"Sir, I—"

"And then you abandoned your men and jumped into the Harlem River. That's the only thing you do well, you know that? You have a real talent for running away from a fight."

Frazier looked stunned. He stood stock-still and said nothing, his face reddening at the accusations. Grant knew it was harsh, but he had to keep pounding away at the guy. It was part of the plan.

"You know what I ought to do, Lieutenant? I should court-martial your ass and replace you with Derek Powell. I should spring Powell from his detention cell and have him take over your command." Grant pointed down the hall, in the direction of Powell's cell. "And you know why? Because Powell did something useful today when he gave us that tip about the Latin Kings, and all *you* did was fuck it up!"

Frazier took another step backward. His cheek twitched. He was struggling to restrain himself. "Sir, I've tried . . . I've tried my best to carry out your orders."

"Jesus Christ! You have one last chance, Frazier. I'm gonna give you a simple job, something a ten-year-old could do. You think you can handle it?"

Frazier saluted him again. "*Yes, sir!* I won't let you down!"

Grant had succeeded. Now Frazier would agree to anything. The man was helplessly loyal to the colonel. That's what made him so perfect for this particular assignment.

Grant pulled the syringe out of his pocket. "You're gonna go to the room where the president is and give him this shot. That's an order, Lieutenant."

THIRTY-ONE

Jenna was in hell. It was the Muslim hell—*Jahannam*—the Fire Whose Fuel Is Men And Stones. The flames crashed into the basement of the police station and blasted through the ceiling of the interrogation room. Bricks and plaster and shrapnel hurtled downward and battered the steel table she cowered under.

Her father lay beside her and screamed. The air blazed and reddened and scorched their lungs. Jenna lowered her head until her lips touched the floor tiles, but even here the air was broiling. She couldn't speak, couldn't breathe. She silently pleaded to Allah for help, but there was no escape from *Jahannam*. The Fire would consume them all.

Then the room went dark, as sudden as a blackout. The air thickened with smoke and soot, which rushed under the table from all sides. Jenna reached for her father and grasped his arm, but she couldn't see him. At the same time, someone grabbed her waist from behind and dragged her backward across the floor. She pulled Abbu along with her, gripping him tightly.

The person behind her started coughing. A wave of cooler air rushed over them, clearing some of the smoke, and the room went from black to hazy gray. Keeping her head low, Jenna took a sooty breath, and then she started coughing too. Her rescuer leaned forward until his lips touched her ear. "*Chica*? Are you hurt?"

It was Hector. Jenna turned around and saw his face through the smoke. She leaned toward him. "I'm okay. Help me carry my dad!"

They positioned themselves on either side of Abbu and draped his arms around their shoulders. Then they rose to their feet and staggered toward the source of hazy light, a wide, jagged hole in the ceiling. It was several feet above their heads, but so much debris had fallen into the room that they were able to climb the heap of rubble to it. They slipped and stumbled on the chunks of brick and plasterboard. Abbu slowed them down, his head lolling and his feet dragging, but in less than half a minute they managed to clamber up to the hole and wriggle through it.

The ground floor of the station had been pulverized. The walls had been knocked down and the ceiling was gone. Fires were still burning everywhere, but they could see enough through the smoke to find their way between the piles of burning debris. Jenna looked down, her eyes stinging, and saw charred limbs scattered across the floor and headless torsos still in their body armor. It was unspeakable.

They lurched forward, coughing and grunting, until they were past the fire and smoke and rubble. Then they collapsed in a shadowy underpass beneath one of the Triborough Bridge's exit ramps. Jenna lowered her father to the ground and rested his head in her lap. He was wheezing and trembling in terror. He clutched Jenna's hand and opened his mouth, but he couldn't say a word. She stroked his forehead and wiped the soot from his eyes. "Shhh, Abbu. Don't say anything. Just rest."

Hector took a deep breath and got back on his feet. He bent over Jenna, but his eyes were on the ruined police station, which was almost completely masked by the billowing smoke. "I have to go back there. For Carlos." He took a wobbly step toward the station. "If I don't—"

But before he could finish the sentence, someone emerged from the pillar of smoke. The man was caked in ash from head to foot. It sprinkled from his hair and blackened his clothes and covered all of his face except for his eyes, which leaked tears that left muddy tracks on his cheeks. Jenna had no idea who he was until he spoke, and then she recognized his flat, trancelike voice.

"Carlos is dead." David Weinberg raised his arm and stiffly pointed at the station. "So is Commissioner Hayes."

Hector confronted him. "What? Are you sure?"

David nodded. "A falling piece of masonry crushed the commissioner's head. A steel rod impaled Carlos." He turned and pointed his arm in the opposite direction, toward the Harlem River. "We should leave this place immediately. We need to go five hundred yards to the west. Those were Raza's instructions."

His voice was so robotic, so empty of feeling. Hector clenched his hands and glowered, overwrought and infuriated, ready to express his grief and rage by beating the shit out of David. But then Jenna heard a loud, thumping noise that roared over Randalls Island. She looked up at the huge plume of smoke rising from the police station and saw a couple of black shapes emerge from the haze, sleek and predatory and moving very fast.

She shot up and yanked her father to his feet. *"Shit, let's go!"*

The helicopters swooped down, and their gunners opened fire.

THIRTY-TWO

Frazier stood by the gurney in the recovery room, with the syringe in his hand. He was alone with the president, who lay faceup on the bed, in a blue hospital gown. POTUS was asleep, lightly sedated.

The nurse had left the room two minutes ago, called away to attend to an emergency that Colonel Grant had invented. Two FSU guards stood in the hallway, just outside the closed door, but Frazier had slipped past them by using a different entrance, a door that connected this room with the neighboring one. No one had seen him go in, and no one would see him go out. Everything was going smoothly.

But Frazier hesitated. He was confused. The unconscious patient on the gurney looked nothing like the man he'd seen on TV.

His head had been shaved. He still had his wispy yellow eyebrows, but his scalp was bare. His skin looked like clay, pale orange and gritty. His eyes were closed, and an oxygen mask covered his nose and mouth. But the oddest thing about him was a stubby metal catheter that jutted from his scalp, just behind his left ear. A long curving tube connected the catheter to a plastic bag full of milky fluid, which hung from an IV pole above the gurney.

Frazier had received training in battlefield medicine, so he was familiar with IV tubes and catheters, but this apparatus was different. Instead of trickling the fluid into the patient's bloodstream, it was dripping the stuff right into his brain. As Frazier stared at it, he raised his left hand and fingered his own scalp. There was a small scar under his buzz cut, just behind his left ear. The doctors had done the same thing to him six months ago, drilled a hole in his skull so they could flood his brain with CRISPR.

He shook his head. He was getting distracted. He needed to concentrate.

He examined the long tube that ran down to the president's shaved head. Near the bottom was the access port, a hollow piece of blue plastic that jutted from the tube. According to the instructions Colonel Grant had given him, Frazier was supposed to fit the tip of the syringe into this port and push the plunger. Then the poison would flow into the man's brain. Grant had said it would only take a minute, and then Frazier should simply detach the syringe and get the hell out of there. And within four hours, the president would be dead.

But before Frazier could do it, something went wrong.

It happened in an instant. As Frazier stared at the blue piece of plastic, everything around him seemed to come unglued. The room spun in vicious circles, slowly at first, then faster. He grabbed the bed rail of the gurney, but he could barely stay on his feet.

No! Not now!

He was cracking up again. His mind split down the seams and disintegrated. His brain burst open and all the memories inside it scattered across the room. They swirled around him like confetti, like a billion bits of colored garbage.

Goddamn it, focus!

Frazier closed his eyes and tried to think. He strained to catch the memories swirling inside him. After a few seconds of struggle, he had some success—he could remember his name and today's date and what he'd eaten for breakfast that morning. He could also recall the specific instructions that Colonel Grant had given him, all the details about the syringe and the access port. But he couldn't remember why he was doing it. *Why kill the fucking president?*

He closed his eyes tighter and rummaged through his mind. This man on the gurney was his commander in chief. When Frazier had enlisted in the army, he'd sworn an oath to obey the president's orders. But Colonel Grant was his immediate superior, and he'd told Frazier that the oath wasn't valid anymore. He said the situation had changed in the past few hours, something very important had happened, and now Frazier had to swear allegiance to a new leader and follow the new orders Grant had given him. It was for the good of the country, he'd said, the future of America.

But what was the important thing that had happened? What had invalidated the oath? Frazier couldn't remember. It was driving him crazy.

Fuck, it doesn't matter! Just follow the instructions!

Frazier opened his eyes. Struggling to keep his balance, he reached for the tube and the access port. He flicked the protective cap off the tip of the syringe and grasped the hollow piece of blue plastic. But then he glanced at the face of the man on the gurney, and he saw that it wasn't the president anymore. It wasn't even a man.

It was a woman, a nurse. But not the nurse who'd been caring for the president. It was the fat bitch from the hospital in Springfield, the emergency-room nurse who'd refused to treat Andy.

She was asleep, lightly sedated. Her skin looked like clay, pale orange and gritty. Her eyes were closed, but she sneered at him from behind her oxygen mask. Someone had shaved her fat head and wedged a funnel into her scalp. Thick white slime streamed through a tube and dribbled into her skull.

Frazier dropped the syringe. He wasn't going to inject the poison into her. No, that would be too easy. Too impersonal.

He was going to kill her with his bare hands.

"*Bitch!*" He clamped his fingers around her neck and squeezed. "*He was my brother, my little brother! Only nine fucking years old!*"

Her eyes flew open. She was groggy but terrified. Frazier smiled when he saw that look in her eyes. It was so satisfying.

And it was familiar too. He'd killed her once before, eleven years ago. Just a week after Andy died, Frazier had tracked down the nurse and surprised her outside her house. He'd chased her into the woods and shot her with his hunting rifle, the Remington he'd gotten for his fourteenth birthday. And as she lay wounded in the mud, he'd choked her to death. He'd punished her for what she did to Andy, and now he was going to punish her again.

She tried to scream, and Frazier felt her larynx vibrate under his hands.

At the same time, he heard someone yell, "What's going on in there?" A moment later, two men in black uniforms charged into the room and pointed their assault rifles at him.

The next second was a blur. He didn't even think, he just let his enhanced nerves and muscles act on their own. He let go of the bitch's throat, leapt toward the guards, grabbed one of their rifles, and shot both men with it. Then he rushed back to the gurney, turned the rifle around, and bashed its stock into the bitch's shaved head.

Her skull shattered. Blood and brains splashed onto the pillow, and a stream of piss jetted from her crotch.

Then Frazier looked closer and saw a cock beneath the hospital gown. *What the hell?*

His head was clearing. He blinked a few times and took a deep breath. His perceptions came back to normal as he stared at his victim. It wasn't the nurse after all.

The president was dead. An alarm was ringing.

Still holding the bloody rifle, Frazier bolted out of the room.

THIRTY-THREE

Jenna and her father ran under the highway that led to the Triborough Bridge. Bullets pounded the steel span above them, and the buzzing of the helicopters echoed everywhere, but Jenna raced ahead and dragged Abbu along with her, following Hector and David as they sprinted toward the Harlem River.

The road above them was a major highway, more than two hundred feet wide, so it gave them plenty of cover. The NYPD, though, wasn't so fortunate. Most of their officers were at the checkpoint on top of the highway, where the toll plaza used to be, and that was the FSU's primary target. The helicopters strafed the checkpoint mercilessly, firing their guns as they flew past the bridge's towers. Some of the bullets struck the baseball fields to the north of the highway, and Jenna could hear the rounds pinging into the dirt.

As they approached the river, the highway above them narrowed. The Harlem River span of the Triborough Bridge had only six traffic lanes and was less than a hundred feet wide. They were more exposed here, and there was nowhere left to run. The bridge arched over a weedy field and a fenced-off lot at the river's edge, and beyond that was the slate-gray water that separated Randalls Island from Manhattan. The sun had set and the shadows under the bridge had darkened, but the FSU's helicopters turned on their searchlights. *We can't stay here*, Jenna thought. *Sooner or later, they'll find us.*

She slowed to a walk, then doubled over, panting. Her father lay down in the weeds nearby, while Hector and David stopped next to the fence at the water's edge. The helicopters' guns had fallen silent—they'd probably slaughtered all the cops at the checkpoint—and a moment later Jenna heard a change in the sound of their engines. The wind picked up and the beams from the searchlights grew brighter. The helicopters were landing. One of them touched down a few hundred yards to the south, and a dozen men in black uniforms jumped out of the aircraft.

Jenna dashed over to Hector and David. "The soldiers are coming! We have to hide!"

David was pointing at a section of the chain-link fence, and Hector was pulling at the bottom of it, creating a gap between the mesh of steel links and the ground. "*Chica*, what do you think we're doing? Get your *papi* over here and make him crawl under this."

She rushed back to her father. He was so tired, she had to practically carry him to the fence and shove him underneath it. Then, after they'd all slithered through the gap, Hector took the lead and guided them across the lot.

It was a boatyard. At least a dozen boats had been taken out of the water and placed on metal cradles, so their hulls and engines could be repaired. Some were large and some were small, and they were in various states of disrepair, but all the boats had something in common: each was painted blue and white, and each had the letters "NYPD" emblazoned on its sides.

Jenna hurried after Hector. "This is the police department's boatyard, right? The place that Commissioner Hayes mentioned?"

"Yes, and that's the marina." Hector pointed at a pair of docks that extended from the boatyard into the river. "Let's take a look at the boats over there, the ones tied to the dock. Maybe we can find something that suits our needs, eh?"

They stayed low and moved quietly. Although it was quite dark now, the FSU officers weren't far away. All the vessels moored to the closer dock were big harbor-patrol boats, at least thirty feet long, but at the end of the farther dock was a small, simple, brownish boat that sat low in the water. It was about the size of a rowboat, but it had a large outboard engine at the stern.

Jenna grabbed Hector's arm and pulled him toward the small boat. "That one would work. Once we're away from shore, no one will be able to see us in the dark. I think it's a Boston Whaler, actually. Looks like a thirteen-footer."

He stared at her curiously. "You know about boats?"

"I grew up on Coney Island, and my father liked to fish. So, yeah, I picked up a few things."

They lucked out. The Whaler had enough room for all four of them, the key was in the engine, and the gas tank was full. Best of all, it was equipped with oars and oarlocks, so they could pull away from the dock without making any noise.

Jenna untied the lines and took the wheel, while Hector manned the oars. The FSU officers were less than a hundred yards away now, but several trees and the boatyard fence blocked their view of the marina. Within a minute the Whaler was in the middle of the Harlem River. Silent and unseen, they floated with the current, which steered them into the narrow strait between Randalls Island and the Bronx.

One of the things Jenna knew about boating in New York was that all the city's waterways were just brackish extensions of the Atlantic Ocean. The currents depended on the tides, which sometimes pushed the water inland and sometimes pulled it out to sea. The rivers around Manhattan could flow one way in the morning and in the opposite direction by the afternoon.

Now the currents pushed them from the Harlem River to the East River. They were headed toward Rikers.

After they rowed far enough away from Randalls, Jenna turned on the Whaler's outboard engine. They were safe now. Although dozens of searchlight beams crisscrossed the island behind them, this stretch of the East River was empty and black, probably the darkest place in New York City. They'd escaped. They were free. They could cruise up the shoreline to Connecticut, or maybe go all the way up to Canada, beyond the reach of the FSU and the whole insane government.

But Jenna wasn't really free, not yet. She had to find Raza first. She had to rescue him.

She gazed due east at Rikers Island, only a mile away. Powerful flood-lights dotted the island's perimeter and illuminated the long rows of buildings in the jail complex. Raza was in one of those buildings right now, most likely mistreated and definitely terrified. The thought of it enraged her. She couldn't leave him behind. It was unthinkable.

I'm coming, Raza. Your baji *is coming.*

She looked at Hector, who'd pulled in the Whaler's oars. He sat with David on the bench at the front of the boat, while Abbu slept on the rear bench beside her, his head resting against her left shoulder. Jenna nudged her father a little, but he didn't stir. He was sleeping soundly—this was probably the first good sleep he'd had since he was arrested—so she didn't have to worry about accidentally waking him up. She raised her voice over the noise of the outboard.

"Hector? Can you do me a favor?"

He leaned toward her. His head was only a couple of feet from hers, but she could barely see his face in the dark. "Anything, *chica*. The Almighty Latin King Nation is at your service."

"I need you to help my father. Can you take him someplace safe? Maybe to the home of someone you know in the Latin Kings?"

Hector nodded. "Of course. I have plenty of brothers in the Bronx, right over there." He pointed at the shoreline to the north. "But there are lots of Latin Kings in Queens too, over that way. They'd be happy to have both of you as their guests, for as long as you want."

Jenna shifted uncomfortably in her seat. Hector didn't understand. "I'm not going with him. I want to land somewhere on the shore and drop off you and my dad. Then you could take him to the safe house. Can you do that for me?"

He was silent for a few seconds. The Whaler rocked in the water, and the wind gusted over the boat, tousling his hair. "And where will *you* go after you drop us off?"

She decided to tell the truth. "To Rikers. I'm gonna save my brother. And get those vials of vaccine." She turned her head and focused on David, who sat rigidly on the other end of the bench, his back straight and his hands on his knees. "You're gonna come with me, David. You're gonna take me to Raza. You know where the FSU is keeping him, right?"

David stretched his arm to the east and pointed at the tallest building on Rikers Island. He moved like a marionette, as if someone were pulling his strings. "As of two a.m. last night, Raza Khan was in Room Seventeen on the fourth floor of the Research Center. I still have the security card that gives me access to the center."

"Good." She turned back to Hector. "So, where should I drop you off, Queens or the Bronx? Which would be safer for my father?"

Hector paused again before answering. Clearly, he wasn't happy. "Excuse me, but I think you're overlooking something. When we discussed this plan with Commissioner Hayes, we all assumed that a team of police officers would raid the Research Center. You know, specially trained officers with military combat skills, probably several dozen men in all. Needless to say, what you're proposing right now is very different."

Jenna frowned. "Well, the NYPD just lost most of its officers. Including Commissioner Hayes. So we need to change the plan."

"Jenna, you don't even have a gun. What are you going to do, just stroll into the jail and ask for your brother?"

"Look, I'm gonna do this, okay?" She tightened her grip on the Whaler's steering wheel. "I'll go to the darkest part of the island to tie up the boat, and then David will get us into the complex using his security card. It's a big place, so maybe we can slip through."

"Well, at least let me go with you. If you run into one of the jail guards, you'll need someone who knows how to fight. I can—"

"No." Her voice drowned out the engine and rang over the water. "I want you to go with my father because I know you can protect him. That's the important thing." She squinted at Hector in the darkness, trying to get through to him. "Do you see now why I asked you for this favor? You're the only one I can trust. I'm putting his life in your hands."

There was a third pause, a silence that lasted for a full ten seconds. Then Hector sighed. It was a shrill, despairing sound, like the wind hissing over the river.

"Ah, *mi querida*. I can't argue with you anymore." He pointed south. "Go that way. To Queens. The Latin Kings are strong in Jackson Heights."

Jenna trembled. She was so relieved and grateful, she felt faint.

"Thank you, Hector."

She docked the Whaler at Steinway Creek, an inlet in a run-down, industrial part of Queens, a mile north of Jackson Heights. Hector helped her dad off the boat, and Jenna promised she'd come right back. Then she turned north and gunned the outboard.

The wind was blowing harder now and the East River was choppy. The Whaler's bow rose and fell, bouncing on the waves, and the brackish water sprayed everywhere, soaking Jenna and David. She looked up and saw a thick blanket of low clouds spread across the night sky. They scudded overhead, rushing out of the southeast, erasing the horizon. She was less than half a mile from the long, low bridge that connected Rikers Island to Queens, but she could barely see it. Then the rain let loose, hammering the boat, and lightning flashed over the water.

Wonderful. Just wonderful. On top of everything else, another storm.

The river was getting dangerous, and Jenna's boating skills weren't that great to begin with. It had been ten years since the last time she'd gone fishing with her father, and she'd never sailed into a storm before. She tried to keep the Whaler perpendicular to the waves, but staying on that course took her away from Rikers, so instead she hit the swells at a forty-five-degree angle and prayed she didn't swamp the boat. She'd hoped to do a thorough reconnaissance of the island to determine the best place to land, but now she would settle for anything. She needed to get out of this storm.

David swayed on the bench in front of her, his rigid body lurching left and right like a metronome. Lightning flashed again, and Jenna got a good look at his face, which was utterly blank. He wasn't afraid of the storm. He didn't seem worried at all. It was as if he knew he was doomed and therefore didn't care if he fell overboard and drowned. It didn't matter to him.

Thunder boomed behind them, very close, and all the floodlights on Rikers Island suddenly went out. A few seconds later, about half of the lights came back on, powered by emergency generators, but the darkness around the island was thicker now. Jenna pushed the throttle forward and sped toward the lights.

Then David shouted something at her. It surprised Jenna—this was the first time he'd spoken tonight without prompting—and she was so startled, she didn't catch what he'd said. She was too busy battling the waves, her hands squeezing the boat's wheel, and at first she thought David had spotted something in the water.

"What was that?" she shouted back at him. "What did you say?"

"Jenna, I apologize." His voice was loud but lifeless. "I shouldn't have done it."

"Done what? What are you talking about?"

"What I did to Raza. I shouldn't have tested him at the Research Center. It's reprehensible to do scientific tests on prisoners. I should've disobeyed that order."

Jenna grimaced. She didn't want to be reminded of this, especially not now. She was fighting for their lives. "Let's just get there and find him, okay?"

"Raza already punished me. He went into my mind and started slashing. He tore out big pieces, the parts of me that were selfish, the parts that wanted success and pleasure. That's how he took his revenge. He instructed me to tell you that."

There it was again, the telepathy nonsense. It confused the hell out of her, all this talk about Raza giving instructions and projecting his voice into David's head. She wanted to dismiss it as rubbish, a fantasy David had invented, maybe because something horrible and traumatic had pushed him over the edge. But she couldn't ignore the fact that her father had said the same thing: that Raza could somehow broadcast his thoughts into other people's minds. And she was humble enough to acknowledge that the human brain was mysterious, perhaps the most complex and mysterious thing in the universe. So how could anyone say for sure what it can and can't do?

But she couldn't think about it right now. She was racing toward Rikers, less than a hundred yards away, and staring at the concrete seawall that ringed the island. The East River crashed against it, the waves battering the concrete and splashing over the top. She steered the Whaler due north, paralleling the island's shore, and looked for a dock or a boat ramp, but the seawall ran unbroken along the shoreline. There was no place to tie up the boat, nowhere to land.

Jenna shook her head in frustration. "David, help me look for a dock. Keep your eyes on the shore."

He obediently turned toward the island. He held the bow rail with one hand and shielded his face from the rain with the other. "Raza instructed me to tell you something else. He wanted you to know how much he loved you. His exact words were, 'Tell my *baji* that I love her more than the stars.' And he promised he'd never stop loving you, no matter where he went."

Now Jenna was even more confused. Although Raza had lost the ability to speak long ago, this sounded like something her brother might've said when he was a little boy. *No, that's just a coincidence! David's hallucinating, making it all up.* But what did he mean by "no matter where he went"? Where could Raza possibly go?

Alarmed, she leaned over the boat's wheel. "David, was something wrong with Raza when you left him behind? Was he hurt?"

Keeping his eyes on the shoreline, he nodded. "Your brother was struggling. Especially after that soldier threatened him. The man was big, and his mind was vicious."

"What soldier?" Now she was in a full-blown panic. "Wait, what—"

"Over there!" David pointed at the shore. "Look!"

It wasn't a dock or a boat ramp. It was a break in the seawall. The relentless waves had cracked the concrete and washed away a ten-foot-wide section, and the East River had poured through the gap. The water streamed across a road on the other side of the wall and flooded a parking lot, but it was less than a foot deep there. The storm had created a shallow inlet on the island.

Jenna turned the wheel and aimed the Whaler at the gap. Then she slammed the throttle all the way forward, and the outboard shrieked.

"Hang on! We're going in!"

The Whaler hurtled toward the shoreline. It jounced against the waves and leapt into the air and dove through the gap in the seawall. Then it skimmed across the flooded road, its hull scraping against the asphalt below. The friction slowed the boat, and a moment later it skidded to a stop in the parking lot.

Jenna stood up, unsteady, her hands still clenching the wheel. David stood up too and turned toward her. In the dim light his face looked unchanged—still blank, still emotionless. His expression seemed especially strange after what they'd just survived. Jenna remembered what he'd said about Raza slashing his mind. Something was definitely missing. This wasn't the David Weinberg she once knew, the brilliant ambitious young man she'd almost married.

Then a bullet smashed into the side of his head. It plunged into one ear and exploded out the other. David collapsed in the Whaler's bow, dead before his body hit the bench.

Jenna spun to her right and saw the gunman. Standing in the ankle-deep floodwaters, he pointed his assault rifle at her. His black uniform was sopping wet.

It was the Angel of Death, here to collect her soul.

THIRTY-FOUR

Vance Keller raised his right hand and placed his left on the cover of a thick black book. It wasn't a Bible. No one could find a Bible anywhere on Rikers Island. It was a very old laboratory reference book, titled *Tables of Physical and Chemical Constants*, but fortunately that title wasn't printed on the book's musty cover, so Vance had brought it to the inauguration ceremony. He knew that everyone would simply assume it was a Bible when they saw it in the photos.

The man holding the book for Vance was an eighty-year-old white-haired geezer named Barton. Judge Barton had an office in the basement of one of the Rikers jails, where his job was to rubber-stamp the FSU's search warrants and surveillance orders. His presence on the island was a lucky thing; Vance wanted to take the oath of office as quickly as possible to solidify his hold on the presidency. And another superstorm had just hit New York City and shut down all the air traffic in the region, including helicopter flights to Rikers. If Barton hadn't already been at the jail complex, they would've had a hard time getting a federal judge there to administer the oath.

The fake Bible shook in Judge Barton's hands. He was gaunt and nearly bald, and his face was hideously wrinkled. He turned his grizzled head and looked around the conference room, which was usually reserved for meetings of the Federal Service Unit's commanders. Now the room was full of Vance's bodyguards, a group of heavily armed soldiers handpicked from the ranks of the FSU and the Secret Service. Also in attendance was an FSU camera crew, which usually shot video of prisoner interrogations but was now recording the inauguration ceremony for posterity. Barton stared at the cameraman for a moment, then turned back to Vance and cleared his throat.

"Please repeat after me." His voice was high-pitched and breathy. "I, Vance Corey Keller, do solemnly swear . . ."

He paused to allow Vance to repeat the words.

". . . that I will faithfully execute the office of the President of the United States . . ."

He paused again, and Vance echoed him.

". . . and will, to the best of my ability, preserve, protect and defend the Constitution of the United States."

Vance repeated the last words of the oath, then added, "So help me God."

Barton managed a feeble smile. He lowered his right hand and shook Vance's. "Congratulations, Mr. President."

This was the moment Vance had been waiting for, the culmination of all his hard work and sacrifice. Through careful planning and diligence, he'd wrested the reins of power from a dangerous bungler and put them in his own capable hands. Now he would steer the country toward a safer, more prosperous future, engineered to maximize harmony and minimize strife. The American people would no longer seethe with discontent nor claw at one another in hatred and envy. Peace and acceptance would flow from one town to the next, streaming from millions of hearts and minds, all tempered by the Serenity sequence.

But, like so much else in life, the moment of victory was a disappointment. Vance felt no bliss. He didn't even feel much satisfaction. He still faced so many problems.

He let go of the judge's hand and pointed at the cameraman. "That's enough. Send the video to the news media and upload it on the White House website." He swung his arm from left to right, gesturing at everyone in the conference room. "Okay, folks, thank you for coming. We need to use this room for a classified briefing now, so everyone but the senior commander has to leave."

Vance declined to shake hands with anyone else. The video crew, the judge, and the soldiers filed out of the room, and Vance's bodyguards took position in the corridor outside. Only one FSU man remained behind, and it wasn't Colonel Grant, who'd disappeared shortly after the assassination. It was Grant's chief deputy, Major Michael Weston, the officer who'd stood beside Vance at the rally at Citi Field. In Grant's absence, he'd become the acting commander of the Federal Service, and he looked the part. He wore black fatigues and a Kevlar helmet, and he carried a semi-automatic pistol in his belt holster.

Once they were alone in the room, Weston saluted him, standing rigid and tall, as dull as dirt but utterly obedient. Like Vance and Grant, he'd been vaccinated against the virus that carried Serenity, but he didn't need the DNA sequence to make him tame. He was born that way.

Vance frowned. Even with his most loyal and efficient underlings, it was his policy to be harsh. If you wanted to get the best performance from your subordinates, you had to threaten them sometimes. Human beings just can't reach their full potential unless they're at least a little afraid.

"Major, what's the status of the search for the suspect?"

Weston dropped the salute but still stood at attention. "Mr. President, I've assigned three hundred officers to look for Lieutenant Frazier. They're divided into ten squads, and each is searching a different section of the island. No one has reported sighting him yet, but we've only cleared half the buildings in the complex so far."

"I assume you're also monitoring the video from the security cameras?"

"Sir, the power outage from the storm has caused a few problems with that. Our emergency generators can't produce all the power we need, so we had to turn off some of the floodlights and surveillance systems."

Vance's frown deepened. He didn't want to hear this. He wanted to tie up the loose ends and move past the ugliness. "Major, this is unacceptable. Lieutenant Frazier assassinated the president. He murdered my father-in-law in the most brutal way possible. You need to find him immediately."

"Yes, sir!" Weston saluted again. "I'll order another hundred officers to join the search."

"And I don't want to see any heroics. Trying to capture Frazier alive would be suicidal. The only way to neutralize the man is to use over-whelming force and shoot him on sight. Is that understood?"

"Absolutely, Mr. President. We won't take any chances." Weston reached into the chest pocket of his fatigues and pulled out a plastic baggie. "Sir, you asked me to notify you if we discovered any evidence from the crime scene. My men found this under the gurney in the recovery room."

Vance felt a bolt of panic. Inside the baggie was the syringe, still loaded with yellowish poison.

He quickly grabbed the thing out of Weston's hand and slipped it into his own pocket. "Thank you, Major. It's probably a dose of the CRISPR treatment, but I'll have the laboratory confirm that."

He took a deep breath, trying not to let his terror show. Along with the fear, he felt an equally strong surge of fury. Not only had Colonel Grant shirked his duty and foisted it on a genetically enhanced lunatic, he'd left a damning trail of evidence. If someone other than Vance had recovered the syringe—an FBI agent, for example, or a Secret Service investigator—then the situation might've turned ugly. Both he and Grant could've been arrested for treason. Maybe even executed.

The colonel's carelessness was unforgivable. Vance had no choice except to take action. "Now let's move on to our next priority. Where the hell is Grant?"

For the first time, Weston's professional demeanor wavered. He shifted his weight from foot to foot and avoided eye contact. "The colonel isn't in his office or his quarters, sir. I've questioned everyone on his staff, and no one has seen him in the past hour. I also checked with our officers on the Rikers Island Bridge, and they said the colonel hasn't tried to leave the island either."

"Then we have to assume the worst. Grant and Frazier vanished at the same time, so it's likely that they're collaborating. I suspect that Grant planned the assassination and ordered Frazier to carry it out."

"But, sir, why would the colonel do that?" Weston's voice rose slightly, betraying his sympathy for Grant. "Why would he want to kill the president?"

The major's attitude was understandable. He was a loyal soldier, and he'd served under Grant for years, so naturally he sympathized with the man. But Vance had to make it clear that the definition of loyalty had just changed. From now on, every FSU officer owed his allegiance to the president and no one else. "This matter is highly classified, Major. Due to national-security concerns, I can't give you all the details. Suffice it to say, Colonel Grant wasn't what he seemed. He had his motives."

Weston nodded. Because he lacked the capacity for independent thought, it was relatively easy to redirect him. "So should the search parties be on the lookout for Grant too?"

"Yes, he's probably hiding with Frazier, so the same rules of engagement should apply to the colonel. In other words, shoot him on sight."

The major nodded again. He didn't look happy about the order, but Vance felt sure he'd obey it. After a couple of seconds, he saluted Vance a third time. "One more thing, sir. Our officers on the Rikers Island Bridge are reporting some unusual activity in Queens. Dozens of young males, mostly blacks and Latinos, are rioting at the intersection of Nineteenth Avenue and Hazen Street, which is just outside the security gate on the Queens side of the bridge."

Curious, Vance cocked his head. "That's odd. They're outside in the middle of the storm?"

"Yes, sir. And they're blocking the entrance to Rikers. They've dragged several junk cars into the intersection, and they've piled up all kinds of garbage to make a barricade. Most of the rioters are dressed in gang colors, bandannas, that kind of thing. So it's probably organized gang activity."

It was just a minor annoyance, Vance thought, but it needed to be dealt with. As soon as Major Weston's officers eliminated Grant and Frazier, Vance wanted to leave Rikers and go back to Washington, by tomorrow morning at the latest. He had to organize his White House staff and meet with congressional leaders and deliver a televised address to the American people. And he was going to bury his father-in-law too, in a grand patriotic funeral at Arlington National Cemetery. But the streets in Queens had to be cleared before any of that could happen.

Vance pointed at the major. "Send more officers to the bridge. Order them to dismantle the barricade and arrest the troublemakers. If they resist arrest, fire on them." He folded his arms across his chest. "If necessary, kill them all."

THIRTY-FIVE

Colonel Grant crouched in the dark lake of seawater that had spread across Rikers Island. He'd found a hiding place behind one of the jail buildings, between a loading dock and a Dumpster. It was a good spot because there were no lights or security cameras nearby, and if any of the search parties came looking for him, Grant would hear them splashing through the water that covered the parking lot. But the floodwaters were already three feet deep and rising, and he couldn't stay here much longer.

He was afraid. No matter how well he hid himself, the soldiers were sure to find him. Probably before midnight, and definitely before sunrise. And they wouldn't bother with arresting him or putting him on trial. No, they would terminate him "with extreme prejudice," as Grant's buddies in the Special Forces used to say. He'd realized this fate was inevitable as soon as the alarms started ringing in the Research Center and all the officers ran toward the president's room. After that debacle, there was no way that Vance would let him live, not even in the darkest cell in the most secret prison in the country. Although Grant fled the Research Center, driven by his strong instinct for survival, he knew he was only buying himself a few more hours.

And he was angry too. He couldn't believe he'd been reduced to this—cowering in the foul water, with garbage floating all around. After all those years busting his ass in the army and the FSU, clawing his way to the top of the bureaucracy, he was now lower than the lowest criminal. He could just imagine what his ex-wife would say if she saw him. *Eli Grant was a bastard, a liar, and an abuser, someone who never cared about morality or basic decency, and now he's only getting what he deserves.* It was a lie, all of it, but no one would ever see the truth. He would die before he could justify all the decisions he'd made.

He shivered. The water was fucking cold. He couldn't see much in the dark, so he focused on listening to the storm—the wind howling, the rain sluicing down, the East River crashing over the island's seawall. And he heard other noises coming from the jail behind him, water pouring into the building through a million crevices, and the muffled screams and curses of the detainees, trapped in solitary-confinement cells that were rapidly flooding.

Grant had put most of those people in jail. He'd ordered the arrest of thousands of illegals and suspected terrorists, and he'd supervised their detention and interrogation. And if he were still head of the FSU, he would've ordered someone to get the prisoners out of their flooded cells and move them to a higher floor. But that wasn't his problem anymore. He wasn't responsible for anyone now, and frankly it was a huge relief. His life was finished, and so were all his problems, all the petty bullshit headaches that used to drive him crazy. So he could ignore their screams.

There was one voice, though, that Grant took special notice of. It was deep and firm and steadfast, and unlike all the other voices, it wasn't full of desperate fear. It wasn't coming from the jail behind him either. It was a familiar, comforting voice coming from inside his own head, and it was telling him not to give up. *There's still hope,* it said. *I can save your life. All you have to do is come to me.*

Grant stood up straight and peered into the darkness, wondering where he was supposed to go. He sloshed around the Dumpster and gazed across the parking lot at another jail building that looked identical to the one behind him. It was dimly lit because it was running on emergency power, but a quarter mile beyond it was a taller building that still blazed with electric light, shining like a beacon in the storm. It was the Research Center, the building Grant had run away from just an hour ago. All the lights were still on there because the Research Center was the

FSU's most important facility, so it received the lion's share of the island's emergency power.

The voice inside Grant's head was telling him to go back to the Research Center. He didn't know why. At first glance, it seemed like a terrible idea. Just north of the Research Center was the FSU headquarters, which Vance used as his office when he came to Rikers, and that whole section of the island was swarming with FSU officers and Secret Service agents. But Grant didn't question the logic of it. The voice was confident and commanding, and it reached out to him like a lifeline.

Besides, what the hell did he have to lose?

So he waded across the parking lot, leaning into the rain and wind. Luckily, he knew the layout of the jail complex better than anyone. He stayed in the shadows, moving as quietly as possible and steering clear of the security cameras. As he neared the Women's Detention Facility, he saw a dozen FSU officers rush out of the jail, and for a second he thought he was done for. He ducked behind a parked car, expecting the officers to surround him and start firing. But they didn't spot him. Instead, they jumped into a convoy of black SUVs, which raced south toward the Rikers Island Bridge. Grant waited until they were gone, then splashed past the jail.

After another three minutes he came to the back entrance of the Research Center, which had its own loading dock. This was where the semitrailer trucks pulled up to the building every morning to deliver lab supplies and cages of white rats. A couple of guards usually kept watch over the area, but now the floodwaters lapped at the building's ground floor and there were no officers in sight. Grant climbed up to the loading dock and examined the doors, which were all locked. But one of the doors had a security-card reader next to it, and Grant still had his card.

He dashed inside and charged up the stairway. He couldn't avoid the security cameras here, because they hung over every landing, and at any moment he expected some FSU officer to spot him on one of the video monitors and raise the alarm. But the building remained silent. Grant supposed that the security forces were stretched thin, with so many officers assigned to search the island or protect Vance or respond to whatever was going on at the bridge. He made it to the fourth floor without any trouble and hurried down the corridor.

He was very familiar with this section of the Research Center. He'd walked down the same corridor earlier that evening, after Vance had given him the syringe, but before he'd passed it on to Frazier. Grant remembered the pain he'd felt the last time he'd been here, the awful twisting in his guts, but now he felt fine. No, better than fine—he was jangling with a fierce, wild hope that pulled him toward the detention cells at the far end of the hall. He used his security card again to open the last door on the right.

Then he approached the gurney where Derek Powell lay.

It had been eight hours since he'd last seen Powell, and Grant was shocked at how much healthier the man looked. Derek turned his head on the pillow and smiled, his eyes clear and focused, his dark skin gleaming. His broad chest rose and fell under his hospital gown, and his arm and leg muscles rippled under his skin. Grant looked at the monitor beside the gurney and studied Powell's vital signs, which were remarkably strong for someone who'd nearly died the night before. If not for the handcuffs that still bound his wrists and ankles to the bed rails, the man could've probably jumped out of bed and run laps around the island. It was a medical miracle.

Grant smiled too. He couldn't help it. He'd liked Powell from the start, from the very first time he'd met the young soldier. Something about him reminded Grant of himself. "Jesus Christ, you're healing fast. It looks like your new genes agree with you."

Derek nodded. "Yes, this CRISPR treatment is much better than the last one. Your researchers finally got it right."

His voice was also strong, although it sounded a bit different from Powell's old voice, more formal and precise. Grant pointed at the man's midsection, where his hospital gown had come undone, exposing a layer of gauze bandage wrapped around his waist. "And how does the wound feel? Any pain?"

"None at all." Powell lifted his head off the pillow and looked Grant in the eye. "Come over here and see for yourself. Take off the bandage."

Grant stepped closer to the gurney. He had no desire to look at Powell's wound, and yet he reached for the bandage and peeled off the surgical tape and removed the gauze. To his astonishment, the gash in Powell's waist was almost completely healed. A long scar ran across his midsection, but there was no swelling or discoloration, and the absorbable stitches had already dissolved.

Grant dropped the gauze on the floor. "Holy shit."

Powell chuckled. He dropped his head back, relaxing on the pillow, but he kept his eyes on Grant. "So you heard me call for you, Colonel? While you were hiding behind the Dumpster?"

Grant's heart thudded. He wanted to back away from the gurney, but he couldn't. "You . . . you did what?"

"You're in trouble, aren't you? And you need my help?"

It was all true, yet Grant couldn't believe it. How did Powell get inside his head? Was it another side effect of the CRISPR treatment that Weinberg had given the soldier the night before? The new DNA inserted in Powell's cells had included the Serenity sequence, which was supposed to reduce his aggression and willfulness, but could it have had other effects as well? After seeing what happened to the Khan freak, Grant was willing to believe almost anything.

Powell shook his head. He'd clearly heard Grant's questions, even though the colonel hadn't said anything aloud.

"Dr. Weinberg didn't put the Serenity sequence in my treatment. I instructed him to leave it out and insert a different strip of DNA instead. The special sequence that Dr. Jenna Khan developed for her unauthorized experiment."

Now Grant started to panic. He felt like he was shivering in the floodwaters again, except now the water was thick with terror, and it was rising inside his skull. He wanted to run, but he was frozen. He couldn't move, couldn't say a word. But Powell heard everything inside Grant's head, even the quietest thought.

"Calm down, Colonel. I'll explain everything in a moment. But first you need to do me a favor. The key is still in your pocket, isn't it?"

To Grant's shock, his right hand began to move against his will. It felt as if someone else had taken control of it and guided his fingers into his pants pocket, where they grasped a small key. Under Powell's control, his hand pulled out the key and fitted it into the handcuffs that attached Derek's right wrist to the bed rail. Then Grant unlocked the other three handcuffs that bound Powell to the gurney and undid the belts strapped across his chest and thighs.

When Grant was finished, Powell let go of him. The colonel's muscles went slack and he sank to the floor, paralyzed, his mouth open in a silent scream. At the same time, Powell sat upright on the bed and stretched his arms wide.

"Ahh! That's better!" He swung his legs over the bedside and looked down at Grant. "Thank you, Colonel. You know, it's a shame you're so small. I need some clothes, but nothing of yours would fit this new body of mine."

Grant was helpless, drowning. He pissed himself and shat into his pants. He'd just realized why Derek's voice sounded so different now. The huge man peering down at him wasn't really Derek Powell.

The man chuckled again. "That's correct. Powell died last night on the operating table. His heart stopped beating, and the surgeons were about to give up. But luckily, the operating theater was right next to Room Seventeen. So I was able to jump into Powell's head just as he expired." He hopped off the gurney and stepped toward Grant. "I left my crippled body behind and streamed into his brain, and my mind was strong enough to revive it. Then the heart began beating again, and now it was *my* heart, *my* body." He slapped his chest and flexed his pectoral muscles. "You have to admit, it's a big improvement. I don't miss my old body at all."

The freak! It's him! He's still alive!

Frowning, the man knelt beside him. "I should punish you for that remark, but I don't have the time. So I'll make this quick." He clenched his giant right hand into a fist and cocked it back. "Goodbye, Colonel. I hope you enjoy *Jahannam*."

Grant writhed. The last thing he saw was the fist coming down.

THIRTY-SIX

The cold barrel of an assault rifle poked into Jenna's back as she waded through the floodwaters. Frazier was behind her, but she couldn't see or hear him. He was like a ghost, blending into the rain and darkness, but the rifle he carried was solid enough. Its muzzle pressed against Jenna's spine, the same gun that had killed David.

They followed a twisting path across Rikers Island. Frazier steered her between cell blocks and fences, down alleys and service roads that had turned into raging streams. Jenna obeyed his orders and walked in silence, confused and terrified. She couldn't understand why he hadn't killed her. Why did he shoot David but keep her alive? Was she more useful to him as a prisoner? But it was pointless to guess his intentions, because the man's brain was damaged. She couldn't even be certain that he recognized her. For all she knew, his memories had gone haywire again and he saw her as someone else entirely, an enemy from his past or a monster from his nightmares. In an instant he could change his mind about her and pull the trigger.

Soon they approached a pair of modern steel-and-concrete buildings, both of them taller and more brightly lit than the surrounding jails.

Frazier whispered, "Get down!" and Jenna crouched behind a car, a waterlogged SUV parked by the seawall. Peering through the car's windows, she saw a Stryker armored vehicle cruise past the buildings and rumble onto the bridge she'd noticed earlier that night, the long causeway that connected Rikers Island to Queens. Several other vehicles were already speeding down the bridge, their headlights pointing south. She felt a sudden stab of hope in her chest—*Hector's doing it! He's drawing the soldiers away!* But then Frazier clamped his hand around the back of her neck and crushed the hope out of her.

"You got a choice, bitch." He pulled her head back so he could growl into her ear. "You can either keep quiet, or you can try to fuck me over by making some noise. But that second choice won't do you any good. If the soldiers hear you, they'll shoot first and ask questions later. So you'll end up dead, understand?"

Jenna nodded. Although she was scared out of her mind, she'd recognized the change in Frazier's situation. He was avoiding the other FSU officers. They'd clearly turned against him. Maybe they'd realized how fucking crazy he was. "What happened? Why are you running from them?"

He squeezed her neck, and an electric spasm ran down her vertebrae. "You're curious? You want to get inside my head, like your brother did?"

She was in so much pain, she couldn't speak. Closing her eyes, she remembered the last thing David had told her, about Raza struggling with a big, vicious soldier. And she imagined the worst.

"That's who fucked us up today, your little freak of a brother. Why do you think you got so lucky at the footbridge? You really thought it was just a coincidence?" Frazier shook her by the neck, and she saw stars against the backs of her eyelids. "No, I figured it out. That little bastard has been manipulating everything. He fooled everyone into thinking he was dead, then he tricked me into chasing you to Randalls Island. But I'm not fooled anymore. This time, I'm gonna kill him and make sure he's fucking dead."

He let go of her, and she collapsed against the SUV. Her head swam and her stomach heaved, and the whole ugly island whirled around her. It was hopeless. She couldn't reason with Frazier. She couldn't even understand what he was saying. Her only hope was to get the attention of the other FSU men. Maybe they could gun down this maniac before he got a chance to hurt Raza.

Frazier grabbed her arm and lifted Jenna to her feet. "Come on, let's go. You're gonna help me do this." He raised his rifle and pushed her forward. "Before I kill your brother, I'm gonna kill you first. Right in front of him."

At first glance, the two brightly lit buildings looked identical, but as Jenna drew closer to them she noticed an important difference. Behind the building to the north, just outside its back entrance, three dead FSU officers floated in the brackish water.

Frazier stopped to examine them, bending over the corpses. He glanced at the building to the south, just a hundred feet away, then pointed in that direction. "He exited the Research Center, over there, and came here to the headquarters. Then he killed these three idiots and went inside." He stood up and pointed at the back door, which was propped open by a fourth corpse that lay across the threshold. "And now we're gonna follow him. He's doing all the work, getting rid of the guards for us."

Jenna was confused again. "Who are you talking about?"

Frazier prodded her with his rifle. "Shut your mouth and get going."

He shoved her toward the open doorway, and she stepped through it, averting her eyes from the dead man at her feet. Then she started climbing the building's stairs, with Frazier right behind her.

Water dribbled off her hair and clothes and puddled on the concrete steps. Jenna looked ahead and listened carefully, hoping to hear the clomping boots of FSU officers somewhere in the building. She was ready to start screaming as soon as they came within earshot, ready to draw their fire. The only footsteps she heard, though, were Frazier's and her own. At the fourth-floor landing she stopped short—rivulets of blood trickled down the next flight of stairs above them. But Frazier poked her with his rifle again, and she climbed the bloody steps.

The officer's body was on the fifth-floor landing, sprawled on its side. Jenna trembled, thinking of Raza. She had to grip the handrail to stay upright. Biting her lip, she stepped over the corpse and kept going up.

The stairway ended at the ninth floor. When they reached the top landing, Frazier lowered his assault rifle and slung it over his shoulder. Then he removed a big black pistol from his belt holster. He grabbed Jenna's left arm and yanked it behind her back. He curved his other arm around her body and jammed his gun against the right side of her forehead.

"Okay, here's where things get interesting." His damp torso leaned against her shoulder blades, and his chin jutted above her head. She looked straight up and saw his face looming over her, looking down the front of her shirt as he wrenched her arm. "You're gonna be my human shield. Keep moving, bitch."

Jenna stepped forward, using her free hand to open the stairwell door. Ahead of them was the ninth-floor corridor, about six feet wide and a hundred feet long. It had a tile floor and several doors on both sides and a pair of double doors at the far end, like a million other office-building corridors. But the sight of this one was so sickening that Jenna doubled over and vomited on her sneakers. At least twenty bodies lay strewn across the floor.

Frazier laughed. "Whoa, this is it! We're in the right place!" He craned his neck and peered over Jenna's head, staring at the far end of the corridor. "Hello? *Hello*? Is anyone down there? Look, I know all these assholes didn't commit mass suicide, so someone must be there!"

He pushed Jenna down the hall. She tried not to look at the bodies, but she had to glance down to avoid stepping on them. Half of them wore the black FSU uniform, and the other half wore dark suits and radio earpieces. Frazier kicked one of the suited corpses and laughed again. "Damn, this was a real party! You snuffed some Secret Service boys too! Nice fucking job!"

It was the longest hundred feet Jenna had ever walked, but by the time she reached the end of the hallway, she could guess who was on the other side of the double doors. She knew only one person, aside from Frazier, who was that good at killing people. A moment later Frazier turned sideways and, without letting go of her, rammed his shoulder against the doors, flinging them open. Then he turned toward the man standing in the middle of the office, a seven-foot-tall black man cradling an assault rifle and wearing nothing but a pair of sweatpants.

Jenna's guess was confirmed. It was Derek Powell.

Frazier glared at him. "Don't even think about raising that rifle, motherfucker. My reflexes are just as good as yours." He pressed his pistol against the side of Jenna's head. "Before you can point that thing at me, I'll blow her brains out."

Derek ignored him. He focused on Jenna. He smiled.

Frazier shook with fury. He pressed the gun harder against Jenna's skull. "And don't try to fuck with my head again either! It won't work this time. I know how to stop it now."

Derek didn't even glance at him. He kept his eyes on Jenna. And then he said something to her, although he didn't open his mouth or move his lips. He just stared at her, and the words rang inside her mind.

Jenna? It's me. Raza.

While Jenna stood there, astonished, Frazier got angrier. He pushed the pistol against her temple so hard that the muzzle dug into her skin. "Bitch! Tell your brother I'm not fucking around! Tell him I'll kill you if he tries to get into my head again!"

The man whom Jenna had assumed was Derek Powell finally took his eyes off her. He turned to Frazier and gave him a sympathetic look. "You're right, Lieutenant. You're enhanced, so your mind is strong enough to defend itself. I got through your defenses last time only because I surprised you. I definitely won't try it again."

And at the same time, he spoke soundlessly to Jenna.

Are you okay, baji? Did the stupid pig hurt you?

She was going crazy. In her desperation, she was imagining her brother's voice. That was the only possible explanation. The constant terror of the past two days had finally gotten to her.

You're not crazy. This is real. Derek Powell died, and I inherited his body. And I'm very grateful for it. I have so many skills now.

Meanwhile, Frazier had calmed down a bit. He nodded a couple of times and relaxed his grip on Jenna. "You're damn fucking right! It won't happen again! Now put your rifle on the desk and back away from it, nice and slow."

The huge man shrugged and did as he was told. He rested his assault rifle on a fancy antique desk, placing it next to a crystal nameplate with the name VANCE C. KELLER etched into it. Then he stepped away from the desk and backed up toward the wall behind it. A portrait of George Washington hung on the wall, and a few feet to the right was a heavy steel door with some kind of electronic lock on it, like the door to a bank vault.

That's a panic room. The President of the United States is in there. I know, it sounds ridiculous, doesn't it? But I'm not joking. While I neutralized all the soldiers who were guarding him, the president ran into that room and locked himself inside.

Frazier relaxed a little more, easing the pressure of the gun against

Jenna's forehead. "You made a mistake, freak. I knew something was off when I saw you after the surgery. You were pretending to be Powell, but you didn't sound like him. I could tell that something funny was going on."

This pig isn't as smart as he thinks he is. He says he was suspicious, but he did everything I told him to do. He went to East Harlem and walked right into the ambush on the footbridge. He's living proof that genetic enhancement can only do so much. Yes, CRISPR increased his brainpower, but he was starting from a very low intelligence level.

Jenna wanted to scream. Her brother had been silent for ten years, and now she heard him chattering nonstop inside her head. It was a hallucination, a nightmare.

Why are you so skeptical? My illness kept me from talking all those years, but I could still think. I listened to everything you said when you took care of me, all the books and magazines you read out loud to me, all the songs you sang. And I learned a lot just from watching and listening. I grew up and became a man, even though no one could see it.

Frazier took a step toward the antique desk, pushing Jenna forward. It was a taunt, a provocation, a dare. He was getting cocky, reckless. "And I saw what you were doing to Colonel Grant. You were sending your fucking brain waves through the air and torturing him. But it kept happening even after the cripple was dead, and that was your big mistake. That's when I started to figure it out."

Here's the problem, baji. *You're suspicious of telepathy and other psychic phenomena, so you don't trust your perceptions. But there's a scientific basis for it. David Weinberg explained it to me when we shared thoughts last night. Brain signals are just electrical impulses. If you make genetic changes that increase the electrical power of those signals, your thoughts can extend beyond the brain and propagate to other people. And under the right conditions, you can transmit all your thoughts and memories to another mind. It's like transferring software wirelessly from one computer to another. You can transfer an entire consciousness. That's what I did.*

Jenna was crying. She didn't want to believe him. It was too much, too painful. Even if she could accept the scientific explanation, how could she believe that her brother's mind had taken over Powell's body? The Raza she'd known had been innocent and helpless. How could he have transformed himself into this calm, ruthless soldier who'd already killed at least twenty men? Where did he learn to do all those things?

When I jumped into Powell, his brain wasn't a blank slate. It still had all his memories and reflexes, all his instincts for combat. And now I'm able to use those skills.

She forced herself to silently respond to him, forming the words in her mind.

Use them for murder, you mean?

I had no choice. It was either kill or be killed. You see that, don't you?

Frazier took another step forward, dragging Jenna along. He was like an executioner clutching his prisoner, or like a high priest guiding a human sacrifice to the altar. "So now I'm here to punish you, freak. You already showed me what happened to your mother on Coney Island, and that was pretty bad. But this is gonna be worse."

Okay, we've run out of time. Whether you believe me or not, you have to follow my instructions now.

Please stop. I can't take this.

I'm sorry, Jenna, but you have to listen. The lieutenant may be an idiot, but he's holding a gun to your head. If you want to survive this, you need to do something for me.

What? What do you want me to do?

Just slide your eyes all the way to the right and take a good look at his pistol. I need to see it from your perspective.

She stared at the gun out of the corner of her eye. Frazier held it firmly, not shaking at all. The pistol was cocked, and his index finger was on the trigger. And the lieutenant was breathing evenly, confident that he was in control of the situation.

"Take a good look at your sister, freak. Say goodbye to her, you fucking—"

Now!

Jenna's right hand reached for the gun. She hadn't planned to do that. It felt as if an invisible force had yanked her hand toward the pistol at fantastic speed. Her fingers moved of their own accord and clamped around the gun's barrel and pushed it upward till it pointed at the ceiling. At the same time, she lunged to the side, under Frazier's right arm, again feeling as if an uncanny force had pulled her body in that direction.

She realized, though, that this feeling was deceptive. The forces actually came from her own brain, specifically her motor cortex, the region that sent nerve signals to her muscles, telling them how to move. Until

this moment, the instructions had always come from her own consciousness, but now someone else had taken over this part of her brain. And as
a result, Jenna could move much, much faster than normal.

Frazier fired the pistol, and the bullet tore into the ceiling. As Jenna
dove sideways, she caught a glimpse of his face and saw the surprise and
bewilderment in his eyes. He was so stunned that he hesitated for a moment, unsure how to handle this new threat. But after half a second he
bared his teeth and let out an awful roar. He ripped the gun out of
Jenna's hand and lowered it toward her head, preparing to fire.

Then a second gunshot rang out, but it wasn't from Frazier's pistol. The
lieutenant stumbled backward, shoved hard by the bullet that had just
plunged into his chest. Five more bullets struck him in quick succession,
tearing five neat holes in the front of his black uniform. He dropped
his pistol and landed on his back, thumping against the office's carpet.
His body convulsed as he hit the floor, and bloody froth bubbled out
of his mouth.

Jenna looked away and turned toward the antique desk. The giant
bare-chested soldier stood behind it, holding the assault rifle that he'd
picked up and fired while Frazier had hesitated and Jenna had lunged
out of the way. He kept the rifle pointed at Frazier until he was certain
that the lieutenant would never get up. Then he looked at Jenna and
smiled again.

Praise be to Allah. You're safe now.

Jenna shook her head. She couldn't deny it any longer. This man was
her brother. Raza was inside him. She didn't know yet whether this was
a miracle or a catastrophe, but it was the truth.

After a couple of seconds she heard a mechanical rumbling outside.
Looking out the window, she saw three Stryker vehicles pull up in front
of the building. A moment later, the soldiers poured out of the armored
personnel carriers and sprinted toward the building's front and back entrances.

Her heart sank. She was afraid of the soldiers, of course, but she
was even more scared that her brother would be forced to kill them.
"Raza, we have to get out of here. We have to find another way out of the
building."

Don't worry. I've prepared for this. He slung the rifle over his shoulder
and stepped toward the door to the panic room. He bent over the electronic lock and stared at its keypad. *Earlier this evening I was sharing*

thoughts with a man named Eli Grant. He was the commander of this facility, so he knew all the security pass codes.

Raza punched the code into the keypad. Then he turned the door's handle and heaved it open.

THIRTY-SEVEN

Frazier couldn't move anything below his neck. One of the bullets must've severed his spinal cord. But as he lay on the floor and his lungs filled with blood, he took one last look at the man who'd shot him, hating the fucker with all the strength he had left.

The asshole smiled at him. Captain Derek Powell, the man whom Frazier had once respected and admired, was no longer inside that huge body. It was the freak who loomed over him, the crippled kid staring at him from behind Powell's eyes, eager to watch Frazier drown in his own blood.

Then Frazier's dying brain shuddered, and the bastard's face changed shape. It narrowed and sharpened until it became the cripple's face, with its beak nose and gaping mouth, tilted backward as if he were laughing in delight.

That little fucked-up raghead! I should've snuffed him in his wheelchair!

Everything was darkening now. His heart had stopped beating, and his blood soaked the carpet. But his brain shuddered again, and another face appeared on the giant's body. Frazier was relieved at first, because this face wasn't nearly as nasty as the cripple's. It was a handsome young man with blue eyes and blond hair, a husky country boy from southern Missouri. *Is that me? Is that my own face?* But no, that wasn't right. The boy looked a lot like Frazier but not quite the same.

Then it hit him. It was Andy. It was his little brother, but at the age of twenty. It was what Andy would've looked like if he hadn't died eleven years ago.

It should've been a joyful sight for Frazier, but Andy was frowning. He shook his head slowly, looking very disappointed. It upset and confused Frazier, because Andy was the only person he'd ever really loved. It struck him deeper than any of the bullets that had torn through his chest. He needed to know what was wrong, what had disappointed his little brother so much.

So Andy told him.

You shouldn't have killed anyone, Rick. That wasn't what I wanted.

But I didn't—

And why did you listen to all those commanders in the army? And the politicians? They all lied to you. You shouldn't have believed them.

Andy! I'm sorry!

No, it's too late. I can't forgive you. You really fucked things up, Rick.

Then Andy turned around and opened a door behind him, and the whole ugly world faded to black.

THIRTY-EIGHT

Vance held his breath when he heard the door unlock. Fifteen minutes ago, just before he'd run into the panic room, he'd used his cell phone to send a distress call to Major Weston. The idiot was miles away, chasing brainless gangbangers somewhere in Queens, but by now he should've had more than enough time to come back to Rikers. Vance had ordered him to return with at least a hundred soldiers, enough to put down the genetically enhanced beast who'd attacked their headquarters.

But then the heavy door swung open, and the beast stood in front of him.

Vance was beyond fear now. His mind was jumbled to the point of madness. He fell back against the wall and slid to the floor, his eyes fixed on the bare-chested giant. But he didn't scream for help or beg for his life or do any of the desperate things that might be expected from a man in extreme peril. No, all he could do was marvel at the monster. The soldier's physique was magnificent. And he moved with such grace and precision, demonstrating the same agility he'd used fifteen minutes ago to slaughter an entire platoon of FSU officers and Secret Service agents. He was terrifying and beautiful.

Standing behind him was a petite, dark-haired woman in wet clothes. She looked vaguely familiar, possibly because Colonel Grant had displayed her photograph in one of his security briefings. She stayed outside the doorway while the soldier stepped into the panic room, but she furrowed her brow. She looked confused.

After a moment she shook her head. "That's not the president. That's his son-in-law."

The soldier looked over his shoulder at her. "There's been a change at the top. Vance Keller ordered the assassination. Lieutenant Frazier was the one who actually killed the president, but this man here set it up." He turned back to Vance. "Isn't that, right? I got the details from your good friend, Eli Grant."

Vance winced. The situation was distressing, but it was also absurd. Was Grant actually conspiring with this creature? Did the colonel really think he could get away with it? Vance saw an opportunity to turn things around, so he suppressed his terror and gave the soldier a serious man-to-man look. "Listen, I don't know your name, but I'll make you a promise. Whatever Grant is paying you, I'll double it. As you can imagine, I have access to vast sums of money. The entire federal budget, in fact."

The soldier smiled. He stepped closer to Vance and bent over him. The giant's handsome face hovered just a few inches away. Perhaps he was ready to start bargaining.

Then a loud, angry voice boomed inside Vance's head.

I don't want your money.

The soldier's lips didn't move. Vance turned his head left and right, wondering if someone else had come into the panic room, but they were alone. He was hearing voices, which was probably another symptom of his distress. He was imagining what the beast must be thinking.

No, it's not your imagination. And I'm not a beast. I outsmarted you.

Vance shivered. There was something horribly alien about this voice. It had snaked into Vance's skull, and now it slithered through his thoughts and feelings and memories. It had penetrated his most private sanctum, a place he'd kept secret since he was a little boy. His stomach churned with shame, and he felt a terrible, helpless fear that he hadn't experienced in almost forty years. He wanted to shriek and wail and scream for his mother, but his throat was so tight that all he could do was let out a strangled cry.

"Please . . . please!" Vance held up his hands in surrender. He was willing to do anything now to make this monster go away. "Just tell me what you want!"

The soldier bent over a little farther and locked eyes with Vance. It was as if he were trying to peer into Vance's head and get a glimpse of the horrible thing he'd let loose inside. It wasn't just wriggling through Vance's brain now—it was drilling holes through his thoughts and slashing his mind, amputating all the memories stored there. Vance twisted and cringed, squirming in pain. He lost his memories of his childhood and his marriage. He lost his strongest emotions and deepest secrets. The soldier was dissecting Vance's consciousness, his identity. He was carving it out of Vance's skull, severing its connections to the living tissue of his brain, slicing it off as if it were a tumor.

Vance flailed his arms and legs. He banged the back of his head against the panic room's wall. "STOP! OH GOD, STOP! YOU'RE KILLING ME!"

I'm afraid it's necessary. At this moment, Major Weston and his men are climbing the building's stairway. They'll be here in a minute or so, and they'll target anyone who's threatening the president. So there's only one safe option for my sister and me.

Now Vance was half gone. The monster had already sawed off millions of thoughts and memories, and he was working on the rest. At the same time, Vance felt a sudden pressure inside his head, an unbearable fullness that was more painful than a thousand migraines. A torrent of strange images and sounds and emotions flooded into his brain and began to reshape its delicate matrix of nerve cells. The new thoughts and perceptions came from the soldier. As he cut away Vance's consciousness, he replaced it with his own. His thoughts extinguished Vance's and occupied the brain's lobes and layers. He was taking control.

Just a few more seconds and it'll be over. I wish I could say I'm sorry about this, but I'm not. You were worse than all the others, worse than Frazier and Grant and even the president you worked for. And you know why? Because you knew what you were doing. You knew how wrong it was, but you did it anyway.

Vance didn't understand. He no longer could. He was just a remnant of himself, a bloody stump, a bit of flesh throbbing with fear and horror.

And then that was gone too.

THIRTY-NINE

Jenna screamed. The immense body that had once belonged to Derek Powell—until her brother Raza poured his mind and soul into it—collapsed facedown on the floor of the panic room. He lay next to the wall, sprawled over the suited torso of Vance Keller, who was also unconscious but lying faceup.

She rushed forward and knelt beside them. "Raza! What's wrong?" She grasped his left shoulder with both hands, getting a good grip on the hard muscle under the skin, and heaved it upward. *"Wake up!"*

It took all of her strength, but she managed to flip him over. As she rolled his body off Keller's, his shaved head clunked against the floor and came to rest on its side. His mouth was open but he wasn't breathing, and his huge limbs were as loose as a rag doll's. Terrified, Jenna pressed her fingers to his neck—no pulse. Then she pulled back his eyelids. The pupils were dilated, a sign of brain death.

"No!" Bending over him, she pushed the palm of her right hand against his sternum. She'd never performed CPR before, and she wasn't sure if she was doing it correctly, but she pumped his bare chest anyway, throwing her whole weight into it. *"Come on! WAKE UP!"*

But it was hopeless. If his brain was already dead, there was no point in reviving his heart. She stopped pumping, closed her hands into fists, and beat them against his chest instead. Her tears and sweat dripped onto his slack face. Grief twisted her stomach, agonizing beyond belief. She'd come all this way for nothing.

Then she heard his voice inside her head again.

Jenna. I'm still here. Look to your left.

She looked at Vance Keller, who'd opened his eyes. Staring straight up, he blinked several times, as if he were shaking off a dizzy spell. Then he slowly lifted his head and propped himself up on his elbows.

I'm all right. It just feels a little strange. This body isn't nearly as strong as Powell's.

Jenna crawled toward him. She looked straight into his elongated face, his dark brown eyes. Then she wrapped her arm around his thin shoulders and helped him sit up. She'd given up her habitual skepticism, her scientific reflex of doubt and disbelief. Now she was willing to believe anything if the reward was getting her brother back. "Raza? You did it again? You made the jump?"

He nodded. He took a deep breath, then swallowed a couple of times and cleared his throat. Raza was testing his new voice box. "It was easier this time, actually. I was right next to him, only a foot away. The first time I did it, there was a wall between Powell and me."

His voice was hoarse, but otherwise he seemed fine. After a few seconds, Jenna helped him to his feet, holding his elbow until she was certain he wouldn't fall. He was still shaky, but getting stronger. He stretched his arms out wide and adjusted the jacket of his suit. He opened and closed his hands and stared at the manicured fingers.

Then she heard a distant clattering, the sound of dozens of boots stomping on the concrete stairs. The FSU officers had reached the ninth floor. They were at the other end of the corridor, only a hundred feet away.

Raza turned to her. He had an urgent look on his skinny new face. "The gun, *baji*." He pointed at the assault rifle, which had dropped to the floor. "Pick it up and give it to me."

She felt a surge of alarm. "Raza, you can't. Don't kill anyone else!"

"Just trust me. Please?"

Jenna picked up the rifle and handed it to him. He aimed the gun at Powell's corpse, pointing it straight at the head. "Get behind me, Jenna. I have to do this right now."

He fired. The shot echoed painfully against the walls of the panic room, and Jenna covered her ears. Raza threw the rifle to the floor, then raised his hands over his head. Keeping Jenna behind him, he turned to face the doorway.

"Help! *Help!* This is the president! I'm over here!"

Jenna heard the soldier before she saw him. He rushed into the office but stayed out of sight, halting a few feet to the side of the panic room's doorway.

"Mr. President? I'm Major Weston of the Federal Service. Is anyone with you in that room?"

Raza backed up until he stood just a few inches in front of her. His new body was her shield. The soldiers couldn't take a shot at her without putting him at risk. "Yes, someone is with me, but she's a friend. There's an assault rifle lying on the floor, but neither of us is armed. There's also a corpse here. He's the man I killed with the gunshot you just heard."

"Okay, tell your friend to lie down on the floor and put her hands behind her head."

"I'll do no such thing. Who do you think you're talking to?" Raza shook his head. His voice was firm. "I'm your commander in chief, and that means I give the orders. Lower your weapon and tell all your men to do the same. Then step over here, so I can see you."

"Sir, I don't think that's a good—"

"Weston, do you want to be court-martialed?"

There was a pause. Raza filled up the time by speaking to Jenna silently.

I've had enough of their bullying. I won't let them push you around.

Then the major stepped into view, his assault rifle pointed at the floor. Half a dozen soldiers in body armor spread out behind him, also with their guns down but ready to raise them at a moment's notice. Weston squinted, his eyes narrowing just below the rim of his helmet. He didn't look too bright. "Uh, sir, who's the woman behind you? Does she have a security clearance?"

Raza shook his head again. "That doesn't matter. This woman saved my life." He turned around, placed his hand on Jenna's back, and nudged her forward. "Her name is Dr. Jenna Khan. She was a researcher for the

Palindrome Project. Your men tried and failed to arrest her two nights ago. But they did arrest her father, and they killed her brother."

Jenna was dumbfounded. Raza was taking command so smoothly, so effortlessly. He seemed to know exactly how to handle the situation.

Believe me, baji, *it wasn't effortless. I started working on this plan as soon as I realized what I could do. And I had to make a lot of adjustments along the way.*

Major Weston pointed at the bodies on the floor. "Is that Lieutenant Frazier? And Captain Powell?"

Raza nodded. He led Jenna out of the panic room, stepping around the corpses. "Palindrome has turned out to be a complete fiasco. Powell killed Frazier and Colonel Grant and dozens of fine officers. And he would've killed me too if Ms. Khan hadn't shown up here and distracted him." He pointed at Weston. "Major, I want you to immediately shut down the project. Cancel Phase Three and begin a cleanup effort. And retrieve the doses of vaccine from the Research Center so we can stop the spread of the airborne CRISPR virus."

Weston hesitated, clearly trying to make sense of all the orders Raza was giving him. But after a few seconds, he saluted the president. He was a loyal soldier. "Yes, sir. We'll shut down Palindrome at once."

Raza stepped closer to the major. "That also means closing the detention facilities on Rikers. I want you to send your men to all the jails in the complex and free the detainees. As soon as the storm dies down, let the prisoners cross the bridge and leave the island. Their detention was illegal in the first place, so they should be allowed to go back to their homes and families."

Weston bit his lower lip. He seemed to have more trouble with this particular order, but in the end he nodded. "I have a question, sir. My top priority is ensuring your safety. How can I do that if thousands of detainees start running loose across the complex?"

Raza shrugged. "It's simple. Contact the Secret Service and arrange my transportation back to Washington. Dr. Khan and I will leave Rikers within the next thirty minutes, and then you won't have to worry about my safety here. If we can't fly through the storm, we'll ride in a convoy of Strykers all the way to D.C."

Jenna stared at her brother. Minute by minute, he seemed to become more at ease in his new skin. He'd already cowed Major Weston into automatic obedience, forcing him to carry out orders that reversed the policies of the former administration. And Jenna guessed that over the next few hours Raza would get even better at it. Once he arrived in Washington he would have plenty of opportunities to intimidate subordinates and bend them to his will.

It was stunning to watch his transformation, and a little frightening too, but it also confirmed a suspicion Jenna had harbored for a long time. During her ten years of taking care of Raza—feeding and bathing and comforting and amusing him—she'd always suspected there was a little genius hidden inside his paralyzed body. Now she saw this genius in action. He was doing everything right, giving orders, making plans, establishing his authority as president. And he was taking the first steps to repair the damage caused by the last person who'd held the office.

But he'd forgotten something. Jenna didn't want to say it out loud, so she touched Raza's arm and sent him a silent message. **We have to pick up Abbu before we leave New York. I left him in Queens with Hector Torres, the head of the Latin Kings. The FSU is fighting the gang on the other side of the bridge.**

Raza nodded ever so slightly. A moment later, he pointed a slender finger at Weston. "One more thing, Major. Send new orders to your officers in Queens. Tell them to stop fighting the gangs there and withdraw from the area. I'm going to send a private message to the gang leaders instead. I think that'll ease the tensions." He put his arm around Jenna's waist and stepped forward. "Let's get going, everyone. There's no time to lose."

All the soldiers saluted him. Then they fell into line, taking position ahead and behind Raza, and the presidential procession marched out of the office.

EPILOGUE

Five weeks later, Dr. Jenna Khan went to the White House for a meeting with the president. It was a cool, clear October afternoon. The trees behind the West Wing were starting to change color, their leaves tinged yellow and orange.

The Secret Service agents at the West Wing's entrance recognized Jenna and waved her through. She'd visited the White House a dozen times over the past month, coming every Sunday, Tuesday, and Thursday. She had a good excuse for seeing the president on a regular basis—he'd appointed Jenna to lead the Office of Science and Technology, which had taken over the laboratories formerly involved in the Palindrome Project. After the shutdown of Palindrome and the evacuation of Rikers Island, the scientists in the government labs needed a new home and a new goal to pursue. It was Jenna's job to draw up a plan for future research.

Today's meeting, though, was going to be different. Jenna felt a cold dread in her stomach as she walked down the West Wing corridor. Just half an hour ago she'd discovered something disturbing. She needed to talk with Raza immediately.

Another pair of agents let her into the Oval Office, and when she stepped inside she saw her brother behind the massive presidential desk, signing some documents. She no longer did a double take every time she saw Raza in his new body. She'd grown so accustomed to the sight that now it seemed more real than her memory of his old body, the twisted, paralyzed figure in the wheelchair. And Raza seemed to be getting more comfortable with it too. In fact, he worked out every day in the White House gym to keep his new body in shape, and he'd developed an unlikely fondness for tailored suits and expensive haircuts.

He didn't look up from his papers when she came into the room. Every week, it seemed, he grew more and more obsessed with his job, more consumed by its responsibilities. But someone else in the Oval Office noticed her.

"Jenna! My sweetness!"

Abbu sprang up from the beige couch in the middle of the office and dashed across the room to embrace her. His enthusiasm was a little excessive—she'd had dinner with him only the night before—but Jenna smiled and hugged him. Abbu had become emotionally fragile since the traumatic events a month ago, and he got very nervous if he didn't see his children every day. Raza had found him a job as a White House steward, giving him a legitimate reason for spending so much time in the Oval Office, but Jenna worried that sooner or later someone would get suspicious.

She looked him over. "You know, Abbu, you're getting heavier. How often have you been visiting that fancy kitchen downstairs?"

He shook his head. "No, hardly ever! The food here is so bland, it has no taste at all. That's the one thing I miss about Brooklyn. Come, darling, I want to show you something." He took Jenna's arm and pulled her over to the couch, where a large leather-bound book lay on one of the cushions. He picked it up and opened it for her. "I started making this. What do you think?"

It was a scrapbook. Abbu had pasted dozens of recent newspaper articles on the cardboard pages. Jenna read the headlines as he turned the pages for her: PRESIDENT KELLER DISBANDS FEDERAL SERVICE UNIT. AMNESTY DECLARED FOR ALL UNDOCUMENTED IMMIGRANTS. MASSIVE REBUILDING PLANNED FOR FEDERAL DISTRICTS IN NEW YORK. PRESIDENT KELLER PROPOSES FAR-REACHING CLIMATE-CHANGE LAW.

"Do you like it?" Abbu looked as proud as a third-grader showing off his school project. "I'm collecting all the best stories. When it's finished, you'll have a record of all the wonderful things you and Raza have done."

A voice in her head interrupted them. From its tone, Jenna could tell that Raza had sent this silent message to her and her father at the same time.

Remember what I told you, Abbu. Always call me Vance, even when no one else is here.

Their father turned toward the desk. "Sorry, Vance. I keep forgetting."

Raza didn't raise his head. He kept his eyes on the documents he was signing. *And I'll keep reminding you. I want you to get in the habit of doing it, so you won't make a mistake when other people are around.* He paused to jot down a note on one of the papers. *Jenna, I'll be with you in a minute. I have to review all these executive orders by five o'clock.*

Jenna stared at him. In all likelihood, he'd already read her mind. He knew why she was here and what was upsetting her, but he didn't want to talk about it. So he was putting it off, trying to avoid the conversation for as long as possible.

Abbu turned back to her and pointed at another page in his scrapbook. "This is my favorite part, the articles from the first few days. Look at this picture of Ra—" He stopped himself. "I mean, this picture of Vance. He looks so handsome, doesn't he?"

The picture appeared below the headline PRESIDENT ASSASSINATED, KELLER SUCCEEDS HIM DESPITE COUP ATTEMPT. The date of the story was September 14th.

> NEW YORK—Vance C. Keller became the 46th president of the United States last night after suppressing a violent uprising by Federal Service Unit officials attempting to take control of the White House.
>
> In a late-night battle at the Federal Service's headquarters on Rikers Island, Keller and his Secret Service bodyguards fought off a rogue group of FSU officers who had assassinated the president earlier in the evening. The leader of the group, Colonel Eli Grant, had apparently intended to seize the presidency, but he and his followers were killed in the shoot-out with the Secret Service.
>
> Keller, a longtime White House advisor, was confirmed as

vice president by Congress yesterday afternoon and then sworn in as president immediately after the assassination. He took part in the battle against the coup plotters and reportedly shot one of the FSU officers trying to kill him.

Jenna frowned. Inventing a cover story had been Raza's idea. He'd rightly pointed out that no one would believe the truth. And this particular story line provided a fairly believable explanation for the violence and deaths that had occurred on Rikers Island that night. The weakest part was the claim that Vance Keller had somehow become a gunslinger, but to Jenna's surprise, no one questioned it. The American people had a soft spot for heroes, especially those who were handy with an assault rifle.

So Jenna understood why the cover story was necessary. What really bothered her were all the things left out of the story. Most important, there was no mention of Palindrome, which remained a classified secret even after the project's cancellation. Raza had argued that revealing the genetic-engineering breakthroughs at this time would only terrify the public. He was particularly adamant about concealing the existence of the airborne virus that carried the Serenity sequence. If the news went public, he said, the whole country would panic. Hundreds would die as they tried to escape the areas where the virus was spreading, mostly in New York and Pennsylvania. The panicking crowds might even massacre the people who were already infected.

Instead, Raza decided to quietly squelch the epidemic. He sent public-health teams to New York and Pennsylvania under the guise of trying to prevent a flu outbreak. Within a few weeks, the teams vaccinated hundreds of thousands of people against the Serenity virus. This made it much more difficult for the infected people to spread the microbe, because so many of their neighbors were immune. Raza also made sure that Jenna and Hamid were vaccinated.

Jenna had gone along with the plan, but she hated the deception and secrecy. And because she was now managing the scientists who'd worked on Palindrome, it was her job to keep them quiet. They all wanted to continue the genetics research and publish their results, but Jenna couldn't let them. They weren't even allowed to talk about it at scientific conferences. Long-term, she knew she couldn't keep muzzling them. Maybe someone like Colonel Grant could shut them up, using threats and arrests to intimidate the researchers, but not Jenna. It just wasn't in her.

Don't worry, baji. *It's only temporary. We won't have to keep them quiet forever.*

She looked up from the scrapbook. Raza had finished signing his documents and stepped away from his desk. He smiled at her as he approached the couch.

You'll see. In a year or two, everything will be different. We're going to change the world for the better, and then there won't be any need for secrecy.

Abbu looked up too. Although the message had been meant for Jenna alone, her father had sensed it. Abbu had such an intense connection with Raza that he could hear his son's thoughts no matter who they were meant for. "What was that, Vance?"

Raza went over to him and patted his back. "Abbu, could you go downstairs for a few minutes? I need to have a private conversation with Jenna."

"Sure, no problem." He closed the scrapbook and put it back on the sofa cushion. "I'll go see if the other stewards need some help."

Abbu tried to smile but failed. There was a lot of tension in the room, and he could sense that too. With a nervous look on his face, he left the Oval Office.

Raza waited until their father was far enough away. Then he sat down on the couch and looked straight at Jenna. *We should do this silently. I know what you want to talk about.*

Jenna remained standing. **Then you know why I'm upset. Why haven't you ordered the production of more vaccine?**

Please, sit down. I'd like to discuss this calmly.

I just saw the report from the director of the vaccination teams. He says they can't stop the spread of the Serenity virus unless they get another two million doses. But when I checked with the manager of the vaccine production facility, he said they were shutting down their equipment. What the hell's going on?

Look, you're throwing off so much anger right now that I can barely understand you. It's like listening to static.

Jenna took a deep breath. She definitely wanted her brother to hear this, so she forced herself to calm down. She sat at the other end of the couch, keeping the scrapbook between them. **They asked you for more vaccine, and you said no. Why, Raza?**

He didn't answer right away. He stared at his neatly pressed pants and picked a piece of lint off his knee. It was difficult for Jenna to read his expression—the pale, slender face was still new to Raza, and he was still learning how to use it—but if she'd been forced to guess, she would've said he was embarrassed. He would've gladly avoided this conversation if that were possible.

I've changed my mind about the necessity of stopping the Serenity virus. I think we may actually be better off if we let it take its course.

She'd been afraid of this. Her anger returned. **So you want the virus to spread the genetic changes to everyone? A whole nation engineered to be docile? That would make your job a lot easier, wouldn't it?**

Jenna, I—

You want a pacified country that won't protest your policies. And that's the same thing Vance Keller wanted. Funny coincidence, right?

No, it's not the same. Don't you see what's going on?

Yeah, I see. You've inherited more than Keller's body. You've adopted his political strategy too.

Raza grimaced. He shook his head firmly. *This has nothing to do with politics. What we're facing right now is bigger than me, bigger than the presidency. Bigger than America even. This is a crucial moment for the entire human race.*

Really? I don't see it that way. To me, this just looks like a genetic atrocity.

Just think for a minute about what we've learned in the past few months. Yes, the first CRISPR experiments were flawed, but they proved that the technique can radically change human DNA. Our species can guide the next step in its evolution. I'm living proof of that, Jenna. Whether you intended it or not, your treatment turned me into something completely new.

Jenna's throat tightened. She'd tried to forget her own responsibility for their predicament, but it was inescapable. She was the one who'd changed Raza so completely. She'd saved his life, but he was no longer human.

I don't blame you for it. Believe me, I'm grateful. And not just because I can walk and talk and tie my own shoes. You also freed me from so many other limitations. Although I'm happy in Keller's body right now, I'm not permanently tied to it. In a way, I've become more of a spirit than a biological creature. In theory, I could jump from one body to another indefinitely. You made me immortal.

She swallowed hard. Raza was frightening her.

No, no, don't worry. I don't think of myself as a god or anything like that. This is more like a revolutionary advance in medicine, like the discovery of penicillin.

And I want to share it. We've discovered a cure for death, and I want everyone to benefit.

She didn't find this reassuring. If anything, it scared her even more. **You do see the problem with this cure, right? In order to escape your dying body, you have to jump into a living one and get rid of whoever is already occupying it. Like you did with Keller.**

Raza waved his hand in a dismissive way, as if brushing off the difficulties. *We can get around that problem. Maybe through cloning. We could extract cells from a dying patient and create a healthy, younger version of his body, but with no higher intelligence in its brain. Once the new body is ready, the patient can make the jump. It would probably take a few years of research to perfect the technique, but it's doable.*

Jenna shook her head. **Maybe the technical problems are solvable, but what about the ethics? A lot of people won't like this idea, Raza. They'll call it a barbarity. They'll grab their pitchforks and come after you.**

He shrugged. *Well, now you see how Serenity could be useful. Most human beings are too stubborn to recognize what's good for them. They resist new ideas and demonize the people trying to help them. But if we modify their DNA and make them a little less resistant, the path to a better future will be smoother.*

So you're already committed to this plan? You won't even debate it?

As I said, this is the next step in human progress. If we don't pursue it, someone else will, most likely a government or corporation that has no scruples whatsoever. The future of our species is at stake, and I think we're the ideal leaders for this task. He leaned across the couch, edging closer to her. *I really hope you'll help me with this,* baji. *You should encourage the Palindrome researchers to take on this new project. They need to study the genetic mechanisms that caused the changes in my brain cells. Once they understand the process, they can try it on other people. Maybe the first test subjects should be terminally ill children. If we can give them the ability to move their minds out of their dying bodies and transfer themselves to healthy ones, it would dramatically demonstrate the value of the technique.*

And in the meantime, you'll genetically lobotomize the American people. No, wait, that's an understatement. Once the virus spreads to other countries, it'll lobotomize the whole world.

Raza sighed. *I admit, the plan isn't perfect. But in this case, the end justifies the means. The human race is in dire trouble. We'll drive ourselves to extinction if we stay on our current path. But we can survive if we're willing to change our biological design. We have the power to do that now.*

Jenna was appalled. She wanted to scream and curse and smack Raza in his new face. How could he seriously consider such an idea? For ten years, he was her innocent and pitiful little brother, mute and paralyzed, totally helpless. And in a mere five weeks he'd become so cold-blooded, so arrogant. It took her breath away, the change was so shocking.

And yet she should've seen it coming. If she'd been thinking more clearly, she could've predicted it a month ago when she saw all the soldiers he'd slaughtered on Rikers Island. If he could do something like that, he was capable of anything.

She rose from the couch. Her knees were shaking, but she managed to stay on her feet. She chose to say the words out loud. "I won't help you. I'm resigning my position. If this is what you really want, you'll have to find a new director for the project."

Don't be rash, Jenna. Take some time to think it over.

"I'm going to fight this. You won't get away with it."

Then, before Raza could slip any more thoughts into her head, she stormed out of the Oval Office.

Jenna left in a hurry. She rushed out of the West Wing and across the White House grounds. After she exited the security gate on Pennsylvania Avenue, she broke into a run and sprinted through Lafayette Square, stumbling past the throng of oblivious sightseers.

She didn't stop until she reached the corner of K Street and Connecticut Avenue. She stood panting on the sidewalk in the middle of downtown Washington, surrounded by soulless, glass-fronted office buildings. It was past five o'clock and the street was full of well-dressed men and women, corporate lawyers and lobbyists filing out of their buildings and heading for the nearest Metro station. The evening light bronzed their faces. They were all blissfully unaware of the fate that awaited them.

After several seconds Jenna caught her breath and looked south. She was half a mile from the White House, but she could still sense Raza's mind in the distance. He hadn't given up on her. She was his sister, after all, and blood was thicker than water. He expected her to come back.

But Jenna turned around and walked another block north. After crossing L Street she came to an older brick building with a large American flag hanging over an ornate awning. It was the Mayflower, one of Washington's most famous hotels, and standing under the awning was the man whom Jenna had arranged to meet there. He was dressed much more stylishly than usual, in a sharp black jacket over an open-neck silk shirt, but she recognized him at once.

Hector stepped toward her. His face was tense and alert, full of concern. "How did it go?"

She shook her head. "Not well. It's what I was afraid of."

He was silent, waiting for more, but Jenna was too distressed to say anything else. Finally, he took her hand. "What should we do?"

"I don't know yet." She looked down at the sidewalk. "I'm still thinking it over."

Hector gave her a few seconds, then bent over so he could look her in the eye. "You'll figure it out. You're good at that, *chica*." He smiled. "In the meantime, why don't we go inside and have a drink?"

Jenna nodded. She squeezed his hand, and they walked into the hotel.

AUTHOR'S NOTE

I used to be an editor at *Scientific American*, so I've followed with great interest the recent development of the CRISPR gene-editing method that's described in this novel. The method uses viruses to insert a lab-designed molecular complex into the body's cells; one part of the CRISPR complex guides it to the targeted gene, and the other part slices the DNA. The first clinical trials of the method are now under way as researchers test whether it can safely alter human genes to fight cancer and other illnesses. Using CRISPR to enhance someone's intelligence is a more difficult challenge, because scientists don't yet understand how genetic variations influence abilities such as memory recall. But the research efforts are likely to accelerate over the next few years, and the temptations of genetic enhancement may be hard to resist.

I'd like to thank my wonderful agent, Dan Lazar of Writers House, and my fantastic editor, Alexandra Sehulster of St. Martin's Press. Once again, though, I owe the greatest debt to my wife, Lisa. After twenty-six years of marriage, she still puts up with my nonsense.